THE STRANGER YOU SEEK

Amanda Kyle Williams

headline

First published in 2011
by HEADLINE PUBLISHING GROUP

1

Cataloguing in Publication Data is available from the British Library

ISBN 978 0 7553 8416 7 (Hardback)
ISBN 978 0 7553 8417 4 (Trade paperback)

Typeset in Palatino by Avon DataSet Ltd, Bidford-on-Avon, Warwickshire

Printed and bound in Great Britain by CPI Mackays, Chatham ME5 8TD

Headline's policy is to use papers that are natural, renewable and
recyclable products and made from wood grown in sustainable forests.
The 'ted to conform
of origin.

THE STRANGER
YOU SEEK

Praise for *The Stranger You Seek*

'*The Stranger You Seek* is filled with rich, evocative prose that transports you straight to the South and right into the psyche of new heroine Keye Street. She's formidable, but poignantly human as she struggles to navigate her present while battling shadows of her past. You can almost feel the Georgia humidity when you read this book, but you definitely feel the heat when the victims of a calculating, relentless serial killer start stacking up. This book burns rubber to the end, so carve out some down time, because you won't want to leave Keye hanging' PJ TRACY

'An exceptionally smart, funny and character-driven debut' KARIN SLAUGHTER

To my dear friends Pam and Miki with all my love.

Acknowledgements

Thanks to my good friend and consultant, Special Agent Dawn Diedrich, and to everyone at the Georgia Bureau of Investigation for your awe-inspiring dedication and compassion for the victims of crime and their families. Thanks to criminal profiler Brent Turvey for answering all those emails. Thanks also to Forensic Solutions, pathologist Lisa Lyons, and Special Agent Steve Watson.

Kelly Chian and Deb Dwyer, thank you so much. Victoria Sanders, you might as well be wearing a red cape. You are a superhero. Thank you, Chandler Crawford. Benee Knauer and Kate Miciak, what you did is too big for this space. I'm forever in your debt. Thanks also to Imogen Taylor and the wonderful team at Headline.

Kari Bolin, Meredith Anton, Deb Calabria, Greg Luetscher, Michal Ashton, Pam Wright, Scott Williams, Adair Connor, Jayne Rauser, Susan Culpepper, Betsy Kidd, Kim Paille, Elizabeth Jensen, Fred Kyle and Betty Williams, Diane Paulaskas, Graham Street, Chuck Bosserman, Heather Rouse, and Susan Balasco: each one of you lent me something for this book. Special thanks to Mary Silverstein for the laptop that set me free. Roy, Jani Faye, and Tricia Watson, I hope you're watching this.

Prologue

The sun had not even burned dew off the grass under the live oaks, but the air was thick and soupy already, air you could swim around in, and it was dead-summer hot.

Inside the car she had not yet noticed parked on her street, a patient hunter dabbed at a trickle of perspiration and watched as Westmore Drive began a sleepy jog toward midweek.

The white-trimmed windows in the small brick house were flung open around seven, and she first appeared as a faint image behind the kitchen window, nearly abstract behind glass and screen, but no less an object of desire. The smell of cooking food drifted from her screened windows – frying bacon and toast and coffee – and Lei Koto's killer felt the first stab of hunger this placid summer morning.

A little before ten the street was silent. The last neighbor had left for work, 9:50 on the dot as always. The smells from Lei Koto's kitchen had shifted from breakfast to something else, something green and cabbagy and rank.

The car door opened, then footsteps on the concrete walk, a briefcase, good shoes, a white smile, a business card.

They always open the door.

Chapter One

My name is Keye Street. First name from my Asian grandfather; my adoptive parents awarded me the second. By trade I am a detective, private, that is, a process server and bail recovery agent. In life, I am a dry alcoholic, a passionate believer in Krystal cheeseburgers and Krispy Kreme doughnuts, and a former behavioral analyst for the FBI. How I ended up here in the South, where I have the distinction of looking like what they still call a damn foreigner in most parts of Georgia and sounding like a hick everywhere else in the world, is a mystery Emily and Howard Street have never fully unraveled for me. I know they had wanted a child so badly they adopted a scrawny Chinese American with questionable genes from an orphanage. My grandparents and guardians had been murdered and my biological parents consisted of two drug addicts and one exotic dancer. I have no memory of them. They took flight shortly after my birth. I can only manage a word or two in Chinese, but my mother, Emily Street, who is as proficient in innuendo as anyone I've ever known, taught me a lot about the subtle and passive-aggressive language of southern women. They had tried for a cute little white kid, but something in my father's past, something they have for my entire life flat-out refused to share with me, got them rejected. It didn't take me long to understand that southerners are deeply secretive.

I embraced the South as a child, loved it passionately and love it still. You learn to forgive it for its narrow mind and growing pains because it has a huge heart. You forgive the stifling summers because spring is lush and pastel sprinkled, because November is astonishing in flame and crimson and gold, because winter is merciful and brief, because corn bread and sweet tea and fried chicken are every bit as vital to a Sunday as getting dressed up for church, and because any southerner worth their salt says please and thank you. It's soft air and summer vines, pine woods and fat home-grown tomatoes. It's pulling the fruit right off a peach tree and letting the juice run down your chin. It's a closeted and profound appreciation for our neighbors in Alabama who bear the brunt of the Bubba jokes. The South gets in your blood and nose and skin bone-deep. I am less a part of the South than it is a part of me. It's a romantic notion, being overcome by geography. But we are all a little starry eyed down here. We're Rhett Butler and Scarlett O'Hara and Rosa Parks all at once.

My African American brother, Jimmy, whom my parents adopted two years after I moved in, had a different experience entirely. Not being white, we were both subjected to ignorance and stereotyping, but even that seemed to work in my favor and against Jimmy. People were often surprised that I spoke English and charmed that I spoke it with a southern accent. They also assumed my Asian heritage made me above average. I was expected and encouraged to excel. The same people would have crossed the street at night to avoid sharing a sidewalk with my brother, assuming that being both black and male he was also dangerous. He'd picked up our mother's coastal Carolina accent, the type usually reserved for southern whites in a pri-marily white neighborhood at a time when diversity was not necessarily something to be celebrated. He couldn't seem to find a comfortable slot for himself in any community, and he spent high school applying to West Coast universities and carefully plotting his escape. Jimmy's a planner. And careful with everything. Never screwed up his credit, never got fired, never had addiction issues, and never rode down Fifth Avenue in New York City after a few too many with his head sticking through the sunroof of a limo yelling 'Hey, y'all' like I did. Jimmy's the well-behaved child. He now lives in Seattle with his lover, Paul, and not even the promise of Mother's blackberry cobbler is an attractive enough offer to bring him home to Georgia.

How I came to be here this night, edging my way along an old frame porch, double-clutching my 10mm Glock, body pressed flat against the house, peeling paint sticking to the back of my black T-shirt and drifting onto cracked wood, is another story entirely.

I had once been called Special Agent Street. It has a nice ring, doesn't it? I was superbly trained for this kind of work, had done my time in the field before transferring to the National Center for the Analysis of Violent Crime (NCAVC) at Quantico as a criminal investigative analyst, a profiler. A few years later, the FBI took away my security pass and my gun, and handed me a separation notice.

'You have the brains and the talent, Dr Street. You merely lack focus.'

I remember thinking at that moment that the only thing I really lacked was a drink, which was, of course, part of the problem.

I was escorted that day to the FBI garage, where my old convertible, a '69 Impala, white-on-white and about half a mile long, was parked at an angle over the line between two spaces. Fire one Special Agent, get back two parking spots. Sweet deal.

Now, four years later, I passed under the curtained front window and congratulated myself on accomplishing this soundlessly. Then the rotting porch creaked. The strobe from a television danced across the windows, volume so low I could barely make it out. I waited, still, listening for any movement inside, then stuck my head round and tried to peek between the curtains. I could see the outline of a man. *Whoa!* A big outline.

Jobs like this can be tricky. Bail jumpers move fast. You've got to go in when you can and take your chances. No time to learn the neighborhood, the routines, the visitors. I was here without the benefit of surveillance, without backup, going in cold with my heart thundering against my chest and adrenaline surging like water through a fire hose. I could taste it. *Almonds and saccharin.* I was scared shitless and I liked it.

Chapter Two

The streetlamps were out, the night draped in billowy white clouds that cast a faint light across the overgrown yard and locked in the heat like a blanket. Atlanta in summer – suffocating and damp. Nerves and humidity sent sweat trickling from my hairline and over my darkened cheekbones. I was grease-painted and dressed for night work, crouching near the front door, searching my black canvas backpack for Tom. Anyway I called it Tom, as in *Peeping* Tom, a thirty-six-inch fiber optic tube with a miniature screen attached to one end, an electronic eye to the other. Tom takes a lot of the guesswork out of jobs like this. As I twisted and turned the tiny tube under the door, I got a pretty good look at the front room.

The subject, Antonio Johnson, was a repeat violent offender. He'd been out of prison for two months when he robbed a convenience store. I had traced him to Canada three weeks ago and lost him. But his ex-wife was in Atlanta and Johnson had a history of stalking her. She'd been getting hang-ups again. A trace of the calls, with the help of a friend at APD, led to a pay phone in a sleazy motel in Atlanta's crack-infested West End. I found people there who knew Johnson. One of them ratted him out for thirty dollars. He was staying at a place off Jonesboro Road near Boulevard and the federal penitentiary. There even locals check their car doors at stoplights and commuters take the long way around after dark.

I could see him on the three-inch viewer, sitting on a ragged couch, feet on the edge of a wooden utility spool coffee table. He appeared to be alone, a beer in his right hand, his left hand in his lap and

6

THE STRANGER YOU SEEK

partially hidden from view. *You hiding something under there, big guy?*

Hovering in the damp air around the front porch, just above the sweet, sick scent of trash and empty beer cans, was the aroma of something synthetic like superglue and Styrofoam.

I triggered off the safety, then tapped on the front door. I was going to use my best woman-in-distress voice, say I needed a phone, say I had a flat, say something, anything, to get the door open. I wasn't sure. I'd learned to improvise since I'd been on my own.

Johnson didn't hesitate. I got a glimpse on my tiny viewer of something coming out of his lap seconds before he blew a hole in the door near my ear the size of a softball. The blast was cannon-loud, splintered the door, and left me light-headed and tumbling off the porch to safer ground.

Another blast. The front windows exploded. Glass flew like shrapnel. I balled up against the side of the porch and felt the sting on my neck and arms and knew I was cut, then rose up enough to get a shot off in the general direction of the front window. I didn't want to shoot him. I merely wanted him to back off a little.

. . . Then silence.

I took the porch steps in a half crouch, made it to the door. Still quiet. I tried reaching through the hole in the door to unlatch it. That's when I heard it, a shotgun, a goddamn pump-action, and if you've ever heard the sound, you'll never forget it – the foregrip sliding back, one shell ejecting, another pushing into the carrier, the bolt closing. It happens in a split second with a good operator, and Johnson had had plenty of practice.

I pressed my back against the house, took a breath, took a moment. A quick reality check is always a good idea in these situations. Did I really want to get killed bringing in this guy? Hell no, I did not, but the adrenal flood of mania this kind of event produces propelled me forward rather than back, which perhaps illustrates most effectively the differences between those of us in this business and the sane population.

Boom! Johnson let the shotgun loose once more. I felt it under my feet, like a fireworks show when the ground shakes. He was probably making his own loads. God only knew what he was firing at me. Another chunk of front door blew out. Then the *pop, pop, pop, pop* of an automatic weapon.

On three, I told myself.

... One ... Two ... Two and a half ... Two and three quarters. Fuck! Three!

I put everything I had behind one of the black combat boots I wear for this kind of work and went for the space just above the front doorknob. It had no fight left, splintered and swung open. I flattened back against the house and waited.

... Silence.

Glock steadied with both hands, heart slamming so hard I felt a vein in my throat tick, tick, ticking against my shirt collar. I stepped around the corner and surveyed the front room, a living room/ dining room combo pack. I could see the kitchen beyond that, a hallway. I was figuring the place for two bedrooms and a bath. I'd poked around outside for quite a while before making my move, counting doors and windows. So where was he? A bedroom, the hallway?

... Then *pop, pop, pop.* I hit the floor and rolled into the tiny dining room, got off a few rounds in case he had any ideas about coming to find me.

'Bail recovery, Mr Johnson! Drop your weapon and come out with your hands behind your head. *Do it now!*'

'A chick?' Johnson yelled back, and laughed. 'No fucking way!'

Then I heard the back door opening, the screen slamming. I rushed into the kitchen and saw the door swinging half off its hinges, and beyond that the white letters on Johnson's T-shirt bobbed across the dark backyard toward the fence.

I took the back steps into the yard and watched with some satisfaction as Johnson neared the fence and the gate. I'd left something back there in case it came to this, which had been a pretty good bet.

It didn't take long. It was a postage-stamp small yard with a chain-link fence and a horseshoe lever on the gate. Johnson grabbed the fence, and just as he tried to hoist himself over, a blue-white explosion knocked him backward. Just a little black powder, some petroleum jelly, a battery and a couple of wires, a few fireworks to slow him down. My ears rang from five feet away and for a couple of seconds I had to fight my way through a million tiny flashbulbs.

Johnson lay there like a slug, motionless. I approached him cautiously, Glock steady, and checked him for signs of life. Breathing fine. Out cold. I pulled his big arms up behind him. His palms were scorched.

'It wasn't supposed to be quite that dramatic,' I told his limp body as I snapped cuffs on his wrists and threaded a belt around his waist and through the cuffs. 'But then I really don't know shit about explosives.'

I rolled him onto his back. With one size-thirteen shoe in each hand, I attempted to drag him by the ankles. *Damn.* The guy was at least two-sixty and dead weight. I'm five-four and a half and one-ten if I drink enough water. I moved him about three inches before I gave up. I could have used my mobile phone to call the cops for a pickup, but the girl jokes would have run for weeks at APD.

I plopped down on the ground and poked him in the ribs with my Glock. 'Come on, you big fat baby, wake up.'

His eyelids rose a full minute before his eyes were able to focus.

'Hi,' I said cheerfully, shining my flashlight into his bloodshot brown eyes. I was holding it cop-style over my shoulder and near my face. 'Remember me?'

He squirmed angrily, then made grunting animal sounds when he realized his hands were locked behind him.

'Now, would you like to walk your fat ass to my car, or you want me to call the cops?'

'Who you if you ain't no cop?'

I thought about that. It wasn't a bad question. 'Soon as I figure it out, I'll let you know,' I promised him, nudging him again to get him on his feet. But he was having trouble getting up without his hands. I got behind him and pushed.

'Ever think about a diet?'

'You like it, bitch,' Johnson slurred. He seemed a little loopy. 'You want some Antonio. You know you do.'

Oh yeah, bring it on. Nothing like a big ole fat man with a prison record.

'Okay, Lard Boy. Lets you and me take a drive.'

Chapter Three

The old Sears Roebuck building is an Atlanta landmark. It took seven months to build it in 1926, and even in its day, the building, which includes a guardlike tower in the center, looked more like a prison than the center of retail activity. Two million square feet of faded brick sprawls for acres and rises up nine floors above Ponce de Leon Avenue on the outer edge of Midtown, where you couldn't stop for gas without getting heckled by street people or hit up for money before the cops moved in. For the last few years the sign out front has read CITY HALL EAST and the building currently houses overflow from our growing bureaucracy and a portion of Atlanta's massive police force. This will soon change. The mayor closed a forty-million-dollar deal with a developer who says it will be the city's hottest new address in a couple of years. Condos, live/work artists' spaces, restaurants. So it goes in Midtown Atlanta, where the landscape is ever changing and scaffolding is a thriving industry. The city was hashing out details on where the current residents will end up, but no one seemed happy about packing up their offices and moving out. At least not the cops I knew firsthand.

A couple of blocks east, a breakfast line was already forming at the community soup kitchen. The temperature hadn't dropped below seventy-eight degrees at sunrise in a month. We were having a real southern-style heat wave, but the homeless line up for breakfast in jackets. It must be hard to stay warm when your stomach is empty. I wondered how the city's hottest new address would get along with the soup kitchen regulars.

At the station with Antonio Johnson, I saw Lieutenant Aaron Rauser watching me from his office across the hall in Homicide. Johnson was fully alert by then, cursing, struggling, trying to make a scene, showing off a little. He'd been fine in the car, quiet in the backseat, still fighting off the drugs and the explosives, but when I was using one of the station phones to call Tyrone, whom I worked with as a contractor at Tyrone's Quikbail, and let him know I'd nabbed Johnson, the rascal started acting up.

Cops, trickling in at the end of their shifts, laughed at the commotion. 'Hey, Keye,' one of the uniforms snickered. 'You don't look so good. You let Fat Boy kick your ass?'

I rolled my eyes and handed Johnson over for printing and then waited for the receipt I'd need to collect my money from Tyrone. When I ducked into Rauser's glass office in Homicide, detectives sitting in their open cubes made kissing sounds. Rauser's relationship with me was an endless source of amusement at the station. I suppose we seemed an unlikely pair. Rauser is white and twelve years my senior. We had come from different worlds and there were whispers around the station that we were lovers. Not true. But he is my best friend.

'Good morning.' I was trying to be cheerful even though my head was pounding. I hadn't had time to wash up and I was still picking glass out of my forearms and wiping away dried blood.

Rauser looked terrible too. He gestured to the desk where they were fingerprinting Antonio Johnson. 'Why you have to take shit work like that?'

'Money,' I said, but he wasn't buying it. The smile dropped off my face. It was his tone. Sometimes that's all it took for Rauser to do that to me, and I didn't like it. He had that look in his eye. He always picked on me when something wasn't right in his world.

'Keye, for Christ's sake. You got degrees and corporate accounts. You don't have to do that crap. I don't get the choices you make sometimes.'

I was playing with the pencil cup on his desk and refusing eye contact, which, in his mind, was dismissive and I knew it, but I wasn't in the mood for all his Daddy stuff.

I briefly ran a mental list of the corporate accounts he was talking about. The retainers were fat. I'd paid down some of the mortgage on my loft with them. But the work was mind-numbing – employment service application checks, nanny backgrounds, lawsuit histories on contractors, workers' comp cases, unfaithful spouses, service of process. The odd subpoena offered a bit of challenge from time to time, but for the most part it was all excruciatingly boring.

I'd been a licensed Bail Recovery Agent since leaving the Bureau. It bought the groceries while I built my private investi-gating business, and it still supplemented my income nicely. My shrink, Dr Shetty, says it's a power thing, that I have a brutal case of penis envy. What can I say? I like strapping on a big Glock now and then.

And the degrees: criminology from Georgia Southern, doctoral studies at Georgia State in developmental psychology. And none of it, even with eight years at the Bureau, would earn me a real position with a law enforcement agency in this country. Not now. Drinking had changed all that. It entered my records as it tore away at my life and discredited me professionally forever. I couldn't even jump on the expert witness gravy train. Expert testimony requires an expert who can't be discredited on the stand. That's so not me. My closet is full of bones.

I was fifteen when I first heard about the Behavioral Analysis Unit (BAU) at the National Center for the Analysis of Violent Crime, and I could think of nothing else after that. I tailored my studies and my life around getting there, and a few years later, there I was. And then I blew it.

Sometimes you only get one chance at something. Sometimes that's a good thing too. When that door slams shut on the thing you couldn't live without, what happens next is when the real education begins. You have to figure out how to make some peace with it all, how to have an interior life you can live with. Digging down deep is never really a bad thing in the end, but it will flat-out kick your ass while it's happening.

'Keep screwing around with bonding-company trash and you're gonna get hurt,' Rauser grumbled, then muttered something that sounded like 'sick fucks'.

I lowered myself gingerly into a chair across from his desk. There were two of them, thin black vinyl cushions with metal armrests. I was sore from the tumble I'd taken earlier and it was just beginning to sink in.

'What's wrong?' I demanded.

Rauser slipped a cigarette from his shirt pocket, stuck it in the corner of his mouth. The flint on his Zippo caught after the third try. He wasn't supposed to smoke in the building, but I wasn't going to correct him. Not today. 'Remember when there was just, like, normal stuff? Somebody shoots the guy in bed with his wife or something? Nothing weird. Just normal everyday murder.'

I shook my head. 'Before my time.'

Rauser pulled open his desk drawer and dropped his cigarette into a hidden ashtray and, head down, massaged both temples. For the first time, I realized that there was more silver than black in his hair. He was nearly fifty, handsome and fit, but a lifetime of caffeine and cigarettes, a lifetime of chasing monsters, had turned him to ash.

'Bad case?' I asked.

Rauser didn't look at me. 'Understatement.'

'You'll figure it out,' I told him. 'Good guy always wins, right?'

'Uh-huh,' Rauser said, with about as much conviction as Bill Clinton at a deposition. 'And maybe Judge Judy will come in here and shake her ass for us too.'

'I'd like that,' I said, and Rauser showed me his smile for the first time today.

Chapter Four

KNIFEPLAY.COM

Your Online Adult Edge Fetish & Knife Play Community blogs > beyond the EDGE, a fantasy by BladeDriver blog title > Purple Cabbage

It was the first time I had been so near to her, although I'd seen her many times. And she had seen me. Whether it was conscious I am not sure, but her eyes had skipped over me in public places. I stood on her porch waiting for her to answer the door. I didn't need to wait. She had not even latched the screen. So safe in your little homes, I kept thinking, and an old song came to mind. *Little boxes on the hillside, little boxes made of ticky tacky . . . and they all look just the same . . .*

She came to the door wearing a pale blue cotton shirt, a dish towel in her hand, perspiration around her hairline. She motioned for me to follow her. A hot breeze from the street rushed through open windows. She took me to her kitchen and offered me a chair at her table. She cooks early before the heat is too bad. The house has no air-conditioning. It is stifling already. The stink of boiling cabbage nearly choked me when we stepped into the room. The countertops were Formica, poisonous yellow and dated. She was chattering about her son coming home from summer camp that afternoon, and all I could think about was how she would smell once the chemicals began their wild run.

'My son is always starving,' she said, and smiled at me as if starving were an endearing quality, a clucking mother hen. 'I'm glad you're here. I didn't realize it would be today.'

I did not tell her why I was there. I did not want to ruin the surprise. The silly cow was smiling at me and using the back of her hand to push sweaty hair off her forehead. I was thinking about her skin, the warmth of it, the texture, the salty taste, the firm resistance against my teeth as I bite into her.

She offered me iced tea and set it in front of me. Sweat trickled from the glass onto the tabletop. I did not bring my hands from my lap, did not touch the glass. I touch nothing. I am invisible.

I had my briefcase on the table opened away from her. She was at the stove stirring a pot of purple cabbage. 'How do you think little Tim will do living with your sister?' I asked. I could not resist the urge to play. These things go so quickly.

She turned from the stove. 'My son lives with me. I don't understand.'

You will.

A shadow crossed her face, something uneasy. Alarm lit up her dark eyes as they moved from the briefcase to my face, to the hands I had kept in my lap, to the kitchen door. Something inside her was clawing, urging, begging for attention, some still, small voice warning her to get out, but she was not going to listen. They never listen. It is absurd, really, utterly absurd. They do not want to offend me. What if they are wrong? It would be so impolite.

I closed my eyes and breathed. Beyond the food and the heat I detected it at last, the onion scent of fear, hers and mine, hanging heavy in our shared air. It hit me like an electric current. The chemicals were surging, cortisol was practically bleeding out through our skin, my heart and hopes clamoring at the thought of what was coming next. I felt a deep and urgent ache between my legs. All I could see was this small woman. All I could smell. All I wanted. She was everything.

I stretched on tight surgical gloves so sheer I could almost feel the air against my warm fingertips, and took my favorite toy from the briefcase – satin finished with a white-gold throat, a crook-back with four and a half inches of high-carbon steel blade. I looked at her narrow back as she stood there stirring her cabbage and wondered if she felt it yet, our connection. I wanted her to feel it, to *know* it, just an instant before my hand reached her.

I think she did. I think she wanted it.

16

The neighborhood is trendy, between the Virginia-Highlands section of Atlanta and funky Little Five Points. My tiny investigating agency is in what was once a row of forgotten warehouses on Highland. A couple of years ago the owner decided to renovate the exteriors, adding aluminum and brushed-nickel peaks and overhangs, a breezeway in bright Miami deco and some metal sculptures. It looks like a demented welder got hold of a crack pipe. They are now named The Studios and marketed as commercial lofts. Our landlord raised the rent on his current tenants – me, the gay theater company next door, the tattoo artist and body piercer next to them with the S/M stickers on his Jeep, and the Hindu hairdresser on the end. The renovation would bring us more business, we were told. More walk-ins now that we appeal to the nearby coffee-and-biscotti crowd. I hate biscotti. I mean really. Has anyone ever once had a craving for *biscotti*? And walk-ins. *Hate 'em.* They're usually total freaks. People with any sense do not window-shop for a detective. It's just not that kind of business.

I love the neighborhood, though. I catch myself humming show tunes all day when the theater company is rehearsing, and when I work late, I sometimes pass costumed people on my way in and out, loitering, talking, smoking. Last night a woman in a mermaid costume watched me walk in. She had a cigar in her mouth and she squinted through smoke at me, but didn't speak. Neither did I. What do you say to a gay mermaid? A dry-erase board propped up on an easel announced dress rehearsals for *Swishbucklers*.

Two doors down, the hair salon operates quietly and during normal business hours. The owner deeply resents terms like 'hairdresser', 'haircutter', or, God forbid, 'beautician', and makes it well known she prefers 'hair *artist*'. In addition, she was recently assigned a new spiritual name by her guru and would very much appreciate her neighbors honoring that. We do try, though having gone from plain Mary to Lakshmi, we mangle it a bit from time to time. The name means something like Goddess of Prosperity and all the neighbors are hoping to hell it's real and good fortune has smiled upon us at last.

I am in Studio A and a small sign on my door reads CORPORATE INTELLIGENCE & INVESTIGATIONS. Inside, computers, printers, a couple of overused fax machines, track and fluorescent lighting, and a huge air-conditioning condensing unit give the place a kind of electronic purr. I sometimes hear the humming in my head when I close my eyes at night.

I began CI&I a couple of years ago after emerging squinty eyed from rehab as if I'd been living in a cave for three months. I was looking for something, anything, any work, any distraction. I never wanted to go back there. Someone asked if it was my first rehab and I remember looking at him, slack jawed, and thinking, *Jesus, it takes more than one?* But I get that now. The outside, it's a whole different deal. It doesn't prop you up and keep you safe. It's no net. It's too many hours in the day. It's being confronted hour after hour by your own glaring weaknesses.

In those first days on the outside, I went to meetings all over town; sometimes all day long, just leave one and head to another. And I hated them. All the God stuff in AA really got to me. I know, I know. They say it's whatever you choose as your own God, but let me tell you that when you're there and everyone wants to hold hands and pray, it sure doesn't feel like a choice. And all of them talking constantly about drinking really made me want a friggin' drink. But you can't get a drink there and that's the point, or at least it was for me. Those meetings and those people to whom I felt so superior and despised at times for their frailties and for their kindness, very patiently and knowingly put up with my shit and saved my life in spite of my bad attitude. I went out into the world then to get the business going rather than going back into the package store on the corner.

CI&I kept me busy, and it caught on – traditional investigative services, missing persons and skip traces, corporate bug sweeping, fugitive apprehension, and the occasional foray into the unadvertised.

'Denver.' Neil chuckled. 'We got him. He bought a house there.'

Neil is blond and usually a little shaggy, with at least a day's worth of stubble on his chin. He was sitting in front of a computer screen, a Cuban shirt unbuttoned to the navel. Neil always seemed a little out of place to me in a city with no beach to bum around on. When I bent over him to have a look at the screen, he smelled like coffee and pot, his own personal speedball.

We had been trying to locate an accountant who'd skipped town with the contents of a company safe, which included quite a lot of cash, for a large corporate entity with headquarters in Atlanta. The company didn't want to file charges and my understanding was that they wanted the matter handled in a quiet way, just find the accountant and turn the information over to them. I didn't ask why. Something in that safe was obviously worth going to some trouble to get back, but it was none of my business. My days in law enforcement were over.

'Guy rips off five hundred grand,' Neil said, and tucked his longish blond hair behind his ears. 'And he goes to *Denver*? Go figure.'

Neil was the first person I called when the idea for CI&I sprang to life. I needed his expertise. He knows his way around a computer, one of those guys who spent high school with his bedroom door locked, a computer in his lap, some drugs, and a teenager's desire to subvert. Neil is essentially a hacker, an extremely successful hacker who got himself on the FBI's list of cybercriminals and then worked for them as a consultant. He's on the payroll of more than one corporate giant who hired him as a security expert when they couldn't shut him down. Neil is paid not to hack. This makes him an extortionist pure and simple. But it's always good to have one around, isn't it? And he works cheap. He doesn't really need the money. He does it because he likes it, but he only likes it when he can control it. This means he works when he feels like working and on his terms. I have no problem with that. He's a huge asset, and we get along most of the time.

He turned away from his monitor and looked at me for the first time that morning. I was wearing cargo shorts and a shirt rolled to the elbows, still very scratched up from the bond enforcement apprehension gone bad. Neil sipped his coffee and studied me seriously.

'You going after this guy in Denver?'

I shook my head. 'I just want to get paid.'

'Ten bucks says they want you to go out there and get what he took from their safe, and I bet it's not the money they're worried about. Maybe they're cooking the books or bid rigging. Or maybe it's, like, sex tapes.'

I thought about that. 'Still not going.'

He smiled and looked up at me through bloodshot eyes and blond lashes. 'Worried you might break a nail?'

'I know you are but what am I?' I shot back.

Neil seemed momentarily stumped by this. ''Fraidy cat,' he rebounded, and so our day began with childish insults, just the way we liked it.

From outside, we heard *hooga, hooga* and moments later the door opened and Charlie Ramsey came grinning into our workspace. Neil looked at me and smiled. We work by appointment. Not a lot of regulars, just Charlie and Rauser and my friend Diane, whom I've known since grade school. Charlie always announced his arrival with the squeeze horn on his bicycle handlebars. He works as a bicycle courier, and as far as I can tell has the intellect of a twelve year old, which made him a very good fit for us. We use Charlie's visits as a way to avoid work. It's nice for everyone.

There were a lot of stories in the neighborhood about how Charlie ended up on a bicycle with a squeeze horn at forty-something. They are all some variation of this: the perfect job, great family, life was sunshine and Skittles until an armored bank truck ran him down at Tenth and Peachtree and permanently damaged him. Wife and kids left, Charlie lost a career, a home. He has a lot of pain in his neck, he once told me, and headaches that stop him cold. He doesn't always speak well. His words get slurred and really loud when he's excited, and combined with the fact that Charlie is also a close talker in a bicycle helmet that sits a little crooked, a conversation with him can be a bit, well, surreal. He seems to have moments of adult clarity, but they are fleeting. Mostly Charlie's just a big goofy kid. I asked about his past one day. He talked about the accident. He talked about *after* the accident, but never *before* the accident. It was as if there hadn't been anything up till then. In a rare and serious moment that day, he told me that the very next second of your life can change everything. He'd spent months in rehab at the Shepherd Center in Atlanta and learned that patients there referred to us on the outside as TABs – Temporarily Able-Bodied – another reminder that life is mutable. It's a lesson I had learned before Charlie pedaled into our lives, but I'll never forget his earnestness that day. We hadn't seen him in a couple of weeks and we always worried about him. Charlie spends his days on a bike in Atlanta's treacherous traffic, and since he seems to have only about half a brain, he's a kind of ticking time bomb. Rauser and Neil have running bets – ten bucks says he gets it this year, etc. I pretend I'm above all this.

Charlie visits at odd times, never really anything to count on – mid-morning or late afternoon, but generally several times a week, always smiling and almost never without a gift. In the summer he might fill up a worn baseball cap with blackberries. In the winter he plants pansies in the planter outside our front door. There's a nursery two blocks away and we think he pinches them at night when the only thing between Charlie and flats of beautiful, bright pansies is five feet of chain-link fence. He seems to like the yellow ones with the deep purple eyes, the same ones, coincidentally, in short supply on the long wooden tables at the nursery.

He came in smiling with his little helmet sitting crooked on top of his head and the thick-rimmed glasses he wears pushed all the way up to his eyebrows. He was wearing his courier's uniform – shorts with an embroidered golf shirt, short white socks. His body was lean and strong, and the muscles in his legs let you know that Charlie was a kind of athlete, but something about the way he

21

held his head, the occasional tic, the open-mouth stare that seemed to grip him at times, made it clear that something was very off about poor Charlie.

He held out his upside-down baseball cap. 'Figs,' he said, too loudly and with enough of a slur so that it sounded like *fligs*. 'You like fligs, Keye? Neil, you like?'

'Fresh fligs?' Neil asked. 'Cool. Where'd you steal 'em?'

Charlie pointed toward the door. 'Off a damn tree,' he said, and looked pleased. Neil roared and clapped his approval. He'd been working with Charlie on how to swear. I shot Neil a look.

'My mom and dad have a fig tree in their yard, Charlie,' I said. 'Want to see how they eat them?' I opened the fridge and found a package of Italian cream cheese. Neil and I ate it on everything from celery sticks to sandwiches. 'You okay with a knife, Charlie? Can you split these in half?'

Charlie nodded. 'I know how to clean fish with a knife.'

'Wow,' I said, and grated some orange zest into the mascarpone, then added a little honey. Charlie carefully dipped a teaspoon in and dribbled it on each fig as instructed. I followed with about half as much chocolate hazelnut cream. We took a moment to admire our work.

'Damn beautiful,' Charlie said.

'I promise you'll love 'em,' I said.

'You keep your promises, Keye?' Charlie asked, and popped a fig in his mouth.

I thought about that. 'I haven't always, Charlie. But I try harder now.'

Neil poured himself a fresh mug of coffee and joined us at the table.

Charlie reached for the plate and picked off another fig. 'These *are* good! Why is your name Keye?'

'My grandfather's first name was Keye.'

'But you don't have a family.'

I didn't remember ever telling Charlie about my childhood, but then I remembered the day I had been brave enough to ask about his past. Perhaps I'd said something then.

'I do have a family. I just didn't get them at first. The family I have now didn't want to change my name.'

'That's good. It's a good name,' Charlie mumbled, and used his forearm to wipe cream cheese and chocolate from the corner of his mouth. 'Besides, it's what you had that was all yours, right?'

I reached across the table and put my hand on his. 'You're a pretty smart guy, Charlie. You know that?'

'Yep,' he answered. 'I clean fish real fast.'

Chapter Five

The door opened and Lieutenant Aaron Rauser strolled in on a shaft of morning light and nearly collided with Charlie.

'Charlie, what up?' Rauser asked, and held up his hand.

Charlie laughed too loudly and high-fived Rauser. 'Gotta go work, Mr Man. Hey, Keye can cook,' he added, and left without further explanation.

'Oooo-kay,' Rauser said, and then in a half whisper, added, 'Hard to believe he was some kind of biomedical something. Poor bastard.'

'I heard he was an engineer, but I never really believed it,' Neil said, and peeked outside to make sure he was gone. 'I just figured him for a retard.'

Rauser chuckled, and I said, 'That's incredibly insensitive, even for you two.'

'Whatever,' Neil said, and returned to his desk with his mug.

Rauser headed for the kitchen, where the coffee was almost always fresh. Neil practically lives on the stuff. And sometimes, when he's in a very generous mood, he makes cappuccino for Rauser and me. He prefers something dark in the mornings, Café Bustelo mostly. After-noons in winter, he likes a nice smooth Jamaican Blue. On summer days, cold-pressed Cuban on ice with cream and sugar. He cuts me off when my leg starts to shake.

But that wasn't why Rauser was here today. He had something on his mind. I watched him chewing the inside of his bottom lip while he stirred half-and-half into his coffee. He looked good with his jacket off, shoulder holster over a black T-shirt, biceps tight against the sleeves, gray slacks. I took a moment to appreciate that while he wasn't looking. Rauser had a few jagged edges, but he was a handsome guy if you're okay with off-the-charts testosterone levels, the kind of guy who has to shave down to the collarbone every morning. He's more Tommy Lee Jones than Richard Gere. More Gyllenhaal than Pitt.

The kitchen where he stood doctoring his coffee was really just a corner of the converted warehouse, with all the necessary appliances, a sink, red marble countertops, no walls or partitions. He saw a couple of leftover figs on the table, glanced at me for approval, then plucked them all off the plate. A raging sweet tooth was just one of the things we had in common.

Big puffy leather sectionals had been strategically placed throughout the wide-open space just beyond the kitchen, along with leather cubes in bright colors – red, purple, mint, red, purple, mint. Most of the main space was painted a very light sage, but the longest, most open wall was periwinkle with a shocking Granny-Smith-apple-green line painted across the center, part lightning bolt, part EKG monitor. I had given away my decorating power of attorney to a local designer based solely on her reputation in the city, a decision I questioned later.

'All we need is a goddamn purple dinosaur!' I'd blurted out upon first seeing our newly designed commercial loft. The designer, standing with hands on hips and her subordinates lined up reverently behind her, had very explicitly and through clenched teeth explained to me as if I had some disability how sophisticated and dramatic the space was. Sure. Okay. I can appreciate drama. Hey, I'd paid good money to have her drag us into the twenty-first century and, by God, I was going to learn to love it. A wide, flat-screen plasma television that lowered itself out of the rafters on demand was the highlight for me. It thrilled me each and every time. Neil, Rauser, me, Diane, even Charlie now and then, we had all spent evenings here watching games and movies, playing foosball on a table Neil and I had ordered and then paid someone else to assemble. Two fights had broken out regarding competing ideas for assembly before we realized we were not equipped for the project. Damn thing must have been in five hundred pieces.

Rauser walked toward us, blowing steam off his coffee and watching us from under arched brows. Neil and I were joking around about something silly and that seemed to irritate him.

'Ah,' he said, loud enough to interrupt. 'The intellectual stimulation here, it's what I come for.'

'Why *do* you come?' Neil asked with a smirk.

Rauser came back with 'To see if you suck dick as good as you make coffee.'

'You wish,' Neil said without looking at Rauser. He was fixed on his computer screen, which was a jumble of shifting letters and symbols and numbers. For all I knew, he was hacking into the CIA. He'd done it before, changed their logo by replacing the word *Intelligence* with one he liked better.

He swung his chair around, folded his arms over his chest, and studied Rauser. 'By the way, I put a mild hallucinogen in the coffee this morning.'

Neil and Rauser seemed to always be in some kind of competition. My presence made it worse, I decided, so I turned for my office before this escalated into scratching and spitting. I had work to do, but Rauser was hot on my heels.

He followed me into the far left corner of the warehouse that is my office. No glass or walls for privacy. Oh no, that would have been too simple. Instead, the design firm simply erected a huge wire fence. It's something like an enlarged version of barbed wire and about ten feet high – barbed wire on steroids, and backlit in deep blue, sort of an artsy East-Berlin-during-the-Cold-War thing. Really different and, I have to admit, beautiful, in a moody anti-corporate corporate way.

Rauser plopped his ancient leather case on the outside edge of my desk and, after wrestling briefly with one of the brass latches, opened it. I was grinning at him and his old scarred-up case. The bottom corners were worn white and the intricate leatherwork on the outside was too faded to know what the original artist might have had in mind. It tickled me. That was the kind of guy Rauser was. The department had offered him a new car, but he liked his old Crown Vic. 'Rauser,' I'd said, 'this car has an eight-track. What are you thinking?' He had shrugged and mumbled something about dreading cleaning out the glove box and the window pockets and everywhere else he'd stuffed notes and maps and papers and cigarettes and junk.

He withdrew a stack of photographs from his case and dropped them in front of me. They hit with a loud smack. No warning. Crime scene photographs just tossed at me. Death on my desk. My smile and my good mood faded fast.

'A stay-at-home mom,' Rauser said as I took a photo into my hand and drew in a quiet breath. 'Nobody special. Know what I mean?' He lowered himself into the chair across from me. My stomach felt suddenly like it was full of granite.

I turned over the top photo, read the date and the name, her age at death, ethnicity. Lei Koto, Asian female, thirty-three years old, stomach-down on a bloody kitchen floor. You could see the edge of an oven in the upper right-hand corner. Her legs were spread, buttocks and inner thighs naked and bloodied, plenty of stab and bite marks. She looked so small and so alone lying there, I thought, and I was struck, as I always am, at what a solitary business death is, and at how stark, surreal, distorted and telling all at once violent-murder-scene photographs are – the wounds and bruises eerily illuminated by the bright lights used by scene techs, the blood and matted hair, the unnatural positions, the screaming absence of life. Even at a glance, before detail emerges, you know it's a death scene. One never forgets.

'Who found her?' I asked.

'Ten-year-old kid,' Rauser answered. I looked up from the photographs, and he added, 'Her son. His name is Tim.'

This would change him, I thought, change the way he sees the world, sees a stranger, a spot of blood, an empty house. It would change this little boy as it had changed me. We are all of us disfigured in some way by the grief that murder always leaves in its wake. I didn't want to think about this child or what he felt or what he will feel. Interest in this sort of thing invites darkness to bleed into your life. And even knowing this, I ached for him. A part of me wanted to help piece him back together somehow, warn him of the nightmares, warn him of the shuffling around that would come. No one really knows what to do with a child who has been made homeless by violence. Will relatives take him? the police would wonder aloud, thoughtlessly and with the best intentions. Adults would whisper and worry and shoot concerned glances his way, increasing his terror tenfold. A stranger from social services would come to sit with him while they searched for next of kin. But no reassurances, no kindness can mend that kind of terrible rip in the infrastructure. It would take years.

The crime scene photographs trembled in my fingers.

'Why are you showing me this?'

Rauser handed me a letter addressed to him at the Homicide Division, neatly printed and without a signature. I looked at him for a moment before I began to read. His eyes were steady on me.

Dearest Lieutenant,

Do you want to know how I did it? No – your forensic experts have determined that much by now. Did you find the details troubling? I have such vivid memories of standing on her front steps smelling her small kitchen. She smiled as she pushed open the door for me.

I know where your mind must be going, Lieutenant, but you will not find a trace of me in her life. I was no part of her inner circle. She died not knowing who I was. She died asking Why? They all want some peace in the midst of chaos. Their chaos, not mine. I do not tell them. I am not there to comfort them.

The papers have called me a monster. I think you know better.

28

What have your profilers told you? That I am intelligent, able to blend into the outer world, and sexually functioning? A pity their methods do not offer you a better yardstick with which to measure mine.

You have withheld certain information about the crime scenes from the newspapers. Did you know their constant and incorrect speculation would compel me to respond? And what does your experience tell you about this letter, this new tool for your investigation? You have either concluded that I am a braggart as well as a sadist or that I have a deep and driving need to be caught and punished. And you must certainly be wondering if I am, in fact, the stranger you seek. Shall I convince you?

The day was hot by ten that morning and the air inside that kitchen was heavy and damp from a pot of boiling cabbage. I felt a breeze from the open window as I stood at the table looking down at her on the floor. She was quiet by then and still and seemed so tiny when I turned her over to make my marks.

The last sound she heard above her own whimper was the click of my shutter and the tiny crack of her neck, like a wishbone snapped in half.

Chapter Six

'He broke her neck,' I said quietly, and sank back in my chair. I held the photo in my hand of Lei Koto twisted up and bloody on her own kitchen floor, her head bent too far left to be natural.

'Cause of death,' Rauser answered. 'The wishbone reference. What do you make of it?'

I pushed through a jumble of emotion. I pushed through it as I always had and I found my trained self, my detached self, and I answered, 'Power, domination, manipulating the victim, the victim's body.'

'Letter's accurate right down to the cabbage on the stove. We never released cause of death or any scene details to the press. Original's in the lab. Hopefully, he left a print or licked an envelope or something. We don't have much so far.'

'You have a letter from a killer. You don't get handed this kind of behavioral evidence every day.'

Rauser nodded. 'It's a different kind of case, Keye. Motive isn't understood. The scene isn't understood. Physical evidence is practically nonexistent. I get that the way we find this guy is to understand what he's playing out at these scenes.'

A tiny alarm was sounding somewhere deep inside me. I felt that familiar tug to unravel the pathology, to contemplate the violent acts of violent offenders until I got one step ahead. Yes, this one is different, I was thinking, and epinephrine shot through my system. My palms felt sweaty. *They all want some peace in the midst of chaos.* 'She wasn't the first,' I heard myself saying to Rauser. Yes, this one is different. This killer's not just some opportunist, not some thug, but something else, something cruel and hungry that schemes and feeds off fear and anguish.

'Four victims we know of.' Rauser's gray eyes were cold as winter rain. 'ViCAP linked them. Detective down in Florida got assigned to cold cases a few months ago and started entering old scenes in the database. ViCAP matched two scenes down there to one here in the northern suburbs, then the flags went up again when we entered the Koto scene two weeks ago. No doubt about it. Same MO. Same signature elements – positioning, multiple stab wounds, staging, lack of physical evidence. Also, the victims are always facedown, legs spread, premortem stabbing to various areas of the body and postmortem stabbing to specific areas, inner and outer thighs, buttocks and lower back. Bite marks on inner thighs, shoulders, neck, and buttocks. Same weapon, serrated blade, something like a fishing knife, four to five inches long. Bite marks are consistent for the same perpetrator.'

'No DNA?'

Rauser shook his head. 'He's using rubber or latex barriers, maybe a dental dam. We're checking medical supply houses, dentists, medical assistants, doctors.' He chewed his lip. 'Four victims *that we know of*. I mean, how many murders out there haven't even gone into a database? Or have different characteristics? If he started killing young, are the early ones going to match? I assume he's been developing and learning.'

'How long since the first murder?'

Rauser didn't have to look at his notes. 'Keye, this guy has been hunting for at least fifteen years.'

How many murders had gone unreported? How many cold cases still not entered in a criminal database? I tried to let this sink in. 'The last one didn't satisfy the craving,' I said. 'So he writes to you about it. He's restless, unfulfilled. He's telling you he's becoming fully active, Rauser.'

'You know what really bugs me?' Rauser rubbed the stubble on his face. 'The way he leaves them. The bastard knew about the Koto kid. He knows enough about each victim to get in and out at exactly the right time to avoid apprehension. He wanted the kid to find her.'

I didn't like thinking about the boy or anyone else finding someone they love torn and broken and treated with that kind of disregard. It took me a moment to swallow down the growing lump in my throat. 'Ritually displaying the body, leaving it for someone close to the victim to find in positions the killer considers humiliating, leaving the body unclothed, postmortem mutilation, it's all part of the domination theme. It absolutely establishes the killer's control over the victim.'

He took more scene photos out of his case, rubber-banded together, each group labeled, and pushed them across the desk. 'Why do you think he turns them over?'

'Maybe he's not okay with their faces,' I answered, and thought about that. 'Maybe it feels to him like they're watching him.'

'Jesus,' Rauser said.

'Positioning the bodies gives him more power. It helps him dissociate and objectify them.'

I went through the photographs one by one. *Anne Chambers, white female, 20, Tallahassee, Florida. Bob Shelby, white male, 64, Jacksonville, Florida. Elicia Richardson, black female, 35, Alpharetta, Georgia. And Lei Koto, Asian female, 33.* Three women and one man of varying ages and ethnicity, all left facedown, stabbed and bitten.

She died asking WHY. *They all want some small peace in the midst of chaos. Their chaos, not mine. I do not tell them. I am not there to comfort them.*

I looked at Rauser. 'Homicide isn't the motive in this kind of crime. It's merely the result of his behaviors at the scene. Manipulation, control, domination – that's motive.'

Rauser groaned. 'Great, that's gonna be easy to track down.'

I looked back at the Lei Koto scene: the little kitchen, pale yellow walls, yellow countertops, white appliances spattered with blood and smeared with her handprints. I'd seen a lot of crime scenes. They

THE STRANGER YOU SEEK

all shocked and disturbed me. They all told a story.

According to the autopsy report Rauser brought with him, there were extensive wounds to the neck and shoulders. The angles suggested that Lei Koto had her back to her killer at some point during their interaction; some of the wounds were clean, some torn and ragged. I looked at the bloodstain analyst's report. Blood pooled on the kitchen floor, then arterial spray and spatter from her wounds, cast off from a bloodied weapon, dotted the stove, the refrigerator. Walls and floor in the hallway were smeared. I understood what this meant. The initial attack came from behind while Lei was still and unprepared, and then she started to move and it continued and continued and continued. The blood spatter proved that she had somehow broken free at one point and tried to get away. Perhaps she'd been allowed that one brief hope of fleeing, just for entertainment's sake, just so the killer would have something to chase. Already I was learning something about the offender. A patient sadist, to be sure. And a disciplined one. The attack had gone on, according to the pathologist, for more than two hours. It went all the way through the house. He had then dragged Lei Koto back into her kitchen, leaving bloody drag marks across the living room floor and down the hallway.

Why? Why did it need to end in the kitchen where it began? I thought back to the letter, to the cabbage on the stove. I looked at the inventory sheets. Ground beef in the fridge in an open bowl. She was making dinner early before the summer sun heated up the house, I realized. That's why there was cabbage on the stove at ten in the morning and why there was an uncovered bowl of hamburger in the fridge. Dinner for the two of them, her son and herself. A wave of nausea washed over me. He not only wanted the boy to find his mother, he wanted to leave her right there where she was making dinner for him.

I closed my eyes and imagined him coming home. The smell of scorched food would have led him straight to the kitchen. *Mom? Mom? You here?* The killer would have considered all this, of course.

The planning, the fantasizing, the act, the time with the victim – all that was only part of it. The attention that comes later is thrilling, validating. *What are they saying about me? What are they thinking?* His imprint on this child's life, that he'd marked someone in an undeniable way, was a huge bonus, invigorating.

I looked again at the autopsy results for each of the four victims they'd linked. A finely serrated knife had done most of the damage, weakened each. But never, not at any of the scenes attributed to this killer, was the knife the actual cause of death. The knife was just a tool, I decided, just part of the fantasy reenactment.

Rauser was digging through his old leather case for his notes. He liked to do this sometimes, just bounce things off me. 'The African American female, Elicia Richardson, she was a lawyer, successful, lived in one of those big Alpharetta neighborhoods north of town, killed in her home. Just like Lei Koto, who was widowed and lived with her son. And the two cases in Florida – Bob Shelby lived on disability and was also killed in his home, and the female student at WFSU, the first vic we know of, killed in her dorm room. All during daylight hours.' He leaned forward, arms on my desk. 'So we know how he kills them and how he leaves them. But we haven't figured out what connected them in life. Maybe it's random. Maybe he sees them somewhere and the crazy sonofabitch just goes ape-shit.'

'I don't think it's random,' I said.

'Victimology tells us victims' lifestyles, ethnicity, neighborhoods, income levels, ages, friends, restaurants, takeout joints, dry cleaners, routes to work, and childhood experiences are too varied to make a connection. I thought the deal with serials is that they choose a type, a race, a gender, an age range, something. These cross all the lines. I can't find the thread, you know? That one thing that draws him to them. There's no forced entry at any of the scenes. So they each opened the door for the creepy sonofabitch. Last victim, Lei Koto, even made him tea.' He pointed at one of the photographs from the kitchen. There were two glasses, nearly full, on the table. 'No prints.

34

No saliva. He never touched it. He never touches anything. The scenes are freakishly clean. Ligature abrasions are from wire at all the scenes, wrists, in some cases the neck.'

'So they're conscious and struggling while he's torturing them,' I said.

Rauser nodded his agreement and we were silent, just letting our minds grasp that, trying not to imagine it and imagining it anyway. We had both processed too many crime scenes to be able to push the images away. What we were better at was pushing away the feelings.

'You send the reports to the Bureau for analysis?' I asked.

Rauser nodded. 'And the letter. White male, thirty-five to forty-five, smart, probably able to hold down a job, lives alone, could be divorced, a sexual predator who is living and probably working in the metro area.' He gave a little salute and added, 'Great work, FBI. That narrows it down to about two million guys in this city.'

'He needs time and space to engage the fantasies that drive his violent behaviors,' I said. 'So it makes sense they're thinking he lives alone. And, according to his letter, he's taking pictures, so that helps keep the fantasy ramped up. What he's doing with them, he's already imagined in vivid detail. It's just a matter of inserting the victim. He probably sees himself in a relationship with them somehow. Are there secondary scenes?'

'Primary scene and disposal site are one and the same. Does all his work on them right there. What does that tell you?'

'He doesn't *have* to remove them to a secondary scene, because he knows he's not going to be interrupted. He's obviously engaging in the kind of precautionary acts that make him feel secure about their schedules, the neighbors, and that the door will open.'

'There's no evidence of rape, no seminal fluid, but the Bureau labeled it sexual homicide. Why? This just ups the wow factor for the press.'

'Well, the stabbing thing is usually associated with sexual behaviors.'

'Jesus Christ,' Rauser erupted, startling me. 'I can't wait to announce that we've got some kind of sexual lust killer out there. We have a press conference in two hours. And I have the pleasure of telling the city we have a serial.'

I remained very still even though I didn't feel calm at all. My desk was covered in death scene photographs and Rauser was emitting stress hormones that were leaping across the desk and slapping me in the face. We did not have a history of being great together when one of us was stressed out. We're a bit like puppies, Rauser and I, much better at playing and not so good at calming each other down. Generally a fight breaks out when we're both cranked up.

Rauser looked away. 'I'm grasping at straws and you're not giving me anything I don't already know.'

I thought about the taunting letter and about the medical examiner's report. I couldn't stand it when Rauser was disappointed with me. I loved and hated the way I felt around him. That Daddy thing again. It was a hook for me and always had been. My father barely spoke a word to me or any other member of our family, and when he did, it was like the clouds had parted and you suddenly felt all warm inside. Both my brother and I spent too much of our childhood trying to draw him out in order to repeat that feeling, and I've spent too much of my adult life looking for that from men. My mother, on the other hand, was almost never quiet. She handed out her criticisms liberally and her approval sparingly, which only seemed to compound our psychoses.

'Violent offenders report having had penetration fantasies while they're stabbing,' I told Rauser. 'The theory follows that the offender uses a knife instead of a penis. The stabbing tends to be around the sexual areas of the body, and in some cases the stabbing has also been postmortem and therefore not about victim suffering but something very different. In criminal psych circles it might be called some-thing like regressive necrophilia.'

'What else?' he asked.

'Writing to you now after being silent for so long, if it really has been fifteen years, playing games with law enforcement – it's all meant to heighten the level of excitement and challenge. Just killing isn't enough anymore.'

'He doesn't just kill, Keye, he mutilates them,' Rauser reminded me, and ran a hand through thick salt-and-pepper hair.

'I'm sorry. I wish I could help. I really do.' I only half meant it, of course. It was just what I said when Rauser was worried about something.

'You can,' he said, surprising me. 'Come to the station and read all the reports from all the scenes. Break it down to something practical I can use to figure out who this bastard is. I'll put you in the budget as a consultant.'

I shook my head. 'I don't think that would be a great choice for me right now. This kind of work, I think it's why I drank so much.'

'Bullshit.' Rauser chuckled, but there was no humor whatsoever in his eyes. He had never been the kind of guy to cut me a lot of slack. 'You drank because you're an alcoholic. What are you worried about?'

'I was fired from the Bureau, remember? Couldn't stay sober. Oh, and my marriage came apart and I spent three months in rehab. 'Member that? You want to derail your entire case? You need a criminologist whose credentials hold up during the trial phase.'

'DA can get some talking head up there on the stand with a prettier past. I need you now, today, in *this* phase. I don't trust anybody else with this pointy-head analysis shit. And I fucking hate it when you feel sorry for yourself.' He started gathering his things with quick jerky movements. 'I know, I know, the Bureau did you wrong. Well, goddamnit, get over it, Street. So you have a drinking problem. You and about fifty million other people. Stop using it as an excuse not to participate. So you had a tough childhood. Welcome to the club.'

Angry and stretched too tight, he shoved his notes and photographs into his leather case. I thought about Bob Shelby, the killer's only documented male victim. He'd lived alone on disability, Rauser had told me. Life had obviously already handed Bob Shelby enough pain.

He shouldn't have had to endure torture and humiliation and terror in his final moments. I thought about Elicia Richardson. Black, female, young, and successful, she'd shattered all those ceilings. Her family must have been so proud of her. Why did she open her door that day? I thought about Anne Chambers just beginning adult life at WFSU. I thought about Lei Koto and the chaos and horror in that kitchen, and Tim coming home to find her. I thought about Rauser's eyes on me now, steel with tiny blue flecks. I knew him. It hadn't been easy for him to ask for help.

I leaned my head back and closed my eyes, took a deep breath. I wanted a drink.

Rauser slammed his case closed, grabbed it by the handle. 'Congratulations, by the way. You're in full agreement with your former employer. Bureau says he's coming alive again too and that this cooling-off phase will be very brief. You know as well as I do what that means.'

It wasn't really a cooling off, I thought. It was a gradual ramping up. And even though APD wasn't turning up bodies at the moment, the killer was out there, and he was fantasizing, reliving his kills, very carefully planning for a later reenactment, and perhaps already stalking his next victim.

Chapter Seven

KNIFEPLAY.COM

Your Online Adult Edge Fetish & Knife Play Community blogs > beyond the EDGE, a fantasy by BladeDriver blog title > Pool Boy

He had not noticed me. He had a tiny phone to his ear and he was telling someone too loudly that his work keeps him so busy. 'I see the wife and kids for five minutes at breakfast,' he said into his stupid phone, and laughed. It was eight this morning and we were jammed into an elevator. Every asshole in town with a briefcase was pressed up against me, and he was showing off for the crowd. I saw him sneak a glance around the elevator, his theater. This was where he thrived. I recognized the pathology. It sickened me. It felt like a heavy, wet blanket just dropped down on me, and it had. Its name was David. What a little prick, a fucking little bragger. Mr Up-and-Coming. No time for the family, but plenty of time for his dick. He had not changed a bit.

He snapped his phone shut and glanced around again. He wanted to make sure he had made an impression. So desperate for approval. *Pathetic.*

He lit up when he saw my face. He remembered. A mutual friend, an invitation to a backyard barbeque. I met his wife and fucked him twenty minutes later behind his own pool house. And now this, a chance meeting. What luck!

The elevator door opened and I stepped out onto the fifth floor with him. He wagged a finger at me. 'You never called.'

We walked in our business suits down tiled halls and carpeted corridors, stopped by a concession stand the size of a closet, and ordered black coffee that came with cardboard sleeves. He was blathering about a promotion. He uses his hands when he talks, slim, manicured hands with a thick gold wedding band on the left ring finger, and he glanced at me to make sure I was listening. He wanted to know I was interested. I was. *Very.* He smiled. He liked the way I was looking at him. My cold aspirations validated and flattered him. I know the type. He too pays a lot of attention to what he wears. The pair of black John Lobbs on his feet must have cost twelve hundred dollars, a Fioravanti power suit in navy blue was probably another twelve grand. He also pays a dominatrix four hundred a month to text him degrading messages, step on his balls, and assault him with a dildo now and then.

We made a date. Dinner. I think I will fuck him for a while before the point of my steel parts his flesh. How deep will it go before shallow David bleeds? I will keep you posted. *BladeDriver.*

Sunsets are dazzling in Atlanta and utterly counterfeit. Nearly five million people and their idling automobiles help stain the city air dusty-yellow on still summer days when ozone smog is so far out of federal compliance that even a big-money bank exec might raise an eyebrow, but at night when the late summer sun catches the chemical air just right, it turns the downtown sky to fire. Each evening, from my loft window on the tenth floor of the Georgian Terrace Hotel, I am treated to the show along with a million or so commuters stuck on the Downtown Connector, ribbons of rolling reds and whites from my perspective, miles of them.

It was raining the first time I looked through this window. It was December and Peachtree Street was dressed up for the holidays. Lights from the Fox Theatre danced off glistening streets as the concert crowd left cafés with frozen breath and long coats to gather under the pale yellow lights of the big red marquee. I love my Peachtree Street neighborhood, where restaurants leave the back doors open to let out the heat and the delicious scents greet me each day, where fried chicken livers and pecan pie appear on the same menu with lobster risotto and fig brandy soufflé, where street vendors and street people take their chances among the polished shoes of the rich, and windshield washers wait on corners with half-empty spray bottles.

But Atlanta can be a hard city in summer, when the days are long and the unblinking sun sends temperatures soaring. Tempers flare. Steam billows from overheated engines, and stepping onto the street feels like stepping in front of a heat blower. Atlanta broils in its own anger. And now, because of what Rauser had told me, I knew another killer was roaming the streets.

I heard a sound in the hall outside my loft and thought about Dan. Even now, a smell, a sound, the turning of a lock, can launch me back into what it felt like to share a life with someone, a home, the prosaic burdens of the everyday, waiting to see his blue eyes in the evening, hear his voice in my ear. It's not like that with us anymore. Not even close. It's work. It's barely civil. It's utterly fractured.

White Trash, the cat I had rescued off Peachtree Street two years ago, came from the bedroom stretching and yawning and rammed her head into my ankle. I call her White Trash because she's white and because I found her having dinner in a pile of trash. I don't know what she calls me. I stroked her a few times and turned back to Peachtree Street feeling pouty and unloved, and I hadn't eaten in hours.

My phone went off. Rauser's ringtone. I didn't want to talk to him or to anyone, but I'm not always good at saying what I need. 'Hey,' I answered without any enthusiasm. I felt a little angry with him for coming down so hard on me yesterday simply because I wasn't giving him what he wanted.

'Well, that doesn't sound good,' Rauser said. I recognized the background noise, phones and voices at Atlanta Police Department, and pictured Rauser in his cube. We hadn't talked since he'd stormed out of my office.

'Not a great day,' I dodged.

'Have lunch with Dan?' Rauser asked, and I could hear him moving, then the elevator dinging. 'That was today, wasn't it? You guys talk?'

41

'I'm so up to my ass in talk,' I snapped.

'Hey, really great attitude, Street.'

'He's in therapy,' I said. 'So am I. Give me a break.'

'Bitter, party of one,' Rauser said.

'Yes, I am bitter. He thinks he's a goddamn analyst now because he's in therapy. And he's so righteous. It's painful.'

'And what was Dr Dan's diagnosis?'

'That I can't be serious. That I have intimacy issues.'

Rauser chuckled. 'How'd you take it?'

I sighed. 'I told him, "I got your issues right *here*," and I grabbed my crotch and walked out.'

'Smart,' Rauser said. 'And grown-up too.' The elevator dinged again, then footsteps on old tiled floors. The wind hit his phone suddenly and I knew he'd stepped outside the building. I wondered where he was going, to what emergency. An urgent need for a cigarette or another crime scene? I thought for the millionth time about those photos he'd tossed on my desk.

We'd had these discussions before, Rauser and I. We understood things about the other no one else but a lover might. My romantic life till now had been a series of tiny wars. The last one, a five-year marriage, left me feeling raw and a little bloodied. Rauser was ten years divorced. Two grown kids. Both in DC. They never visited Atlanta. He saw them when he could. He said he still loved his wife. I knew he'd called her a few times over the years and hung up when she answered. He knew I'd slept with Dan, even mad as hell at him, and each time it had whittled away at my self-worth. Rauser and I were both woefully unqualified for a lasting romantic relationship. We were moody, appallingly self-indulgent and self-absorbed. Our kinship, we had decided over doughnuts and coffee at Krispy Kreme, was in our defects.

'Dan's a jerk,' he said, and exhaled. I imagined a cloud of cigarette smoke around him. 'A namby-pamby pain-in-the-ass jerk. I've been meaning to tell you that.'

I considered that for a moment. Dan was small boned with the fluid movements of a dancer, dark hair he always wore below the collar, and just handsome enough in an artsy, rakish way as not to be perceived as effeminate. I thought about the way he had always managed to twist his fine features into a perpetually bored expression whenever I introduced him to someone.

'He really is a jerk,' I agreed.

'So what's the attraction?'

'He has an enormous cock.'

Rauser laughed. 'Listen, Keye. I'm sorry about yesterday. I just . . . I don't know. I don't mean to take it out on you, okay?'

It was in these moments, these small gestures, that Rauser revealed himself. When he showed up with takeout or called for nothing else than to find out what I was doing and suffered quietly through a complete explanation of my day while in the midst of a high-pressure investigation. He was a very sweet man and I was glad he had called after all.

'Shit,' he said suddenly. 'Gotta go, Street.'

Chapter Eight

I wasn't sure how long I'd been asleep when my cell phone sounded. White Trash was lying on my chest. I generally didn't mind, but lately she'd taken to pointing herself in the wrong direction, so that when I woke, I had the distinct pleasure of looking directly at her butt. Aerosmith's 'Dude (Looks Like a Lady)' blasted out of my phone, the ringtone I'd assigned to Rauser. I wasn't sure he would fully appreciate the humor in this, so I kept it to myself.

'You okay?' I asked, looking at my bedside clock. Three a.m.

'I got another letter. Guy's a total whack job, Keye.'

I was silent.

'Keye? You back asleep?'

'Yes,' I lied. I honestly was not sure if I wanted to rush in to help or slam down the phone. I had tried in the past and without much success to establish boundaries around his work and my life and where it's okay and not okay that the two meet, but I'd given mixed signals, I knew. Cop work pulled at me like a drug, like warm lemon vodka, and I had both loved and hated this thing I'd spent my life learning.

'I'm faxing it to you, okay? Just please look at it. I won't ask you again, but I need your brain tonight. He gave us a timeline. Three days until he kills again.'

I let that fresh horror sink in for a second, then sat up in my bed and thought back to the murder scene photos, to Lei Koto on her kitchen floor, and Bob Shelby and Elicia Richardson, and Anne Chambers brutalized in a dorm room. I thought again about their blood, their final horror. I'd sensed it when I looked at those pictures. *Three days.*

In an old pair of Dan's boxer shorts and a T-shirt, I made my way to the kitchen. My blood sugar was about ankle high. I found a bottle of grape juice and thought about those first days in rehab while they were detoxing me. They supplied plenty of replacements, phenobarb and grape juice to name just two. A nurse told me grape juice would slam into my system the way the cognac used to and trick me. She was right. On day four they started removing the crutches. The phenobarbital was first. Day five, they came for my grape juice. I'm still kind of pissed about that. My first trip to the market when I was released, I stocked up. Rauser pours three fingers of it in a whiskey glass for me when I go to his house, and fills his own with cheap bourbon, and we clink our glasses together and pile up in front of the TV in summer to watch the Braves.

I thought about Rauser and sighed, leaned against the kitchen counter with my grape juice, felt the guilt seeping into me. Guilt, another gift from my days as a practicing drunk. Was I really being that selfish? Rauser had available to him great investigative minds if he would just tap them, but he wouldn't trust easily. He hadn't been exactly thrilled with the psychological sketch he had received from the Bureau. He'd be protective of his territory, reluctant to open the door any further to an outside agency, and the truth is, local cops solve local problems better than anyone else.

From the living room, I heard the whine of my fax machine. White Trash bumped my ankles, waiting for the splash of half-and-half she'd grown accustomed to in the morning. That we were up four hours early seemed to make no difference at all to her begging schedule and her relentless pursuit of dairy. I put a little cream into a saucer for her and walked into the living room.

What was I so afraid of? I asked myself. Was I afraid I couldn't do it without drinking? That I couldn't let my mind run in that savage terrain without it? Had alcohol made me a better profiler? I was certainly more attuned to unleashed destructive power back then,

45

but unfortunately a lot of that destructive power was my own. Perhaps it was learning that dark craft in the first place that had pushed me into something my genes had been poised and eager to receive already. Might it push me there again? I never wanted to go back there. Not ever. *And* I wanted a drink every day, which is the torment of addiction, the constant tug, tug, tugging of rival desires. It was pulling at me now as I took two neatly typed, double-spaced pages from the fax machine. I felt the familiar quickening in my pulse, a ticking in my temple. No, this wasn't dread or fear, this was something else – exhilaration.

I switched on a floor lamp and sank onto my couch with the letter.

Lieutenant Aaron Rauser
Atlanta Police Department
Homicide Unit, City Hall East

It wasn't planned. I wasn't there for him. Providence intervened. You want to understand, don't you, Lieutenant? You want me to explain the selection process.

'What is it, what nameless, inscrutable, unearthly thing is it . . . ?' Melville wanted to know, just as you do now. The why of all this must drive you mad.

It was an elevator, an innocent encounter, him smoothing his black hair, performing, and me so close I could smell his aftershave. His self-importance made me want to laugh, and then it made me physically ill. His need was suffocating.

I watched him and I listened. I know the type. There's a stack of bodies buried under the ladder he's climbed. Eighty hours a week at the office and he still finds time to cheat on his wife. He has to have it, that extramarital thrill. He uses sex to fill in the vacancies. And there are so many vacancies. He says he loves his wife and children, but he hasn't the capacity. He's pretending, just as I am. What are the profilers calling it these days? A successful social veneer? Smiling,

46

exchanging small talk with coworkers and neighbors, resting a chummy hand on their shoulder. Would it surprise you to know I have developed friendships? Nothing honest, of course, no deeply shared intimacy or any other disposition that defines friendship, merely the appearance thereof. And I'm so good at it. People like me, Lieutenant. Is that why they open the door?

Shall I toss you a tidbit? Here's something your analysts will want to know: when I am with them, when they beg me to stop, when they tell me I'm hurting them, when they ask why, I ask back, 'How does it feel? What does it feel like inside?' They never know what to say. They don't even understand what I'm asking. I dig deeper. I press on. I don't let them rest. I want to know. How Does It Fucking Feel? At least I give them something tangible to grieve, some pain that can be pinpointed, heroically endured. People forgive you for pain. Sometimes it's good to have an ache you can really sink your teeth into. This is why people cut themselves, I now understand. We are practically bleeding all over everything most of the time anyway. Might as well see the goddamn trail of arterial spray we leave behind.

No empathy, you decide. Totally egocentric. But how would I know how to hurt them if I did not myself have a comprehensive understanding of pain and degradation? One must have a non-egocentric viewpoint in order to enjoy the true pleasures of egocentricity. Sick, sick, sick, you say. Don't judge me by your own values. It won't help you to find me. We merely employ a different set of ideals, you and I. Someone so terribly ill would have trouble, wouldn't they, avoiding detection for so long? And I have been at it longer than you think, Lieutenant.

I said hello to him on that elevator morning and we shook hands. Did your heart jump at reading that? A public setting, witnesses, video cameras. Oh, how that must intrigue you. What building and what elevator? Had we met before? He gave me his wolf smile and I knew at that instant he was every bit as much of a predator as I am.

47

Shall I give you a clue to make that hopeful heart of yours skip a beat?

David, black hair, expensive suits, up and coming.

Three days, Lieutenant. Tick-tock.

The light from Peachtree Street casts a stained glow over my loft at night and I love the warmth of it and the marquee at the Fox across the street outlined in fat, round bulbs. But tonight my home seemed eerily dark and silent as I sat with notebook and pen and this uninvited guest, another letter from a murderer.

When I answered my phone an hour later, Rauser said, 'You speaking to me? I'll make the coffee if you'll let me come up.'

He had called from the lobby and appeared two minutes later in Levis and a royal blue T-shirt with APD embroidered on the left sleeve in bright yellow, looking like he needed a nap and a shave. He went straight to the kitchen and dumped espresso beans in the coffee grinder. He knew where to find things here. We'd both spent a lot of time in the other's home.

'Coffee,' he said, and put our cups down on the coffee table, sat, turned toward me, and put his hand on mine. 'Thanks, Street. I just need to talk this through with somebody who understands this shit.'

I nodded. What else could I have possibly said to that?

He crossed an ankle over his knee and slurped the coffee he'd loaded with cream and sugar. 'I don't think this guy'd be letting off warning shots if there was time to find David,' he said flatly. 'But we're sure as hell gonna try. I don't care if we have to look at every tape from every building in this city, we're gonna catch this bastard.'

We were quiet for a moment. I thought about what that arduous process would be, about the time and resources it would gobble up, about some unlucky cop from each shift sitting for hours watching surveillance tapes, grainy and indistinct. And what exactly would they look for? Someone shaking hands on an elevator, walking the halls and talking? And then what? Spending hours, perhaps days, running down the names of those individuals, getting statements? The killer was putting out just enough information to keep APD chasing their tails.

Three days, Lieutenant. Tick-tock.

'Maybe the entire scenario is bullshit and he's just playing us. The bullshit factor's high with these guys.' Rauser was making notes on his own copy of the letter, chewing on his pen. 'That's the problem with killers. They're all a bunch of goddamn liars. Maybe there's an elevator and maybe not. Maybe there's a David, maybe not. We have to run it down, though, every bit of it.' Rauser had already pulled together more investigators than had ever been assigned to a task force in Atlanta, something the mayor had announced proudly and the media had criticized as excessive spending. Rauser had also set up twenty-four-hour tip lines. The most expensive task force ever wasn't getting results, or so the reports claimed.

'Something to think about,' I said carefully. 'He may have a good understanding of what this means in terms of manpower.' My heart rate spiked a little. Was the person killing and bragging about it in letters to Rauser familiar with law enforcement? And if so, how familiar?

Rauser looked at me, then shot me with his forefinger and thumb. 'Good point,' he said, and called one of his detectives. 'Williams, you and Bevins start checking out every denied application for the police academy in the last fifteen years,' he said into the phone. 'Run 'em down. All of them. Cop wannabes on file, *CSI* freaks, find them too and check their alibis. And I want you to personally and very quietly, please, get a list of everybody we've had disciplined because of excessive force, sexual harassment issues, abusive language or sexual assaults, anyone on probation or paid leave with that kind of stuff pending, I want their files on my desk by noon.'

Rauser took the crime scene photos from his case and spread them around my coffee table. 'Guy's obviously intelligent,' he said, arranging them in groups from first to last murder – Anne Chambers,

Bob Shelby, Elicia Richardson, Lei Koto. 'FBI talked about him being a frustrated underachiever. Is that what you see?'

'No,' I answered. 'I see a perfectionist. Someone careful and focused who wants to appear brilliant, who wants to impress others. The two letters tell us that. I don't see some guy who still lives in his mama's basement.'

Rauser nodded his agreement. 'So I've got a potential victim named David and a goddamn elevator, that's what I got from this shit.' He thumped the letter with his forefinger.

'Well, there are a couple other things to get from it. For one, this person would be extremely controlling in life,' I said. 'Family members, lovers, coworkers, would have experienced this on some level. Also, the sadistic behaviors probably need acting out with sexual partners even in the cooling-off periods. He probably pays for this or finds them in S/M communities where there's curiosity play with pain and bondage, but he wouldn't like his partners having boundaries or using safe words. People like this get bad reputations in communities where it's controlled. I'd start asking questions there. He's probably also looking at websites that help him fuel the domination fantasy. He's careful, though. The whole social veneer idea, it's really true, Rauser. On the surface, I think he is what he says he is. Extremely good at the game.'

'All the other victims were fairly easy access, but if David has a family and wears expensive suits, it'll be different. He'll have a security system, maybe a nanny or a stay-at-home wife, a dog or two.'

'Elicia Richardson had a security system,' I said, and picked up a picture of her lying facedown with her legs spread, bruised and bitten. Dark-stained oak floors surrounded the Chinese rug where she'd been left like an abandoned rag doll. Savage bite marks covered her shoulders and inner thighs, stab wounds on the thighs and buttocks, on her sides and lower back. I imagined him walking into her home. Had she been expecting him? I closed my eyes and tried to be there, see Elicia in life, through his eyes. I ring the bell and wait. She's pretty. She smiles. Does she know me? She wants me here.

Why? I step into her home. I'm nervous, but then my lungs fill with the air she's breathing and I feel the power. I know I own her now just like I own the doorway I've stepped through and the air we're sharing and the rug under my feet. All I can think about is when, when will I hit her that first time? I like the blitz. I like the surprise. I like seeing her plead while I get out my wire and my knife.

'Yeah, but the security system wasn't activated,' Rauser objected. 'Because she opened the door for the creepy sonofabitch just like the other three. She lived alone, though. David doesn't.'

'He won't take David at home. He's stepping out of that box, which makes him even more dangerous.'

'We're looking into the bisexual thing. But, truth is, it's the most closeted community out there. Lot of guys might want it, but they don't necessarily advertise that. We're hoping David does or the killer does. We're canvassing bars – straight, gay, S/M – questioning hustlers, male and female.'

'This is not about sexual preference or sexual attraction,' I said, and thought about all the violent serial cases I'd worked with the Bureau. 'It's about power.'

'How do I find him?' Rauser asked. 'How do we get to David in time?'

'Release the letter,' I answered.

Chapter Nine

I felt like I'd been out jogging all night. Rauser stayed until almost six. I was supposed to serve a restraining order at nine. Normally, these things aren't scheduled, but I got lucky on this one. The target, one William LaBrecque, had been forced to agree to church counseling sessions and to accept the documents I intended to hand him, a restraining order he'd dodged from the sheriff for weeks, in order for the State to consider supervised visitations. Easy money.

I found him in the chapel, sitting ramrod straight, staring ahead. A carpenter, I knew from his file, and a strong block of a man. William LaBrecque didn't seem particularly happy to see me. The feeling was mutual. I had not been inside a church in fifteen years.

'Don't you dare hand that to me in a house of God!' He practically hissed at me. His top lip curled.

'Look, we both know you have to take this or you'll never get to see your kid, so don't give me the house-of-God crap,' I whispered. 'Take it or I'll leave it sitting here. Either way, you've been served, Mr LaBrecque.'

Uh-oh. I was beginning to think we might have a problem. A lovely crimson rose up from his neck and a bulging blue vein in his temple started doing the Macarena.

'I'll just leave it,' I whispered.

'Screw you,' he snarled, and quite unexpectedly grabbed my wrist hard as I tried to squeeze past him in the pew. I didn't like his hands on me and I didn't trust his eyes, glossy and lit up now like lava. So much for the house-of-God thing.

'*Hey*.' I twisted my wrist free. 'I'm just the messenger here, pal. You knew this was coming. Your pastor made the arrangements. I don't think a big ole scene in church is going to help your case.'

'You know why that bitch lawyer and the pastor wanted us to meet in the church?' LaBrecque asked. 'So I wouldn't be tempted to cut your Chink ass into little pieces and stuff you in the fucking sewer.'

Oh boy.

That was my morning. Maybe later I could poke myself in the eye three or four hundred times just for fun.

The sun is streaming in through windows. The room is quiet as the killer leans back and reaches for the iPhone. There's video there, video of the black lawyer and video of the Asian bitch, the fussy mother hen cooking stinking cabbage for her son. That one was a favorite. Lei Koto on her knees begging and pleading. No dignity at all.

The killer smiled and slipped a hand into expensively tailored pants, and switched on the video of Lei Koto. *Everyone needs a release now and then.*

'Put on the gloves. That's right. Now give me your hand. Touch me right here just like this. *Do it!* Yeah, that's right. Keep doing it, baby. You stop and I'll fuck you up. You hear me? Stupid fucking bitch. You like jerking me off, don't you? Say it. Tell me you like it. *Tell me*.'

'I do. I like it.'

'Like what? *Say it!*'

'I like jerking you off?'

'Oh no. That's no good at all. You know what happens when you don't do this right? I get the knife back out. Is that what you want? Now, try again with some conviction this time. *Say it*. Say it like you mean it. You like jerking me off, don't you? You *love* it. You want me to come, don't you?'

'Please, just let me go. I'll do anything you want. I will. I swear. I won't make a sound. Just tell me what you want me to do.'

'I want you to say it right or I will end this now. Do you under-stand, Lei?'

'I do. I understand. I'll do whatever you want. Please.'

'Good. Now tell me how much you like touching me. Tell me you want me to come. *Tell me!*'

'I like touching you.'

'Say you like jerking me off. I want you to use that language. You think you're too good to say it? *Do it!* Say "jerking off". I want to hear it from your fucking bitch mouth.'

'I love it. I do. Please let me go and I'll do anything. I'll put my mouth on you. I'll be good. I promise. I'll let you do whatever you want and I won't make a sound. Just please don't hurt me anymore. Please! I'll be quiet.'

'That's good. The crying thing really works. Keep that hand going. I'm so close. I'm so close. Don't stop talking. Tell me what you love.'

'I love jerking you off. I want your come on me.'

'Oh yeah. Tell me you want it. Keep saying it. *Tell me.*'

'I want it. I want you. I love your come on me . . .'

'Oh yeah, yeah, yeah. *Fuck!* Now, wasn't that nice, baby? Look at the camera for me and smile. *Smile, bitch!* Excellent. Now take the gloves off and hand them to me. That's right. Don't want to forget these, do we?'

'I feel so dizzy.'

'Yes, I bet you do. Are your lips tingling yet? You're losing a lot of blood.'

'What happens now?'

'I'm going to stop your bleeding.'

I pulled in to the parking lot at 1800 Century Center Boulevard in the Century Center Office Park off the Northeast Expressway, a seventeen-floor glass building, triangular and black, baking in the midday sun. A few things needed to be picked up at a client's office, a small law firm but reliable about tossing work my way. Larry Quinn specialized in personal injury suits and his partners handled a lot of divorces. I'd been scratched up by a few rosebushes trying to get a good shot of an unfaithful spouse, and served divorce papers and subpoenas and restraining orders relating to those very cases. Time plus a hundred and fifty a pop for the paperwork, good work if you can get it.

The day was dry like most of our days had been since a three-year drought had kicked in. The weather patterns were changing now, I'd heard, and rain would come back to us. I knew I should care more about our trees, about Lake Lanier, our main source of water in Atlanta, being sixteen feet down. The local news crews were practically hyperventilating over this. Every day the papers treated us to a chart showing just how low the lake was and how long we had until we would run out of water and start eating one another. I secretly and very selfishly enjoyed the drought. It meant I could ride in my old Impala with the top down.

I headed for the revolving doors and felt the hot sun on my shoulders. It had some work to do burning through the morning smog, but it was doing just fine and was almost at the front side of the building, the side that faces I-85 where Larry Quinn's office was positioned. I sighed. I'd been in Larry's office when the sun had moved to his side of the triangle. Even with air-conditioning, it was tough to cool the glass-walled offices. We'd had meetings around his conference table with sweaty hairlines and pushed-up shirtsleeves. AT&T, the Atlanta field office for the Bureau, tons of doctors and lawyers, and the Marriott all called this office park home. Executive Park and the Druid Hills section of Atlanta were nearby, and in the opposite direction, was Buford Highway, which was hands down the best area for authentic ethnic cuisine, anything you want, miles of it, Korean, Malaysian, Indian, Chinese, Cuban, Peruvian. If you can dream it, if it walks, crawls, slithers, swims, grows on trees or vines, above or underground, somebody on Buford Highway is putting it in a savory sauce and cooking the shit out of it.

Larry Quinn's office was on the fifteenth floor, a long shoulder-to-shoulder elevator ride on busy mornings, at lunch, at five o'clock, but today I'd squeezed in quickly between the rush hours. Quinn's legal secretary, Danny, was at the front desk, a handsome guy in his mid-twenties with a headset and fingers that were always busy on the keyboard. Danny seemed to be able to do twelve things at once without skipping a beat. He put in forty hours a week at the offices of Larry Quinn & Associates, juggling work for three attorneys, but on the weekends, Danny shaved himself from cheek to ankle, slipped into heels and something slinky, and strutted like a runway model at one of Atlanta's drag clubs. He was the most beautiful woman I'd ever seen.

'Morning! I'll let Larry know you're here. He's in a mood, though.'

'Something happen?'

Danny shrugged. 'You know Larry – girl, he can go from silly to mean bastard in fifteen seconds. Unfortunately, it's the mean bastard that's been hanging around for a couple months now.'

'Maybe his panties are too tight,' I whispered, and we both laughed.

'What's so funny?' Quinn demanded from his office door.

'Girl talk,' Danny said. 'You wouldn't understand.'

Quinn was in his early forties but could pass for younger, a dirty blond with a southern accent who had become famous in Atlanta for his eye-rolling TV commercials. *Divorce, personal injury, tax problems. Make one call before you fall.* Practically everyone in town recognized Larry. I couldn't accompany him anywhere without some jerk-off saying 'Hey, Larry,' and then repeating his slogan word for annoying word.

'Danny, bring the Bosserman file, would you? Thank you,' Quinn said, and we walked into the conference room. Vertical blinds had been installed and it must have been ten degrees cooler than the last time I was here. 'How 'bout some coffee or bottled water, Keye?'

'I'm okay, thanks. You all right?' Larry was generally a happy guy, joked a lot, a mischievous little glint in his brown eyes. Today he seemed drawn.

He opened a bottle of water and sat down, smoothed his purple tie. 'It's showing, huh? Market tanked. I took a hit. Don't get me wrong. I'll be fine. But I don't own a damn thing that's not worth about half what it was. Know what I mean?'

'Everyone knows what you mean.'

Danny handed Larry the file and quietly closed the door on his way out. Larry looked it over. 'So the claimant's position is this. She goes to one of the Laser Treatment Centers of the Southeast to get the hair on her top lip removed. The technician in charge of this procedure improperly uses the equipment, has the setting way too high, something normally used for less sensitive areas like legs. The result is second- and third-degree burns above her upper lip.'

I shuddered. 'So now she has a burned-on mustache?'

Larry's trademark smile stretched out across his face for the first time today. 'I swear to Jesus, Keye, she looks like my uncle Earl now.'

We took a moment to enjoy his client's misfortune. It was wrong, of course, but funny doesn't know any better. 'You want the history on this treatment center and the technician, right?'

Larry nodded. 'Complaints and in what form and if this guy appeared in any of them, statements from individuals harmed, court records and any settlements you can dig up. Danny copied the file for you.'

Quinn was staring at his cell phone when I walked out of his office. I felt good about the file under my arm. It was something mildly interesting for a change, and with plenty of billable hours.

Neil was in his usual position at the computer when I walked in. I saw an extremely large fruit basket on the conference table where we sometimes worked and sat with clients, but generally it was where we ate and socialized and sometimes spread out pieces of jigsaws. Neil was a whiz at jigsaw puzzles. He could spot the right shape in a mountain of pieces. I think his brain must be shaped something like the state of Texas.

'What's this?' I asked stupidly. Neil didn't bother answering.

I pushed aside a satsuma orange to find a card. It was heavy stock, embossed, expensive, a thank-you for a job that had ended to their satisfaction, and signed by Margaret Haze, my first big client and now my most prestigious reference. There were law firms and corporate headhunting agencies that used my services now thanks solely to the weight of a hard-to-get recommendation from Guzman, Smith, Aldridge & Haze.

I would have to hire help soon. I needed another pair of eyes and ears for those long surveillance hours, cramming sugar and caffeine to stay awake and listening to crappy books on tape, someone to take over the errands, research and schedule gigs, someone to actually be nice to new clients when they call, which doesn't always happen now. I dreaded bringing a new person into my business and into my life. Change is, at the very least, inconvenient.

I dug through the fruit basket looking for something I wanted. 'People really eat this stuff?' I would have preferred a bag of Krispy Kremes. 'Freaks,' I muttered, and reported to Neil that the basket was a gift from Margaret Haze's office.

'That's why you're the detective,' he said grumpily.

It was going to be one of those days with him, I thought. Neil could be, well, a bit of a moody little bastard at times. But then I'd always been drawn to little bastards.

I sat down at my desk, picked up the phone, and heard the pulsating dial tone. My voice mail was full when I checked for messages. Neil doesn't take messages. He simply transfers the ones that hold no interest for him to my mailbox.

I listened to a batch of messages, client stuff, most of it, and then I heard Rauser's voice, stretched so tight it seemed about to snap, and realized I'd let the charge on my cell phone run down. I called him immediately.

The *Atlanta Journal-Constitution* had received a copy of the first letter from the killer, the one describing the Lei Koto murder, and they had decided to run it nearly in its entirety. Rauser was furious for the loved ones who might read this cold account of the killing, and he was afraid, too, that the publicity would only motivate the killer further and damage the investigation. 'And the mayor and the chief are so far up my ass it hurts,' he complained, enraged.

When would the second letter show up in print, the one about David? Rauser told me he had tried to get APD onboard with releasing the second letter to the press, but Chief Connor and the mayor had flat-out refused. They said they would all be eaten alive if APD wasn't able to find David after being handed a set of clues.

I retrieved the morning paper, slid it out of the plastic sleeve, and unrolled it on my desk. **Wishbone Killer Taunts Police**.

It was front-page stuff. The papers had given him a name, something grisly to live up to.

The last sound she heard above her own whimper was the click of my shutter and the tiny crack of her neck, like a wishbone snapped in half.

A chill started between my shoulder blades and snaked down my back. No wonder Rauser was going nuts. The pressure from his superiors would increase now. He'd have to work with them second-guessing his every move. He'd take the heat when the killer struck again. And the killer *would* strike again. Right now he was probably imagining himself on the minds and lips of the city, of the country. Celebrity is an aphrodisiac to someone seeking it.

Would he write again, to taunt, to display his superiority? This one likes the game, I thought, and the more it's played, the greater the likelihood he'll screw up.

I pulled a fresh legal pad from my drawer and began a list.

1. Precautionary acts, surveillance, schedule research . . . Victims alone.
2. Daylight attacks. Risk taking to obtain victim.
3. Locations – 1st vic school dorm, three victims' homes, first floor.
4. Method of approach: con. No forced entry. No witnesses. Chooses time of day with fewest people. Disguise? Someone familiar? Mail carrier, landscaper . . .

5. Victims' diverse backgrounds.
6. Different gender & age groups.
7. Lack of physical evidence, added precautionary acts
   – staging, cleaning scenes – hinders investigative efforts.
8. Communicates with police. Motivation unknown.

Note: Arrange access to autopsy photographs, crime scene sketches, videos, detectives' interviews & lab reports from all scenes.

I was sure APD had already checked all shared services – electric, gas, mail, cable, anything that might connect the victims in some way. Rauser had pulled teams of detectives off everything that wasn't a priority. Had they also checked photography supply houses, camera and electronic stores? If the killer's taking pictures, he's probably using a digital, something small and high res. Is he printing out hard copies? Yes, of course he is. He'd need the freedom of hard copies. *Photo-quality printers, electronic and photography stores.* He's probably arranging stills in some sequence that is meaningful, masturbating, reliving, but why settle for stills when all he needs is a decent camera phone for video? It was a small thing, but one of those head-slapping moments nonetheless. I knew I'd just moved a tiny bit closer to understanding something about the interior life of this killer. And a phone would be so easy. On the train, in the office. I thought about this. I didn't like it. It gave the killer the ability to keep the fantasy charged up. He could watch anywhere, anytime, without special equipment. No one would look twice at a guy staring at his phone. Half of Atlanta never looks up from their BlackBerry even to cross the street.

Anne Chambers had been killed in Tallahassee and Bob Shelby murdered in the Jacksonville area. Double-checking those dates with airline and rental car records made sense. Also, if the killer had relocated from Florida, there would be records. *Check Motor Vehicles, Postal Service, IRS.*

Breaking a neck is an unusual choice, especially for a serial.

To break someone's neck required some expertise as well. *Martial arts studios, military service, med students . . . doctors?*

And why are they opening the door? A repairman? A delivery person? Had APD checked uniform rentals and costume rental receipts in the days leading up to the killings? Were there any neighborhood disputes, local elections, anything that might have petitioners knocking on doors? *Zoning board, real estate records. Read detective interviews with neighbors.*

I leaned back in my desk chair and closed my eyes. What the hell was I doing? This carried too much risk. In some ways I felt I needed to relearn my years at the Bureau, redo them sober. It wasn't remembering my craft that was the problem, it was knee-jerk issues, like someone who can't talk on the phone without lighting a cigarette. I'd spent my years at the Bureau as an active but functioning alcoholic. I wasn't even sure how to think about this, what to do with the emotions surrounding it, without a drink waiting at the end of the day. And yet here I was on the fringes of this investigation and I realized suddenly that I would know and discuss in detail with Rauser every scene this killer left behind. My heart would both ache and delight at each new discovery. I rolled my neck a few times, but the cables weren't letting go. Just one drink would fix that. Just one. I was back in it, sucked back into the violence again. *Damn you, Rauser.*

I needed to move, physically move. 'Hey, Neil,' I said from my office. I could see him at his desk in the main room. He didn't budge. 'Want to go to Southern Sweets?' No answer.

Southern Sweets, a tiny bakery in Avondale Estates, had things in their display cases you'd have to be made of iron to resist. 'I'll buy you cake. Come on, Neil. We'll both feel better. Jump on Dekalb Avenue and we can be there in fifteen.'

Neil was one of my very favorite people to eat with besides Rauser. He was enthusiastic about food. Very. He smoked a lot of pot.

I saw him stir in his chair. 'Cherry pie?'

'You got it,' I said, and grabbed my keys. 'I was thinking old-fashioned chocolate or sweet potato cheesecake.'

Neil frowned. 'Cheesecake is wasted on sweet potatoes. Might as well just smear some peanut butter on it. Cheesecake deserves something more sophisticated.'

'Riiight,' I said. I'd seen him standing at the refrigerator just last week dipping raw hot dogs into yellow mustard but decided not to bring it up.

Chapter Ten

The War Room was makeshift but organized. It had been thrown together quickly when FBI databases linked the four killings. Wound patterns, tool marks, scene staging all added up to the same signature, same killer, same knife. This one wasn't an opportunist like Gary Hilton or someone who worked within strictly defined parameters like Wayne Williams – an ethnic group, an age group – and therefore likely targets could be protected. This one was different. Atlanta had never seen anything like it.

I stood at the door, unnoticed except for a nod here and there from familiar faces. Rauser was on the telephone, his back to me. The long table in front of him was littered with papers. Crime scene and autopsy photographs, numbered and dated, covered an enormous bulletin board. Pushpins marked the murders on maps of Georgia and Florida. Another board was devoted to leads, witnesses, interviews, detectives' reports. Yet another was for the victims – candid shots of them in life. Elicia Richardson standing at an outdoor grill with a metal spatula in her hand, smiling shyly at the camera. Bob Shelby with his feet on a coffee table and a beer in his hand, shorts, shirtless and sunburned. Lei Koto with her son, Tim. The boy was holding a swimming trophy in his hands. Here they all were, laughing, playing, breathing. We'd put up family photos at the Bureau too. It was meant to remind everyone that these people hadn't always been victims, that they were real people who'd left behind them daughters and friends and grieving parents and lovers and stunned husbands and gardens half planted, papers half written, groceries still in the bag, dinners on the stove, and full lives. Rauser had told me he'd practically been living in this room. He wanted to surround himself with the information. Maybe it would make sense after a while, sink into him by osmosis.

The department today had the atmosphere of being under siege. Pressure was crashing down from offices high in our local government. Detectives with already knee-buckling caseloads pushed by me and hustled in and out of the War Room, drinking from Styrofoam cups, posting reports, tapping at keyboards, kicking around ideas. One posted a sign over the bulletin boards that read WISHBONE MURDERS, and for a moment everyone in the room fell silent. Harsh reality had suddenly slammed into an odd and disconcerting sense of history in the making, of a terrible bloody legend still forming.

'Christ,' Rauser muttered.

I pulled a chair from the conference table and sat down beside him.

'Let's get to work, huh?' I said.

Rauser stared at me. Then he pushed back his chair and stood up. 'Attention, people,' he said, and movement ceased. A couple of detectives left their cubes to stick their heads in. 'For those of you who don't know, this is Keye Street. She's an experienced criminalist trained in interpreting physical evidence. Keye's coming on as a consultant to our task force, so play nice, full transparency, please, and share your doughnuts, people.'

With that, he sat back down and we went to work. I spent the afternoon in Rauser's War Room, and my notes quickly filled a couple of spiral notebooks – pages jammed with bad artwork and fat question marks and nearly indecipherable stream-of-consciousness stuff. It was the way I had always worked. I'd take it apart later. The important thing was not to edit. Not yet. Just keep it going, lay the foundation for a coherent assessment. Instinct and training, an instructor at Quantico once told me, you couldn't trust one without the other.

'I'm looking for the interviews with the first officer or the EMTs,' I said to Rauser, shuffling through mountains of paper at the messy War Room conference table. I was starting to hurt from a shortage of sleep. I couldn't imagine how Rauser was functioning at all.

'I handed you their reports. Jacksonville didn't do interviews.'

I pointed to one of the crime scene photos pinned to the board. A coffee table was flipped on its side next to the body. Bob Shelby. I glanced up at the board and studied him in life, beer, baseball cap, same couch, same coffee table that was at the death scene, only pushed several feet away from the sofa. The room was in disarray. Furniture out of place, according to the impressions left on the carpet. The remains of a fast-food dinner were spilled on the floor; bloody footprints led from the area where the victim lay facedown near a pool of blood to the front door and then toward the back of the house. The victim was completely naked. Bruising stained the top and inside of his upper arms. Sharp force and incised wounds on the pale white skin of his lower back and buttocks, thighs. And bite marks.

'If you had to reconstruct this scene, what would you say?' I asked.

'Guy liked Taco Bell?'

'Funny.'

Rauser didn't have to think about it long. He'd looked at these pictures a thousand times, read the files again and again, and clearly formed his own conclusions. 'Bob Shelby,' he said. 'Sixty-four. Not many defensive wounds. Contusion on the back of the skull. Some food and furniture got turned over, control bruising on the top of the arms. Ligature marks around the wrists. Pooling on the floor. Cast-off on the furniture and carpet. Killer beat him senseless, stabbed him about twenty times while he was still breathing and another thirty-three times after he was dead, slit his throat, then tracked the blood out and left us a size-ten impression.'

'Was the first officer male?' I asked, and Rauser nodded. 'Do you know what he did on arrival?'

'He followed first-officer protocol, notified dispatchers, secured the scene.'

'Did he step in the blood? Do you know what size shoes he wore and what type? Do you know if the EMTs moved the furniture and knocked over the food?' I used my pen to point out details in one of the photographs. 'Body's over here near the sofa. So did the med techs push this table out of the way to get to him or is this the way the killer left it? Do you know what size shoes *they* wore and what type? Also, that could be therapeutic bruising on the arms. There can be some postmortem bruising. You need to get clear on this with the ME.'

Rauser said, 'What's bugging you?'

'Well, if the offender gained control using a blitz, and from the blunt-force trauma here it looks that way, there wouldn't have been a struggle. Shelby was down, unable to fight back. It doesn't make sense. So without interviews, we don't know if we're reconstructing victim and offender interactions or if we're actually just analyzing the first officer's and med techs' effect on the crime scene, *and* because of this, we don't have an ice cube's chance in hell of being certain the killer's in a size ten.'

Rauser sighed and made a note. 'This wasn't our case,' he reminded me.

'So where are the interviews on the cases in Atlanta? I haven't seen anything but written reports from first responders, which are bare bones. You know that. These people won't take the time unless you force them.'

'We'll follow up with the officers and the med techs on the Koto and Richardson scenes here.'

'Remember Locard,' I told him. Locard's Exchange Principle states that everyone entering a crime scene both takes something of the scene with them and leaves something behind. It was one of the founding principles in crime scene investigation. 'I hate to say it, but the offender more fully understands Locard than the Atlanta Police Department. He's highly skilled, Rauser. The scenes have to be processed with that in mind. Your people have to know what kind of evidence to collect, and part of that is a detailed interview from *everyone* who steps into your crime scene.'

Rauser nodded. 'I'm onboard,' he said with that restless, nearly kinetic energy of his that was both contagious and a little disconcerting. He stayed revved up during cases like this, barely slept, had a flood of ideas. But he paid for his manic episodes. In the next few days or weeks or whenever this project no longer needed him, he'd bottom out, hit a low so debilitating that just getting out of bed was overwhelming. He called it 'the flu' and I had seen those moods knock his feet out from under him. I called it hypomania, but he wasn't interested in my opinions regarding his mental health.

I called Neil from the station with information about the victims – date of birth, Socials, full names. Neil had laserlike focus when it came to anything that remotely resembled spying. We needed to examine the lives of each of these four people in a more intimate way, profile each as thoroughly as the offender, and complete an in-depth risk assessment. If we understand the victim, we understand the killer. He gets something from them. What? What need is he fulfilling? What does his behavior say about motive? What is he acting out and how does that behavior work in relation to the physical elements of his crimes? At what point were these victims first at risk? Just answering that question alone would solve a hundred others about what the killer's willing to do to acquire his victims, about location and triggers and motive.

Movement caught my eye. Jefferson Connor, Atlanta's twenty-fourth police chief, was walking heavily down the hallway toward the War Room. Connor was in uniform, which he always wore for press conferences. I wondered if that accounted for the sour expression on his face. Perhaps it was the two-hundred-million-dollar budget or the twenty-four hundred employees he managed. Perhaps it was a serial offender at work under his watch. I had never met him personally, but I'd seen him calmly fielding questions on everything from homicide investigations to corruption inside the department, and Rauser had talked a lot about him. They had been friends and partners in DC as uniformed cops. Both had twenty-plus years in law enforcement. Connor had wanted to climb through the ranks. Rauser, on the other hand, had refused promotions in order to do the work he still loved. Rauser came to Atlanta, while Connor went to LA, where he rose to chief, created positions for community liaisons, began a Public Integrity Division and, through partnerships with the community, drastically reduced homicides under his watch. The hype that surrounded the chief's coming to Atlanta was memorable – the press surrounding him like he was a rock star when he passed through the gate at Hartsfield-Jackson, the mayor beaming at their first press conference together.

He was a big guy, six-four, wide shoulders, with a veiny round nose and the ruddy complexion of someone who'd spent some time either in the sun or at the bar. Trailing closely behind Chief Connor was Jeanne Bascom, APD's official spokesperson. Bascom gave daily press briefings, handed out progress reports, worked damage control, and according to Rauser, she was generally pummeled for her trouble. Bascom not only took a daily battering from the press, she was the person who took the calls from the families of victims and answered to the chief and the mayor for any public misstep. I could not imagine what attracted anyone to such a position.

The chief pushed open the door and nodded at the tangle of detectives in the room, let his gaze settle on me for a moment, and then said to Rauser, 'Powwow, Lieutenant, before the press conference. You gotta stand there too. They like seeing us all lined up. It's like target practice.' He nodded again to the room. 'You've got about two minutes, Aaron.'

Rauser looked at his team. 'Listen up. Street's been working on a psychological sketch. Pay attention, please, listen, make notes, and then I want you back out there. Thomas,' he said to one of only two female detectives on the task force, 'go back to Lei Koto's neighborhood, talk to the neighbors again, and keep talking and walking around until something makes sense. There was a car watching that street or a motorcycle or a bike. Some neighbor, some kid, some nosy old lady saw him. Maybe they don't even know it. Maybe they just need the right question to jog their memories. I want to know everyone who ever stepped in that neighborhood in the two weeks before this lady was killed. Stevens, make sure we got all the interviews Cobb County did when Elicia Richardson was killed. Track them all down. Neighbors, paperboys, service people, first responders, whatever. There was five years between Richardson and Koto, so you gotta track everyone down and talk to them again. Bevins, communicate with every jurisdiction in the Southeast, then branch out state by state. Maybe it hasn't been five years. Maybe we got more vics out there. Maybe we got a crime scene somewhere that's not so clean. Williams, Balaki, if you gotta go to every elevator in the city until you figure out where this freak is doing his hunting, do it, 'cause the only thing we know right now about David is that we don't know shit. You get any sense at all of what building that bastard is writing about, I don't care if it's just a feeling, put in requests for the surveillance tapes. We got nothing to lose.'

He left us there and headed down the hall. From the War Room we could see Jeanne Bascom perched on one of the vinyl chairs in Rauser's tiny office. Chief Connor was in Rauser's desk chair.

'Poor Lieu,' Detective Andy Balaki said. He had a swampy southern drawl and a Braves cap. 'That don't look so good.'

I cleared my throat and addressed the room. 'This person's family, his friends, and possibly his coworkers would have experienced his tendency to be hypercritical, moody, perhaps even verbally abusive.' No one even bothered to look up. Everyone kept on doing what they were doing. I was an outsider, no matter what Rauser had told them. 'Okay, listen,' I said, louder. 'I want this sonofabitch off the streets just like you do.' A few heads turned. 'I'm not going to get in your way. I don't want to direct your investigation. I'm here to assist, not to interfere. I used to do what you do. My background is in law enforcement. I know how hard you work.' A few more detectives gave me their attention. 'His crime scenes and his letters, they have a story to tell. He's skillful, this guy, and careful about showing his temper. He doesn't want to be observed losing it.'

'What about his personal life?' Detective Thomas wanted to know. She was in jeans and athletic shoes, an army green hoody. 'Are we looking for somebody married, divorced, gay, straight?'

'Never been married,' I replied. 'Intimate relationships are fraught with obstacles. They don't last. He dates and is sexually active, but this is about appearances. He's straight, but his orientation has nothing to do with victim selection.'

I had their attention now. One by one, the twelve detectives assigned to this task force came back to the table. Detective Brit Williams, well dressed and handsome with very dark skin, spoke up. 'Koto and Richardson and both murders in Florida happened during the day. So we assume he works the night shift.'

'Well, he needs both daylight and evening hours for surveillance purposes, planning and fantasizing. So the most important consideration in his work is mobility and freedom. He could have a mobile profession like sales, construction, route driver, but I think it's more likely he has these freedoms because he's in upper management. He's educated, and it's very important to him how the world sees him. There's also knowledge of evidence collection and forensics, obviously, since the scenes are spotless. How much knowledge? It's hard to determine, but at the very least he will subscribe to trade journals in these areas. So the mailing lists for these kinds of publications and the traffic at these websites could be helpful.'

Williams nodded and scribbled a note. Detective Andy Balaki frowned. 'What about the blogs? I mean, he's such a fucking bragger. These letters are all look how smart I am.'

'Yes!' I agreed. 'That's exactly what they're about, and there's a very good chance he's blogging or at least making regular hits on websites devoted to him. My tech guy tells me there are dozens already. And now he has a name – Wishbone – so the websites will multiply. This is part of the thrill for him. He'll want to know everything law enforcement is saying and everything the profilers are saying, so he'll be extremely dedicated to the news. Check children's organizations too. He may donate to them since he experienced abuse as a child. Those mailing lists up against the trade journals' mailing lists might net you something.' I paused, looked at each face in the room. 'The killings are becoming more frequent and the cooling-off periods shorter in duration. It's not an unusual pattern in the active years of a serial, but it's a dangerous one.'

Chapter Eleven

KNIFEPLAY.COM

Your Online Adult Edge Fetish & Knife Play Community blogs > beyond the EDGE, a fantasy by BladeDriver blog title > Good Wine

The restaurant was small and famed for its chef, who had begun a kind of culinary revolution, the New Southern, no rules whatsoever. I knew the place. Getting a table was nearly impossible but he had done it. He bragged about this over dinner. He bragged about everything.

He was near the back when I walked in late, and he was wearing Brioni, well-tailored gabardine in navy, a quarter inch of pale blue shirt cuff showing and not a millimeter more. I couldn't wait to get my hands on him.

He checked his watch before he spotted me. He looked annoyed. There were two full water goblets on the table and bread and butter. He wanted to make sure everything was right. That's the kind of guy he was. I knew other things about him too. He owed two hundred and forty thou on his home, had a couple kids, liked good wine, played golf, cheated regularly on his wife, hit the gym five days a week, owned a German shepherd, and liked to brag about being made partner in some shitty law firm. I do my homework. It's part of the fun.

He lit up when he saw me, stood to shake my hand, gave me his most dazzling smile, and searched my face. He wanted a signal. I gave him my eyes, but only for a second, just enough to make him believe I'd revealed something vital about my intentions, then a quick downward glance, a flush of color. It's not hard to do, that look, even though my ears were ringing and it felt like a hundred degrees in the restaurant. I let my eyes fall to his beltline and linger there a moment too long. The wolf smiled. He thought he was going to get lucky. I liked that idea too. After all, that's really why we were there. Just like it's why you're here now reading my fantasies. You want the fucking and the cutting too. Just like he did.

He smoothed his tie as we sat, motioned for the waiter, nothing flashy, a tiny movement. The wine was ordered without bothering to consult me. He was working the staff, working me, managing all of us. *Mr Up-and-Coming. So in control.*

We chatted our way through dinner, both of us lying about who we were and what we wanted. We knew we were lying and we liked that too. There was no pressure to lift the mask. Neither of us really gave a damn what was underneath. And then the wine began to do its job, our eyes and minds were wandering, our knees touching under the table. He grinned at me. I was a sure thing, he was thinking. And why not? We'd already been half naked behind his pool house while his wife entertained guests a few yards away.

He put his hand on the table and scarcely touched my little finger with his, very discreet, but it shot through me like a laser. The blood was pumping to all the right places.

'Want to go somewhere?' he asked.

Oh yeah, somewhere in your mouth, somewhere in your pants.

'I'll meet you outside,' I said, and left him with the check.

His eyes burned into my shoulder blades as I walked out. I felt it. I felt his desire and his need.

Control *that*, David, you little creep.

I fell into a sweaty, disturbed sleep that night. I had gone directly from the blowout at Southern Sweets to the War Room and hadn't eaten again. White Trash wanted to sleep on my legs. I felt trapped. I think I remember seeing her flying off the bed once. One of my feet might have been responsible for this, that and a hot flash. Christ, is it time for hot flashes already? Forty wasn't far away but that seemed young. I wondered if my biological mother had had them, if she'd transitioned early and easily or if she'd knifed the father I'd never known during a hot flash and wound up in jail. It was really the only time I thought about them, when I had some question about our medical history. I wasn't emotionally devastated by the fact that they'd given me up. They did it because they were incapable of caring for a child. I mean, with the prostitution and stripping and drugs and all, they were really busy. I guess I was a little pissed I'd grown up on cheese grits and gravy instead of the soy protein that might have helped me glide through hormonal shifts, but generally I had been incredibly blessed by their handing over their child. It might have been their one totally unselfish act in life.

I made coffee and poured honey and sliced nectarine into a container of Greek yogurt. I called Rauser while I dressed for an appointment. Still no leads on David, he told me, sounding grim and tired.

I wedged the Impala into a garage adjacent to SunTrust Plaza at 303 Peachtree and walked to the light at the corner of Baker Street and Peachtree Center Avenue. Crossing Peachtree Center without the light was just a little more excitement than I wanted. Hell, I'd grown up in the South, had a mighty bout with alcohol, and married an actor. Why tempt fate further?

I passed empty tables and chairs at sidewalk cafés and glanced through windows at packed bar stools. In the spring and fall, the street was lined with full tables and chatter, martinis and iced coffee and espresso. Not today. No one wanted to sit in the heat and humidity and the code-red smog alerts in business suits on a workday. And no one wanted to become the target of a serial killer whose selection process seemed so terrifyingly random.

I walked through the revolving doors at 303 Peachtree, grateful for the cold air-conditioning. Atlanta has some extraordinary office towers, with lobbies and elevators of mahogany and Italian marble and crystal, hand-woven rugs and stunning original art. SunTrust Plaza was one of them, and was famous for its occupants too – mostly big-money law firms and investment bankers. Because its fifty-three floors of gleaming blue glass and a center poking through tiers of

74

jagged lower floors happen to sit on an elevated piece of real estate between Peachtree Street and Peachtree Center Avenue, it plays a very significant role in the city's skyline.

I stepped into one of the mirrored elevators, inserted the key card that would allow me to access floors 48 through 53, all of which belonged to the law firm of Guzman, Smith, Aldridge & Haze, my biggest client and the people who essentially bought the groceries and paid the mortgage every month. I checked my reflection. Not bad – Ralph Lauren in banker blue, professional, with a crisp white shirt. It probably wouldn't get me a date, but it said that I care, that I am serious about my work, and that I'm not interested in competing with my clients. The shoes, however, probably said more to me than about me. Right now they were saying, *Hey, you up there. You're going to have to skip some things this month.* Okay, so I spend a little too extravagantly on shoes now and then, but I know people who spend thousands each month on cocaine, so comparatively speaking, it really isn't that big a deal.

I was buzzed through a set of glass doors and pointed toward the partners' offices. I had an appointment with Margaret Haze, who was one of the hottest criminal defense attorneys in the country right now.

Haze's assistant, Diane, saw me and smiled. She was blond, a little Peter Pan-ish, and wearing a gray suit I thought I'd seen in Macy's front window. Diane had the body for off-the-rack clothes. No problem. She was adorable.

'Hey, girl,' she said, and handed me a couple of folders from her desk that some of the attorneys had dropped off for me.

Diane Paulaskas had been my friend since grade school, and she'd kept me up on the office politics at 303 Peachtree. She was a relentless gossip and the reason I now had work from a firm like Guzman, Smith, Aldridge & Haze. She had slipped my business card into every file and office on the top five floors, and when an attorney asked for a PI, Diane gave them my name as if I was the gold standard. She could down two gin and tonics for every one of my club sodas, and she didn't pull her punches either. Diane Paulaskas was one of those people who would actually give you the truth when you asked for it.

'So, you get any lately?' she asked.

I rolled my eyes as if I was above that sort of thing.

The door opened to Margaret's office. Diane and I both drew breaths. People seemed to dissolve like gelatin in hot water when Margaret Haze entered a room, and we were no exception. She was over six feet in heels, hair cascading below her shoulders, red highlights, looked like a goddamn L'Oréal commercial. And she was, well, gorgeous.

'Please come in, Keye,' she said warmly, and shook my hand. She always shook my hand and she had always insisted on speaking to me personally. The other lawyers were content with scribbling out some instructions and leaving a folder for me at Diane's desk. Not Margaret.

'Thank you, by the way, for the excellent work you did on the Stoubart case,' she said, and ushered me to a chair in the sitting area of her enormous office. 'You gave me so much to use against the prosecution's witnesses, it's not even going to trial. I sent a little something to your office.'

'You didn't have to do that, but thank you. It's a beautiful basket. We're enjoying it very much,' I lied. I'd already given the fruit to Charlie.

She smiled, took a chair next to me, and crossed mile-long legs. 'I see you were able to file the paperwork on LaBrecque. Was he a problem to serve?'

I shrugged. 'It would have been worse had we not been in church.'

Margaret nodded. 'I was afraid of that.'

'He's not a nice man.'

'Was he aggressive?'

I showed her my bruised wrist. 'I'll feel it for a day or two.'

Her nostrils flared ever so slightly. 'This man's wife is a friend of a friend and she asked me for help,' Margaret explained. It was not the kind of case she would normally take on. At this point in her career, she could pick and choose from a long waiting list. Her windowed office atop this gleaming office tower in downtown was a testament to her success. 'He has been abusing his wife and child for some time. The restraining order is just the first step. I've handed it to one of our attorneys here. The wife will hopefully follow through and file divorce papers. I'm sorry he hurt you.' She rose and moved to her desk. 'I think I remember it's Diet Pepsi you like, right?' She pressed the intercom button on her phone. 'Diane, would you please find Keye a Diet Pepsi.'

'Sure thing,' I heard Diane say cheerfully.

I read for a few minutes, then looked up from the papers she'd handed me. 'You've taken a client who shot his boss twenty-three times?'

Margaret nodded. 'We're going for self-defense.'

'Uh-huh.'

'His boss was a frightening brute and my client feared for his life. The whole company is a bunch of thugs. Most of them carry weapons. Towing company. Very tough guys.'

There was a tap on the office door, then Diane came in smiling and handed me a drink on ice. She saw the papers in my hand. 'Oh, you're working on the tow truck driver case? It's going to be tough to find an impartial jury on that one. Everybody in the city hates the tow guys—'

'Thank you, Diane,' Margaret interrupted, straightening a stack of papers on her desk, then handing the papers to Diane. 'That will be all.'

'Of course,' Diane said with a smile.

I watched her leave, then looked back at Margaret. 'So he shot him twenty-three times with a Glock nine? He had to reload. That implies calm and purpose. Not terror.'

A thin smile. 'This is why I use you, Keye. You understand the challenges we face. Now go find some scary stuff on my client's boss.

We've got about three months to prepare. I'd like something from you within the next four weeks.'

I stood, took a sip of the Diet Pepsi and set it on the glass table next to my chair, then walked to Margaret's desk. 'You want me to keep this information?'

'Yes. That's your copy.'

I picked up a framed picture from her desk and studied it absently. It was of a couple in swimsuits. The man was holding a little girl who had Margaret's eyes. They were on the deck of a boat, both of them good looking and very tan. The woman looked especially familiar.

'You and your parents?' I asked.

'Those were the days,' Margaret said, and smiled. 'I didn't have to have a day job.'

'Great-looking family.' I put the photograph back and tried to position it exactly as it had been. Margaret had already moved on to a thick stack of papers on her blotter.

'We'll talk in a couple of weeks, okay?' she said without looking up.

Diane stopped me on the way out. She was leaving work to meet Neil and Charlie at my office to watch something on the big screen and wanted to know when I'd join them. My office had been a gathering place for us all, especially during baseball season – me, Rauser, Diane, Neil, Charlie. I thought about the television my designers had installed lowering itself by remote control from the rafters on a silent silver pulley system like a seventy-two-inch flat-panel love slave.

'I can't,' I told her. I wanted to find Rauser. I wanted to go back to the War Room. New reports from follow-up interviews on Wishbone scenes would be in, and the tip lines had started ringing. It was day two on the search for David, two days since the threatening letter had promised to murder him, and Rauser and his detectives had become so desperate they were searching Motor Vehicles and telephone records for anyone named David and attempting to contact them, a biblical name in the southern Bible belt and a metro area of nearly five million. *Three days, Lieutenant. Tick-tock.* We had twenty-four hours left if the letter was true. There wasn't much room for optimism.

'I'm seeing someone,' Diane told me. 'It's serious.'

'Hey, that's great,' I said, but what I was thinking was that it was always serious with Diane, who fell hard and fast and was too clingy and too willing too quickly and generally got her heart trampled for her trouble. I checked my watch. 'I'll call you in a couple days. I promise. I want to hear all about it.'

Chapter Twelve

It was nearly two in the morning. Rauser had his lights flashing but no siren, no need to wake the natives. We took Peachtree into Buckhead and cut over to Piedmont Road, silent on our way to the scene of another murder – a male victim, facedown, visible bite marks, stab wounds. The Crown Vic's windows were lowered, warm air blowing our hair, the squawking police scanner making for strange background music. Rauser's severe profile in the flashing blue light looked like something out of *Dick Tracy*. Nothing seemed real. A crime scene when it's new is an invaluable tool. Seeing it just the way the killer left it, smelling it, feeling it, listening to its story. Crime scene photographs don't always slap you in the face with first impressions and subliminal connections like a fresh scene. And they never give you a sense of angle and distance and space. But there's never much time. Once discovered, the landscape of a scene begins to change forever. Lights are switched on, evidence is bagged, the air begins to circulate, the body is disturbed. Trace evidence is collected, some drifts away.

I glanced at the speedometer. Rauser was doing seventy-five down Peachtree and barely slowing at the lights, but it wasn't fast enough to suit me. I just wanted to get there. Like Rauser, I was thinking only of the prospect of new evidence, the seconds ticking away on a perfectly preserved scene. I wasn't contemplating the loss of life or the shame and sin and horror in that. That part comes later. One learns to compartmentalize emotionally for the sake of efficiency. Unfortunately, that particular talent doesn't translate well in personal lives. The divorce rate is high for people like us.

We had been in the War Room with detectives and interviews and coffee mugs and cold takeout cartons, and the victims, all four of them up there on the bulletin boards, reminding us constantly what could happen to David, when the call came. I watched Rauser's face change. The War Room had emptied out in seconds as Rauser shouted out instructions. He was already on his cell with a blood-stain analyst as we skipped the elevators jammed with detectives and ran down the stairs. Minutes later, his Crown Vic screeched through the parking garage at City Hall East.

'I want to process the shit out of this scene,' Rauser told me. 'No mistakes this time. First officer secured the scene. No one gets in. I got CSI techs waiting for us and our spatter analyst on the way. We need anyone else there?'

'No. But you'll want a good forensic odontologist at the morgue for the bite marks.'

Rauser was quiet for a few blocks. 'I wanted to find David, Keye, find him alive, save his life.'

'Lots of people end up dead on their stomachs, Rauser,' I answered, and turned toward the window in time to see the huge fins on Symphony Tower glowing like something from *Star Wars*. 'Lots of folks get stabbed and bitten. Doesn't make it a Wishbone scene. Doesn't mean it's David.'

Minutes later, Rauser whipped the Crown Vic into the parking lot of an upscale extended-stay hotel off Piedmont in Buckhead. Immediately ahead we saw a tangle of police and emergency vehicles, lights in blue and red, officers stringing crime scene tape, dealing with arriving news crews and a gathering crowd. Unmarked vehicles, Crown Vics in different shades and in different states of disrepair, were pulling in – task force members. Rauser handed me a pair of surgical gloves from the scene case on his backseat, and I followed him across the parking lot past half a dozen police cruisers with blaring scanners. I watched him say a few words to some of the officers outside. Rauser had the heart of a beat cop. In his memories and in his stories, he was happiest back then. He missed feeling the grit in his shoes and still thought of himself as climbing into 'civilian clothes' each morning even though he'd been in Homicide twelve years.

We passed a crowd at the roped-off entrance. 'Someone filming?' I asked.

Rauser nodded. 'Williams and Balaki were in the area when the call came, so they got things moving. Let's hope this one likes to hang around. Lots of 'em do.'

A chill suddenly lifted the hair on my arms. I looked back at the crowd. Something out there looked back. I felt it, and tried not to let my hopes sink. The signature elements and the physical evidence, tool marks, wound patterns – that would tell us if this was another Wishbone murder.

Guests had gathered in the lobby. The night shift manager was doing her best to keep some order amidst a storm of rumors. In the background there was a constant, faint ringing of the switchboard while the clerk stood idle and gaping at the front desk. Detective Brit Williams was standing next to her with an open notepad in his hand, but she wasn't talking, wasn't looking at him. Her face was gray, expressionless. I'd seen the look. She'd found the body, I realized, and she'll never be quite the same, never push open a darkened door without remembering. I thought about Tim Koto finding his mother stabbed and beaten next to the stove where she had cooked for him. Who was taking care of him now? The night shift manager had started to sob. Murder disrupts everyone in its path forever.

More than thirty years ago, I sat on an old tiled floor watching as my grandparents' blood drained from them and pooled up around me. I don't really remember them or anything much before that moment. It's like being born into a crime scene at five years old. I had been playing behind the counter when I heard the door open, heard angry voices. *Where's the money, old man? Give us the fucking money.* Grandfather had pressed his palm firmly against the top of my head that day and held me down so I wouldn't pop up and get it blown off. When he fell next to me, and when another shot collapsed my grandmother too, I didn't make a sound. In obedient silence, I watched the blood soak through my clothes and the pale pink shoes I wore.

Now, lights from television crews lit up the street and reporters spoke into cameras with the hotel and the crime scene tape as their backdrop. Uniformed officers kept them as far from the scene as possible. Already there were whispers about it being another Wishbone murder, and it seemed that everyone outside the ropes had a phone to their ear.

'It's that freak who wrote to the newspapers,' someone said into their BlackBerry, and Rauser and I exchanged a quick glance. He was chewing on his lip.

We followed one of the officers through the parking lot and walked past a few buildings. Uniformed officers and plainclothes cops fell silent as we passed them on our way to Building G, Suite 351.

Rauser had strict instructions that no one should notify the ME's office until the scene had been properly processed. All hell would break loose over that, I knew. He'd had disputes before with the medical examiner over jurisdiction and procedure, but preserving the scene and whatever evidence was left on the body was crucial before it was released.

We stood outside the doorway while the first officer briefed us. He had followed Rauser's instructions to the letter. No one, not even an annoyed crime scene investigator, had been allowed inside. Everyone who had come in contact with the scene had been detained and was now unhappily waiting to give a detailed interview.

'Victim's name is David Brooks,' the officer told us.

Rauser glanced at me. The muscle in his jaw was busy. He gave the officer a pat on the shoulder and said quietly, 'Good work.'

I spoke briefly at Rauser's request with Ken Lang, the specialist from the crime lab. I told him a bloodstain analyst was on the way and that no samples or scrapings or any kind of blood evidence should be collected unless there was pooling. In that case wet and pooled blood could be swabbed without jeopardizing other spatter evidence. I let him know Rauser wanted it processed thoroughly and as if it were a Wishbone scene. Lang promised if there was a fiber, any DNA, a fingerprint, any trace at all, he would find it. I wasn't so confident.

If David had a family and the killer couldn't take him as he had the other victims, in their own environment, which he had meticulously surveilled, then what better place than this? Hotel property covered a couple of acres. The lobby was small and freestanding, and two-story brick buildings were spread out with what appeared to be only a couple of town house-style units per building. I hadn't seen any cameras except at the lobby entrance and inside at the front desk. And even with a good housekeeping staff, hotels are crawling with DNA and fiber and trace evidence.

Rauser was handing out assignments to the detectives and uniformed cops. The parking lot entrance was now blocked off. 'Nobody leaves the hotel,' he ordered, 'and everyone in the place is interviewed no matter how far away their room is from the crime scene. Split up two to a building and get the guest interviews,' he told the cops. 'Make sure we got statements from everyone on staff before anyone goes home. Balaki, get the credit card receipts from the front desk. Somebody needs to talk to the businesses around here and see what they saw. Looks like the Krystal and the pancake house are open. Bevins, you and Velazquez check out all the vehicles, search the property again.'

The tension was palpable. Rauser patted his shirt pocket for a pack of cigarettes, then stopped himself. You can't smoke in a closed crime scene no matter how bad you want one. 'Move your ass, people. Maybe we got a perp still hanging around.'

Rauser looked at Lang, who stood with a video camera in one hand, an aluminum case in the other, a digital Nikon hanging around his neck. He'd already slipped into a paper cap, booties, and a lab coat designed especially to reduce the transfer of fiber evidence.

'Thanks for waiting,' Rauser told him. 'We'll suit up and be right behind you.'

A woman carrying a scene case in each hand was speaking to a couple of the uniforms. She was wearing jeans, tennis shoes, and a worn Army T-shirt with the sleeves cut off and the bottom shortened.

'That's our blood-splatter guy,' Rauser said, and grinned at me.

He shook her hand, then wrapped an arm around her. She was pretty with a strong jaw, five-tenish or more with the lean V-shape of a swimmer, short wavy hair, creamy skin, looked like she ate nuts and berries. Probably had soy milk in her fridge, and absolutely never touched a Krystal cheeseburger.

Rauser walked her back to me and introduced us. 'Keye, I want you to meet Jo Phillips. Jo, this is Keye Street, our friendly neighborhood profiler. Jo here used to make an honorable living. Now she's just one of the ghouls.'

'I was a cop. It was seven years ago,' Jo Phillips said, and smiled at me. We all pulled paper booties over our shoes and slipped into coats. Jo stretched examination gloves over long fingers, then elbowed Rauser and added, 'But you know how old men are. Always trying to relive the past.'

Her voice was husky and soft all at once, southern smoky. Kind of Lauren Bacall. I hated her already. Let me count the ways. Who comes to a crime scene in the middle of the night with their belly button showing? And what's Jo short for anyway? I hoped it was Joseph. And the familiar elbowing thing she did with Rauser, *hated* that. And the way she used his first name. They were just way too chummy for my comfort.

Rauser pushed open the door to the suite and Ken Lang went in first with video, maneuvering around carefully. Trace evidence is a delicate matter. Just the breeze created by someone crossing a room can dislodge trace.

The rooms looked expensive. They were clearly designed for upscale business travelers, two levels with fireplaces and full kitchen, a bar, a wireless office, a conference table in the dining area. Was this rendezvous site the killer's idea? Or the victim's? Which one of them was familiar enough with these hotels to make this choice? No – the location would not have been left to chance. Not with this careful and precise offender. The killer chose this place deliberately. We were looking for a professional, someone with enough successes and enough of an expense account to accommodate this type of hotel, I told Rauser.

The room was chilled, a dramatic contrast to the eighty-seven-degree soup we'd just waded through outside. Humid Georgia nights dampen your clothes, bead up around your hairline, sit heavy on your chest. Walking into a room air-conditioned to sixty degrees gets your immediate attention. A gas fire was burning in the fireplace. I thought about that for a moment, remembered going away with Dan for a romantic weekend and doing the same thing with the air-conditioning. Nothing inspires a romantic evening like a fireplace. I wondered if the killer enjoyed the fire before or after the murder.

It was an odd feeling, standing here and knowing this space was something very different before it became a crime scene. How did it begin? I wondered. Was it gentle with a kiss? Or violent and instantly intense? So far there was no sign of a struggle. A two-story suite like this would take ten, twelve hours to process. Only then the story would come to light and we would understand what happened here. Lang would handle collecting the bulk of the physical evidence apart from bloodstain; he was in for a long night.

Standing at the bedroom door while Lang made the first video of the room that appeared to be the primary murder scene, I let my eyes skip over the bedroom. The body was facedown on the queen-size bed. A large bloodstain had seeped deeply into the sheets and mattress around his neck and chest and was turning the color of old brick. One sheet was pulled up to the waist, tucked around his open legs to outline the lower body. The fabric was peppered with blood. Somewhere in the suite, music played softly.

I saw a sweaty bottle of fifty-dollar Chardonnay and two moisture rings on the bed table near the phone. I didn't see any glasses, and stood there thinking about that for a moment. The crime scene specialist followed my eyes to the bed table.

'Two rings and only one glass,' Lang said, and continued his work. 'It's over here on the rug next to the bed. Looks like the victim might have dropped it.'

One missing glass? The killer took a glass away from the scene? Why? A souvenir, something for his trophy collection? Or was it just for safety and speed? Never know when you might leave behind a bit of saliva, a partial print, an eyelash, some tiny piece of DNA evidence in the rush to leave a scene.

I looked down at the corpse on the bed. David Brooks was white, the pale blue dress shirt was pushed up on his lower back, exposing a perfect set of bite marks. One arm hung off the bed, one arm was raised above his shoulder. He'd been muscled and fit.

'I know you must be the reason I'm here,' Jo Phillips said from behind me, then lowered her voice so no one else could hear. 'Most of the time APD just uses their own people and they're pretty good, but this is my thing. Spatter is *all* I do. Three years, I've been telling 'em bloodstains are the physical manifestation of the inside of a perp's head, that it's physical *and* behavioral evidence and it deserves an expert.' She laughed a soft, frustrated laugh, then shook her head. 'All I get is it's not in the budget. Man, you must have some pull, Keye.'

'Pull? With Rauser? He's desperate,' I answered.

'I think I'm going to like working with you,' she said, and gave me a good, long look, then brushed against my arm, stepped in front of me, and leaned over the body. She pressed a cotton swab into the sheet where blood had first pooled, then became absorbed into the sheets and mattress. I watched as the swab in her hand slowly turned dark. She allowed it to air-dry before placing it into a sterile test tube. She looked up at me and smiled again. It crossed my mind that she might have been flirting with me, but this was work, a death scene, and that would have been, well, creepy.

She stooped to look at the headboard and the bed table. 'Cast-off here,' she said, and scraped a few samples off each piece of furniture and dropped them into a test tube, then filled out labels for each sample. She took pictures from several angles. In the next couple of hours, Jo Phillips would have what she needed to set up an elaborate system using string to help fashion a three-dimensional point-of-origin determination, precisely measuring distance of blood drops from the body, the distance of the stains from one another, on the victim's clothes, the sheets, the headboard and walls. She would identify each type of stain – spatter saturation stain, drops, arterial spray, or cast-off from a bloody weapon and the associated edge characteristics. By drawing a line through the long axis of a group of bloodstains, the point of origin could be determined. So could trajectory and impact angle. Back at the lab, she'd use a computer to make the calculations that would finish telling the terrifying story of victim and offender interaction. Analysts like Phillips played a huge part in a thorough reconstruction. And bloodstain patterns were nearly indisputable in court. I stepped back to give her room to work. She was methodical, careful – everything you wanted in a spatter analyst. God! If she'd been any more perfect I think I would have gagged. Already I felt a rash coming on.

'What do you make of the sheet?' Rauser asked from the bedroom door. 'We clearly got wounds under there, so why cover him up?'

I had no idea how long he'd been standing there. Rauser was one of those guys who could memorize the scene, close his eyes, and envision it later inch by inch. Scenes made sense to him. He was a natural and instinctive investigator.

'He was protecting the victim. Trying to minimize his humiliation by not exposing him,' I answered. 'That could indicate a prior relationship. Or the victim may symbolize someone significant to the killer – a parent, a spouse, a brother, someone thought of with genuine affection. It's a protective and loving gesture.'

'Hell of a way of showing love,' Rauser muttered. 'Even I could do better than that.'

'So you say,' Jo Phillips answered without looking up from her work.

Rauser grinned and said something about never breaking his word, then took his time looking around the bedroom. 'Brooks checked in about eleven, according to the front desk. No reservations. Appeared to be alone.' He got down on hands and knees and picked up the wineglass with an ink pen from his pocket, examined it, and returned it to the same spot on the floor. 'That's pretty late for a check-in. Maybe they went out first, had dinner, and then came here.'

'ME's report on stomach contents should tell that story.' I looked around at the drawn curtains, the radio set to a local jazz station, the bottle of wine. 'This was definitely a date. It was on someone's appointment book or at the very least there are calls on his cell. This wasn't spur-of-the-moment. It was planned.'

'I agree,' Rauser said just as someone called for him from downstairs. When he returned, he told us, 'Williams interviewed the desk clerk who found the body. She noticed the door open, stuck her head in, and called out. When no one answered, she got worried, came upstairs and walked into the bedroom, found the body, then ran like hell. Swears she didn't touch anything but the door and the railing.' Rauser thought for a minute. 'He left the door open. Bastard wanted to make sure the scene was discovered right away. How come?' He paused, and then answered his own question. 'So he could hang around and watch us pulling in, lights going, all of us falling over ourselves to clean up his mess. Probably took off as soon as we started filming. But let's hope not, huh?'

Two and a half hours passed before Jo Phillips let us know she'd gotten her measurements and was ready to have the sheet pulled back. Ken Lang slid brown paper lunch sacks over David Brooks's hands and secured them with rubber bands to reduce loss of evidence when the corpse was moved and eventually transported to the morgue. Evidence is hard to come by in fingernail scrapings. On television, scientists get loads of DNA cells and fiber evidence from under fingernails. In life, what you usually get is so much dirt and gunk you can't distinguish real evidence.

Rauser peeled the sheet away and Jo Phillips stiffened when we saw for the first time the signature stab wounds on the dead man's legs and buttocks.

'Guess that answers that,' Rauser said quietly. 'Somebody turn off that damn radio.'

Another scene tech had arrived and taken over the videotaping of the scene. Ken Lang spoke into his recorder as he snapped stills. 'Sharp-force injuries, incised stab wounds to the buttocks, back of the thighs, sides, and lower back. Minimum blood and bruising there. Probably postmortem. Bite marks back of neck, shoulders, buttocks, lower back, and inner thighs.'

All the signature elements were in place. The stabbing and the bite marks were in the same areas as on the previous known victims, and the positioning of the body, the scene staging. This was Wishbone all right, but this victim was different. I was certain of it. There were no abraded ligature marks. No struggle, I thought. Why? I had a feeling knowing that would answer a ton of other questions.

'Jesus,' Rauser said, when Lang had finished examining Brooks's back and the body was finally turned over. An ugly stab wound appeared in the area of the jugular notch. That explained the amount of blood that had soaked the mattress. Brooks's expression told us nothing, gave away no secrets. He looked as if he'd fallen asleep. There were multiple stab wounds around the groin and deep bite marks on the fleshy areas on both the right and left side of his body between the ribs and pelvic girdle.

Someone called for Rauser from downstairs again, and this time I followed him. I needed air. I wanted to get out of that room. One of the detectives had found Brooks's car unlocked in the parking lot, which told us that David and his killer had taken separate cars or the killer had left on foot or – if we were lucky – by cab or bus. Rauser opened Brooks's suit coat and slid a wallet out of the inside breast pocket with his gloved hands as lovingly as a pickpocket. 'And what do you know: business card says he's an attorney.'

Our eyes met as we made the connection. A moment later I was on my phone waking Neil up. David Brooks was not the first lawyer to be among the Wishbone victims. My heart beat faster at knowing it was the first time we'd found any commonality regarding selection. Was this it, the link that would finally blow the case wide open?

'Hey, Lieutenant,' Detective Brit Williams called out. He held up a newspaper. 'Early morning edition, *AJC*.'

Rauser jerked the newspaper out of his hand, looked at it, and thrust it at me. 'At least they had the decency to black some of it out this time.'

The headlines read: **Do You Know David? New Letter Vows More Killing**.

Chapter Thirteen

It was daylight when I left crime scene techs and investigators at the scene of David Brooks's murder. I heard Rauser complaining loudly to the ME about the way his people were handling the body and their effect on his crime scene. Lieutenant Aaron Rauser was going to have another long day, I knew. Day three and David Brooks was dead. Day three and the *Atlanta Journal-Constitution* had the second letter. *Tick-tock, Lieutenant.*

I caught a cab back to the Georgian. The news about the murder and the second letter were all over the car radio. The driver wanted to talk about it too. He feared for his own safety. He'd gotten good, he claimed, at judging a fare, at knowing whom to pick up and whom to leave standing, who might rob him, who might tip. Now he didn't know what to look for. The news was telling him the killer might be the guy next door, the cashier at the grocery store, the man standing at the ATM behind you.

The cabbie dropped me in front of the Georgian. I wandered into the café off the lobby, exhausted.

The story of Brooks's murder was on the television in the coffee shop, and I waited for my double-shot latte, transfixed like everyone else in the line. That these brutal killings appeared random, that the killer's motive was unknown and therefore unpredictable and not something one could protect against, seemed to plant a seed of terror in everyone. Foreboding choked the air we were all breathing. A thirty-second spot on the local news with a criminologist from Georgia Southern told us that no one knew who was next, but that it would happen again and soon. A contact number was displayed for runners who wanted to form groups rather than exercising alone. It was suggested that parents wait at bus stops with their children, and there were warnings about how vulnerable scooter and bicycle operators were after dark. MARTA stations had added security, we were told.

Atlanta had a long history of spree and serial murders – the Black Butcher in the early 1900s; the Atlanta child murders in the seventies and eighties, twenty-one children and teenagers killed; Brian Nichols's rampage, which began at the Fulton County Courthouse and branched out into the burbs; day trader Mark Barton taking out his family and Buckhead coworkers. All of us had grown up with or read the stories of Atlanta's violent past, but this was different. This killer was writing to us, describing the ways he was torturing his victims. He was telling us that he talks to them, that he asks them, *How does it feel?* This insight into his interaction with the victims and this latest letter ratcheted the city's anxiety up to another level.

And if we weren't near enough panic, *Good Morning America* opened with '*The serial murderer in Atlanta known as the Wishbone Killer has struck again after letters taunting the Atlanta police and to the Atlanta Journal-Constitution detailing his plan. Was it politics that prevented Atlanta police from using their best resource, the public, to prevent this latest brutal murder? This morning nationally known criminal profiler Jacob Dobbs weighs in on the investigation and the menace known as Wishbone . . .*'

I sank into a cushioned chair and glared at the television. I had worked with Jacob Dobbs at the Bureau. Dobbs was a full-on sonofabitch, in my opinion, unfit to weigh in on any aspect of the investigation, since he had no insider knowledge of the investigation and 'weigh in' really just meant 'speculate'. I wondered if the killer was watching. The story had gone viral now. It must have been heady stuff for someone who had allowed the media to name him.

KNIFEPLAY.COM

Your Online Adult Edge Fetish & Knife Play Community blogs > beyond the
EDGE, a fantasy by BladeDriver blog title > Sweet Sixteen

There is so much work left to do and so much pressure. They say they
want it to stop, but do they really? No. They cannot wait to read about the
next one.

Want to know a secret? I was sixteen the first time. Sixteen years old and
my grades never dipped a point. I wasn't like other children.

I showered, shared some breakfast with White Trash, who loved
scrambled eggs with chives and cream cheese, then called Neil.
I still had a mortgage and a business to run, calls to return, promises
to honor, money that had to be made in order to keep my head above
water regardless of what else was happening in the world, and I
needed his help this morning. It was after eleven before we got
started.

I took Piedmont Avenue through Midtown while Neil took long
hits off a joint in the passenger's seat, held them in, and coughed
them out. It was hot already and humid, and I was tired from the
long night. Neil was tired too. He had been working with a couple of
detectives from Rauser's task force to develop a complete picture
of the victims' lifestyles, anything that might help unravel
Wishbone's selection process. The top was down and the air felt good
on my face. I'd pulled my hair back and put on a white button-down
tucked into khakis, with the logo of a nonexistent courier company
embroidered over the left pocket, and a pair of Tod's that had set
me back four hundred bucks, but if you're forced to wear khaki
and loafers, it's only fair.

I glanced at Neil, then back at the road. 'How do you inhale that
stuff all day? Are you going to be able to drive?'

He blew smoke at me. 'Hell, yes, I can drive.'

We were coming up on Tenth Avenue – Outwrite Books' patio

packed with coffee and raspberry scones and cute guys, the Flying Biscuit on the right, Red Tomato and Nickiemoto's and Caribou on the left. Brunch was in full swing and the lunch hour just beginning. The street smelled like melon and baking dough and frying bacon, and I had a moment when I remembered exactly what a Bloody Mary tasted like at this time of day.

Neil opened the background folder on the person I was to serve with a witness subpoena. We had her home address, work address, vehicle description and tag number, a passport-size photo, a copy of her driver's license, a brief summary of the attorney's experience with her thus far, copies of court documents that told us why she was being served, and copies of the sheriff's report.

'Oh, I remember running her for alternate addresses,' Neil commented after he'd studied it for a while. 'Sheriff tried to serve her three times.'

There are a lot of reasons people duck subpoenas. Nine times out of ten it's about convenience. Who wants to take the time to show up for a long deposition or sit in court and wait for hours to testify? There are exceptions, of course. Sometimes witnesses are frightened. Sometimes they're being paid to stay quiet. Sometimes they're thugs and criminals themselves.

'To be honest, I don't think it'll be much of a challenge.'

Neil grinned at me. 'Really? What do you know that the sheriff doesn't?'

I smiled and winked as we passed Piedmont Park, hung a left on Monroe, then turned into an apartment complex across from Ansley Mall.

Several of the law firms I worked with used me for hard-to-serve subpoenas when the sheriff's office had failed. I wasn't under any restrictions at all as far as method or, well, ethics, so I could get creative when I needed to. Plus, I had the time. They don't. They have too much on their plates already. Last Christmas I'd stuffed a subpoena inside a fruitcake, and not long ago when Rauser and I ordered pizza, I talked one of their drivers out of his cap. With that cap and a pizza box, I was able to serve a man who had dodged the sheriff's office for three months. I mean, who doesn't open the door for pizza? Today the subpoena I intended to serve was folded inside a coffee cup that was inside a gift box that I'd wrapped in brown postal paper. A bright foil sticker read SWEEPSTAKES AWARD HEADQUARTERS and listed a fake address in Illinois, thanks to some help from a very resourceful guy at Kinko's.

Helen Graybeal and her husband lived in C-6, ground level. I parked one building over, got out my clipboard, and stuck a pen in my shirt pocket.

'Careful,' Neil said. 'Place is kinda nasty.' He put his head back against the seat and closed his eyes.

The door opened after the first ring. 'I have a delivery for Helen Graybeal.'

'I'll take it.' The man was wearing red plaid shorts and a T-shirt. He had a cigarette between his fingers, thick forearms, and a suntan. Not the kind you get from tanning salons or sandy beaches. The kind you get from working outside.

I pretended to read delivery instructions on the clipboard while tilting the box so he could see it. 'Sorry,' I said. 'Gotta have her signature. Just have her come down to the warehouse tomorrow and pick it up.'

Mr Graybeal seemed to be wrestling with what to do. He looked at me uneasily, then back at the box. 'Helen, it's one of your sweepstakes,' he called over his shoulder. 'You gotta sign.'

In the background, I saw a quick-moving shadow, and then it was gone. *Bingo!* Her head came around the corner, then a foot, and finally she came to the door. She was thin and tough looking, leather skinned from too many cigarettes, with lines that webbed out around her top lip. She paused long enough to give her husband a hate look, then handed him her full coffee cup. She took the box and scribbled her signature on my fake courier log.

I quick-stepped it back to the car as soon as the door closed. One thing you don't want to do when someone has been dodging a subpoena for a long time is hang around while they discover what just happened. All that cocky you've-been-served stuff can bounce like a football if you're not careful. You never know which way it'll go.

Neil had turned the car around and was waiting in the driver's seat with the engine running.

'I got her,' I told him, and climbed into the passenger's seat. 'Husband totally folded when he saw the return address. She's into sweepstakes, buys lottery tickets, stuff like that.'

'And you knew that how?'

'Hey, you're not the only one capable of doing a little research. I am a detective, after all.'

'Which means you poked through her trash?'

'Exactly.'

We were waiting for a break in traffic to pull out of the complex and onto Monroe Drive when I heard shouting behind us. I checked the visor mirror and saw Helen Graybeal barreling toward us. She was waving the coffee cup I'd just seen in one hand and the subpoena in the other, describing the ways in which she was going to shove both up my ass. Her husband came running up behind her and attempted to restrain her without success.

'Jesus, let's go,' I told Neil.

Then *thump*. The coffee cup she'd been holding sailed over my old convertible and clipped the back of my head near my left ear. For a couple of seconds the world was nothing but little gold specks. 'Fucking *go*,' I yelled. 'Bitch has an arm.'

Neil was laughing. 'I can't just pull out in traffic—'

Then *pop, zing*. A perfectly round hole appeared in the windshield. A bullet had passed between our heads and gone through the windshield. We exchanged a quick glance, then Neil punched the gas hard, spun out onto Monroe Drive, shot across four lanes of traffic, and burst into the Ansley Mall parking lot amidst honking horns and screeching tires and middle fingers in the air. He bounced over six speed bumps, got us onto Piedmont, and then pulled over a few blocks down on Fourteenth near the park.

I think we were silent for a full minute, both of us staring, stupefied, as the hole spiderwebbed out across my windshield.

'Goddamn,' Neil whispered finally.

I ran a hand over the growing lump on the back of my head. 'That was a brand-new windshield.'

My phone rang. Tyrone's Quikbail number showed up on the display.

'What up?' Tyrone asked.

'Well, I'm not sure you'd believe it if I told you.'

'Try me.'

'Okay. I just got nailed with a coffee cup. There's a fresh bullet hole in my windshield, and Neil looks like he's going to puke.'

'Riiight,' Tyrone said. 'Okay, well, this will seem easy, then. Guy violated a restraining order, they picked him up, we bailed him out, and guess what? Weasel didn't show for court. You need a few bucks?'

'Family or criminal court?'

Tyrone hesitated. Not a good sign. 'Criminal.'

'So it wasn't just an order violation. There was an assault?'

'Ex-wife,' Tyrone admitted. 'Beat her bad. You get him, you make sure he accidentally bumps into some shit on the way to the station.'

'What's his name?'

'Some faggy French-sounding shit,' Tyrone said.

'It isn't LaBrecque, is it?' I asked, rubbing my head. 'William LaBrecque?'

'Yeah, that's the creep. Billy LaBrecque.'

Chapter Fourteen

Forty-eight hours ago David Brooks was found in a bloody hotel bed and the second letter to Rauser hit the news. It had been a week since the first letter about Lei Koto gave the killer a name the media loved, Wishbone. The threat was real. A killer roamed our streets. To ratchet up the city's boiling point, Atlanta was baking at a hundred degrees for the second straight week. The assault rate was soaring as it always does when big cities and blazing hot summers collide, and the news was full of warnings. *The owner of a downtown convenience store shot . . . Another case of road rage on Atlanta's highways . . . Code-red smog alert.*

No one felt safe. It seemed Atlanta's streets would find a way to get you. The atmosphere was pure crisis.

At my office, things were piling up. My desk was a mess. I couldn't find evidence that I'd paid the electric bill, a bank deposit had been waiting for days, and I hadn't done any billing in three weeks. I hated billing. I do it only because I have to. The agency was growing and seemed determined to become a roaring success with or without me.

Truth is, I'd never really had my heart in the business. I hadn't had my heart in anything since Dan and being fired and getting sober. Most of the messes I'd made as a practicing drunk had been cleaned up, but I realized during those hot, anxious weeks that there was a chunk of me missing still, a disturbing lack of emotion. Life seemed to blow right past me without leaving anything behind. When I shut down – *why* I shut down I don't know exactly – but that night, driving to the Brooks scene with my heart slamming against my chest, and walking into that room where a killer had killed so recently that the body was warm and the wine hadn't lost its chill, I was alert, alive again. I felt something. That it takes a dead body to bring me around is screwed up, I know. But then Dan lay under me like a corpse for five years and I still managed an orgasm most of the time. To be fair, he did offer the occasional pelvic thrust when duty called, but he'd long lost his appetite for anything that was readily available. My ex-husband was all about the hunt, which meant one day after the wedding ceremony he had absolutely no challenges.

I wanted to get as much done as possible at my office before the lab reports came in from the medical examiner and the crime labs on the Brooks murder. It would take some time to piece together all the information in an assessment that might help guide investigative strategy. The reports would take time too, I knew, but I wanted to be ready. The proper way the scene was processed, the ability to more fully understand victim/offender interaction, would give us all a greater understanding of motive. If we could pierce this killer's motive, I was convinced, it might lead us to him.

I was planning the trip to Denver, going through my closet, thinking about what kind of clothes I would need. Neil had been right: the corporation that hired us to find their thieving accountant wanted me to deal with him personally, and I needed the money. Their former accountant was in for a big surprise when I showed up at his house. The plan was to fly in one night and fly back out the next. Easy, I hoped. The imprint of Helen Graybeal's coffee cup on my head and the bruised wrist William LaBrecque had given me hurt enough to serve as reminders that these things do go wrong from time to time. And Larry Quinn's laser-treatment-gone-wrong case and another date with William LaBrecque were still waiting for my attention. I wondered how agreeable LaBrecque would be to being hauled into APD for processing.

My phone warbled. 'Sorry, I haven't had a chance to call,' Rauser told me. I had sent him a text message before going to sleep last night and never heard back. It wasn't like him. 'Busier than a one-armed paper hanger,' he said. 'ME's report on stomach contents is in. Trout, crab, turnip greens, some kind of sweet potato dish, and a good amount of white wine. We're showing Brooks's picture around to all the local restaurants, especially in the Buckhead area where he was killed.'

'Turnip greens and sweet potatoes in Buckhead?' I asked.

'Probably one of those whoopee-shit fusion places that make little designs in sauce. And get this: there was evidence of a condom on the body, Keye, but it wasn't in the suite. Also, soap residue all over the body and all over the sheets under him. Brooks was squeaky clean except for some of his own semen. No other DNA on his body. Fingernails trimmed and brushed out. We got a load of stuff from the room, though, but it's going to take weeks to break it down. Probably got stuff from three years ago in the carpet. Soap on Brooks was consistent with the hotel brand, which is also missing from the room. Oh, and something else interesting. Housekeeping says they put three washcloths in the room. All missing. No condom, no washcloths, no open bar of soap, one missing glass.'

'A sponge bath,' I said. A clearer picture was emerging of this killer, who was capable of more than just a con to get a front door open, but also of a clever, manipulative seduction. 'That would account for the seminal fluid and the soap residue on the sheets. Must have been part of their sex. It's one more thing that separates Brooks from the other victims.'

David Brooks was spared hours of torture. His body was covered in a loving way. He meant something in the life of this murderer – real or symbolic, he was significant.

'Killer came from behind, right?' I asked.

'Exactly right. Reached around from behind and stuck the knife blade into the substernal notch. Wounds are consistent with the knife used at prior scenes.'

The others had known what kind of danger they were in, what kind of monster had entrapped them. They had experienced the terror that comes with that knowing and been left naked with their legs spread. Brooks was different. Brooks was special. The killer didn't want him to see death coming. Why? I shared my thoughts with Rauser and we grew quiet.

'Lobby cameras show Brooks checking in alone,' Rauser said finally. 'No other outside surveillance except at the lobby. The unit next door was empty, and since there are only two of those units per building, it's isolated. Somebody shoves a knife blade into my chest, I'm gonna scream like hell. The hotel was a good choice.'

'That kind of stab wound paralyzes the diaphragm,' I told him. 'Air can't pass through the vocal cords. It's impossible for the victim to make a sound. Death is instantaneous. It wouldn't have mattered where they were. It's a completely silent kill.'

'That's some creepy shit right there, Keye,' Rauser complained. '*Christ*. I don't think I even want to be hanging out with somebody that knows that shit.'

'Hey, I'm just spreading the sunshine,' I said.

'We've been poking around in Brooks's private life, and he was one womanizing sonofabitch. The guy would do anything that moved. No evidence that he was bisexual, but most guys hide that anyway.' I could hear the tension in his voice. And the exhaustion. 'To be honest, I don't feel one step closer to understanding how he picks them.'

'No,' I said. 'We know one thing we didn't know two days ago. The killer had feelings for Brooks. That's huge, Rauser. You may have a victim who knew the killer in his life. What did he call it in the first letter, "the inner circle"?'

'So you don't think this is the beginning of him having intercourse with the victims. You think this was specific to Brooks?'

'I think he knew him and I think that Brooks symbolized someone significant. Someone he loved and lusted after.'

'God,' Rauser complained. 'What the fuck am I doing in this business?'

Chapter Fifteen

The Midtown house near Tenth Avenue didn't look like a battered women's shelter. I had driven or walked past it a million times over the years. It was ten minutes from my loft at the Georgian, but there was nothing to distinguish it from the other sprawling old Victorians that dotted Atlanta's neighborhoods.

I'd packed for my Denver trip, then spent what was left of the morning looking for William LaBrecque. I went by the home he had once shared with his Russian wife, Darya, in Candler Park. A neighbor said it had been empty for a couple of days, that Darya and the boy left as soon as they found out LaBrecque had been released on bail. She knew he'd come back for her, said the neighbor, he always came back. I tracked down his parents and quickly discovered that Billy boy came by his rudeness and anger honestly. I hadn't really expected them to help me haul their son off to jail, but I wasn't prepared for them to be so utterly vile. They did share some thoughts on their daughter-in-law, and when I sifted through all the expletives, it was the words *whore* and *slut* that surfaced again and again, apparently favorites of theirs. It crossed my mind that LaBrecque probably called Darya these things while he beat her. I did learn that LaBrecque met his wife in Germany while hospitalized on an American military base during his last year of service. A hero, his parents called him. *Right*. He had found Darya on the Internet, one of those cyber-bride websites. She went to Germany for the meeting; they fell in love and came to the United States together seven years ago. I knew a few things his parents had omitted. The police had responded to three

103

domestic violence calls at the LaBrecque home in the last year and a half. They had once arrested Darya even though she was bleeding and bruised, because LaBrecque met them at the door and told them she'd started the fight in a jealous rage and he'd simply defended himself. Gender does not guarantee the cops will be on your side. Child protective services had sent a social worker to the hospital once after a doctor reported suspicious bruising and broken bones on the boy. Darya finally filed a restraining order, which had done absolutely nothing to protect her.

There wasn't a lot in LaBrecque's folder to point me in the right direction. His parents gave me nothing. He didn't have friends, but I figured his wife would know where he'd hide, so I started calling and leaving messages at women's shelters all over the metro Atlanta area. No one at them volunteered any information, of course. Women's shelters do everything within their power to protect the anonymity of their residents. But when my cell rang and the number showed up as restricted, my gut told me it was Darya.

I walked up the empty driveway toward the rambling white Victorian with the lacy peach-colored shutters. A motorized iron gate was closed and locked and I assumed staff cars and resident vehicles were parked behind the house and out of sight. I saw sections of a privacy fence surrounding the backyard, nicely painted to match the house. A security camera, barely noticeable in the upper-right corner of the enormous front porch, watched me while a tiny light under the camera lens blinked green. Traffic on the Midtown street, one of the city's busy one-ways, was sparse this time of day. At rush hour all lanes would be crawling bumper-to-bumper.

'I'm Keye Street,' I told the woman standing behind the screen. 'Darya called me.'

'Hey,' she said, and with just one word, I heard Louisiana in her accent. She pushed open the door for me. 'I'm Adele. I work with CADV.'

'What's CADV?' I asked as she ushered me inside. She was thirty, perhaps, lanky with spiky hair and bright blue-green eyes. An elaborate stained-glass tattoo ran down one bare arm. In the background, I heard women's voices, children, a television.

'Coalition Against Domestic Violence,' Adele answered. 'I'm one of the social workers on rotation here. Another brick in the wall,' she added, smiling.

She led me down the foyer past a bedroom that had been turned into an office. I saw two desks, a woman at one talking into a headset. 'We have a twenty-four-hour crisis line in there,' Adele explained. 'We all take turns. It's brutal.' I looked again and noticed three security monitors, with views of the front porch, back porch, and driveway.

We turned a corner and stepped into the main living area, where several kids played on the floor and a row of women on a couch barely looked up from *The Jerry Springer Show*. The furniture was used Salvation Army, mismatched, long out of date. A couple of folding card tables added to the mix.

'Donated funds don't care about decorating,' Adele said. We walked past several bedrooms with lines of single beds and cots, and through the kitchen, where two women played cards. Adele pointed to the door. 'Darya's on the back porch.'

She might have been pretty before LaBrecque went to work on her with his fists, but it was hard to tell now. Darya was smoking a cigarette, her face so bruised and misshapen that her lips wouldn't close completely around the filter. There was a little sucking sound of air when she took a drag. My stomach did a flip-flop.

I sat down next to her on a porch swing. A dark-haired boy about seven worked resolutely on a toy car, taking it apart and reassembling it at a bright green and red child's table. 'Thank you for calling me back.'

'I want you to find him.' I detected her Russian accent even through the slur from a swollen jaw and lips. Her bruises were ugly and hard to look at. I looked instead into her eyes. She'd been shown enough disrespect. 'I think I know where he will be. There is a lake near Lawrenceville in the Gwinnett County. There is a cabin there. It is private and owned by his friend who is wealthy and travels. Billy stays there sometimes. He likes to fish.'

The boy lifted his head to me for the first time when I stood to leave. 'Are you going to keep my daddy from finding us?'

His fearful dark eyes set off an ache in me. 'Is that what you want?' I asked gently.

His attention turned quickly back to the toy car. I thought I'd lost him, that he was too timid to answer. Perhaps he wasn't accustomed to being asked what he wanted. But then he found his small voice. 'Yes,' he answered simply.

'Well, then, don't you worry, kiddo. You and your mom are safe here, okay?'

I waited, but it didn't seem he had anything more to say. Darya ran her fingers through his hair, then bent to kiss the top of his head. I left feeling like a hole had been blown in me.

It was just after lunch when I pulled onto the dirt drive on Webb Gin House Road in Gwinnett County. We have a saying in Atlanta: *Stay inside the perimeter where it's safe.* Not from muggings and murder and robbery, of course. That we have up the wazoo in the city. We mean Jesus freaks and guys named Bubba who only change their overalls once a week. Interstate 285, the perimeter highway, makes a big circle around the city and gives us a false sense of protection. We stay in. They stay out. That's the way we all like it. Most of us who are non-white, non-blond, and non-Baptist would rather stomp through a shit blizzard in snowshoes than spend time Outside the Perimeter (OTP), yet here I was looking for a guy named Billy who'd already called me a Chink.

The sky had gone gray and a steady drizzle had begun. Steam rose up off the lake as I drove toward the cabin. My wounded windshield had started to fog up. The midday heat was unreal. I reached under the seat for my Glock and put it in my lap. LaBrecque wasn't going to have a chance to do to me what he'd done to his wife. I thought about Darya's world-weary eyes peering out behind that contused black-and-blue mask, and the anger felt like a hot iron in my throat.

I wasn't happy with the driveway. It was three quarters of a mile at least and rose and dipped in a way that gave me glimpses of the cabin and could have easily given someone inside the same view of me, but the rain was starting to come down hard, as it often does when a cold front meets the tropical systems that hang over us in summer. I hoped it would hamper visibility and cover the sound of gravel crackling under my tires. Another hill, another bend, and I could see the cabin getting close. I decided to stop there and take the last couple hundred yards on foot. I pulled over to the side of the narrow dirt lane and wiped my windshield clear with a napkin from Krystal. Between swipes of the windshield wipers, I could see the cabin roof was tin. I stuck the Glock 10 in the back of my pants and pulled on a gray, waist-length hooded rain jacket that helped me melt into the scenery on days like this but still allowed me mobility. The wind was beginning to act up as I started down the muddy road. Rain pelted my jacket. Lightning slashed over the lake for one stunning millisecond, and I did what I've done since I was a kid. I began to count. *One, two, two and a half*, and then came the boom. A tactic my mother used when I was little to take the fear out of thunder. I've counted my way through many southern storms.

Deep ruts gouged the saturated red clay earth. Someone had driven here recently. Perhaps LaBrecque had come and already gone. LaBrecque drove a dark blue Dakota pickup truck, I knew from the file, but there was no way to tell now what size tire had left these marks, the ruts softened by rain and indistinct.

I walked down a hill and around a curve and got my first good look at the cabin, brick red and larger than I'd anticipated, one of those vacation homes the rich call cabins or cottages that really just look like houses to the rest of us. I saw no lights in the windows even though the day had turned dark with thunderclouds. LaBrecque's blue pickup was parked near the front lawn, streaming with rain. A hill with stone steps cut into it sloped down to the lake. Anyone who fishes in the warm months knows it is best done early morning, late night, or after the rain comes and cools things down. Two rowboats had been pulled up to shore and flipped over near a wooden dock. I imagined LaBrecque inside getting his gear ready, a few cans of cheap beer and a hat with hooks and lures.

As I neared the cabin and started down the pebble sidewalk, I saw it. *Shit.* The front door was cracked open a few inches. My pulse quickened. I moved in a half crouch toward the side of the house for cover, releasing the trigger safety on my gun as I did so. It was stifling under the gray jacket. Rain dripped off my hood in front of my face and blurred my vision. I waited. Nothing. No movement, just the rush of wind and rain battering the roof and bouncing off me. Could this day get any shittier? I was about to find out.

I moved to the front door and pressed my back against the outside wall, used my foot to gently inch the cabin door open, waited a few seconds, then stuck my head round and peered inside. Cold fireplace on the right, a sofa, a recliner. A picture window looking out onto the lake provided the only light. A food bar on the left, a kitchen, lots of cowboy art on the walls. No Billy LaBrecque.

Normally I would have called out, let someone know bond enforcement was in the house, but my gut was telling me something was off. I eased my way through the kitchen into a large open space, Glock double-clutched cop-style. A staircase was railed off in the center of the room and there were four doors right and left of it, all closed. I decided to cover the obvious opening first, the stairs, which – unlike the planked cabin floor upstairs – were carpeted. They led down into an enormous game room paneled with rustic bleached wood, an impressively stocked bar, a pool table, a TV, and an antique pinball machine. No LaBrecque.

Moving slowly back up the stairs, I paused at the top. The main room was exactly as I'd left it – empty and dim except for the natural gray of the day bleeding through the big window.

I went for the door on the left first, stood to the side, tried the knob, found no resistance, pushed it open quietly, and stepped around fast, Glock steady. I was sweating. The rain jacket was clinging to my skin; my heart was pounding in my temples. My body, in all its genetic wisdom, had the nerve cells rapid-firing. Fight or flight? I wasn't sure yet.

I checked the closet, the bathroom. Empty. I peeled off the jacket and left it, then twice more I went through this excruciating process, freezing each time the floorboard creaked under me or a door hinge complained.

When I opened the last door, I saw LaBrecque right in front of me, and it felt like I'd been smacked with a two-by-four. His face was turned away, but I instantly recognized his build, the thick neck, his heavily muscled arms. But this wasn't the threatening bully I'd seen at the church, the man who had brutalized his wife and child and grabbed my wrist with an infuriating sense of entitlement. This William LaBrecque had had everything stripped from him. Naked, he lay on the floor, his legs pulled open, his buttocks and thighs bloodied, spattered with vicious bruises and stab wounds.

Wishbone had been here before me.

I stepped in and spun quickly, heart trip-hammering, Glock ready to open up on anyone behind the door. No one there. I checked the closet and bath, then came back to LaBrecque, touched his neck with two fingers, held his wrist for a moment. No heartbeat, but his skin was still warm. I thought about this. He was a big guy, the cabin was hot, so even naked and with no blood pumping through him, his body would stay warm a while. I thought again about the ruts I'd seen in the road.

I stooped to see his face. I was careful to disturb as little evidence as possible while remaining alert to any sound, shadow, movement in the cabin. Sometimes I think there's a block of ice inside me, perhaps in the heart of every investigator, something ghoulish and coldly voyeuristic.

LaBrecque had been beaten viciously with some kind of weapon. His face was battered and bloodied, unrecognizable. A fist couldn't have done this kind of damage. I studied the spatter in the room.

Cast-off on the walls and ceiling and floors, medium-velocity spatter all over, the result of blunt trauma, an intense external force. It was consistent with the pool that had formed under his head.

I used two fingers to lift his chin off the floor. There it was. Blunt-force trauma, a cave-in just above the temple that must have fractured his skull. Why the rage? I thought about Darya. Was that the connection? Had the other victims been abusers of some kind? Only one other victim, the first that we knew about, the student at West Florida State University, had had a lot of facial bruising. What was it about LaBrecque and the first victim that had enraged the killer so?

I pulled my phone out of my pocket and pressed Rauser's numbers, then noticed a bloody rolling pin on the floor a few feet away. Another connection to that first killing in Florida. When he'd killed Anne Chambers fifteen years ago, the killer had used something at the scene as a weapon. Perhaps it was just for efficiency. A rolling pin here, a lamp there. Not like you can carry those things around in your pocket. I got to my feet. There was something else that intrigued me about this scene. It was contained. It seemed to have begun and ended here in this one room. The rest of the cabin was free of spatter, undisturbed, furniture in place. Had the killer found LaBrecque asleep here in the bedroom, drunk in the middle of the day, let go the controlling blow before he could come to? Or had it been another seduction like Brooks? LaBrecque didn't seem the type, but what was the type, really?

Rauser was on his way. He was calling Gwinnett County Homicide. I stayed there memorizing the crime scene as long as I could. When I heard the sirens, I took a shallow breath, stuck my Glock in my waistband and my hands behind my head. Then I headed out to greet the Gwinnett County cops, who didn't know me from Ted Bundy.

Chapter Sixteen

I was exhausted. I'd spent hours at the LaBrecque scene, being questioned hard by detectives who wanted to know how it was that I happened to be consulting on the Wishbone cases while tracking a bail jumper who, it certainly appeared, happened to be the newest Wishbone victim. None of this was explainable, but I did my best until Rauser arrived at the scene and saved me, followed by Ken Lang and the CSI van. There was no small amount of tension. The Gwinnett County cops didn't like having APD on the scene and Rauser wasn't at all happy about someone else processing it. They finally reached some agreements but until then it was a full-on pissing contest.

It was very late in the afternoon before I got away. Rauser hadn't wanted me to leave the scene, but there was nothing I could do there, and I still had a business to keep afloat and work I hadn't even begun. I was also starving.

I called Neil. 'Want some breakfast?'

'It's after five,' he answered.

'Tell me about it.' Happy hour was tapping at my shoulder once more. It rarely passed unnoticed. And how I wanted one today.

'Rough day?' Neil asked.

'Not at Waffle House,' I said in a singsong way to tempt him, knowing full well it was one of his weaknesses. If there's one thing you can count on down South, it's Waffle House. The grill is cranking 24/7 – eggs, bacon, waffles, and hash browns scattered, smoothed, and covered, crispy outside, soft inside, and glistening with oil. Eat

111

them every day and they'll flat-out kill you. But from time to time there's nothing like them alongside a pair of eggs scrambled with cheese, over-buttered white toast angles, and a couple cups of thin Waffle House coffee surging through your system like Liquid-Plumr.

We talked about LaBrecque over a pile of food, kicked it around for a long time. We knew a lot about him. That knowledge gave us a jump start, a first: the other victims had been big question marks. Not this guy.

'Can you run the vics' names for anything like domestic abuse calls?'

'Yeah, but Rauser can get this stuff easy.'

'Let's see if there's any merit to it before I put anything else on Rauser's plate. How about hospital records? Emergency room visits? Can you dig those up on all the victims? And on their immediate families?'

'Depends on how old they are.' Neil made a face as I squeezed yellow mustard over the hash browns I'd ordered scattered with jalapeños, then he asked our waitress for a second pecan waffle.

'I have to go check out the laser treatment gone wrong for Quinn,' I told him. 'Want to come? No bullet holes this time.'

'Man, that was cool,' Neil said.

'Uh-huh. That why you turned that pretty shade of green?'

'Yeah, well, it's like your first roller-coaster ride, you know? You kind of want to hurl but you keep going back.'

We left Waffle House big eyed and hopped up with our stomachs rumbling from too much rank coffee. The storms had moved through the way late summer storms do, and I folded the top down on my old Impala. It was just before seven. The heat was slacking off finally.

Vincent Feldon lived off McLendon in the Candler Park section of Atlanta near Little Five Points, where it is not uncommon to see within a stretch of blocks gleaming Vespas, nicely dressed gay and straight couples with strollers, tattooed street people, corner musicians, teenagers pierced from toe to tongue, and the homeless curled up shoeless on the sidewalk. 'Diversity run amok,' Rauser said one afternoon while we ate on the patio at Front Page News along with a couple of trans men, their soft packs looking like enormous boners; Whitney Houston and a recording team that was apparently following her around for some reality TV thing; a group of lesbian writers fresh from a book signing at Charis Books, the lesbian feminist bookstore around the corner; a table of really loud beer-drinking athletic types; and a guy sitting alone with a parrot.

I pulled over a few doors down from Vincent Feldon's address, put the top up on the Impala, then parked one house away and cut the engine. 'What are we doing here?' Neil wanted to know.

I nodded toward the house. 'That's where Feldon the laser tech lives.'

Neil squirmed. 'I know that house.' I looked at him and waited. 'My guy John lives there,' he added reluctantly.

'Your guy John? What does that mean?'

'Well.' More squirming. 'He's kinda my pot dealer.'

'You are kidding me! Vincent Feldon lives with a pot dealer?' I laughed. 'Quinn is going to do cartwheels. Oh my God, no wonder she has a permanent mustache. Good Lord.'

'I didn't know he had a roommate,' Neil said. 'I never saw anyone there, but it's a big house.'

We heard a door close and keys rattle. A heavyset guy in jeans with the crotch at knee level was locking Feldon's front door. The big guy turned and waddled down the walk, a tiny phone to his ear. I reached for the file in the backseat and studied the picture I'd received in the file from Quinn's office.

'That's him,' Neil said.

'Oh, so you *have* seen him?'

Neil gave me a pained look. 'That's John.'

I looked back at the picture. Neil's guy John and Vincent Feldon were one and the same.

I opened my phone and called Larry Quinn's office. Danny,

Quinn's assistant, told me Larry had been out of the office for hours. Did I have his cell phone number? I did.

'Look,' Neil was saying as I scrolled for Quinn's cell number on my contact list. 'I didn't sign up for this. I don't want any part of him getting busted.'

'Nobody wants to bust him,' I told Neil, and heard Larry Quinn answer. 'Larry, hey, it's Keye. Got a minute?'

'Keye, you okay? I heard about the murder and you finding the body. Christ, how awful for you.'

'How'd you hear that?'

'Murder's all over the news, kiddo.' Quinn spoke in that slow southern accent he'd made famous on his commercials. 'And, well, being in the legal biz and all, I've got a few friends in law enforcement. You all right?'

'I'm fine,' I said. I didn't want to talk about it. I hadn't even had time to think about it beyond trying to work out why William LaBrecque had been lying on the floor naked and beaten to death. The very last thing I wanted was for someone to try to comfort me. Just pushing through it was usually a better choice for me. Whatever was left, I'd give to Dr Shetty during our next hundred-and-eighty-dollar hour. 'I wanted to talk about the laser center case, the med tech.'

'Okey-dokey,' Quinn said.

'He supplements his income by selling pot and I have reason to believe he smokes a good amount of it too.'

'I'll be goddamned,' Quinn said. 'That's why he didn't show for the pee test. Said he had the flu or something. We had to reschedule the deposition too.'

'He looks healthy to me,' I told Quinn, and made sure the time and date stamp were active on my camera. Then I snapped a few pictures of Vincent Feldon standing in his yard talking on his phone, pacing back and forth, then folding his big body into a tiny Chrysler Crossfire and driving away. I waited a few seconds, then pulled out behind him.

We followed Feldon down Moreland, took the turn for Reynoldstown, curved into a residential section, and watched him pull up to a small white frame house, get out, and knock. When the door opened and Feldon disappeared inside, I grabbed my camera and got out. Neil sank down low in the seat.

'Hey, look on the bright side,' I told him. 'Feldon loses his job at the treatment center, he's going to have to keep dealing pot.'

Through one of the windows, I saw Feldon talking to a woman, then sitting down on the couch and tossing a sandwich bag with a zipper top onto the table. It looked like pot in the bag. I'd seen a lot of it since Neil and I had been friends. The series of shots I took showed Feldon opening the bag, filling a bowl, lighting it, blowing out a huge cloud of smoke, passing the bag over, and receiving cash. Less than that had gotten Michael Phelps into a world of trouble. I didn't think Quinn would need anything else.

I called Rauser to check in. They were still at the LaBrecque scene. I told him I had to leave for a day, fly to Denver for a client. He didn't want me to go. He never wanted me to go. Unfortunately, what APD was paying me as a case consultant wouldn't even buy my groceries.

Denver had always seemed to me a surprisingly ordinary city. One can spend days here and almost forget entirely that the city happens to be surrounded by extraordinary scenery. From the streets of downtown, the pedestrian's view is of corporate office buildings and unending development, with lots of coffeehouses tossed in for atmosphere.

When I leave Atlanta, where downtown real estate ran short years ago and buildings had to grow tall in order to grow at all, everything looks as if a giant weed whacker had sheared the tops right off the buildings. Here, a mile high, Denver seemed a bit stoop-shouldered as I drove from the airport to the hotel at Logan and Eighteenth.

I was standing on my balcony soaking it in when the sun began to set and light switches and streetlamps all over the city seemed to flick on at once. The thin, dry air rushed my lungs like a football team, and I saw the Rockies in silhouette against Colorado's broad night sky. Nothing at all like my last assignment here, when my view had been the laundry room on the back side of a Best Western and room service meant picking up something from the greasy spoon across the street and bringing it back in an oily paper sack. By Bureau standards, that was first-class treatment of an agent on assignment.

I showered, settled into the soft terry-cloth robe I found hanging in the bath. My room was one of several corporate suites leased year-round by my client; my assignment was to strike up a deal with an accountant named Roy Echeverria, who, I had recently been made aware, had not only run off with a huge amount of cash, he'd also stolen audiotapes, a dozen of them, of private executive meetings. I'd been authorized to offer Echeverria as much for the tapes as he'd snatched initially, five hundred thousand, and once I had his signature on a confidentiality agreement drafted by company lawyers, I was done. My client was betting that the tapes, which were apparently inflammatory enough to have every corporate executive wetting himself, would surface eventually. Why not track the thieving weasel down, make an offer, make it high, nail down an agreement, and be done with the little traitor? At six hundred a day plus expenses and a luxury suite, it sounded like a pretty good plan to me.

I ordered pan-roasted asparagus, rosemary and goat cheese mashed potatoes, and seared rare ahi, then turned on the television and sank into the couch while I waited for room service. A brief but energetic craving for a drink resurfaced and caught me off guard. I could almost hear the ice tinkling against a glass as a uniformed member of the wait-staff balanced a silver tray toward my room. At the height of my drinking, I had used hotels for privacy, to be alone with what I loved most back then. Tonight, I would settle for a Diet Pepsi.

I opened my laptop. My friend Madison from Quantico, my only cordial relationship left at the Bureau, wanted to check in. She had once been a deep-cover operative for the CIA, had her cover blown wide open. She'd ended up at the Farm, the CIA's training center, trying to teach a bunch of kindergartners, as she had called the new recruits, the deceptive and dangerous trade of intelligence. Madison had been later lured to the Bureau, where I met her by chance. We'd become instant friends. Her email today was blunt. *Desperate for someone who doesn't leave a diamond on their desk chair.* Her proper British way of saying she was working with a bunch of tight asses.

I had mail from my mother, who had only recently discovered the joys of the Internet, and now faithfully forwarded religious messages to me. I never read them. If I receive something with three hundred other names on it, I'm not reading it. I don't care if it says Jesus is coming back. My father, thankfully, has not yet shown an interest in the Internet.

Where have you been, child? the subject line in my mother's message asked, and I could almost hear her thick drawl. Emily Street had grown up on the Albemarle Sound of North Carolina, not far from Virginia, where words like 'about' sound like 'a boat.' Her voice was butter and swamp water all at once, soft and strong, and when I was a child, it calmed me. She read me to sleep at night and insisted I read to her in the afternoons, all kinds of books, magazines, newspapers. Words were her flying carpets. Wherever she wanted to go that day, we went. She taught me about that kind of escape and I grew up loving it and books.

I didn't call her back. I have to build up to it with Mother, the princess of passive aggression, especially when she perceives neglect from her children. A real live southern belle, my mom makes true the expression that southerners can say anything to anyone no matter how insulting as long as it begins or ends with 'bless your little heart' or 'you poor darlin''. Emily Street has turned it into a kind of art form. Honey drips from her lips as she extends her long claws and prepares to pounce. *Melanie, you poor darlin', are you still struggling with that awful weight problem? And with Harvey cheating on you and all,*

bless your little heart. Don't you worry, honey. You'll have lots of support.
I've told everyone.

When my phone rang, I was watching blooper reels and using my asparagus instead of a fork to eat mashed potatoes. This is what I do in hotels now instead of crack open the little bottles in the minibar.

Neil sounded breathy and hyper.

'By George, I think I've got it,' he said in a bad Hollywood accent. 'The link, old girl. I've got it. Elicia Richardson and David Brooks were both attorneys, as you know. *Civil* attorneys, both of them. Richardson was *not* in criminal law, which is what the file says. It was incorrect.'

'Okay, and . . . ?'

'The second victim, Bob Shelby, lived on disability, barely scraped by, but he had a huge payment pending on a personal injury suit he'd won four months before his murder. Another month or two and Shelby would have been able to afford some stuff. Now here's the interesting thing: Lei Koto won a wrongful death suit against the electric company her husband worked for when he was killed on the job. The litigation took almost six years.'

I tried to wrap my mind around this. 'So there's no connection to the domestic abuse thing at all. But you're telling me there's a link to civil lawsuits or civil law in general?'

'Looks like it. Weird, huh?'

'Very. Maybe the killer sees civil cases as being about greed, as being frivolous. Really sets him off, he sees the plaintiff as the problem. Interesting.'

'Maybe he got a raw deal, got screwed over by the system, or some judge or jury found against him. Maybe it trashed his business or livelihood. Whoa! Just got a big idea. Maybe that's how our guy gets them to open the door, he goes with this injury thing, and pretends to be disabled. Who wouldn't open the door for someone in a chair, right?'

It was something to consider. We were quiet thinking about it. 'Where were the suits filed?'

'Shelby's was in Florida, but Koto's was in Fulton. And it

looks like the bulk of the cases filed by Brooks and Richardson went through Fulton as well.'

'What about LaBrecque? And the first vic in Florida, Anne Chambers?'

'No connection with LaBrecque and, well, it's not all that easy to find anything on Anne.' He paused, and his voice had softened a little when he spoke again. 'She was just a kid, you know? Why would someone do that to her?'

If you think about it, really allow yourself to contemplate the violence and terror in murder, to feel any of the fear and confusion the victim might have felt or consider what they left behind, all that collateral damage, the shock and loss and lives derailed, it will break your heart. Neil had never been this close to it. I was quiet while he collected himself.

'Find out where Anne Chambers's family is now, would you, Neil? I want to speak with them. I'm going to call Rauser and let him know what you found. He's going to be bouncing off the walls. This is huge. You did good, Neil. Really.'

I set my phone down for a moment and thought about this. Had David Brooks and Elicia Richardson been murdered because they practiced civil law? How many more victims were out there that hadn't been logged into a database or didn't fit the MO and signature? We knew now that this killer was adaptable. Did Lei Koto's young son find her butchered on the kitchen floor because his mother had decided to sue an electric company over her husband's death? I remembered the pot of cabbage left burning on the stove, scorched and stinking, as the boy called 911, and then waited alone with her body for the police to arrive at the scene. I can still envision my murdered grandparents when I close my eyes, smell the nervous sweat of their killers, the blood, the piercing sourness of a shattered jar of cranberry juice that had fallen from a grocery shelf. To this day, I can't get near cranberry anything without my stomach doing flip-flops. Murder marks and orphans children, and it rips families apart. I wanted this killer off the streets.

My mind was clicking along. Civil suits and civil attorneys. What did they have in common? Judges, clerks, process servers, steno-graphers, a courthouse. And then it hit me. *The courthouse.* Is that the elevator mentioned in Wishbone's second letter? Is that where the killer saw David Brooks? Was Atlanta's Fulton County Court-house the hunting ground for a serial murderer?

Chapter Seventeen

No one else had ever answered Rauser's phone when I called. Not ever. Her voice seemed vaguely familiar, but I was too dumbfounded to place it right away.

'Aaron, it's for you,' she had called out.

Aaron? I heard the rustling of fabric, a receiver dropped and retrieved, muffled laughter. 'Who calls you that?' I asked when he finally answered.

'A friend,' he said mysteriously. His voice had a gravelly sound I'd heard a million times, too much whiskey and too many cigarettes.

'You know what's wrong with that, Rauser? You don't have any friends,' I joked, but I felt like screaming at him, balling up my fists and pounding on his chest. Jesus, it felt like he was cheating on me. He hadn't even told me he was seeing anyone.

'It's Jo,' he whispered, and I recognized the locker room tone. He was bragging, actually *bragging* to *me* about his conquest, and whispering so she wouldn't hear.

Jo? Who the hell was Jo? Mystified, I ransacked my shaken memory until the connection was made. *The blood-spatter analyst! That's who calls him Aaron. Jo Phillips, the big tall Amazon fucking bloodstain analyst!* So that's why they were so chummy that night at the scene. They probably had a history. Rauser cheerful and joking around at a murder scene. They were flirting, actually flirting, while David Brooks lay growing cold on a bloody bed. And I thought she was hitting on me. *I'm an idiot.* Then I remembered texting Rauser a couple

121

of nights ago and not getting an answer. I collapsed onto the hotel couch. Over the phone line, I heard ice rattle in a glass. Rauser loved iced tea. He could drink gallons of it, sweet southern iced tea with mountains of sugar. I pictured him wandering into his backyard with the phone on his shoulder, sitting on the deck he'd built himself, with the sun on his back and a glass in his hand. He liked wearing wife-beaters, the cheap ones that come three in a package at Target. I didn't want to think about her there with him.

I told him what Neil had discovered and that the courthouse might be the common ground, the place where the offender hunted for his victims, and where David Brooks and the others with lawsuits in Fulton might have met their killer.

'He's probably getting transcripts from the file room. Do they keep a log of who checks out which files?'

'I'll sure as hell find out,' Rauser said excitedly. 'Maybe we got a courier. Couriers go there to pick up court records. And anyone with a case number, a date, and three bucks can get transcripts. Sweet Jesus, Keye, this is big. I owe you guys. Man oh man. I'll get the security company that handles Fulton to get the tapes to us. Lot of cameras there. We'll have a presence on duty there in ten minutes. Deputies covering the metal detectors will help. They know who goes in and out. Hang on, would ya? I gotta tell Jo bye.'

I felt the blood rushing to my head. My eyes might have bulged out a little. I heard muffled voices, laughter. *Oh, please*. Then, after leaving me on hold too long, the ungrateful ass returned to the phone and said, 'Sorry, Jo had someplace to be.'

'New episode of *Xena*?' I asked without even trying to hide my resentment.

Mr Sensitive laughed, and made hissing and yowling sounds, the kind that mean catfight to men everywhere.

I paced around my room after we hung up, obsessing about Jo and Rauser, about me delivering that kind of news to him, news that would redirect the entire investigation, and he had the nerve to put me on hold to say goodbye to her. I was livid, and I wasn't even sure why. I had no right to be. I knew it, but knowing it did nothing to help. I ended up in the café downstairs eating two slices of lemon pound cake, which was better than sitting in the bar across the lobby drinking lemon vodka, and yet it was still something Dr Shetty would have disapproved of, I was sure. I realized that somewhere in the back of my mind, I'd been saving Rauser for myself. He was my backup. It never occurred to me that someone might come along and threaten that. If I could have, I would have lifted my leg and peed on him right then and there. I ordered a third slice of cake.

I didn't sleep well, and I wasn't in the mood to cut deals with accountants this morning. For that matter, I wasn't in the mood for anything. I felt upended and I had never been the kind to bury myself in work when something troubled me. I was far more likely to close the blinds, crawl into bed, and eat a bunch of Twinkies. I wasn't drinking anymore, but in many ways, I still cycled through the behaviors I'd learned back then, isolating and self-indulgence being at the top of the list.

Denver was sunny and sixty-five degrees when I left my hotel and climbed into a rented Jeep Liberty. It was Saturday, a day when the chances were better of finding the man who had ripped off my client at home.

And I got lost. Somehow my brain never seemed to register direction like the rest of the world. I had real trouble with maps. This, combined with the natural tendency to wander, resulted in me doing quite a bit of unintended sightseeing whenever I traveled. Today was no exception. A half-hour drive had turned into three times that, and I was distracted, my mind anywhere but on the case I was working and the agreement I needed to make for my client this morning. I'd been obsessing about Rauser and Amazon Jo and I didn't want to be this far from the War Room. It would be an exciting time in the investigation and it pulled at me. Was I drawn to this investigation because I really deeply cared? Or was it tugging at me because it filled the gaps in me, because it was another thing an obsessive mind and a bend toward addiction needed to grab on to?

123

By the time I turned the rented Jeep into Roy Echeverria's driveway, I wasn't in a good place. I did not give a damn about some sleazy little accountant who got caught with his fingers in the corporate cookie jar, no matter how fat and succulent those cookies were. This man had used the money he took from my client to buy himself a new identity and put a sizable down payment on a home in the Westridge section of Highlands Ranch, twelve miles south of Denver, a sprawling master-planned community with golf courses, open space, and the eighty-five-hundred-acre Wildcat Mountain Reserve. Not bad for a junior-level accountant.

Echeverria was on his knees spreading wood chips around the shrubbery under his front windows. He was wearing gardening gloves and blue jeans and rubber-soled gardening shoes without heels, half loafer, half sandal. He was olive skinned with large dark eyes and black hair and couldn't have been more than thirty. Attractive enough in a dark, brooding way and thinner than he'd been in the file copy of the photo on his employee badge.

'Mr Echeverria,' I said as I approached. 'My name is Keye Street. I'd like to talk with you about some property in your possession belonging to your former employer.'

He rose slowly to full height, slipped the gardening gloves off and let them fall to the ground, dusted his hands off on his jeans.

'You are mistaken,' he said calmly and with an even smile. His accent was thick. I knew from his file that he'd come from Basque country in Spain. 'My name—'

I held up the copy of his employee badge. 'Your name is Echeverria. Can we just cut the crap? Do you want to talk here or should we go inside?'

'*You* cut the crap!' he yelled to my utter astonishment, and very aggressively stepped toward me, shoved me hard with both hands, and shrieked '*No!!!*' the way they teach you to scream it in self-defense classes. I went down on my backside in his front yard and he took off. The heelless gardening shoes slapped the ground like flip-flops and Echeverria had to raise his knees very high to keep

124

from tripping over them. He looked like some kind of demented waterfowl, a seabird gone berserk.

Me, I'm little, but I'm fast. Two lawns down, I caught up enough to make a dive for his ankles. He tried to kick free and lost a shoe. I held on until he hit the ground chest-first with a grunt. The air rushed out of him and I climbed onto his back, tried to hold him down, reached around for my cuffs while he flopped around like a fish in a rowboat. He shook me off and got himself turned over. I wrapped my arms around his head and we rolled several times until he bit my shoulder so hard I yelped and had to let go. Then he ran toward the golf course and hijacked one of the carts. He gave me the finger as he disappeared over the green.

'*Shit!*' I climbed to my feet and brushed myself off.

Standing on a porch a few yards away, I noticed a woman with two young children staring at me, slack jawed. The children crowded up close to her legs when I took a step forward, as if I might cook them and eat them.

'We're family, Roy and me,' I offered by way of explanation, and smiled. 'It's just a thing we do.'

All three of them kept staring.

I moved the Jeep out of sight a block away, then returned to Roy Echeverria's house. The door was unlocked. He obviously had not expected to wrestle a girl and run off in a golf cart. I searched the upstairs bathroom for a first-aid kit, then, armed with peroxide, I stretched out the collar of my shirt and inspected the bite on my shoulder.

'*Sonofabitch.*' The bite was ugly, already turning a nice rich purple around the broken skin, and it hurt. The peroxide's sting brought tears to my eyes. 'That's it,' I grumbled, and headed for the bedroom, where, after a few minutes of searching, I found a 9mm and ammunition in a shoebox in the closet. I loaded the gun and headed downstairs.

There was a canister with coffee on the kitchen counter, so I made a pot and waited. The guy was wearing one shoe and driving a stolen golf cart. I didn't think he'd stay away long, and I was right. It took only an hour for the front door to open very slowly. I heard him walking lightly through the house, heard closet doors opening, shower curtains jerked back. Then his big eyes peered round the corner at me sitting at his kitchen table. They dropped briefly to the gun, then to the coffee cup, the coffeemaker, and back to me.

I rested my hand on the 9mm. 'Have a seat, Mr Echeverria.'

He cursed softly, slumped into the kitchen shoeless, and plopped down at the table. 'Nothing ever works out for me.'

'Oh, great, a whiner,' I said. 'Could the day get any better?'

He would tell me later that he had tried to buy himself a normal life when he bought his house and his new name. But nothing had been normal since he fled. He was frightened all the time, always looking over his shoulder. He believed they might kill him one day for what he'd done.

The tapes were in a safety deposit box. First thing Monday morning, he promised, he'd make a withdrawal, sign my agreement, swap me the tapes for the five-hundred-thousand-dollar cashier's check I offered him. I invited myself for the weekend just in case he changed his mind. He objected weakly at first but soon settled into the idea when he realized I wasn't leaving.

By Monday morning, I understood what he'd done and exactly how he'd justified doing it. I understood everything in excruciating detail. His entire life! I knew his sister's name and that he'd had chicken pox at thirteen. I knew the birth date of his second girlfriend and his grades in high school. I knew the names of every cat he ever owned and their litter box habits. The sonofabitch was never quiet. I thought about killing him myself.

'The tapes will tell you,' he said for the thirtieth time over coffee in the breakfast nook that the money stolen from my client had paid for, 'how they feel about anyone with different skin color or, God forbid, an accent. They told jokes in those meetings. Racial jokes. But it wasn't just the jokes – it was what was happening at policy level to discriminate.' He stared at me. 'They would laugh at you too.

126

They would refuse to promote you or pay you an honest wage just because you are not white.'

In my face he'd seen the heritage that I myself knew nothing about. He was hoping to tap into some hidden rage inside me. He was out of luck. There wasn't any rage. I was numb by then to him and to the sound of his voice. If he'd said he planned on whacking off in a giant vat of peanut butter, I would have nodded and said, 'That's nice.'

I didn't listen to the tapes once I had them in my hands. I didn't want to know. My job wasn't about saving the world from assholes. I just wanted to bill out the two thousand bucks I had coming and walk away from Roy Echeverria without a lump in my throat. I stuffed the tapes inside my suitcase, locked it, and carried them onto the plane with me. I'd done my job. I was comfortable with that.

By dusk on Monday evening, I was watching the sun sink behind the western slopes through the smudged window of a 767 about to take off for Atlanta. I was tired from sleeping with one eye open on a couch at Echeverria's house, and it wasn't long after the plane shot into Colorado's wide, flat sky that I drifted off to sleep.

I dreamt I was in a little diner, the kind that serves salad on thick white plates with cherry tomatoes and little packages of saltines. Sitting at the lunch counter next to my plate was a pistol on a paper napkin and a martini glass with a wishbone inside. In my dream, I understood the wishbone was significant, that it had been left as a warning, and I felt suddenly afraid.

I woke to a flight attendant asking if I wanted dinner. Her name was Barbra, according to a brass plate pinned to her navy blue blazer, and Barbra had gone a little heavy on the lipstick. Big, scary red lips are not what you want to see when your heart's already doing a hundred and fifty.

'Decaf,' I answered, and flipped open my laptop. Dr Shetty had a blast dissecting dreams. She'd spent days on the last one. I'd been riding a Twinkie into a brick wall. I decided to shoot her an email. It would make her day.

. . . And then I saw it. Something dropped in my mailbox just like the wishbone in the glass in my dream. I felt my throat tighten. The woman at my elbow wanted to know if I was all right. 'Yes, yes. I'm fine,' I told her.

The style of the letter was unmistakable. The rhythm of it instantly told me its author was the same person who had been writing Rauser and torturing and killing.

And now in life as in my dreams, I felt danger draw very near. The letter was addressed to Rauser. My name appeared on the copy line.

> *Dearest Lieutenant,*
>
> *You're wondering why David was different, aren't you? What I did with him, where I did it, how I left him. All different. And William LaBrecque. He was different too. Have you even begun to figure out how? Here's what they had in common. Both were the kind of scourge that needs eradicating. Admittedly for very different reasons, but both a blight nonetheless. Really, you must be haunted by all this. What have the analysts told you? That MO changes, that motive changes, that we learn and evolve, that humans are multi-determined?*
>
> *Your analysts know nothing about me and neither do you.*
>
> *I've learned a few things, however. Let's begin with your new consultant. I gave her LaBrecque. Did you know that? And what a thrill that must have been for the profiler to walk into. She was all alone out there on that land, in that cabin. I could have so easily come back for her. Ah, I have your attention now. What surprises you most? That I knew she was there or that I know about her FBI past? I saw you arriving together to find poor David. Why would a private detective show up at a death scene? I wondered. Now that was something to investigate. Does your task force feel the sexual tension between you? Does your chief or the mayor? I do. Do you get hot when she deconstructs my scenes for you? Do you talk about me in bed? Business and pleasure, Lieutenant. Really, you should know better.*

You think I made mistakes with David, don't you? Taking him to a public place and using him that way. Yet you found nothing in that hotel room. Don't despair, Lieutenant. It wouldn't have helped anyway. I am in no database. My DNA can do only one thing for you: give you some reference for the next one.

By the way, this Wishbone thing, the name, it's absurd, don't you think? Isn't it so like the media to take something out of context without telling the whole story? What will they leap at next? W.

I leaned back and took a shaky breath. The woman in the seat next to me seemed to have disappeared, and it crossed my mind that as my anxiety and tension had increased, so had my body odor. I tried to do one of those quick under-the-arm sniffs without being too obvious. Perhaps she had gone in search of an open seat elsewhere. One could hope.

I looked back at the words on my laptop screen, the words of a psychopath. He'd made fun of the name given by the media, but he'd adopted the W as a signature. He was embracing this new identity.

What did the email mean? The point, I assumed, was to deliver two threats. First, a promise of more killing. *My DNA can do only one thing for you: give you some reference for the next one.* Second, a slightly more cryptic threat about something else. *What will they leap at next?* Was this about Rauser? Or Rauser and me?

I clicked on Properties and hit the Details tab on the email program in an attempt to trace it. The email had gone to Rauser's address and my address; no other addresses visible. I looked at the return path, one of those free email addresses, temporary, of course, but I knew every effort would be exhausted to trace it. It was gutsy using the Internet. Neil and cyber detectives like him would be able to find the source, the computer where the email originated. Wishbone must be getting bored.

I thought about that night at the Brooks scene when I'd turned to the growing crowd outside the scene tape and felt the killer's presence there. The air had a wild feel that evening. Something rank and restless had been stirring out there. I was certain APD had been over the video of the crowds at all the scenes, run background checks and comparisons. Maybe a second look was a good idea. I thought about pulling in to the dirt drive in the rain at the LaBrecque scene. I searched my memory. There were cars on the main road, but I hadn't suspected I was walking into a murder scene. All I was going to do was pick up a bail jumper, a wife beater. I'd been looking only for his blue pickup truck. Why LaBrecque? How did he fit in? How did the killer know I was coming for him?

I gave her LaBrecque. Did you know that? And what a thrill that must have been for the profiler to walk into. She was all alone out there on that land, in that cabin. I could have so easily come back for her.

Is it true that you 'gave' me LaBrecque? Or did you simply get a hold of the police reports and decide to make this boast? A little more drama just for fun? Trying to rattle the profiler? What is it about me on this case that bothers you so much? And why didn't you come back for me that day?

I used the decaf Barbra with the big red lips brought me to swallow a couple of Advil. My shoulder still ached from Roy Echeverria sinking his teeth into me, and my head was pounding. The dream, the letter, the case, this killer – it all fascinated and repelled me, like wiggling my toes around in a shark pool, which was, of course, the attraction and the terror of this kind of work.

You're wondering why David was different, aren't you?

Yes. Tell me. Why was Brooks different? He's another key to your past, isn't he?

The killer had referred to him in the letter by his first name only. Again, something that indicated familiarity, even affection. Was it real or symbolic?

And William LaBrecque. *He was different too. Have you even begun to figure out how?*

No, goddamnit, I haven't even begun to figure it out, but I'd known the moment I'd seen LaBrecque in that cabin that it was you who'd been there before me. I saw your marks all over him. *Why do you turn them over?* Rauser had asked me this once. I still didn't know the answer.

I got out my notebook and made another list of the victims in order of their murders, then drew columns for date, location – living room, kitchen, hotel, cabin – cause of death, time of death, number of antemortem and postmortem wounds, and approximate survival time after the first assault according to the autopsy. A check mark identified those victims with a connection to civil law. A star next to Brooks's name reminded me there was sexual contact.

I drew an arrow from the first name, Anne Chambers, to the last, William LaBrecque. Both had been treated to an extraordinary amount of rage, both beaten savagely with a heavy tool, both died from blunt-force trauma. Did these two people have some personal connection to the killer? To each other? I tried to remember the details of Anne Chambers's file. I'd been over the police file, the autopsy and crime scene reports and photographs, reviewed the physical evidence. It had been determined that the primary crime scene and the disposal site were one and the same, which was typical for this offender. Anne's murder took place in her dorm room and it was a particularly brutal killing. There were deep ligature marks around her neck and wrists, and she was so badly beaten with the fat end of a lamp that the bones in her face and skull were crushed. I thought about LaBrecque's face, about the bloody rolling pin. Only at these two scenes was the weapon recovered. After each victim was beaten badly enough to be half conscious and manageable, they were restrained so the killer could begin what we now know is a ritual – the stabbing and biting to the sexual areas of the body. But even that was different with Anne Chambers, the first victim. With Anne, the brutality went beyond the lower back, buttocks, inner thighs. Anne had been penetrated with the knife. Her clitoris and nipples had been removed. The medical examiner counted over a hundred stab wounds – inconceivable rage and lust, a frenzy like we have not seen in four of the more recent organized scenes, as if, in this first killing, there

131

was some connection in life, some extraordinary hatred and anger. I needed to compare the lab reports on LaBrecque to see if the humiliation theme ran as deep with him.

David Brooks had known a different killer from Anne Chambers. His killer had ended his life quickly and from behind, silently, and then covered his body to protect his dignity. There was no physical evidence to indicate any sadistic behavior. Sadism is about victim suffering, about getting off sexually on the victim's terror and pain. By definition, sadistic behavior cannot include postmortem activity because the victim is no longer conscious, cannot suffer, cannot beg or cry out to their tormentor. All the bites and stabbings to the sexual areas on Brooks had been postmortem. David Brooks couldn't have felt the pain of them. So they were about something else, something sexual and ritualistic, something the killer craves.

Anne Chambers suffered more, was kept alive longer and sexually mutilated. LaBrecque was so badly beaten I hardly recognized the mush that had been his face. Brooks suffered less. He was the only one of the three to share a link to civil law, yet they all had one thing in common: Wishbone's signature staging, stabbing, and biting to the same areas of the body. What did it mean?

I leaned back and closed my eyes. I had to speak to Rauser. I wondered if he'd read his copy of the third Wishbone letter yet and what he thought about it. I prayed it wasn't already on the way to the newspapers. Dread swelled up, then turned to sandpaper in my throat.

Chapter Eighteen

From the southbound lanes of I-85 just a couple of miles south of downtown and Turner Field, the airport was a glowing smear in the distant, jet-streaked sky. Atlanta's Hartsfield-Jackson Airport is a mammoth, bustling municipality all its own, a borough without community or heart, a city of unnamed passersby, and an excellent place to blend in.

Hartsfield-Jackson overwhelms. The very place we are told to be most vigilant these days is the place that also makes it nearly impossible. From the moment the sliding glass doors open into the enormous terminals, one is confronted with announcements, posted instructions, recorded messages, moving sidewalks, bars and lounges, escalators, video screens, security checks, shops, food, underground trains, the roar of forty-three thousand employees, soldiers, cops, bomb-sniffing dogs, and travelers. One of the world's busiest international airports is sluggish in all the wrong places, and everywhere else it is a blizzard of information and sound and light. Unless one is there to observe, to watch while others are absorbed. The singular concerns of travelers render them only vaguely conscious of those around them, despite the new threats and heightened awareness. With some simple changes to the appearance – a pair of glasses, a baseball cap, plain clothes, unremarkable in design and color – one could pass a close acquaintance without detection or linger in the same newsstand without a glint of recognition. In a place like this, people don't really look at one another. They see in categories and stereotypes – a traveler, a customer, a cop, a businessperson. Being invisible in a public place is a very easy thing to do.

A couple of hundred yards away from the gate where I arrived with other passengers on the flight from Denver, Concourse B took an abrupt dive into steep escalators that led to the underground sidewalks and trains. From the top of the slow-moving metal steps, I surveyed the crowd of strangers. I was trained for this. I knew how to spot a sudden movement, the odd footfall, something off in the crowd, someone paying too much attention. I was wearing Levi's and a sleeveless pullover and still my body temperature had hit about two hundred, it felt, on the plane, and had not yet normalized. My black leather computer case hung from one shoulder. The scrolling digital signs overhead read one minute until the next train. I could feel it coming under the slate floors in the transportation lobby, a barely perceptible vibration accompanied by a low rumble a moment before it rolled into the dock and the glass doors hissed open.

I quickly slipped through the crowd to make the train before the doors sucked shut again, and grabbed on to one of the poles in the center for balance. My eyes swept the compartment. It wasn't hard to suppose an egoist, a voyeur, a violent sociopath like the one we sought might like to see me when I returned. Might want to check my face for fear, for stress. The whole game – and it was a game – was really about changing and maiming the lives of others. Now this killer had both Rauser and me in his communication loop. He'd want to play cat and mouse for a while. Was I really feeling someone watching me or was this merely a reaction to the email I'd received? I had read it over and over on the plane and it was enough to raise the hair on my arms. *My DNA can do only one thing for you: give you some reference for the next one ... Isn't it so like the media to take something out of context without telling the whole story? What will they leap at next? W.*

It made for a long walk through the airport and across the long-term parking decks, which even during the day are shadowy and uninviting, but just after midnight when air traffic is down and there is only the occasional ghostly whine of a jet engine to interrupt the sound of my suitcase rolling and bumping over concrete, the feeling was . . . sinister, like someone was about to jump out of the bushes. Okay, so I realize there are no bushes at Hartsfield-Jackson. The point is, I no longer seemed capable of distinguishing between real and imagined danger.

Was I next? I kept thinking. No. I didn't fit the victim profile at all, but then, what really fit with this offender? How was *he* profiling his victims? We had one connection with some of the victims but not all, not enough to understand the selection process. I willed myself to move casually at a normal pace, not to turn around. Just get safely to my car. Occasionally I'd hear a door slam shut or an engine growl to life. Every sound seemed to be amplified. Perhaps he didn't want me at all. He'd already passed up an opportunity, or so he bragged, at the LaBrecque scene. Was this about watching? Watching was fuel.

Watching was power.

I imagined eyes burning into my shoulder blades as I neared my old Impala. It took everything I had inside me not to just dump my suitcase on the concrete and run like hell. With this killer, a line had been crossed. In my experience working on all types of serial offender cases with the Bureau, profiling serial murderers, child molesters, rapists, I'd never been pulled in personally. There was always a barrier between the offenders and the criminologists. Emotionally, my work had taken its toll. I'd taken it home with me and into the bed I shared with my husband. Night sweats, a drink to settle my nerves, to put in perspective the horrific acts I'd spent the day reconstructing in excruciating detail. A drink before work to numb the exhaustion, the depression. A drink to kill the hangover. Anyone capable of empathy, I am convinced, is marked by the ability to comprehend victim suffering. Some of us handle it better than others, that's all. But that dark existence had never physically knocked on my door as it did now.

I unlocked the car, slung my suitcase across the seat, and hopped in with my heart slamming. Thank God my father had taken the beat-up Impala I'd driven in high school – V-8 with four hundred and twenty-seven horses – redipped it in chrome and completely restored it for me just before I went off to college. So it certainly had what I needed to ditch a tail. Even now with the bullet hole in the windshield, my old Impala gave me a thrill. It rumbled like an underground train and I loved the sound when the top was down. After all, I'd come of age in Georgia, surrounded by muscle cars and guys in tight jeans. Mother packed picnic baskets for the drag races at Yellow River on Saturday afternoons when Jimmy and I were kids. We ate cucumbers with black pepper and white vinegar, potato salad out of plastic containers, and little black hamburgers that my father charred the shit out of on a portable charcoal grill. We came with a card table and a checkered tablecloth, which were meant, I think, to add class to our operation. The smell of exhaust and burning rubber was part of the meal. And the sound was absolutely deafening. But Saturdays at Yellow River Drag Strip, my father was a happy man. It was about the only time he wanted to leave our garage, where he tinkered constantly, and the only time he could not hear my mother's voice.

I was eleven when he decided I should learn to drive. He stuck me in our beat-up Chevy pickup truck on a dirt road and nearly peed his pants laughing when I tore down part of a cornfield before I found the brake. Later, as teenagers, my brother and I would take long, silent drives with him. We'd stop for boiled peanuts and fresh peaches at roadside stands, then climb back into the truck and keep going, just me, my lily-white father, and my black brother, while the locals stared after us. Sometimes for me even now, tires humming against a paved road sound like the ocean. I can drive and drive, forget everything.

I found my phone and called Rauser. He was notoriously grouchy about wake-up calls. Cops at the station usually flipped a coin to see who had to wake him. It was after midnight now and I had the honors.

'This better be good,' he answered.

'It's me,' I said as I paid the cashier and eased my old ragtop toward the airport exit. 'I opened an email on the plane, a Wishbone letter addressed to you. A new one. Then I had the feeling I was being watched, but I'd already had this crazy dream, so I was totally creeped out. By the time I got to the parking deck, it was like he was all over the place. I felt him, Rauser. I think Wishbone was waiting for my flight. I don't know why. I just felt it—'

'Whoa, whoa, whoa. There's another letter?'

I paused at the exit and looked in my rearview. Three cars were coming out of different parking decks and approaching the cashier lanes. One pulled out behind me; the driver leaned on his horn when I didn't move. Reluctantly, I pulled out into the stream of airport traffic and moved toward the ramp to I-75/85 North.

'Talk to me while I get dressed,' Rauser ordered. 'And slow down. A letter came to you from Wishbone? Hmmm. This could be good news. We can trace that.'

I explained in detail and with a bit more calm the email I'd found in my mailbox, the letter Rauser hadn't read yet, which included the promise of more killing.

The vibration in his voice told me he was walking fast while he listened. I imagined him locking his front door and heading down the sidewalk to the Crown Vic. 'You think you're being followed now?'

'I don't know. It doesn't really make sense, I guess. Lot of cameras here. He would know we'd look at surveillance.'

'Well, I'm not taking any chances. Take your time getting out, give us a few minutes if you can. You're coming 75/85 North, right? In the Impala?'

'Getting on the ramp now.'

I heard Rauser on his radio calling for backup. 'Okay, Keye, go to the Capitol Avenue exit, hang a left on Pollard, and curve around past the ballpark. You'll hit some traffic lights. Stay alert. Lock your doors, for Christ's sake. We've got units close by. I'm working on getting the exits covered. Hopefully, I can get someone to pick up your tail before Langford Parkway.' He paused. 'You sure you're not just paranoid?'

'I think he wants to see if the letter's spooked me. He needs to know that he's gotten under our skin. There's control in that, like moving the game pieces around.' I checked my mirror again. Nothing.

'Don't stop for anything, Street. I don't give a shit if Tonya fucking Harding skates out in the middle of the road and shakes her ass. You don't stop.'

I knew what Rauser was worried about. We both knew too much about the ways killers acquire their victims. My mind automatically began a risk assessment. Almost no traffic on a Tuesday after midnight. It takes mere seconds to shatter a car window, disable the driver. And I had no weapon. It didn't matter that I was licensed in fugitive recovery and had a permit to carry. Unless I had a fugitive in custody, I couldn't have a weapon on an airplane, and even then it took some doing since 9/11.

'Would the fat guy with the bat be there too?' I asked Rauser. 'Or are we just talking Tonya skating out by herself?'

I make jokes when I'm nervous. It was one of the things my ex-husband hated. Dan believed that I used humor as a way to cut off any real dialogue, anything that might lead to a deeper understanding of my core issues. *Jesus*. Dan doesn't have the depth to recognize a core issue. Rauser doesn't always appreciate the timing or flavor of my jokes either. He didn't laugh this time.

'What if the fat guy shook it for me?' I asked. 'Do I stop for that?'

Rauser chuckled finally. 'There's something really wrong with you, Street, you know that, right? I'll call you back in a couple minutes,' Rauser told me, and disconnected.

In my rearview mirror, headlights looked back at me like cat eyes in the dark. Every car behind me, every car that passed, sent my heart racing. What was it, this feeling, this terrible feeling? God, how I wanted to floor it, get away from this menace, this thing I felt at the back of my neck, burning my skin. I didn't want to be this close. But maybe that was a lie. Maybe the life I had lived, the thoughts I'd let occupy my mind, the things I'd read and studied and talked about and talked about and talked about, had created some kind of magnetic field that drew it to me – violence, the thing that frightens me so profoundly it sets my teeth on edge and intrigues me so deeply I cannot run from it.

I considered taking the next exit, killing my lights, making a quick turn into the first side street, and trying to figure if I was really being followed. But I stuck with Rauser's plan. The benefits of teamwork had been drilled into me at the Bureau, and for good reason. Any individual action might risk an offender avoiding apprehension, and when the offender was killing people, risky rogue behaviors were unpardonable.

A couple of miles ahead, the downtown skyline looked like a jagged checkerboard turned upright. Another hot August evening, the stink of jet fuel still fresh in my nostrils. On a normal evening, I would have lowered the top, cranked up 102.5, but this wasn't a normal—

A sound as hollow and unmistakable as a rifle shot ripped through the quiet night and interrupted that thought, sliced up my nerves and spit them out again. The front end of my car swerved toward the pavement. I fought to keep control. I saw my tire and wheel bouncing off the road without me. I was skidding at sixty miles an hour on three wheels and a fender. My telephone started to ring as I screeched across white lines, bumped hard on and off the shoulder.

I remember sliding sideways toward the metal bridge railing ahead, remember not being able to get control of the wheel, remember the headlights behind me creeping ever nearer.

I don't remember hitting the windshield.

Chapter Nineteen

It may or may not surprise you to know that I am a very good patient. I'm not one of those people who complain about lying still and gripe about wanting to get right back to work. Nope. Not me. I have absolutely zero problem with sleeping, watching TV, and eating dinner off a tray. I would have appreciated a side order of Demerol in one of those little paper shot glasses, but apparently they don't give drugs for concussions. Oh no. They like to keep you up. A couple days of immobility and someone peering into your pupils every half hour or so, that's what you get. When Rauser told me how lucky I was because the patient in the room next door had twenty broken bones from a car accident and had to take heavy painkillers, I fantasized about lifting a few Dilaudids off her bed table while she slept. It seemed like such a waste to be here and not get at least a little messed up. It's the hospital. It's guilt-free drug use.

Neil, who had spent most of his adult life testing mood-altering substances on himself, took my complaints so seriously that he disappeared for most of the day and returned with a batch of his homemade hash brownies and some green and white capsules that he swore would make my eyes roll back in my head. I tossed the unidentified pills into the garbage when he wasn't looking and put the brownies aside.

I was in Piedmont Hospital in Midtown with no memory of the trip here. I had been out cold for four hours before I opened my eyes to a throbbing headache and the men in my life staring down at me – Rauser, Neil, and my dad, all three needing a comb and a fresh shirt and reeking of tobacco smoke. I was quite surprised to be here, to be anywhere, really. I remembered seeing the railing coming at me and in a moment of terrifying clarity thinking I'd been wrong, that it was about more than just watching, the whole thing was a setup, that this person was behind me and wanted to kill me, disable my vehicle, acquire and toy with me, torture me and God only knows what else. In those spinning-out-of-control seconds, I think I flashed on every crime scene and bloody photograph I'd ever seen.

'Am I in heaven?' I whispered weakly, really playing it up.

Rauser rolled his eyes. 'She's normal.'

My father, an earnest man who never really got my sense of humor, kissed my forehead and touched my face with his rough hands. 'No, baby, you're in the hospital.' He said it slowly and very loudly, as if I had been brain damaged.

Thanks, Dad.

'Your mother's gone for some coffee. She'll be right back. Diane's with her.'

'You let Mother have coffee? Oh, good. That should help my headache.'

'I shoulda had some decent seat belts put in that old car,' my dad went on. 'I didn't even think about it. Those old lap belts just don't do the job.'

After almost forty years with my mother, my father had learned to accept responsibility for everything. If it went wrong, Dad was to blame. There were rarely exceptions. Guilt was just part of life with Mother.

'This isn't your fault.' I held his hand – it hurt to move – and looked into his pale, watery blue eyes. 'Teaching me to drive like a redneck, now *that's* your fault. How's my car?'

'Beat up bad as you are,' he said, and tilted his head toward Rauser. 'Aaron had it towed over to the police station until we send it somewhere for fixin'. Sure is a good thing he saw you on the road.'

Rauser gave me a wink and I realized he had lied to my parents about what had happened out there on the interstate. But what exactly had happened out there? An accident? Or had the Impala been tampered with? Had I been followed? Had they captured a stalker? Was it Wishbone? I wouldn't get the answers until I had some time alone with Rauser. And that wasn't going to happen as long as my parents were hanging around. Might as well settle in and let everyone fall all over themselves to care for me.

A muffled ring came from Rauser's pocket. He pulled out his phone and answered, listened, said 'Give me a half hour,' and snapped the phone shut.

He leaned over me and brushed my cheek with his fingertips. 'Chief wants to see me,' he said, and rolled his eyes again. Rauser never liked being invited to Chief Connor's office. He said it was never good news. He respected Connor but their paths had split years ago. Jefferson Connor understood the politics of success, knew instinctively when and where to insert himself. Rauser had done quite the opposite thing, butting his head up against rank and policy a little too often. Connor not only enjoyed the privileges of position, the guy clearly loved the responsibilities of a bureaucracy. Rauser had resisted anything that might prevent him from working a case hands-on. When he had finally accepted the promotion and the responsibility of the Homicide unit, he'd made the chief agree that he wouldn't be chained to the establishment. Connor had reluctantly agreed. Jeff Connor had not finished his climb, Rauser said. Connor intended to be attorney general one day and Rauser believed he'd get there.

'I'll check on you later,' Rauser told me. 'Howard, you make sure she stays in bed, okay?'

'You bet,' my dad answered as the door opened and my mother walked in balancing coffee cups. Behind her, Diane had a stack of vending-machine doughnuts in cellophane. Rauser grabbed one out of her hands on his way out.

'Oh, you poor darling. You look just awful!' Mother exclaimed. She had a beaming round cherub face, Debbie Reynolds on prednisone.

She set the coffee down and patted my hand. 'Bless your little heart.'

Diane was smiling down at me. 'Shouldn't you be at work?' I asked her.

'Not when my best friend is in a car wreck. Margaret's fine with it. How do you feel?'

'Like I've been dipped in shit and rolled in cornflakes.'

Everyone laughed except my mother, who slapped my father's arm and scolded, 'My Lord, Howard, do you see what you've taught your children?'

'Jimmy doesn't talk like that, Mother. Just me,' I said.

'Yes, but Jimmy's *gay*,' Mother cried, and, inexplicably, hit my father again.

My convalescing came abruptly to an end two days later. Having found nothing more in my condition to cause concern, Piedmont Hospital was kicking me out. Weary of daytime television and Jell-O, I had decided to leave peacefully.

I was moving slowly, packing the few things I had into a small roll-on. My head ached, and the bite on my shoulder from the yappy accountant still burned. I slipped into the shorts, black sleeveless V-neck, and sandals that Rauser had thoughtfully retrieved from my apartment along with a few essentials – notebook, pens, toothpaste, hairbrush, underwear, and tampons. I hadn't asked for the tampons, but Rauser assumed, as he always did, that when I appeared grumpy, I needed tampons. I decided to present him with a box of his very own the next time he so much as raised an eyebrow at me.

I brushed my teeth and looked in the mirror at the scrapes and bruises on my forehead, chin, cheeks, and arms. Had I rubbed elbows with the killer that night at the airport? Had I made eye contact, maybe even smiled at him?

I had been reading the Wishbone letters obsessively and I was more convinced than ever that the next murder would come soon. The killer was in a ramped-up state, writing, taunting, feeling invincible. And because I had appeared at a crime scene with Rauser, because I had been hired to help explain the killer, he was trying to pull me in too. He wanted to show me, and everyone, that we weren't so smart after all.

Neil had delivered background files on Anne Chambers, Bob Shelby, Elicia Richardson, Lei Koto, David Brooks, and William LaBrecque. Six victims now that we could name. Six victims! Six human beings slaughtered to satisfy a psychopath's appetite for blood. It made my heart ache. Reading the files, I trawled the information we had to piece together psychological sketches and risk assessments based on each victim's lifestyle – friends, social gatherings, professional life, habits, even illnesses. Notes on three-by-five cards clung to the hospital wall with pieces of blue painter's tape someone on the hospital housekeeping staff had turned up for me.

APD was not able to determine if I'd been followed from the airport the night the wheel came off my car and took off without me across the interstate. By the time the first officer arrived, followed minutes later by Rauser, it was all over. A civilian had seen the accident and pulled over to help me. The police, knowing they were there to intercept whoever might be following and intending me harm, assumed the worst when they found a man opening my car door. They forced the good samaritan to the ground on his stomach, cuffed him, and hauled him into the station, where he was questioned so thoroughly and for so long we are all certain he will never again commit a good deed. He said he saw the Impala swerve without warning and run off the road into the bridge railing. No one else had stopped, he swore, although several cars had shot by, not even slowing. He might have saved my life that night by stopping. I would probably never know, but I imagined the killer driving past the scene, disappointed by the presence of a do-gooder he hadn't counted on.

The crime lab concluded that my left front wheel had been tampered with. Not surprisingly, they hadn't found any physical evidence beyond the marks that suggested tampering with a tool that wasn't made to fit the nuts on my wheel. No DNA. No prints.

We knew now that while the hourly parking decks at the airport are under constant surveillance, the long-term parking decks have cameras placed only in strategic areas – the entrance, the exit, the elevator and stairs. Cameras at the entrances and exits are pointed in two directions – at the driver and down, to record the rear of the vehicle and plate numbers. All those tapes would be carefully examined. However, there were dozens of other ways to get into and out of Hartsfield-Jackson. MARTA trains ran directly into the airport, and of course there were taxicabs and shuttle buses.

We were hopeful about something else, though. Inside, the Hartsfield-Jackson terminals are like a Vegas casino, Rauser said. No place to hide. The tapes from several cameras and locations inside and out of the airport were at APD, and Rauser had a couple of cops going over them, following my route from the gate to the exit, studying the crowds milling around me. Anything of interest would come to Rauser's attention.

I was beginning to think about the piles of mail that would be waiting at my office and the voice messages. I still had not even delivered the tapes I'd confiscated from Roy Echeverria in Denver to the rightful owners. I so did not want to do that looking like I'd been in an automobile accident. Bribing Neil into tucking in his shirt-tail and delivering the tapes seemed like a good idea. Old-fashioned chocolate cake from Southern Sweets usually broke him down.

'Hey, you,' Rauser said from behind me. I spun away from the notes on my hospital room wall. 'Let's sit down and talk for a minute before I take you home, okay?'

Uh-oh. Nowhere in my memory had Rauser ever uttered those words. He was standing in the door looking massively serious. 'So you know what the political climate's like here, right? These cases are attracting a lot of attention and everybody's upset and worried.'

'About me?' I asked, and felt myself sinking. I'd always felt a little outside the circle anyway. It didn't take much to make me feel even more outside. It suddenly occurred to me perhaps that's why I'd agreed to get involved at all – my own insecurities. Was I trying to patch up my own ego, prove at last to myself and everyone else that

I wasn't really the fraud I felt like deep down? 'This is what the chief wanted to see you about?'

'Here's the thing,' Rauser said. 'Television journalist over at Channel Eleven got some background on you. Personnel records from the FBI, information about the rehab center you checked in to.'

Oh boy!

'File just showed up on the reporter's car,' Rauser said. 'It was enough to make them start digging.'

'What do you mean *just showed up*? Who made it show up? Those records are confidential.'

Rauser was silent for a few seconds and I knew there must be more. 'Listen, Keye, Channel Eleven put together this, well, this goddamn report about the investigation and the individuals involved. They got an on-camera interview with Dan. He talked about your marriage and your drinking.'

'Dan?' I repeated, and the fiery hot sting of betrayal burned my eyes.

'If it helps at all, it's not just you they're slicing up,' Rauser said. 'I look like a goddamned idiot. Channel Eleven was decent enough to send us a preview so we'd have time to patch together a response before the shit hits the fan. I gotta tell you that what I saw isn't good. The chief's pretty hot about it.' He poked at my pillow with his fingers. 'We need you to not have a visible presence at all, but I could still use your advice . . . unofficially.'

I was silent, sensing another shoe was about to drop.

'The chief hired Jacob Dobbs to be the public face of the task force.' Rauser waited, just letting that hang in the air. I didn't look at him. I couldn't. 'He the one you told me about at the Bureau?'

'Yes. He's the one.' I made a quick sweep of the room to be sure I had all my things.

A woman in pink scrubs bustled through the door with white roses, a couple dozen of them, long legged and stunning against dark green foliage. 'I'm so glad I caught you,' she exclaimed, in the high sunshiny voice that volunteers use on the sick and injured. She looked like a blond cupcake with pink icing. 'Aren't these gorgeous? Somebody must love you.'

She set them on the table, beamed at Rauser and me. When neither of us smiled, her smile fizzled and she left the room. I felt like I'd just kicked a puppy. 'What exactly does *no visible presence* mean?' I asked Rauser, and plucked the card from the center of the roses. 'And *unofficially* – what does that mean, Rauser? Because you needing my unofficial advice sounds to me like I just stopped getting *officially* paid.' I tore open the envelope, getting a nasty paper cut for my efforts.

'Now just hang on.' Rauser held up both palms. It was the only calming signal he seemed to know – palms up, body moving slowly backward as if he'd accidentally cornered a coyote.

A gift certificate from Goodyear tumbled out of the card. It was for a tire rotation and inspection. I sighed. I fully expected to see my father's scrawl for a signature, but I was wrong.

Regular maintenance is so important.

Sorry to hear about the accident, but congratulations on your prime-time debut!

W.

Chapter Twenty

Rauser and I barely spoke on the drive home. I was trying to shake off the news he'd flattened me with at the hospital – the investigative report, my ex-husband's TV interview, Jacob Dobbs being hired to replace me now that I'd been *officially* removed from the case. Or was it unofficially? The two dozen white roses with the familiar W signature on the creepy card was the icing on the shittiest cake ever made.

My phone rang. Rauser kept his eyes on the road. 'Guess what I got?' Diane asked me. 'Reservations at Bacchanalia. We're overdue for a good, dirty gossip.'

Bacchanalia is a five-star restaurant near 14th on the outskirts of Midtown and so far over my budget I need to stand on tiptoes, but Diane and I pool our funds and treat ourselves once a month, regardless.

I looked in the mirror at my cuts and bruises. 'I still look awful.'

'Perfect.' Diane laughed. 'I'll pretend I'm your abusive lover.'

A couple of hours later, we sat down to the white linen tablecloths and low lights at Bacchanalia, which is great for catching up but does nothing to disguise the sucking sound created by the arrival of the check and the departure of our disposable income. And it's worth every penny. One bite tells you the chef is in love with her craft. The menu is big and bold, seasonal and local, and the meals are four courses.

Diane ordered arugula salad, cured Virginia flounder with water-melon relish, ricotta cavatelli, and asparagus cake with lemon gelato.

I started with the potato gnocchi, because when it comes to bad carbs, I like doubling up, and moved on to grilled snapper, a salad with Pecorino Romano, fava beans, and young fennel, and a blood orange soufflé for dessert – exactly what I wanted after fake eggs for breakfast, fake potatoes at dinner, and all the Jell-O I could hold at the hospital. I was starved.

A white-coated member of the waitstaff delivered a warm loaf of rosemary bread and sliced it at our table. Diane ordered an elderflower cosmopolitan for herself and coffee for me.

She listened intently as I told her about my feeling of being followed, about how I really wrecked my car, about the white roses, about how some TV muckraker was about to splatter my tattered record and disemboweled marriage all over Atlanta's TV screens. Her drink came and she sipped it, blue eyes steady on me. She was wearing a wrapped linen jacket cinched at the waist with a black pencil skirt and patent pumps with ankle straps. Diane had never minded getting a little attention. And she was dressed for it tonight. Her blond hair was short and tucked behind her ears, with little wispy sideburns.

'Do you feel safe?' she asked when I'd finished.

That's why I loved Diane. Since we'd met at age six, she worried about me. I ran my knife over a mound of softened butter and spread it over the warm, scented bread. 'I know this may sound strange, but I don't think he really wants to hurt me. I think he just wants to scare me away.'

Our starters arrived and we dug in. The gnocchi was heaven.

'So enough about me,' I said.

Diane laughed. 'Don't be ridiculous. It's *always* about you.' She drained her drink and signaled the waiter for another.

'So? Tell me about the new guy,' I demanded.

'It's fantastic so far. Notice I have to qualify it? God knows it's been forever.'

I chuckled. 'Um, I think it was only like six weeks ago you dumped Brad.'

149

'Blake,' Diane corrected cheerfully. 'What was that about anyway? He was so grungy.'

I nodded my agreement. 'It was a look.'

'Great kisser, though.'

'You look fabulous, by the way. Is that Armani? You get a raise or something?'

Diane broke out her big white smile. 'There's more where this came from. We spent a whole day shopping last weekend.'

'He took you shopping? Wow. That's so . . . so Richard Gere in *Pretty Woman*, isn't it?'

'Oh, come on, Keye. Let me enjoy this, okay? I think it's sweet.'

The waiter delivered Diane's second elderflower cosmo in a wide martini glass. It had a lovely lavender tint and a thin layer of ice on the top. I could smell it. Diane held up her glass. 'I drink for those who can't,' she told me. 'Cheers.'

'So selfless.' I smiled.

'This one's different, Keye. It feels like the big one.'

Diane believed fully in love, believed everyone had a soul mate, a perfect match – the big one. I had believed it once too, but that was a long time ago.

'Tell me everything. Name, rank, serial—'

'Good evening, Dr Street.'

'Jacob!' I dropped my fork. I couldn't have been more shocked if he'd hit my thumb with a hammer.

'Pardon the intrusion, but I couldn't let the opportunity pass.' Jacob Dobbs stood at our table, looked at Diane. 'My, aren't *you* lovely.' He was wearing a perfectly tailored suit with strong shoulders to project the power he so enjoyed. Dobbs was fair skinned with light eyes. He looked like he'd just shaved. I could smell his cologne.

Diane smiled and extended a hand to shake Jacob's. Instead, he bent forward and kissed the top of her hand. Diane's fair skin reddened.

I intervened. 'Diane Paulaskas, this is Jacob *Dobbs*. My *old* boss.'

The information had to wade through the cosmos she was drinking, but I saw it register. Her smile withered.

Jacob pulled a chair from the empty table next to us without asking, smoothed his shirt and tie as he sat. 'Well, then, it's nice to see you looking so well,' he said to me in his Masterpiece Theatre British accent.

One of the staff arrived with our salad selections, and Dobbs announced in his showy way that our check should be delivered to his table. Diane ordered another twenty-dollar cosmo on Dobbs, then winked at me.

It had been years since I'd spoken to Jacob Dobbs. I'd seen him, of course, like the rest of the country, when television needed a talking head with a photogenic face to explain why killers kill. The media loved to employ Dobbs as their expert witness. He specialized in sounding so sure of the labyrinthine ways of killers. Oh, what the hell, I decided. It had been a long time. Why not bury the axe? Besides, if I was rude now, after being thrown off the Wishbone case, I'd appear bitter and jealous.

'You're looking well too, Jacob. Are you alone for dinner?'

He nodded. 'Never miss Bacchanalia when I'm in town. The chef is an old friend. Would you like to meet her?'

'I'm good, but thanks.'

A slightly bored smile from Dobbs. His eyes skipped over me. I felt my entire body tense. The bastard. His eyes moved away from me and to the table, the coffee press, my water glass, then to my breasts and neck and face, very deliberately and very slowly. 'Still sober, then, are we?' he asked, and his eyes finally rested on mine.

So much for burying the axe.

Diane accepted delivery of her third cosmo. 'I don't mean to be rude, Mr Dobbs, but—'

'Please call me Jacob.'

'It's girls' night, Mr Dobbs,' she persisted to my surprise. Diane was usually all aflutter around power types. I thought her coolness

151

now spoke volumes about her loyalty to those she loved. 'But it's very nice of you to pick up our check,' she added.

'I didn't mean to intrude. A pleasure meeting you, Diane.' Dobbs rose, then looked down at me. 'You'll be asked to turn over your notes and files to me, Dr Street. Let's make time for that very soon.'

'Of course,' I said. 'And Jacob – it was nice to bump into you. It reminded me what a sonofabitch you are.'

Dobbs touched my shoulder lightly. 'Have a drink, Keye. It always calms you down.'

And then he walked away, shoulders square, head up, expensive suit, expensive shoes.

Diane blew out air. 'Whoa! That was intense.' She was beginning to look a little tipsy.

I decided it would be best if I drove us back to my office after dinner. Diane had two more drinks and held on to my arm as we left the restaurant.

Neil had popped a theater-size barrel of popcorn for the occasion and tried hard to lighten my mood when we arrived. It wasn't working. The three of us sat on leather sectionals in front of the big television and watched the special report in stunned silence. The media had hired 'experts' to second-guess APD's forensic team, the ME's office, the crime lab, the detectives. They even questioned the way the uniformed officers handled the scenes. My name was tossed into the pot with a psychic APD had once consulted years ago and we were all put under a microscope. The talking heads made it sound like Rauser had hired a bunch of drunks and palm readers to consult on the Wishbone murders. Dan made an appearance, explaining gently and with tears in his eyes that my drinking had destroyed our marriage and that my FBI job might have been too big for me. They cut to a clip of Neil leaving our office carrying an open beer. Families of the victims were shown all this for an on-camera reaction, and they were understandably shocked and outraged by our glaring ineptitude. Tears were shed. The public was cautioned to be wary while a killer stalked Atlanta's streets.

My phone started ringing even before the credits rolled. Rauser called to check in. He hadn't watched. Better things to do, he said. He had been ordered to lay low. The mayor, the chief, and APD's spokesperson, Jeanne Bascom, would handle the press briefings from now on. He told me he was sorry, so, so sorry he'd gotten me into this. He wanted me to agree to regular reports regarding my location. Rauser's view was that there was physical danger to me. My view was that the killer was getting exactly what he wanted from me at the moment. The headlines, the TV clips, the chief wanting me to disappear, the email, the roses, all of it orchestrated by him, designed to embarrass APD and me, to outsmart, to gloat. All of that fun would come to a grinding halt the moment he seriously hurt me. I was betting that was not part of his plan.

Dan called to console me after he'd seen the 'embarrassing' special report documenting my precipitous decline from Special Agent to hostile rehab patient. He claimed he couldn't have known it would be that kind of show, that his words had been taken grossly out of context. He had told them a story of strength and recovery, he said. The truth was, he confessed, he had just wanted some face time on camera to kick his career back into gear. He'd had no idea it would sound the way it sounded. This, unfortunately, could have actually been the truth.

Mother called. My father isn't really a telephone guy. He's more of a grunt-and-nod guy. 'I swear, Keye, you could have buttered us up and called us biscuits, we were so completely astounded. We were watching Joyce Meyer and your father, you know how he is with that remote control, started flipping around. He's intimidated by women preachers even though he won't admit it. Admit it, Howard. You don't like women to have any power at all, do you? Anyway, all of a sudden we see you. Our daughter on television! And the things they said! Oh my Lord. Bless your little heart. Your brother called too. He said the story was picked up way up in Washington. You believe that?'

'Sonsofbitches, reporters,' I muttered bitterly.

'Keye, for heaven's sake, when did you start talking like that all the time? It's just not attractive. Howard, did you hear that? I hope you're happy. Your daughter talks exactly like you.'

I asked Neil to drive Diane home. The alcohol was settling in on her. She had been very quiet for the last hour. I didn't want her behind the wheel, and I couldn't wait to sink into my own bed with White Trash, stare at mindless television. In the last couple of weeks I'd picked pieces of glass out of my neck and forearms with tweezers after being shot at by a bail jumper with a pump-action shotgun, been hit in the back of the head by a flying coffee cup, and shot at by an angry skinny woman over a crummy witness subpoena. I'd stumbled on a Wishbone murder scene, wrestled an accountant who sank his teeth into my shoulder, been hurled through the bullet-wounded windshield of my Impala, officially fired, hospitalized, released and handed over to the media, watched my ex-husband on TV dissecting our dysfunctional marriage, watched strangers on TV discussing my rehab and FBI records. And I was getting roses, white roses, from a violent serial offender. *Oh joy*. What was the significance, I wondered, staring at the screen without seeing it as White Trash snored on my stomach. White roses were used at weddings – the purity of a new bond of love. Was it about him thinking we were in a relationship, as he probably felt with David Brooks or Rauser or anyone he pulled into his twisted fantasy life? White roses were used at funerals too.

Rauser had chased down the volunteer who delivered the flowers to my room. They had arrived at the front desk and passed through many hands to get to my room on another floor and in another wing. Rauser had ordered the surveillance tapes from the hospital and taken the roses and the card to the station.

'Check it out,' Neil said, nodding toward the television. He was looking for the orange flip-flops he loved to wear while Diane used the door frame for balance. A banner at the top of the screen read *Breaking News*, and there stood Jacob Dobbs on the white Georgia

154

marble steps at Fulton County's courthouse wearing a six-thousand-dollar suit and talking to reporters.

Dobbs had been one of the pioneers of the original behavioral science unit at the Bureau. The last few years he'd been a partner in a private forensic investigating organization and was known all over the world for his work in and out of the Bureau. He'd sold out since he'd started making his living in the private sector. His conclusions were no longer evidence based. He had developed profiles for a considerable fee without ever examining the physical evidence and without qualifying his theories as equivocal. His profiles looked more like press kits, and anyone with any ethics left in the business knew it. In my opinion, he had betrayed his science and totally suckered the press.

I watched, feeling a flicker of anger, as he bent forward slightly to speak into a handheld microphone that advertised one of the national networks. He stood alone. No mayor, no police chief. Just Dobbs with his pale, creased face and sharp jaw, and the famous scar on his right cheek he'd earned when a killer had gotten very close to his private world. His wife and children had been home when the window shattered downstairs and the subject of one of Dobbs's profiles had broken in to kill them. But Dobbs saved the day, of course, hero that he was. It was a grim and electrifying story and I'd heard him tell it in his modest understated way, discuss the terror of discovering and then killing a murderer in his own living room with his family in peril only inches away.

'I've been invited to Atlanta by the police department to profile on the Wishbone case,' he announced into the cluster of microphones and cameras in his proper British accent. 'I'm looking forward to getting to work straightaway.'

'Mr Dobbs,' a reporter yelled. 'Any comments on the investigation?'

Jacob Dobbs knitted his brow into an expression meant to convey the gravity of the situation. 'I have enormous respect for this department. I was privileged to work in Atlanta during the child murders some years ago and, I might add, with great success. Wayne Williams was incarcerated and those murders stopped. Just as this killer will soon be stopped.'

Another reporter pressed him. 'Were you hired because APD mishandled the Wishbone investigation?'

Dobbs answered with a thin, almost remorseful smile. 'I think it's best for the city and for the families of the victims if we move forward, don't you?' He looked directly into the camera. 'The evidence is now being *professionally* evaluated.'

Dobbs began his self-assured descent down the courthouse steps – the man with the answers. I flung the bowl of popcorn in my lap at the TV screen.

I was at the office early. I had a lot of catching up to do. Payables and receivables, bank deposits, my personal bills, mail, phone messages, it had all piled up to almost unmanageable levels. I considered sweeping it all into a big trash can and starting over. Maybe it would just go away. Truth is, I'm not cut out for office work. Filing is torture. It almost hurts. I actually start to itch. How I admire the OCD types who keep neat desks and file everything right away. That wasn't me and it wasn't Neil either. Jesus, I needed to hire someone to manage all this, but I dreaded it. It's not like you hire just one person. You hire their family and their problems, their illnesses and financial issues and weird habits and friends. You're forced to share a bathroom with them. It's like sleeping with someone without the obvious benefits.

Hooga, hooga. I smiled. Charlie was a happy distraction. I wondered what he had pilfered and from whom, what he had folded up in his baseball cap to treat me to today. It was too late for blackberries, the figs were gone, and the weather was still too warm for winter pansies.

'Where were you? 'Member we were going to eat at Fritti?' Charlie had his hat in his hand and a worried expression on his face. He was talking too loudly as usual. No volume control.

Fritti is the Neapolitan pizza place down the street. I can smell the dough when the wind blows just right, and it makes me crazy some days. They have an artichoke-and-black-olive pizza that will make your head spin around. The panna cotta is like velvet on your tongue.

'Charlie, I totally forgot. I'm so sorry. Did you wait long?'

'I waited for twenty minutes,' Charlie said. He closed the door behind him. I noticed his hair was beginning to thin at the crown. There was nothing in his cap for me.

'I'm really sorry. I have so much work piled up and everything has been just kind of nutty. I just forgot. We could go now if you want.'

'I'm not hungry anymore,' Charlie said. I'd rarely seen him without his goofy smile. 'I was worried. Were you with Mr Man? Is he your boyfriend?'

'Rauser isn't my boyfriend, Charlie. You know that. He's my friend. Want something to drink?' Charlie nodded and followed me to the kitchen, where I found a Diet Pepsi for us both. 'I would never stand you up on purpose. You know that, right?'

'Yeah, I guess so,' he mumbled, and sat down.

'Maybe I could find us something to eat, huh?'

He shook his head.

I sat next to him and put my hand on his forearm. 'You know, you're my friend regardless of what's going on with Rauser.'

'Okay,' he said, and laughed too loudly. 'I'm sorry. I'm hungry now.'

I smiled. 'You got it.'

I stood and Charlie stood too. He reached for me and I let him hug me. I hugged him back. It was no secret that Charlie had a crush on me from our very first meeting. I was in the parking lot when he rode up on his bike one day a couple of years ago. I found him absolutely charming then and now, and a little heartbreaking. Neil, Rauser, and Diane all teased me about Charlie's infatuation. I didn't mind.

I gave him a kiss on the cheek and turned away, but Charlie pulled me back into his arms and pressed his lips against mine. I couldn't have been more shocked if he'd pulled a live lizard out of his ear. His hands were squeezing my arms.

I said firmly, 'It's not okay to kiss me like that, Charlie. Now let me go.'

'Because we're just friends,' Charlie said. 'Like you and Mr Man.'

I started to twist free. One of his hands quickly moved to the back of my neck and grabbed a handful of hair. The other held my upper arm tightly. He pressed his mouth against mine again. He was strong, his teeth cutting into my lips, his hands digging into me.

He jerked hard on a fistful of my hair, forcing my face up to his. His eyes behind his glasses were greenish brown and without any emotion at all. Nothing.

'I think I should fuck you the way Mr Man fucks you,' he said, gripping my hair with his right arm and using his left to get his fly unzipped. I felt his erection pressing into my stomach. His slur was gone. His goofy smile had vanished. I'd never seen this Charlie Ramsey before. 'Does he have a big cock?' he asked, and something inside me, something pressurized and unstable, went from a spark to a bonfire in a split second. I didn't wait, didn't take an extra breath before I slammed the top of my knee into his crotch. His reaction was predictable and instantaneous. He doubled over just as we'd been assured would happen in agent training, and when he did, I raised my knee again and rammed his forehead with as much force as I could muster. I had no reservations whatsoever about using what I'd learned. I didn't like being handled, and Charlie no longer had the benefit of the doubt. His intentions had been made abundantly clear.

He staggered. When he raised his head, wheezing, the flat of my palm hammered into his nose and practically pushed it into his eyeballs. He tumbled backward. 'I'm sorry,' he moaned. His hands covered his face and he was making gagging noises. 'I keep forgetting to take my meds. I'm sorry. I'm sorry. Don't tell Mr Man.'

I stormed to my office and came back with my Glock, furious. 'You ever touch me like that again, you won't have to worry about Rauser. I have no problem at all using this. You got it? You take your meds, Charlie.'

Neil walked in and saw my face. His eyes dropped instantly to the gun in my hand, then to Charlie writhing in pain. Neil looked at me as if I'd just peed on the floor in church.

'Get him out of here, Neil. Rauser's coming over. He'll freak out.'

Neil bent over and looked at Charlie. He straightened, gathered up a bunch of tissues from a box on his desk, then stuffed them under Charlie's nose. Charlie held them there pitifully.

'Jesus, Keye, what the hell?' Neil asked.

'I thought he was an intruder,' I said. Neil eyed me skeptically. 'I'll explain later. Just get him out.'

Charlie sat up holding the blood-soaked wad of tissues to his face and gagged some more.

'Jesus,' Neil said again.

Chapter Twenty-One

It was an odd feeling cleaning Charlie's blood off my floor. Sweet Charlie, the guy who brings me presents in a baseball cap. My goofy friend Charlie.

Neil helped scoop him up and agreed to drive him home, wherever home was. I felt a pang of guilt. I'd nearly broken the man's nose and I didn't even know where he lived. We all had the idea he was on some kind of assistance, but I'm not sure why. God, what would I do about Charlie now? He'd been my friend. He was part of our weird group. I had never ever had a moment's pause about being alone with him. So this was Charlie off his meds? It was going to change everything between us. What had happened to his brain in that accident? Who was he before that truck ran him down in the street, before all the surgeries and the lost job and the lost family? I made a mental note to speak with Neil about getting a hold of Charlie's medical records. Apparently, confidential files weren't all that hard to come by. After all, mine had just been aired out in vivid detail on Channel 11. Suddenly I wanted to understand more about what had happened to Charlie. We all loved him in our own way. I wanted to believe it really was just his medication.

The door opened and Rauser walked in. 'I gotta eat,' he announced. 'And we need to talk. Look, Keye, I know you're pissed off, but just so you know, I argued for you to stay on the case. This was not my choice. You gotta cut me some slack here.'

I was silent.

'Want to blow this joint and grab some Chinese food?' He grinned at me. 'Ever hear of it?'

'We just call it food,' I said.

He wrapped an arm around my shoulders. 'If that joke wasn't so old and lame, I'd laugh,' he said, and laughed anyway. 'How you feeling? Hell of a fucked-up week, huh?'

A shadow in the open door drew my attention. Jacob Dobbs was standing there. He looked like someone had pooped in his Cheerios.

'Oh joy. It's the Prince of Darkness.' My blood pressure started a series of wind sprints. Let it go, I told myself. Hatred is unhealthy.

Rauser snickered, and Dobbs said, his eyes on me, 'Professional and charming as ever, I see.'

'We were just on our way out,' Rauser replied coolly. I didn't think Dobbs had done himself any good with Rauser when he'd arrived in town and put on a press conference before even discussing the murders with the department investigating them. I had hated seeing Dobbs on those steps too, the pompous bastard, but the press conference had been brilliant in design. Dobbs understood that giving that conference on the courthouse steps sent a message to the killer. *I know where you're hunting now. I'm coming after you.* And it would make all kinds of subliminal connections with the families of the victims – safety, protection, authority.

Dobbs ignored Rauser. 'Nice place,' he said of the old warehouse that had been converted into a modern loft. 'If you like concrete. Really pulled yourself back up by the bootstraps, I see. Well, except for all the unfortunate media coverage.'

'What can I do for you, Jacob?' I'd pinched my face into a tight smile. I thought I might be developing a twitch.

'I'd have thought you'd be expecting me. I did say I'd like your notes and any other information that might be in your possession relevant to the Wishbone case.' He removed his suit coat and draped it tenderly over the back of Neil's desk chair.

Rauser threw up his hands. 'You got anything in your fridge? I'm starved.'

161

Dobbs followed Rauser to the kitchen. 'Good idea, actually. I'm famished.' He rolled his shirtsleeves up while Rauser and I rummaged through the refrigerator. 'It's this business of the letter being sent to you,' he continued. 'I don't like the idea of you being pulled back in.'

I bet you don't.

'And I'd like to know,' Dobbs went on with a wafer-thin smile, 'why this offender attempted to communicate with you. Is it merely that you are accessible and involved in the investigation and therefore fair game? Or did you offer some encouragement? You must have felt . . . disregarded after you were fired.' He paused, then added, 'Again.'

'Encouragement?'

'You've had no other communication with this murderer? No letters before this email you allegedly received from him?'

'That's ridiculous and you know it.' My temper spiked. I slapped cheese and lettuce on bread, squeezed on mustard, and dropped it unceremoniously on a plate in front of Dobbs.

'He sent roses to the hospital,' Rauser added, and described the card.

'Florist?' Jacob asked.

Rauser nodded. 'Florist found an envelope with written instructions and a cash payment when they opened yesterday morning. So they delivered the roses. We got the envelope, but it's clean.'

Dobbs turned his attention back to me. 'Roses too? An email, a tire adjustment, and now roses. Fascinating. Anything else you'd like to tell us? You wouldn't actually obstruct, would you?'

'Now wait just a goddamn minute.' Rauser pulled a chair out and sat down across from Dobbs. 'Keye's not obstructing. She didn't ask for this. She's the victim here.'

Dobbs's smile thinned even further.

I hit my palm against the tabletop. Dobbs's sandwich jumped on the plate. Rauser looked at me as if I'd slapped him. 'I am not a victim.'

'Well, well, look at that. Lovers' quarrel?' Dobbs's eyes had the happy sparkle of confrontation and they held me in a way that made me uncomfortable, had always made me uncomfortable. His eyes, his words, his stories, his hands. I'd spent a lot of time at the Bureau dodging them all.

Rauser was on his feet. 'Just what are you trying to say, Dobbs?' His right fist was clenched.

'Whoa, whoa, whoa.' I held up my hands. 'Just calm down. Rauser, *sit*, please. Let's just take a minute, okay?'

Rauser grabbed his sandwich off the counter and sank back into his chair, scowling.

I looked at Dobbs. 'I would never intentionally engage in any communication with a suspect outside an investigation. *Never*. That would be improper, unethical, unprofessional, stupid, and extremely dangerous.' And then, in an effort to keep the peace, I told him I understood that he was *the* man on the case. In fact, he'd earned it, deserved it, he was just about the most deserving gosh-darn guy in the whole world. I stopped just short of slobbering all over him. Rauser groaned a little, stuffed some stale Pringles into his mouth. I went to the refrigerator, peeled the plastic wrap off a plate of brownies, and pushed them in front of Jacob Dobbs like a peace offering.

Dobbs eyed me skeptically for a moment before his sharp features softened. Then, palms together, chin rested lightly on his fingertips, something calculated to show depth of thought, the self-serving little bastard said, 'Let's lay our weapons down, then, shall we? What do you say?' He picked up a brownie, took a bite. 'You'll give me your notes and we can do some brainstorming?'

I knew his MO. Dobbs would grab the credit for anything I handed him, and, of course, I would have to give him anything and everything I could to benefit the case, Rauser, the victims, potential victims.

'Absolutely,' I agreed, and set another brownie on his plate next to his sandwich.

Rauser had a sour expression on his face and we ate in silence.

Eventually, Dobbs finished his sandwich and four brownies, stood and politely excused himself to the restroom while I struggled to unravel Neil's espresso machine.

Then the three of us, Rauser, Dobbs, and I, moved into the main area with coffee. Dobbs yawned and propped his feet on a cube.

'Anger excitation,' he said, and made one of those mysterious *hmmm* sounds that doctors and mechanics have mastered. He was reading aloud from the preliminary profile and victim assessments I'd finished in the hospital and then printed when I'd gotten home, as if he was grading a paper. I didn't mind. If your work can't withstand peer review, it shouldn't be out there, and however selfish and lazy Dobbs was, he had once been one hell of a criminologist, someone I had admired, even trusted. I wondered when he had stopped needing to find the truth in a case, any case and any truth. When had his fame become the most important consideration in his work? What had changed him?

'You don't see it as retaliatory at all?' He looked up to ask me.

Rauser leaned forward. 'Like, somebody hurt me so I'm taking it out on you 'cause you remind me of them?'

'Exactly,' Dobbs answered.

'We're seeing a lot of stabbing. We're seeing attacks that last an extended period,' I said. 'That's not simply retaliatory. It's about needing to experience the victim's suffering.'

Dobbs *hmmm*ed again. 'Perhaps sadistic behaviors are emerging at the scenes. But the amount of rage evidenced suggests that it's personal. Given the link established between your victims, it makes sense that the killer came from a family involved in similar lawsuits at some level – plaintiff, defendant, mother or father or siblings somehow impacted by an unfavorable ruling, perhaps. Somehow this tore away at something in the offender's life, directly or indirectly.' Dobbs looked at Rauser. 'This will be one of the things you'll look at in a suspect's past. Once you actually have a suspect, of course. Along with the other things Dr Street has already listed, such as mobility of profession, maturity, only child, donations to children's orgs, et cetera.'

'First victim and the last two victims triggered some kind of emotional response in the offender,' I pointed out. 'Anne Chambers, the first victim we know about, experienced far more brutality than all the others until LaBrecque, the last one. What was the trigger? We know it wasn't about some civil lawsuit. LaBrecque had none in his past and neither did Anne Chambers. Then there's David Brooks, who was shown care and respect, killed quickly and apparently silently and tucked into a sheet. I have some theories, but that's all they are at this point.'

'Oh, come now, Keye, let's not be so modest.' Dobbs shook his head. 'Toss them out. Perhaps they will lead us somewhere.'

'Okay, well, as you said, this kind of rage is usually about some personal connection. Because of the way Anne Chambers was killed, because her nipples were removed, which is all about Mommy, and she was sexually mutilated, I believe she's representative of the mother figure in the offender's life, of a very interruptive and intensely competitive relationship with the mother figure. David Brooks might represent a loved and desired father, or even an incestuous relationship with the father. Only Brooks was allowed to die without suffering. With the others, victim suffering was the turn-on. That says something vital about the killer's pathology. Suffering's all about anger excitation or sadism. Victim needs and desires aren't important to him. Killing the victim is just another precautionary act. He's just tidying up, really, and acting out his fantasies.'

'And what's the fantasy again?' Rauser asked.

'The fantasy is undoubtedly complicated,' Dobbs answered, then used the index finger on each hand to rub his eyes. They were red when he was done. 'The phrase "multi-determined" was used in one of the letters and that's very accurate. It's about a lot of things – sex, revenge, eluding law enforcement, needing validation, involving journalists. Seeing his letters in the newspapers, hearing about what he's done – that must feel almost as good as returning to the scene of his crime. And communicating with you both must really be a thrill. It feeds our man's delusion that he's on the inside, in the power structure, keeping you two in his intimate little circle. The circle must widen now that I'm here,' Dobbs added. 'Wonder how that's sitting with our killer.'

'You're extremely visible,' I reminded Dobbs. 'I would expect him to include you now in his communications.'

Dobbs bristled. 'I remind you that I am visible because I am paid to be visible.'

Oh sure. No one would ever accuse you of showboating.

'So where does LaBrecque fit?' Rauser wanted to know.

'I don't know,' I admitted. 'The selection processes we've identified, like the link to civil law, just doesn't fit with LaBrecque. Whatever the link is to him is too personal to identify at this point.'

Rauser said, 'Our tech guy ran down the address of the computer where the email was generated. An Internet café with a stationary computer in Midtown. No cameras. We'll have surveillance there by the end of the day.'

Dobbs sank back comfortably into the puffy chaise. 'Yes, well,' he muttered, and didn't finish his sentence.

Rauser pulled his ringing phone from his pocket, answered, and left Dobbs and me alone while he took his call.

Dobbs tucked his hands behind his head. 'Well done, Dr Street.' He smiled at me. 'You've worked hard on this and it shows. I couldn't have painted a better picture of our unsub myself.'

'I had some time on my hands in the hospital.'

'How are you feeling, by the way?'

'I'm fine,' I answered. His concern made me uneasy.

'I am sorry, Keye, about all that happened between us at BAU.'

I was silent. I didn't believe he felt remorse and I certainly was not ready to let him off the hook. I'd had some problems my last few months at the Bureau. I was struggling. I was under review. Jacob Dobbs had written quite a scathing report about me in which he recommended I be dismissed. If I'd slept with him, he would have recommended a paid furlough rather than dismissal. He had been quite clear and unapologetic about that. I had needed rehab, a hand up, not a kick in the head. He had made my time there nearly unbearable with his constant comments and advances, and then he had turned his back on me completely.

Rauser rejoined us. 'We got the restaurant where Brooks ate the night he was killed. A waitress recognized his photo. She seated him and took a wine order because the shift was just changing and the waiter wasn't on yet. She said the reservation was for two, in the name of John Smith. Original, huh? Said Brooks drove her nuts picking out the right wine like someone on a date. Waiter showed, so she left. Never saw his dinner partner. We have the waiter's name and address. Balaki and Williams are on the way there now. We weren't able to locate a credit card receipt. Brooks was paying cash for everything – dinner, drinks, the hotel. Married, obviously didn't want a paper trail.'

'Anything from the courthouse?' I asked.

'Our people are still going over the surveillance tapes. Brooks is the only vic to show up on the courthouse tapes, but we've only gone back sixty days so far. Brooks was in the courthouse almost every day. Unfortunately, there's no surveillance on the elevators themselves, but all the elevator lobbies are crawling with cameras. We're running checks on any nonemployee who appears more than twice. It's going to take time to look at it all.'

The door opened. 'Well, that was totally weird,' Neil said, and walked past us into the kitchen. He opened the fridge, then looked at Rauser. 'I had to take Charlie home.' If he wondered what I'd told Rauser about Charlie's attack, his face didn't show it. Instead, his eyes settled on Dobbs.

'Neil Donovan, this is Jacob Dobbs,' I said.

'Ah, Dobbs.' Neil clearly recognized the name. 'Big man on campus, right? Nice to meet you.' He gave Dobbs a nod and turned back to the refrigerator.

'Speaking of Charlie,' Rauser said. 'He's on courthouse video a lot, must be in there several times a week. Detectives brought it to my attention.'

I went cold. Today Charlie had just reminded me that you never know about someone's interior life. Charlie had a mean streak. I'd seen that. Charlie the courier. Charlie who was in the Fulton County Courthouse frequently.

Rauser nodded. 'Gotta check everyone. No exceptions.'

Neil laughed and popped open a soda can. 'Total waste of resources. Come on, Charlie can barely remember to bathe. Anyway, he's there all the time because the courier company he works for does real estate deed searches and a lot of simple filings for attorneys. I know this because I actually bother to talk to him about his life.' He looked at Rauser. 'Keye tell you she put some Bruce Lee on his ass today? I had to pull over and let him throw up on the way home. It was brutal. I'm just sayin'.'

'Who's Charlie?' Dobbs asked.

'A friend,' I said.

'What happened?' Rauser was frowning, picking up vibes the way he always does.

'He got a little out of line, that's all,' I told him.

'Out of line how?'

I rolled my eyes. 'Settle down there, cowboy. I handled it.'

'You know he lives down off Dekalb Avenue in some pretty nice condos?' Neil asked. 'I thought the guy was in public housing or something.'

'Because you know so much about his life?' Rauser asked.

Neil was rummaging around for food. 'You guys decided to eat some brownies after all?' He grinned. 'Dang, there's only a couple left.'

We all looked at Dobbs. He had fallen asleep, just drifted off with his hands behind his head, mouth open.

Rauser looked at me as if my head had just done a three-sixty and I'd spit up pea soup. 'Tell me you did not give him the stoner brownies! I hope you realize that raises about a trillion ethical issues for me.'

'Oh, please,' I said. 'You were on your feet two minutes ago ready to smack him. That didn't bring up any issues?'

'That was just good clean fun,' Rauser retorted.

I studied Dobbs. 'He's such an angel when he's snoring and drooling, isn't he?'

'He wakes up stoned and figures out you gave him spiked brownies, he's gonna be a real pain in the ass.' Rauser was still indignant.

'Or not,' I said. 'He could wake up bright and sunny and eager to help.'

'Uh-huh, and maybe Madonna will come in here and shake her ass for us too.'

I considered that. '*The* Madonna or just Madonna?'

Rauser shrugged. 'Which one would you want?'

'To come in here and shake her ass?'

'Uh-huh.'

'Definitely not *the* Madonna.'

We gathered keys and things to leave, both of us heading in separate directions. 'Hey,' Neil called. 'What am I supposed to do with Sleeping Beauty?'

'Give him some strong coffee and call him a cab when he wakes up,' I said. 'Oh, and Neil – don't mention the brownies, okay?'

Chapter Twenty-Two

How I came to own two thousand square feet on the tenth floor of Atlanta's Georgian Terrace Hotel is a testament to, well, blind luck. I had done a job for the property owner that required some diplomacy and discretion during a divorce. He had a mistress, a wife, a child, a boyfriend, and lots of property. Fortunately for him, I discovered the wife also had a mistress *and* a boyfriend. He paid me to negotiate her down privately without the attorneys squabbling over his massive assets. Miraculously, I pulled it off without a hitch. In the course of doing business with him, I discovered his intent to return the private space he kept for himself in the hotel back into hotel suites. The building had been converted to luxury apartments in the eighties, and when my client bought the property, he turned all but one apartment into hotel space. I had fallen in love on my first visit with the white-bricked walls, the hand-carved crown molding, the marble bathrooms, the twelve-foot ceilings, the glistening wood floors, the rows of Palladian windows with their view of Peachtree Street. I offered to waive my fee, all future fees, and promised to surrender to him my firstborn just to have the chance to make a bid. I had some cash at the time. An insurance company had just paid me a percentage of what I'd recovered on an art fraud case. Still, swinging a down payment on a place like this took every penny I had, every penny I could get out of my parents, and nearly everything I owned that could be converted to cash. I mortgaged myself up to my ears and spent the next three years in chaos, knocking down walls, living with carpenters and sawdust and tools. The experience had permanently marked White Trash, but it also turned the apartment into the rambling loft I now call home. It hasn't been decorated. That'll happen when I am flush again, maybe in fifty years or so. In the meantime, a bed, a dresser, an enormous couch, a Moroccan-tiled table that I found irresistibly attractive in Piedmont Park during the Dogwood Festival, a television, a CD player, a computer, three rugs, one scraggly white cat, and me. It's enough for now.

I am the only permanent resident to inhabit the hotel, and I know most of the people employed here by name. I eat dinner downstairs at Livingston Restaurant quite often and sit on the restaurant's terrace on Peachtree whenever possible, breakfast and dinner a few times a week. I have none of the privileges of a guest, however. Not during the day anyway. The hotel manager seems to resent my presence here. He makes sure the weight room, the media room, and the pool are off-limits to me. The months of workmen stomping in and out of the Georgian's pristine lobby might have something to do with the manager's hostility. But the second- and third-shift managers let me have the run of the place. Rauser and I have a midnight dip in the pool now and then, and sit on the roof hugging our knees and talking with a view of the downtown skyline that takes your breath away at night when the city is lit up. The Georgian provides a soft landing on those days when I've been attacked from several directions and retaliated by slamming a knee into a mentally challenged man's forehead and feeding stoner brownies to the public face of APD's Wishbone task force. Good Lord, what was I thinking? Charlie had earned a smackdown, but the brownies . . . well, that was a shameful lapse in judgment and in ethics. And I'd been so judgmental and righteous about Dobbs.

It must be the pressure, I thought. Only three days ago I'd received the Wishbone email and wrecked my Impala. Yesterday two dozen very expensive white roses had sent a distinctly chilling message. *I'm the reason your tire came off. I'm the reason your dirty laundry landed in the hands of a reporter. And I know where you are right now.* It was a lot to take in. And then handing my notes over to Dobbs, the victim

171

sketches I'd worked hard on, hearing his disdain for my preliminary profile. What a dick! Suddenly I wasn't feeling so bad about the brownies.

Oh, for an Absolut martini, dirty. Or a Dewar's and soda with a twist. Either would do the job after a long day. Just one. What's the big deal? Is it true what they tell you about never being able to handle just one? Not ever? I didn't want to believe it. At least at that moment I chose to not believe it, to believe that I could have this again in my life and control it. My deceptive addict's brain was searching for loopholes. I decided to call Diane, who had been an unwavering support for me while I was getting sober. Diane was a devotee of Al-Anon. She had liked the meetings. Too much. She began twelve-stepping her way right through Debtors Anonymous, Shopaholics Anonymous, and Sex Addicts Anonymous. I actually began to seriously worry about her the day she asked if I could go to a CoDA (Co-Dependents Anonymous) meeting with her because she hated going alone.

I reached for the phone to call her.

I told her about the cravings and that the desire to drink again had intensified. I told her I really wanted to go downstairs and sit at the bar, that I wanted to laugh and feel free again. She reminded me gently but in vivid detail what that kind of freedom had to offer, about how I had been chained to a bottle. Then, in case I had missed the point, she went on to cover some of my more disgraceful behaviors – scenes that included toilets and bathroom floors and hanging out car windows and crying and passing out and making scenes. She finished up with the Serenity Prayer. Suddenly a drink didn't seem like that great an idea. I thanked her and we made a lunch date for next week. I'd forgotten again to ask her about the new person in her life. I was a crappy friend, I decided. It was always all about me.

My phone rang and Neil didn't even wait to say hello. Instead, he began with 'I was thinking about something. Charlie came in one day, said his computer wasn't working and he likes to email his folks, so he wanted to use ours. Doesn't take skill to email, right? So I didn't think anything about it. You know he can type? Uses all his fingers. I guess the brain is pretty specialized. Anyway, when he was finished, I figured I'd check out what he did on the Internet, you know? Just for fun look at what a guy like Charlie does. But it took some time. You know why? Because Internet history, browsing history, cookies – all of it was cleaned out.'

I sat down on my couch and stared out the long windows facing Peachtree Street and the Fox. It was dusk. The streetlights were on.

Neil continued. 'So, one – he's smarter than I give him credit for. And two – he didn't want anyone to know what he was looking at on your computer.'

'Wait a minute. He was on *my* computer?' I'd had to log in recently to all the websites that usually recognized my computer – online banking, email accounts. Now I understood why. The tracking cookies had all been cleaned out.

Neil hesitated. 'This is why I didn't want to tell you. I figured you'd be pissed off, but I was using mine, so I let him use your desktop. Anyway, it was pretty harmless stuff. A Hotmail log-in screen, some news reporting sites.'

'You look at the sites? You remember the stories he was reading?'

'Nope.'

'Could he have been in my documents?'

'If he had more than half a brain, he could have, since you don't password-protect your shit. What are you thinking, Keye?'

What I was thinking was about the email to Rauser with my name on the copy line, about feeling watched at the airport, about my dossier being delivered to a reporter. Why me? *Because the killer knows me, that's why.* That's why my appearance at the Brooks scene set off alarms and why I was copied on the next letter. Someone who knows me saw me there or saw the footage and suddenly I was too close. That's why the killer had to then do anything possible to get me off the Wishbone case by trashing my reputation, by embarrassing me and the department publicly, by frightening me by loosening the lug nuts on my tire, sending the roses. Was this why Charlie needed to get to my computer? To find out if I had notes about the investigation and discover if he was a suspect? My pulse quickened. A tiny window flew open in my brain and I leapt through it.

Was Charlie capable of that kind of deception, the kind required to evade law enforcement for so long? To be successful, a serial offender must have the ability to disassociate entirely from their violent self and live an outwardly harmless life. Today, for the first time, I'd seen violence in Charlie. I'd seen his eyes. I'd seen sadistic pleasure in them, but his volatile impulsiveness was inconsistent with the organized killer I'd been profiling. And I couldn't see the killer choosing Charlie's lifestyle and façade for himself. I saw him as vain. He'd want to appear educated, successful. That wasn't Charlie. Charlie elicited sympathy. But I knew too that an investigator must never attempt to sway an investigation in order to meet some theory. That's something Dobbs would do. I had to be open to the evidence – whatever it was and whether I liked it or not.

I took a moment to reconsider the growing list of things that did make sense. Charlie had gained access to my computer with a ruse. He could have emailed my history in letters and documents for the last several years to himself and put together enough information to entice a journalist into doing more digging. He was the right height – the angle of the stab wounds at each scene put the killer at about five-ten. He'd bragged about his ability with a knife, a fishing knife. It would be serrated and about the right length. I'd seen him slicing figs with amazing dexterity considering his normal bumbling. The knife and the bragging fit. People trusted Charlie. He had enormous freedom and mobility. Who notices the brain-damaged guy who pedals around the city all day? Everyone and no one. I thought about William LaBrecque, about the rolling pin, about his shattered face, the bloodstain under his head, the edge characteristics of the pool. His blood had begun to react to the outside environment. Serum separation was taking place even though his body was not yet cold. This kind of thing sticks in your mind. Could Charlie have murdered

LaBrecque, exhibited that kind of rage? Why? Had Charlie seen the bruised wrist LaBrecque had given me or read my notes about the incident at the church when I'd served LaBrecque with the restraining order? I knew an event like this – feeling the object of one's pre-occupation had been mistreated – could set off someone nurturing a love obsession. Was that what it was? Had Charlie's crush on me turned deadly? Yes, I'd glimpsed something in Charlie today I hadn't known existed – violence and jealousy. But even if he did kill LaBrecque, could he have killed the others? Why? Was I too close to see the motive? I thought about the aggression Charlie had displayed toward me today, the mobility in his job as a bike courier, his invisibility, his regular visits to the courthouse. He couldn't have done what Wishbone had done on a bicycle. The area was too wide. The killing was not confined to the city limits. Was Charlie hiding a car somewhere?

A thought brought me to a screeching halt. Charlie was educated. An engineer or something scientific, so the rumors went. Charlie once had a highly functioning brain. He'd had a career, a family. Then the accident that had changed his life forever. And after that? Had there been a suit filed against the company whose truck very nearly killed him? Could that be Charlie's connection to the justice system? Did he get a bad deal, hate those who had done well within that system? Could Charlie Ramsey, the guy who steals pansies just to see me smile, really be a killer?

I closed my eyes. My throat ached. I remembered Neil saying, 'I did some checking around and, well, there's some stuff you need to look at. I'm sending it now.'

I pulled out my laptop and began to open the links and attachments Neil had emailed. The first one reached out and grabbed me by the neck.

Star Player Charged with Rape. Community Shocked.
Charlie Ramsey, Winston Upstate University star running back, was accused of sexually assaulting a fellow student

Friday night at the Ramsey estate near Ithaca. Warrants were issued to search the property after a WUU cheerleader reported to local police that she had been given drugs and was incapable of having consensual sex. Two other players were named in the complaint.

The article, archived from the local newspaper, was more than twenty years old. I went to the next.

Ivy League running back guilty of assault. Rape charges expected to follow.

And the next one.

Star player leaves Orange Crush for biomedical engineering program with 4.0 grade point average.

This article had a photograph. It was not the Charlie I knew, but there was little doubt this was the young Charlie Ramsey, powerful and handsome, smiling, holding his orange helmet against his uniformed chest. There were other articles too, ones that detailed his troubled and sometimes violent career in college football, which included three rape charges – two settled out of court, one withdrawn – and two assault charges – one that stuck and earned him eighteen hours of community service for putting his fist through someone's car window at a stoplight. Neil had included copies of court documents outlining a settlement between the university and a seventeen-year-old woman who claimed Charlie raped her when she refused sex with him at a university event. There was another settlement between the Ramsey family and another young woman a year later. Then a long gap in reporting on Charlie. Five years of no headline-grabbing at all elapsed after the Ramsey family settled the last lawsuit with a check from the family trust for $300,000. The next story reported Charlie's parents had been killed in the crash of a private plane in upstate New York. Charlie was the sole heir to a considerable estate. He had told Neil he wanted to use my computer to email his folks. Another lie.

Local Football Star Blames Athletics for Derailment.

This article came eight years later and talked about his troubled past with drugs and alcohol, trouble with the law, his recovery, losing his parents and finally turning his life around. He'd flown through WUU's master's program and moved on to a Ph.D. in biomedical engineering. At the time the story was published, he was preparing to move himself, his wife, and two young children to Atlanta, where he'd been offered a job in biomedical product design. His specialty was tissue design, artificial skin. But the headlines were about his claim that the athletic programs there encouraged a culture of no responsibility, of drugs and violence, and that lawyers were on retainer to do nothing but get the players out of trouble for everything from breaking and entering to assault and rape. He was quoted as saying, 'It doesn't matter if you leave the university drug addicted or mentally and physically broken by steroids. It doesn't matter if you leave without an education or unable to function normally in society. All that matters is that you play well. It took me years to find myself and to find some calm.'

One tiny blurb surfaced a couple of years later. It was a human interest piece in the Living section of the *Atlanta Journal-Constitution* about an old friend from WUU searching for Charlie after hearing he'd been disabled in an accident and had come upon hard times. The article was two years old now, mentioned briefly Charlie's college football career, but focused on his work at the university with a vascular surgeon developing artificial skin and artificial heart valves for vessel grafts. 'Everyone knew Charlie's impact in artery design and artificial tissue would be substantial. He was going to save a lot of lives.'

I thought about that and felt terribly sad. The next attachment was a lawsuit. *Charles E. Ramsey v. Wells Fargo* in the State of Georgia, County of Fulton, City of Atlanta. I scanned the original petition, and found what I had already learned about Charlie. An armored truck had run a light and struck him while he crossed the street on a walk signal at Tenth and Peachtree. There was a weak Answer on file denying responsibility but soon after that the case was settled.

I went back to the complaint that Charlie's lawyers had filed in Fulton County and took a closer look at reports from the physicians, which detailed months of physical therapy, pain, problems with cognition, memory, and reasoning, sensory-processing difficulties – sight, hearing, smell – communication and comprehension problems, depression, anxiety, personality changes, aggression, acting out, and social inappropriateness all due to traumatic brain injury. Some issues might or might not be temporary; others were permanent disabilities. There were still a lot of unknowns about the brain, about whether it was capable of healing itself over time. The petition also talked about loss of income, career, and any semblance of normal family life. He'd lost everything and then they'd handed him a couple of million dollars to shut him up. I didn't think he'd been able to enjoy it much. I thought about the day he talked about how quickly life can change. Was Charlie bitter enough to kill? Perhaps. But did he still have enough brain power left to pull off this kind of crime, to leave a scene clean? It would mean being fully lucid. Was Charlie that? I didn't think so and I didn't think the signature characteristics of these scenes – the stabbing to sexual areas and other staging elements – fit with Charlie. And there was no physical connection to Florida where the murders began. Or did they begin in Florida? How many more people had fallen victim to this killer who had not yet been connected? I thought about the day we ate together at my table. *I clean fish real fast.* Was Wishbone that simple? Was I just overthinking it?

I called Neil back. 'Can you check the New York area, particularly Ithaca and central New York, for murders involving sexual assaults and stabbings during the years Charlie was at school there?'

'Already on it,' Neil said.

I needed to know more about Charlie Ramsey, where he lived, *how* he lived. I looked at the windows over Peachtree Street. It was dark now, the late summer sun was gone. Must be about nine. What the heck.

Chapter Twenty-Three

I had driven past the town houses where Charlie lived every couple of days since they were built three years ago. They faced Dekalb Avenue, which ran straight from downtown Atlanta into Decatur, where my parents lived, but I hadn't known Charlie lived there, of course. We'd all assumed that with Charlie's special issues there would be financial problems too. Had we assumed or had this seed been planted? I tried to remember how I came to this idea and the notion he lived in public housing. Charlie had told me once that a local church had accepted him into an employment program. Perhaps I'd made the leap from there to arranged housing. A lot wasn't adding up with Charlie. I thought about this. He'd need a job whether he needed money or not to become a functioning part of the community. Part of his diagnosis included emotional problems. I assumed he was in therapy. It made sense he would need assistance to get work. Not that easy for a guy with a crooked walk and a slur, I imagined.

I was sitting on the street in the car I use for surveillance purposes, a white Plymouth Neon. There are about a million of them in Atlanta and no one looked twice. The Neon might not be a great choice for a perfectly manicured Buckhead community, but it did the job within the diverse, infilled city limits of Atlanta. The white paint was graying and the hood was slightly dinged up, which made the car even less remarkable. I'd run up under the spare tire on an SUV at a stoplight while driving and texting. Lesson learned.

I wasn't alone out here tonight. Two of Rauser's detectives, Balaki and Williams, were parked half a block up. They weren't easy to spot. The street was lined with parked cars, but my headlights had hit them just right when I'd pulled onto the street from the other direction and I'd seen Williams clearly, then realized Balaki was behind the wheel. Rauser had said nothing to me about having Charlie under surveillance. Was he hinting at it earlier when he mentioned seeing Charlie so frequently on courthouse surveillance? He did seem very concerned when I'd told him Charlie had gotten out of line, but that was just Rauser, I thought. I'd seen that muscle in his jaw start to work. Did Rauser know more about Charlie than he was letting on? Or was it simply that a routine background check had pulled up Charlie's violent college years, his parents' death, the huge inheritance, details on the armored truck accident that had damaged his brain? That would be enough to start some bells ringing at headquarters.

I looked again at the tidy row houses that backed up to Edgewood Avenue where I was parked. Occasionally another light came on or off. I tried to imagine Charlie getting up for a snack or the bathroom, but I couldn't. I couldn't picture him anymore. I'd had to let go of the idea that I knew this man and had begun to look at him from an investigator's perspective. While Neil had searched for killings in New York, I'd gone online to the Fulton County real estate records and found the deed for this town house. A local lender had financed the $340,000 'townhome' with fifty grand down from Charlie and a guarantee from a law firm called Benjamin, Recworst, Stickler, and Paille.

By eleven I was bored; while one earplug quietly transmitted a book on tape to help keep me awake, the other ear was free to hear the neighborhood. In the seat next to me, two Little Debbie wrappers, a testament to my nutritional concerns. I didn't know what I was waiting for on Charlie's street. I had just wanted to get a feel for where he lived. It was late. I really didn't expect anything to happen. Tomorrow I'd come at different times when I could observe Charlie's life in action.

A light appeared near the entrance that faced Edgewood. The front of the row houses looked out at Dekalb Avenue, which had no parking. The town house door opened. I picked up my binoculars and zeroed in. Charlie was pushing his bicycle through the door onto the porch steps. I cringed. White tape ran up and then across the bridge of his nose. He turned to lock his door, then carried the bike down the steps and pushed it, silent and agile, down the walkway. My blood pressure spiked. Where was the funny walk, the way he held his head to the side, all the ways Charlie moved that told you his disfigured brain was misfiring? Perhaps what was wrong in Charlie's brain wasn't at all what we had believed. The thick tongue slur had been gone earlier today, I suddenly remembered. *I think I should fuck you the way Mr Man fucks you.*

He jumped on the ten-speed and turned right, down Elizabeth Street, heading deeper into the Inman Park neighborhood toward Highland, which was only moments from my office. All those visits from Charlie, all those times he'd ridden in with his squeeze horn honking, it had been a five-minute ride. I had just assumed, like we had all assumed, that Charlie lived in housing for the disabled. No. It wasn't merely an assumption. All at once I remembered the moment Charlie had planted that seed. He'd told us a local church got him into their employment program and found him the courier job. And then he'd said, 'They make sure I have a place to live.'

I saw Balaki and Williams pull out after Charlie, so I eased the Neon into gear, kept the lights off, and slipped into the space they'd left open, which was a full half block closer to Charlie's town house.

A MARTA train whizzed by on the Dekalb Avenue side, inside lights bright, the passengers in silhouette. All those lives zooming past, all those destinations. How many of them would be afraid tonight when they stepped out of their train stations because another monster had fixed murderous eyes on our city? Across those tracks, on the edge of Cabbagetown, which was a millworkers' district in the early part of the century, the huge old cotton mill had been turned

182

into lofts like just about everything else in Atlanta. The area was littered with cool restaurants pushing fresh, local fare, farm-to-table, inspired. A few years ago an Atlanta fireman made the Cotton Mill Lofts famous when a five-alarm fire broke out and CNN filmed him plucking a trapped crane operator off his equipment while dangling from a helicopter rope inches above the flames. More recently a tornado had added to the history, cut a path through downtown Atlanta and ripped the top four floors off the old mill.

My phone went off. *Jesus.* The volume was way too high and Rauser's 'Dude (Looks Like a Lady)' ringtone scared the crap out of me.

'Look, we know he's moving, Keye. We're on it, okay? My guys made you, by the way. I don't mind another pair of eyes, but you cannot pursue, understood?'

'Understood,' I said, and hung my equipment bag over my shoulder, stepped out onto the street, closed the car door quietly.

'By the way, Dobbs slept off the brownies. He thinks he's coming down with something. Poor bastard.' Rauser chuckled. 'I almost felt sorry for him.'

'Can we just never talk about that again?' I was moving along the east side of Edgewood, staying in the shadows.

'Ah, she's capable of remorse,' Rauser said. 'Good to know.'

I ignored that. 'Hey, nice of you to tell me you had Charlie under surveillance.'

'Yeah, well, you haven't exactly been forthright, have you? What are you doing right now? Sounds like you're moving. Keye? You're out of your car! No, you are *not* breaking and entering. Tell me you're not.'

'You don't want to know,' I answered, and worked my way through a couple of well-tended backyards and headed for the town houses.

'Shit,' Rauser spat. 'I'm on my way.'

'Oh, that's smart. Chief Connor would love that. Better keep your distance in case this doesn't work out. I'm putting my phone on vibrate. Make sure somebody gives me a heads-up if he's coming back, would you?'

'Keye, *wait*—'

I dropped the phone into the pocket of the black cargo pants I wear when I'm working at night – loose with plenty of pockets for my tools, easy to move in, dark, soft cotton and practically noiseless. I studied the town houses. There were tall privacy fences around twelve-by-twelve backyards. Unless I was ready to scale a ten-foot wooden fence, I wasn't going to be lucky enough to have access to the private garden doors, the ones that were more likely to be unlocked.

I moved quickly back around the building, staying close in the shadows, found the main entrance, and pulled on tight vinyl gloves. I knelt to examine the lock. It was a standard cylinder lock, pin and tumbler, the kind of deadbolt most people used, easy to open with a key and not so easy without one. I opened my kit, withdrew a tension wrench and a long pick. I twisted the wrench enough to apply pressure to the lock and slid the pick in over it. One at a time, as each pin inside was pushed up with my pick and aligned, I heard a tiny *click*. One, two, three, four, five clicks, a little more pressure with the wrench and the cylinder, and I pushed open Charlie Ramsey's front door and heard the last sound in the world I wanted to hear at that moment. Steady warning beeps. An alarm system. Charlie-with-only-half-a-brain had an alarm system. *Crap.* I figured I had forty-five, maybe sixty seconds at the most before all hell broke loose.

The town house was nicely furnished, earth tones mostly, guy stuff. Leather furniture with beefy steel rivets and a recliner facing a huge television mounted over the fireplace. The television was on.

I had to make the most out of a few seconds. I went straight for the steps. No one puts anything they want to keep out of sight in a common area.

Two bedrooms upstairs. In the second, a mattress on the floor, no frame, unmade. It was strewn with newspapers and magazines,

184

clippings, a laptop, a couple of Coke cans. A bottle of Astroglide sat on the bed table.

I wasn't even sure what I was looking for. Something, anything, to exclude Charlie from my dark suspicions. He was my friend. Funny goofy Charlie who forgot to take his meds and simply freaked out when I stood him up. Charlie with a sweet crush on me. I didn't want to believe the churning in my gut.

I pulled open a bedside drawer. Magazines – porn, hetero leather stuff, bondage, S/M. Under the magazines, a hardback written by none other than Jacob Dobbs titled *The Criminal Behaviors of Serial Rapists*.

I kept looking. I found the safe on the floor near the closet. A small one, eighteen inches deep, the kind you buy at an office supply store to protect documents. It was locked, of course. I moved it a little to check the weight. Heavy. I was running out of time. How long had I been here? Twenty seconds? Forty?

On the mattress, next to the laptop, I saw clippings from the *AJC* and the *New York Times*, *Time* magazine. All of them were about the Wishbone case. I rifled through them, desperate to get a feel for what was going on in this room, in Charlie's head. And then I saw a shot from the *Washington Post* of Rauser and me walking toward the crime scene tape at the Brooks scene. The caption: *Crime scene investigators approach another bloody scene associated with a serial murderer dubbed the Wishbone Killer*. A circle had been drawn around us with a fat black pen. The words *lying bitch!!!* were scrawled over the picture in bright yellow highlighter.

Queasiness hit my stomach hard. I swallowed it back and stuffed the clipping in my pocket, then jiggled the laptop mouse. It asked for a password. No time. My phone vibrated. Rauser's warning? *Shit*.

I felt for the Glock 10 I'd wedged in the back of my pants as I raced toward the front door, taking the stairs two at a time. The beeps on the alarm system had gotten closer together.

It's odd what the brain registers when normal timekeeping stops. I remember thinking that there were no pets here in Charlie's house.

No family pictures, no art. Bare walls. And the television had been left on some true-crime station. A cop wannabe? A *CSI* freak?

And then the world exploded in my ears, a blaring, whirling siren accompanied by a loud male voice shrieking *'Intruder! Intruder! Get out!'* The alarm system blasted it all to the neighborhood. *'Intruder! Intruder! Get out!'*

I grabbed the doorknob and felt resistance, heard keys jingling. Through the peephole, I saw Charlie's bike dropped on the front sidewalk, the bike I'd seen him ride away on.

I tore through the living room, pushed open the sliding glass doors, then remembered there was ten feet of solid wood fence without a gate. *Intruder!* Expletives I didn't know I knew flew out of my mouth. Caged, I made a couple of stupid circles. Then I grabbed a heavy iron patio table and dragged it to the fence, scrambled on top and pulled myself up. It wasn't pretty. My muscles were trembling. I needed to join a gym, really. The ground on the other side nearly knocked the wind out of me, but I kept moving as fast and far away from Charlie as I could, scrambled into my car and pulled out without lights, nearly sideswiping a Volkswagen. The phone in my pocket vibrated again.

'Hey,' Rauser said when I answered. 'Great work. Discreet too.'

I pulled over near the Candler Park MARTA station and tried to stop trembling. My heart was still going great guns. Serve me right if I had a heart attack. 'At least you've got a reason to go in now, right? You've got an alarm.'

'I don't expect him to invite us in, do you? We'll know in a second or two, but I'm not optimistic.'

'The things I go through for APD. And for what?'

'Uh-huh. Always thinking about everyone else. And maybe Hilary'll come down here and give me a spanking.'

'Power types. Fascinating. This is why you're always on CNN, isn't it?'

Rauser was quiet for a minute. 'That was some stupid shit, Keye. Jeez. Don't do that anymore. I can't protect you when you act crazy.'

'I don't need protecting,' I reminded him, but my heart was still doing about one eighty-five.

'Hang on. We've got uniforms at Charlie's door. They're talking, talking, and just like I thought. He's telling them everything's fine and sending them away. He's doing the brain-damaged thing.' I heard him hit his cigarette. 'So, tell me what you got.'

'See, I knew you wanted me to go in there.' I smiled and, feeling calmer, pulled my car back onto the road. Rauser had never been a strictly by-the-book guy, but he was a good and honest cop. I wasn't under the same restrictions. Not anymore. The private sector has its advantages.

I told him about Charlie's town house, about the clippings, particularly the one I still had in my pocket. We couldn't use it, of course. Rauser couldn't even order DNA testing on it without having to explain how he got it.

'Look,' he said when I finished. 'I need you to press charges so we can haul him in, shake him up a little.'

'Press charges for what?'

'Assault, sexual battery, attempted rape.'

I was silent.

Rauser said, 'Isn't this exactly the kind of fraud you've been talking about? Duplicitous lifestyle, just a pack of lies under the layers. It makes sense – the accident, the roses. You press charges, Dobbs'll want to see him interviewed, and the chief can't say anything about you being there since you're filing the complaint. Did you see how he was moving?'

Rauser was excited. I could almost feel his energy through the phone. 'This guy got well, Keye. He recovered from that accident and kept on playing sick.' He paused. 'You don't think it's him.' It wasn't a question.

'I don't know what he is yet,' I answered quietly.

'Fair enough,' Rauser said, but his voice was tight. I'd heard this voice before. Rauser trying not to blow. He didn't want caution right now. He wanted me to go with him to this place of excitement at having a suspect. 'But you agree we got to find out what he is, right?'

'Yes.'

'Look, I get you like this guy. We all liked Charlie. Poor harmless Charlie, right? Is that why they open the door?'

It started as a chill, a shiver, then turned electric. *She smiled when she opened the door.*

Chapter Twenty-Four

The air-conditioning system had been out for a couple of hours when we arrived at City Hall East. The third floor was as torrid as a restaurant kitchen. Rauser used his investigative skills to uncover a stand-up oscillating fan in a broom closet a couple of floors down and hauled it up before anyone else could grab it. It was metal and rusty and squeaked with each full rotation, and it rustled the notes Rauser had anchored with an ashtray in the observation room where I waited with Rauser and Detectives Andy Balaki and Brit Williams behind the one-way mirrored glass. Rauser didn't want fans in the interrogation rooms. He liked it hot in there and wasn't above turning on the heat in the summer just so no one got too comfortable.

We were using Observation Room 3. The center section of a wall had been converted to a one-way mirror, but apart from this addition, it looked like most of the scruffy old offices in the building. A row of windows along the back side let in light and looked out onto North Avenue. The walls were queasy green with a moldy green trim. The paint chipped off if you so much as brushed against it. We had three monitors on a long table if we chose to watch the interview that way. Video was also available in the detective cubes, where they had a choice of observing room 1, 2, or 3. Rauser was pacing around, anxious for Charlie to be brought in.

'Where's our world-famous profiler?' Detective Brit Williams asked, reaching for his coffee cup.

'Trying to find a place to park his white horse,' Balaki said with a smirk.

'He's supposed to be here.' Rauser looked at his watch and shot me a look. 'But he hasn't been feeling that great.'

'Well, I'm okay if he just stays in his nice hotel room, 'cause if assholes could fly, Dobbs would be a seven-sixty-seven,' Williams shot back, fighting with the old roll-out windows as he talked. The windows were winning. 'How long these suckers been closed, anyway? A hundred years?' His white dress shirt clung to his back. He pressed on the windows, tapped the edges, ran his hands along them, tried to force the crank to turn. His fingers found a massive patch of sticky cobwebs in the corner of one of the windows and he cursed aloud, tried to find somewhere to wipe them off.

'Hey, Einstein,' Balaki said. 'That thing down there looks like an elbow, it's a lock. You gotta lift it before they'll open.'

Williams swore again, lifted the lock, turned the crank, and the window separated into three sections and opened out toward the street. A hot wind rushed in and Atlanta's chemical air filled our sinuses. My eyes burned. Down on North Avenue, the sun and the heat on a sea of automobiles creeping through the midday traffic made the street shimmer like water. It looked fake.

Balaki came over with his hands shoved in his pockets, stood there a moment watching the scene with me. 'See the dialysis clinic across the street? Saw a guy out there yesterday peeing in the parking lot. Something about that ain't right. You know?'

Having opened all the windows along the west wall, Brit Williams pulled a chair to the table and sat down facing the glass. Sweat glistened on his very dark black skin. He had rolled up his shirtsleeves and opened his collar, which was as dressed-down as I had ever seen him. He put a legal pad in front of him and slid a pen from his shirt pocket, clicked it with his thumb a few times.

Rauser kept pacing.

The interrogation room door opened and Charlie was escorted in by a uniformed officer. Balaki and I went back to our seats. An enormous bruise blossomed around Charlie's right eye. Medical tape still crisscrossed his nose.

'Dang.' Balaki's South Georgia drawl made it sound like *Da-ang*. 'Kicked the shit out of him, didn't you, Street?'

Charlie's crooked half smile was back. And so were the odd way he cocked his head, the knees that turned in just slightly, all the things that made it register instantly that something wasn't right with Charlie. This was the Charlie I'd grown accustomed to, and had even grown to love. If he was acting right now, if he'd been acting these last couple of years, he was very good.

Charlie had been arrested at six-fifteen that morning. Cops had banged on his door, read the charges, assault with intent to commit rape. Then they read him Miranda and hauled him off. Rauser wanted to make sure this happened very early. He didn't want Charlie well rested. Charlie's attorney, Ricky Stickler, had argued at the arraignment that Charlie posed no flight risk, did not even have a driver's license or credit card, and that he was under a doctor's care. An assistant DA had counterargued that Charlie had a history of violence against women and was also a person of interest in other crimes and should be bound over, but the judge said there was neither sufficient evidence nor probable cause to hold the suspect in custody, that old closed cases from other states were inadmissible, and as long as Charlie had absolutely no contact with the alleged victim – me – he would consider bail. If Charlie agreed to questioning, bail would be set at fifty thousand dollars.

Ricky Stickler swaggered into the interrogation room and sat down next to Charlie, patted his hand. 'You'll be out of here in no time, Charlie. Paperwork is being taken care of now.'

Next to me, Williams folded his arms and leaned back in his chair, nodded toward the one-way mirror and Charlie's lawyer. 'Big-money law firm. Pricey group for a bicycle courier.'

We watched the two men on the other side of the glass for a few minutes. Stickler loosened his tie, took off his jacket. The hot room was having its effect. His pale blue shirt was damp and rumpled when the jacket came off.

Rauser checked his watch, pressed some numbers into his phone, and waited. 'Where the hell is our new superstar? Bastard's not even answering his phone. Williams, you come with me. We're not waiting.' He tucked in his shirt-tail and grinned. 'How do I look?'

'Real purdy, Lieutenant,' Balaki said, and they all chuckled. Cop humor. I didn't always get it.

I watched Williams stroll into the interrogation room, then Rauser. The room was stark, just a table, four chairs, a couple of old HVAC registers on the walls. No windows. Rauser took a chair across from Ricky Stickler and Charlie and dropped a manila folder on the table. Williams sat at the end of the table.

'Sorry about the heat, guys. Old buildings, you know? How 'bout some water or something?' Rauser waited for the answer, which came from Stickler and was 'No, thank you,' then looked at Charlie for a moment, gave a gentle smile. I saw the lines gathering at the corners of his eyes. 'Charlie, my man, what the heck happened? You fall off your bike or something? You're beat up pretty bad, buddy.'

'I know you're mad,' Charlie told Rauser. The familiar slur was back. Very subtle, like someone with a glass of wine too many in them. 'I'm so sorry. I'm so, so sorry. I love her. I didn't mean it.'

Rauser picked up the folder and appeared to read it. 'Says here you've done something like this three times before, Charlie. Did you mean it then?'

'Lieutenant,' Stickler piped up. He was a nice-looking guy, thirties, strawberry-blond hair. 'My client has already been evaluated numerous times. We have brain scans showing the damage from way back. He takes about twenty anti-psych drugs. He went off his meds. He's not an aggressive guy. Are you, Charlie?'

Charlie shook his head. 'Nope. I'm a nice guy.'

'You get real mad sometimes, Charlie? Just want to rip something up, really tear into somebody?' Rauser pressed.

'Don't answer that,' Stickler ordered.

'Yeah,' Charlie said, really drawing the word out – Dustin Hoffman in *Rain Man*. 'I do get real mad.'

'Shit,' Balaki muttered. He had taken the chair next to me that

192

Williams vacated. 'He's not showing any defensiveness at all. *I do get real mad.* Be hard to make a jury believe he's okay to stand trial.'

'You ever kill anybody, Charlie?' Rauser asked.

'No, sir, Mr Man.' Charlie shook his head violently.

'Oh, so you're sayin' you're just into rape?'

Stickler held up a hand, raised his voice. 'Don't answer that. Lieutenant—'

Williams interrupted, speaking for the first time. 'Your client is a person of interest in a homicide investigation, Counselor, and we had an agreement. You should advise him to answer or we will just pick him up again tomorrow and the next day and the next day until we have clarification. You get it?'

'Let's talk about some dates,' Rauser said to Stickler. 'If your client has a credible alibi, well, then we got no problem.'

Stickler's color crawled all the way up his neck and flushed his cheeks. Wet patches were showing under his arms. 'You have got to be kidding! Charlie? Charlie wouldn't recognize his own ass if you handed it to him. Of course he doesn't have an alibi. He can't remember what he had for breakfast, can you, Charlie?'

'I didn't get any breakfast,' Charlie said. 'I'm hungry.'

Rauser looked down at his notes. 'Charlie, you kind of made everyone believe you were living off the church, didn't you? You implied they were supplying housing for you, then I find out you're living in a fancy condo up by Inman Park.'

'It's not against the law to be protective of a fortune,' Stickler said. 'Charlie inherited quite a lot of money when his parents were killed. He has to be cautious. We've lectured him on this. Our firm handles the trust.'

'So how about this sob story about the wife and kids leaving you and all that?' Rauser shook his head. 'Not true. You filed for divorce, Charlie. I've got the papers right here. And you had to be hunted down and served by the court before you would pay support. See why I'm wondering about you, Charlie? Sometimes you act like a dumb shit and other times you're just a mean bastard.'

'Well, since I can't find a question in there, I think we're done here,' Stickler said, and looked at Charlie. 'Come on, Charlie. It's too hot in here anyway.'

'Yeah, it's hot as a damn fuck in here,' Charlie said, and let loose the laugh we'd all come to know. 'Neil likes it when I say *fuck*. I like Neil. Do you like Neil, Mr Man?' He started to rise.

Rauser's arm shot across the table and he grabbed Charlie's wrist. 'All that money and you're pedaling around town in a courier uniform.'

'Work is an essential aspect of his ongoing recovery,' the attorney said. 'These people have to have some sense of self-worth, Lieutenant.'

'Save it,' Rauser told Stickler. He hadn't let go of Charlie. He was staring into his eyes. 'That gets you in, doesn't it, Charlie? That why Elicia Richardson and Lei Koto and the others opened the door for you? You delivering a package? You looking hot like you need some water?'

'I don't know those people,' Charlie answered. He tried to withdraw his arm, but Rauser's grip must have been like a vise.

'Poor Charlie at the door with a package, looks so hot and thirsty.'

'Lieutenant Rauser, release my client.'

Rauser stood. He leaned across the table, very close to Charlie's face. 'I hear you're pretty good with a knife, Charlie. I need to see your knife.'

'Can you put him at the scene?' Stickler demanded. 'That's what I thought.' He pulled his jacket off the back of the chair and put his card on the table. 'You have more questions, you call me, Lieutenant. Let's go, Charlie.'

'That went well,' I muttered.

Balaki said, 'Lieu just wanted to rattle his cage a little and see what he does next.'

But Rauser wasn't done yet. As Stickler and Charlie prepared to leave the interrogation room, Rauser stepped in front of Charlie. He said very calmly, 'I'm gonna get a warrant for that fancy town house and we're taking it apart down to the pipes. I dare you to dump some evidence. You're done, Ramsey. Just a matter of time.'

Then he stalked out of the interrogation room.

'No confession?' Balaki said with a grin when Rauser and Williams joined us.

'Uh-unh,' Rauser growled. 'Be more likely Nancy Pelosi will come in here and give us a lap dance.'

'Yeah, baby,' Balaki said, and pumped his neck. 'Now we talking.'

We all looked at him. A moment of awkward silence followed, then Rauser said, 'We gotta cover this guy twenty-four/seven and we gotta do it in two shifts. Pull Velazquez and Bevins in.'

Groans came from the two detectives. It meant twelve-hour shifts doing excruciatingly boring work. They were used to long hours. It's the sitting and the waiting that makes cops nuts.

'We'll take the first shift at dusk, okay?' Balaki said. 'Give us time to kiss our wives and get a thermos of coffee.'

Rauser reached for the observation room door, then turned and looked at me. 'What the hell happened to Dobbs anyway? Where is he?'

'Count your blessings,' I said.

Chapter Twenty-Five

We had taken the elevator to garage level, where Rauser's Crown Vic was parked. As we reached the car, I heard heels against the concrete and spun around.

'Oh shit,' Rauser said.

She was coming at us fast across the parking garage. A heavyset guy was huffing behind her with a camera on his shoulder, and she was holding a microphone out in front of her like it was an Olympic torch.

'Wait, Lieutenant, wait, please,' she was yelling. 'Lieutenant, is it true you have a suspect in custody in the Wishbone case?'

Her name was Monica Roberts and she liked following cops and city workers around to make sure they were doing their jobs. I'd watched her reports and rooted for her. Not so much at the moment, however. My mind was clicking. Rauser's must have been too. Here we were together again on camera. When Chief Connor got wind of this, I imagined a giant black cloud spinning with debris like a twister over City Hall East.

'No comment.' Rauser had been well warned that only officials much higher up than he were to speak to the press regarding the Wishbone investigation.

'But you've interrogated a suspect.' It was not a question.

'Press briefings are at noon every day,' Rauser said. 'You know that, Monica.'

'Can you explain why the profiler hired by the Atlanta PD, Dr Jacob Dobbs, was not present for the interview?' Monica looked at me and the camera followed. I eased the car door open and sank quietly into the passenger seat.

'No comment,' Rauser repeated.

'Okay, then can you explain why the profiler who was sacked from the case was present at the suspect's interrogation?'

Rauser climbed in and threw the old Ford into gear. 'Christ,' he groused, slamming his door. 'Where's she getting her intelligence? If she knows that much, she already has Charlie's name.' He seemed to think about that for a minute. 'Actually, more pressure on Charlie boy may not be a bad thing.'

He pulled left out of the garage onto Ponce de Leon and headed toward Peachtree. It was that odd time of day when the city seems buttoned up. Lunch was over and it was still a couple of hours before quitting time, when the office buildings would empty out and jam our streets. The afternoon was so still and cloudless it might have seemed entirely without weather but for the stinging heat. The tires on Rauser's Crown Vic were a steady crackling against the city streets. The windows were down. Rauser had had bad luck with air conditioners lately, he said. The police scanner was chattering in the background. We were silent. I was tired and maybe even a little depressed. I thought Rauser must be too.

'*Ten-fifty-four-D-B, possible one-eighty-seven,*' the scanner reported, and got Rauser's attention. '*Juniper and Eighth.*'

'Two-thirty-three responding. ETA two minutes,' he said into his radio, and glanced at me. 'Possible dead body, possible homicide. It's just around the corner. I gotta take it.'

He flipped on his lights and siren and the cars in front of us began a paranoid migration into different lanes. Rauser barreled up another block and turned off Ponce. Moments later we were pulling up on Eighth Avenue near Juniper. I saw two women standing in the front yard of a Victorian with baby-blue shutters. They were big eyed, both of them, with their arms folded across their chests. A cruiser pulled up and then another unmarked Crown Vic. A silver Lincoln was parked on the street.

Rauser used his radio. 'Two-thirty-three, Dispatch. I'm ten-ninety-seven,' he said. 'I'll get you home as soon as I see what we got here, Street. Wait, okay? I don't want you walking.'

I could have walked home in less than ten minutes, but I said, 'I'll wait.'

Rauser's car was like a furnace. I got out, leaned against the door. It wasn't much help. A whiff of a breeze rustled a leaf from a pecan tree, then died. I watched Rauser approach the two women, speak to them a moment. Then he talked to the uniformed officer and two detectives. They all walked toward the silver Lincoln. Rauser unsnapped the holster that was almost always at his ribs and opened a door. For a split second, I thought I saw him react physically to whatever was in that car. It was almost imperceptible, a slight stiffening, something with his shoulders. Whatever it was, I saw it, and I didn't like it.

Rauser pulled away from the car and walked to the back, looked at the tag. He was on his phone. The crime scene unit showed up, then a station wagon from the medical examiner's office. Frank Loutz, Fulton County's ME, got out.

I watched Rauser take a few steps away and wipe his forehead. He had never fully adjusted to Atlanta's long, smoldering summers. Another crime scene van pulled up, followed by Jo Phillips in a gold Ford Taurus. Oh great, Jo the flirty spatter analyst. Rauser didn't seem to notice. He turned and looked at me, then turned away, frowning.

The ME approached him and they spoke, then Rauser walked toward me.

'It's Dobbs,' he said.

'What?'

'He's dead.'

Fifty yards away, two of the uniforms started sealing off the area around the silver Lincoln with yellow crime scene tape. In the distance, car horns and brakes told me the afternoon rush hour was picking up. The officers worked quickly to secure the scene. They needed to establish boundaries that would keep out the cameras and onlookers who would swoop down on it as soon as word got out.

'Liver temp indicates he's been here ten, twelve hours, and there's rigor in the limbs,' Rauser told me. 'That's a couple hours before we picked Charlie up this morning. There's multiple stab wounds.'

Evidence techs and detectives were still pulling up, getting out of their cars. I remembered the way I'd treated Dobbs the last time I saw him, leaving him asleep at my office. I thought about the brownies. *God*. Had that broken down his defenses enough to make him vulnerable to an attack? I slid down the Crown Vic and sat on the curb, feeling suddenly gutted.

Rauser's hand was on my shoulder. He wanted to drive me home.

I looked up at him. 'I want to see Jacob.'

He looked annoyed. 'So now it's *Jacob*? Because usually it's just Dobbs. Why do you have to romance everything? He was a sonofabitch, Street. And just in case you're taking the blame, Dobbs wasn't stumbling into walls and shit because he had a little THC in his system. He slept it off. I'm sure he woke up on your sofa his clearheaded bastardly self.'

'Well, that's a shitty thing to say, Rauser, given what's happened.' I scrambled to my feet. 'I need to see the scene.'

I didn't wait for Rauser. I stalked toward the Lincoln – the disposal site. A casket on wheels.

Rauser caught up and handed me a pair of surgical gloves. 'Okay, sure. Have at it. And if the press and the chief see you down there at my crime scene and the fallout interferes with *my* job, no big deal, right? As long as you get what you need.'

'*Screw you.*'

'Fuck the investigation.' He was walking fast next to me. 'Fuck my job. Fuck me. Keye needs closure. It's always about you, Keye, isn't it? Or maybe you just want to supervise. Is that it? You can do it better than everyone else, right?'

I stopped. 'Goddamnit, Rauser. You're the one that asked for my help.'

'Yeah, so tell me that wasn't a mistake, because right now I'm asking you to fucking stop.'

I slapped the gloves he'd given me into his palm. 'Fine. I'll walk home.'

I didn't answer the phone for hours. I heard Rauser's ringtone a couple of times, but I ignored it. I wasn't mad at him anymore. I was just furious at how right he'd been. About everything. It wasn't the first time he had accused me of romanticizing the shitty things in my life, especially my relationship with Dan. I get all gooey when I'm lonely and forget what life with Dan was really like. I don't think the human psyche has the capacity to fully recollect pain. There are pros and cons to this, of course.

Sometime around midnight, I decided that swallowing a little pride and calling Rauser back was the right thing to do.

There was exhaustion in his ragged voice. 'I called Dobbs's wife. A couple of local cops were there so she wouldn't be alone when I told her. She seemed really weirdly calm, Keye, and then there was a noise like she dropped the phone. Officer told me she'd fainted.'

I thought about what that must have been like for Rauser. I thought about the pain Dobbs's wife must be feeling knowing how brutal and squalid her husband's death must have been. I didn't know Jacob's wife personally. I knew only that she ran the sociology department at a Virginia university and that they had been married for many years.

'I'm sorry,' I told Rauser, and I meant it.

'I fucking hate this job sometimes.' I heard Rauser's shoes against a hard floor, squeaky hinges, and a heavy door closing.

'Where are you?'

'Pryor Street,' he answered, which meant he was at the Fulton County Medical Examiner's Center, the morgue, one of his least favorite places to hang out, I knew.

'Was the Lincoln a rental?'

'Yep. It's at the crime lab. Spatter says he was killed in it.'

'I don't get it. What was Dobbs doing in that neighborhood in the middle of the night? Did he pick someone up? Was he forced to drive there? Was he meeting someone?'

'We're working on it. We have a witness says he was alone at the hotel valet station a few minutes after midnight when he asked for his car. We know he'd consumed enough alcohol to be impaired. Here's what I think. He slept half the day away on your sofa, so by late last night he's wide awake. Strange city, he's alone so he goes out to cat around a little, drinks too much, and lets his guard down. We've canvassed the street. Nobody knew Dobbs except from the news and no one remembers exactly when the Lincoln showed up. I think the location was random. The street was quiet. Killer forced him to drive to the site. So we've got three, maybe four hours we haven't accounted for yet between Dobbs leaving his hotel and the DB call.'

I closed my eyes. It was still hard to wrap my mind around a dead body call for Jacob Dobbs.

Rauser said, 'Fatal wound in about the same place as Brooks, the substernal notch. Angle tells us the killer was in the passenger seat and reached across the car. Had to be right handed to get enough power to sink the blade.'

'He's upping the ante,' I told Rauser. 'The pictures he says he's taking, the letter writing, using the Internet to copy me on emails, tampering with my car, dealing with a florist, and now a high-profile target like Dobbs. His need to fuel his evolving fantasies is escalating. It's trumping his instinct for self-protection. He's taking risks. His illness is progressing.'

'Which means he's not being as careful. Loutz got fiber evidence. He thinks it's a carpet fiber. I went to Dobbs's hotel and got a carpet sample. It didn't match. I'm trying to get a warrant to get samples from Charlie's place. Fiber evidence may be all we got by the time we get in there. I got a feeling he dumped the knife and the pictures and anything else the little freak likes to hold on to even before we arrested him this morning. That's what I woulda done if I'd just stuck a knife into a big shot a few dozen times.'

I thought about Charlie's town house and remembered seeing a fireplace downstairs, an easy place to destroy pictures. Erasing them off a phone or digital camera would be easy too. And it wouldn't be hard for a bike courier to ditch a knife. APD could not possibly cover every step Charlie took. He was in and out of office buildings, commercial centers, and public restrooms all day. Rauser was probably right about the evidence disappearing.

'What else do you know about Dobbs?'

'Wound patterns are consistent with the knife from the other scenes. But get this: no bite marks. None.'

'Not enough time for the rituals.' I was thinking aloud. 'Residential neighborhood, foot traffic.'

'Keye, there's something I haven't told you yet. It was a pretty bad mess, what happened in that vehicle.'

I remembered watching as Rauser leaned into the car at the crime scene and his physical reaction. Mentally, I braced for what was coming.

'Dobbs's pants were down,' he said. 'And, well . . . his dick was gone.'

Chapter Twenty-Six

It had been determined that the black fiber the Fulton County medical examiner had pulled from inside one of Dobbs's wounds was from automotive carpeting. My theory, Rauser told me, agreed exactly with his – the killer probably had the knife on the floorboard of his own vehicle before attacking Dobbs. Fibers clung to the knife, and when it had been plunged into Dobbs's chest and pulled back out, a wisp of carpet fiber had attached to wound tissue. The ME's office had entered the microscopic characteristics of the recovered fiber into the FBI's automotive fiber database, which has over seven hundred samples from new and used cars. The origin of the fiber had been narrowed to fifteen models. Unfortunately, the database didn't have enough searchable samples on file to nail down a year. It might have been a Jeep Wrangler, a Chrysler LeBaron, a Dodge Challenger, a Toyota Camry, or any one of eleven other models. The field was still too wide, but it was the first bit of fiber evidence ever recovered from a Wishbone scene. And Frank Loutz had gone from zero to hero in Rauser's book overnight.

The bad news for Rauser was that the DMV didn't have a vehicle listed in the name of Charlie Ramsey, his prime suspect. Charlie also had no driver's license, which he would need in order to rent a car. Rauser's gut was telling him Charlie was right for these murders, and he wasn't going to stop until he proved it. If Charlie didn't have a car of his own stashed somewhere, then he had probably stolen one, Rauser thought. Detectives were going over all the stolen vehicle reports and comparing them to the list of models with carpeting that matched the fiber.

Rauser asked me to stay with my parents until he had Wishbone in custody. He was worried that the next contact I had with Wishbone might be more than an email or a wrestling match in my office or a wheel on the highway. He wanted me to stay out of sight for a whole host of reasons. I had considered for all of two seconds staying with my parents. Wishbone was inching closer: Dobbs's death was a message for everyone involved in this investigation. I didn't want to expose my parents to that. And I'd become homicidal myself if I had to spend that much time with my dear, sweet mother. Bless her heart.

Whatever Wishbone's motive, I knew it was a good bet that Rauser and his detectives could become targets too. Wishbone had veered out of one lane and into another. It wasn't just civil suit plaintiffs that set him off now. Rauser was the biggest threat to the killer's freedom. He was the head of Homicide, of the task force, and the adversary with whom the killer had already established a cat-and-mouse relationship through letter writing. And it was no secret that Rauser and I were close. Wishbone's letters had suggested Rauser's relationship with me was sexual, just as Charlie had suggested it in my office the day he attacked me.

Rauser promised me he was looking over his shoulder.

I met a locksmith early at my office and called Neil to ask him to come meet me for the new keys. I told him we were going to have to change the way we did things. He couldn't work with the door propped open anymore. The door was to stay closed and locked.

The locksmith followed me back to the Georgian, and by eight-thirty my locks had been rekeyed at home too. I made coffee and cleaned out White Trash's litter box, gave her fresh food and water, then flipped on the television.

Dobbs's murder was all over the news. The networks were running the juicy interviews with him they had on file. It was excruciating even for someone who had disliked the man as I had. I thought about

Dobbs's wife and children watching while newscasters described the gory details of his murder and sexual mutilation. I couldn't even guess at what they must be feeling.

Why hadn't I been skilled and smart enough to provide concise enough information for APD to stop this killer before he struck again? The question weighed on me. And another one too: could Charlie Ramsey really be the cruel, bloodthirsty killer we called Wishbone?

He'd been so rough and so profane when he'd grabbed me in my office. How cold his eyes had been, his grip. I thought about the Brooks scene, then about finding Billy LaBrecque beaten to death, about Lei Koto's child walking into a blood-spattered kitchen, about the wreck on the interstate, about Jacob Dobbs.

Fear as sharp as a switchblade stabbed at me. I didn't want to be afraid for Rauser, for myself, for Neil or my family. I didn't want to live that way.

Start at the beginning, I told myself. That's where you always go on a case – back to the beginning.

I called my mother and asked her to take care of White Trash for a few days. The two had formed an alliance. White Trash accepts handfuls of Pounce and anything else Mother hands her, bumps her ankles, and consents to snuggle sessions. Mom disapproves of her name and refuses to use it. She calls her White Kitty or White One or Whitey.

I made some phone calls and cleared my schedule for the week and sloughed off as much work on Neil as he was willing to take. White Trash followed me to the bedroom and watched me pull out the suitcase. She fully understands it is a prelude to my leaving and she doesn't appreciate this betrayal. She watched me steadily, her bright green eyes resentful slits.

I was headed south. The first two murders attributed to Wishbone were in Florida. A full victimology had been unattainable on Anne Chambers, the first murder on record. The files available from that time had been thoroughly reviewed, but Anne's private life was still

205

very much a question mark. If the murders began in Florida, there was a reason. Chambers appeared to have no link to our court system. She was the victim treated with the greatest cruelty and shown the most rage. Fifteen years ago a young woman had been brutalized, then sexually mutilated. The pattern was almost identical to Dobbs's murder yesterday. Whatever this was, it had started in Florida. I needed to know why.

The peal of the front door buzzer did nothing to improve White Trash's mood. She scurried underneath the bed. I went to the door in shorts, an old T-shirt, no shoes. When I stood on tiptoes to peer through the peephole, I found myself looking at my ex-husband. It was like licking my finger and sticking it into a light socket. I think my eyes even bulged a little.

Not once during our relationship had I looked at Dan and felt nothing. He always stirred something in me. What it stirred wasn't always positive but it was always superconcentrated. I swallowed the cotton ball stuck in my throat and opened the door.

'Cold?' he asked, and gave me that sexy, impossibly white smile. I realized with great displeasure that my nipples were staging some kind of coup d'état over my good sense.

He handed me the flowers I'd already spotted behind his back, a bouquet of fresh-cut ones, bright yellows and purples and reds, no fillers. Dan actually knew flowers by name, had probably requested each one individually, possibly even supervised the arrangement. When we were married, he brought them home whenever he'd been unfaithful. Flowers became a sort of subspecialty for him; his specialty, of course, was bullshit.

I folded my arms over the insubordinate little traitors poking through my shirt, looked at him, looked at the flowers, then turned on my heel and returned to the bedroom.

'Listen, Keye, I know I wasn't a good husband to you.' He didn't follow me. He simply raised his voice so I could hear.

'You've done something horrible, haven't you?' I asked. I was only half kidding.

'No, no. It's nothing like that. I've just been thinking about things. Listen, I know I haven't been there for you. I was a crummy husband and an even crummier friend. Hell, I've had trouble just being a decent man half my life.'

I was silent, waiting, cautious as I always am with Dan. White Trash, on the other hand, was fearless. Hearing his voice, she slipped out from under the bed, stretched, and sashayed out. She had always adored Dan. A minute or two later when I came back into the room, Dan was kneeling, stroking her back. He was wearing boot-cut Levi's that fit him just right. His skin looked dark against a crisp banded collar. White Trash had her paws stretched out in front of her and her butt in the air.

He rose slowly to full height, all of about five feet nine even in his western boots. 'She missed me,' he said.

I rolled my eyes. 'You probably smell like fish.'

He smiled gently. 'I'm changing, Keye. I'm working hard to turn my life around. To make things right.'

I ignored that. 'Why do cats like fish anyway? It's not like they're out there trout fishing in the wild. Ever see a cat rip a fish out of a stream on *Wild Kingdom*?'

Dan was undeterred. 'I don't know how you can forgive me for the kind of man I've been to you, but if you'll just try, I won't let you down this time.'

Of course he would. It's what we do. We make promises, he breaks them, I'm wounded and pissed off. Then we start all over. Sick, I know, but I didn't care suddenly. I just wanted him. I didn't exactly stretch out my paws and stick my butt in the air, but I must have signaled him in some basic animal way, because he came to me, held my jaw, and kissed me. His mouth tasted like Starburst, the orange ones he loved and probably had a bag of in his banged-up old car. He smelled like drier sheets and soap, and when he pressed against me, when he whispered, 'I'm crazy about you, Keye. I always have been,' he was already hard. He didn't ask why I'd been packing when we moved to the bedroom and pushed my suitcase onto the floor.

Dan was a submissive lover, sweet and silky and hard. He liked kissing. He liked being undressed. He liked to be restrained. He liked letting me do whatever I wanted with him for as long as I wanted. In some circles, he was called a Bottom, and it was one of the things I adored about him. There was something boyish and wounded in him when we made love. He was responsive and open, eager and utterly awed by me – everything I wanted from him in life and more than I could ever expect.

We were silent for a while after we'd made love. My head was on his chest, his fingers skipping lightly over my bare shoulder. 'You awake?' he murmured finally, but I didn't answer. I didn't want to talk. I just wanted to fall back asleep like this, in the softness of this moment.

He shook me a little. He wasn't giving up. 'What's with the suitcase?'

I kissed his neck, pressed a finger against his lips. The sun was setting and I was sleepy. White Trash jumped on the bed and immediately went for the exposed half of Dan's fuzzy chest. She paused briefly to sniff my eyelashes, then put her butt in my face and relaxed her whole body on top of him. The phone began to ring. So much for the moment.

'Want a failure to appear with priors?' It was Tyrone from Tyrone's Quikbail. 'Money's good,' he added. 'Meaty.'

Tyrone could say things like 'meaty' and still sound cool. I rose up on my elbow. 'What priors?'

'Assault, armed robbery.'

I hadn't exactly been running down new work. I was sucked into the Wishbone investigation and all the crap that always swallows up my life – background checks, service of process, and about a hundred applications to verify for Rapid Placement, the employment agency that used up a couple thousand dollars' worth of my time each month. I needed them, but the work was so excruciatingly boring that I always put it off until the last possible minute every week, drooling into my keyboard till I fell asleep on Sunday nights, groggily turning in my reports on Monday mornings.

I told Tyrone I wouldn't be available for a few days. He took the news well. He had a long list of agents who wanted work. He had called me first because he liked me. That was the rumor anyway. It's hard to tell with Tyrone.

I curled back up to Dan and the scraggly white cat that seemed to no longer give a damn about me. 'It's a business trip,' I said before Dan had to ask again. 'A few days maybe. I'm not sure yet.'

He moaned a little, kissed the top of my head, pulled me closer. 'And just when we're getting along so well.'

I smiled. 'This is the easy part, remember?'

'No, it's not. It's what reminds us how connected we are and it kills me later, Keye. I ache for you. I do. Why can't it be like this all the time?'

Maybe he was sincere. Maybe it was a line from a play. Maybe he was back in daytime television. I couldn't tell anymore. I wasn't sure he could. He'd been acting for so many years, rehearsing for one role after another, always waiting for *the* role, the one that would put him over the top.

'So what do you think about me staying here?' he asked. It came out of nowhere. I must have looked at him as if his lips just fell off, because he added hastily, 'I mean, just for a week or so. There's a gas leak or something in my building. Everybody's kicked out. They're digging up the street.'

I got up and yanked my bathrobe around me. White Trash caught a bad vibe and leapt off Dan's chest onto the floor, fighting hard for traction on the hardwood. She vanished under the bed.

'So that's why you showed up with flowers and all the I-was-such-a-bad-husband crap. This was just another goddamn audition.' I smacked my forehead with my palm. 'Sonofabitch. I bet you've got a suitcase in your car. You do, don't you?'

'Wait, Keye, listen. It's not how it looks.' He was out of bed, hurrying behind me naked as I stomped toward the kitchen. There was Greek yogurt cheesecake with a pomegranate glaze in the fridge from the restaurant downstairs, and I meant to have it. Some people reach for a Xanax. Cheesecake is my mood elevator.

'I said those things because they're true. And the apartment thing, I hadn't even planned to ask. Really. It just crossed my mind and I blurted it out without thinking.'

'Uh-huh.' I opened the fridge and found the cheesecake. 'So, what's the truth about your apartment, Dan? Did you let the utilities go? Or forget a little thing like rent again? You need money?'

The telephone rang.

'Don't answer it,' he ordered.

I grabbed it before the second ring and Dan threw his hands up and stalked to the long windows that face Peachtree and the Fox Theatre.

It was Rauser. 'You busy?'

I covered the mouthpiece and told Dan, 'Would you get dressed? Peachtree Street is probably only half as interested in your dick as you are.'

'Gee, sorry to interrupt,' Rauser said. 'I really would love to hear more about Dan's tiny cock. I was beginning to think you no longer liked men.'

'I don't.'

'Maybe you're a lesbian.'

I looked at Dan's exposed genitalia and considered that seriously. I had never been given cause to label my sexuality. I'd never suffered through a sexual identity crisis or needed therapy to reach orgasm. In my most liberal assessment of myself, I like to think I could fall in love with a woman. But I've never tested it, unless you count a college make-out session after four lemon Jell-O shooters.

'You always think women are hitting on you,' Rauser continued. 'You know you do.'

'I do not.'

''Member that waitress at Hooters?'

'She *was* hitting on me.'

'Uh-huh, and what about Jo? You thought she was hitting on you too, didn't you? That night at the Brooks scene?'

210

'How'd you know that?'

'She could tell.' Rauser chuckled. 'She told me you got all weird when she touched your arm. Like you were gonna curl up in a goddamn fetal position or something.'

I sighed. 'Great.'

'Homophobes are usually just big ole closet cases,' he said, and made some kissing noises.

My front door opened and my mother walked in. I looked at her, looked at my nude ex-husband sulking at the window, then back at my mother. I hung up on Rauser.

'*Mother!* What are you doing here?'

'Neil gave me the new key. I thought you were leaving town.' She glanced at Dan, then at her own shoes. A smile played lightly at the corners of her lips.

Dan turned from the window, nodded at my stunned mother, and said, 'Nice to see you, Mom.' His calm took me by surprise considering the thing he was most proud of in life had withdrawn to about the size of my thumb. He and his poor shrunken penis walked past us and down the hall. Mother held a covered dish in one hand and a small suitcase in the other. She seemed unable to speak, a rare occurrence and one I might have enjoyed had I not been so completely irritated.

'I'm glad you two are working things out,' she said, her eyes following Dan's bare ass, which was, thankfully, almost to the bedroom, where I hoped it would find some clothes.

I raised my voice so he could hear my opinion loud and clear. 'We're working out how fast he can get dressed and leave, that's what we're working out.'

'My Lord, Keye. You don't have to be so rude, do you?'

'Mother, why are you here?'

'Why are *you* here?' she countered. 'I'm taking care of White Kitty, remember?'

'It's White Trash. Not White Kitty or Whitey or White One or Snowflake or whatever you're calling her today. It's White *Trash*.'

'I was going to stay here while you're gone so she won't get lonely,' Mother said, then shook her head. 'And, well, it will give your dad some time alone.'

Uh-oh. Mom and Dad having problems? Visions of Mother living with me danced through my head.

'Are you and Dad okay?'

'Howard's very upset, Keye. I'm sorry to tell you that your grandfather Street was killed.'

My father's parents had always referred to me as 'the little Chink', so this news didn't exactly rock my world. We had never been close, but I knew my father loved his father and must be hurting. 'You left Dad alone?'

'You know your father. He can be just inconsolable. And it doesn't help his fool father got himself run over on his own lawn mower. Can you believe it?'

'Somebody drove into Granddaddy's yard and ran him over on the lawn mower?' I tried not to laugh, really I did. I knew in my heart of hearts that would be wrong. At the very least, Mother would consider it inappropriate.

'No, no. He was on the road, the *main* road, going to see your grandmother.'

'Going *where* to see Grandma?'

Exasperated, my mother puffed out her cheeks, set her suitcase down, and took her covered dish to the refrigerator. 'They split up after Granddaddy Street got that snake. Your grandmother wouldn't live in the house with a snake and I don't blame her. Idiot was half blind too. They took his driver's license away a few years ago, so he started riding around town on that hideous green thing. Damned old fool. And your poor grandmother, Keye.' She shook her head again in disgust. 'Just one humiliation after another.'

'Granddaddy had a snake?' I struggled to keep up.

'Oh, for heaven's sake, Keye. Don't you know anything that goes on in this family?'

Chapter Twenty-Seven

KNIFEPLAY.COM

Your Online Adult Edge Fetish & Knife Play Community blogs > beyond the EDGE, a fantasy by BladeDriver blog title > Only the Lonely

I love watching her. She is so dedicated. We both are, but to different aims, of course. For her it's all about a flat stomach and a hard ass to pull her little tights over. For me, I know when her neighbors are home, when her housekeeper comes. I know her cat. I have so come to enjoy these evening runs. She pretends not to know I'm there, wears her little headphones in her ears all the time, but I know she can feel me. She loves the attention. She wants my blade parting that cosmetic skin as badly as I do.

I crank up my stereo. It's our song, mine and Melissa's. *Only the lonely. Dum, dum, dum, dum-de-do-wah. Know the way I feel tonight. Only the lonely. Dum, dum, dum, dum-de-do-wah. Know this feeling ain't right.*

I ease my car into gear and trail along behind her. I play it for her, for us. I sing it too. I can't help myself. I'm so happy to see her.

There goes my baby. There goes my heart . . . Oh, oh, oh, oh yeah . . .

Tallahassee didn't seem to know that summer was fading dully away in most of the country. The sun was blazing, the temperature around ninety-five, a hot breeze. In Atlanta, we're deep enough into the South to have mild winters and long summers, and far enough north to get full color in autumn and a bright, budding spring. I had considered moving to Tallahassee and studying. WFSU has an excellent criminology program, but in the end I didn't think I could live somewhere without the clear division of seasons to tame my moods and keep the depression away.

I went to the WFSU Visitors' Center, explained my presence as best I could, and was directed to Mary Dailey in Admissions.

'I'm looking for information on a former student,' I told her. 'Would have been a freshman sixteen years ago. Am I in the right place to get help with that?'

Mary Dailey was, perhaps, fifty years old, hair brown except for a gray streak in the front, brown eyes showing just a little crinkle at the edges.

'You said you're a detective?'

'Private.' I nodded. 'I'm consulting on a case in Atlanta that—'

'May I see some identification?'

'Sure,' I said. 'APD can verify also. Lieutenant Aaron Rauser in Homicide.'

I scribbled Rauser's cell number down for her. Since I was not here officially, I didn't want her going through the police department switchboard.

She took the number and studied my ID. 'You want to know about Anne Chambers?'

I nodded again. 'Whatever records you have on her. Do you know anything about her friends, family, life off campus? I understand she was a sophomore when she was killed.'

'Sixteen years is a long time, Ms Street. I've only been here five.'

'But you knew her name and why I'm here.'

'Yes,' she replied. I could hear the regret in her tone. 'We've been expecting this since her murder was connected to the ones in Atlanta. Honestly, no one here was looking forward to it. It's not the sort of thing one wants publicized.'

'I understand,' I said. 'No one else has been here?'

'A detective from Jacksonville was here maybe six weeks ago after they connected Anne's murder to the ones in Atlanta and the one in

214

Jacksonville. But with all the news from Atlanta now, we knew someone would come back.'

' "We"?'

'The staff here. We talk about it, of course.' She hesitated. 'I can point you to yearbooks from her years here, if that will help, and give you some general information, but our records are private.'

'Uh-huh, well, a court order wouldn't take long,' I said agreeably. 'And right behind it comes a team of investigators who walk around campus looking very coplike. Or you could help me. I promise to be very unobtrusive and discreet.'

The corners of her mouth twitched almost imperceptibly. 'May I call you later? Where are you staying?'

'I haven't made arrangements. I drove straight here from Atlanta.' I wrote my cell number on the back of a business card and handed it over her desk.

'I understand Anne lived on campus. Any chance I could see the dorms before I go?'

Mary Dailey rose stiffly from her chair. 'I'll have to find out which hall she lived in. It's a very large campus. Would you excuse me, Ms Street?'

I hurried around to her desk the second she stepped out. The Visitors' Center had clearly called before I got here. There was a note on her desk pad with my name, Anne Chambers's name, the years she'd attended the university, and the words *murdered, Roberts Hall, W. Campus*, which made me wonder why Mary Dailey had really stepped out of her office. I hustled back to the proper side of her desk and tried to look as innocent as possible.

'Will you follow me, please, Ms Street? I'll show you to Ms Chambers's residence hall. We've done quite a lot of renovations since she was here, but I don't suppose that matters to your investigation.'

'General layout pretty much the same?'

'I can get you a campus map from that time, but, yes, it hasn't changed that much.'

'So whoever you stepped out of your office to speak to told you—'

'To cooperate. That's right,' she interrupted evenly.

'I'd love a map. Did Anne Chambers have a roommate?'

'Room*mates*,' Mary Dailey said crisply, then gave me their names. 'Ms Street, no one here wants to get in the way of a murder investigation. We just want to be certain the investigation isn't something that could affect us in a negative way. The general public had forgotten all about Anne Chambers. The focus is on Atlanta. We'd like it to stay that way.'

We climbed in a golf cart and she drove us across the lush, tree-lined campus where a twenty-year-old Anne Chambers had lived and died a savage death. I thought about her family, the people who had loved her. They hadn't forgotten, Ms Dailey. One never forgets. I kept my thoughts to myself, though.

Mary Dailey led me to Anne Chambers's old room and left me there alone. The walls were minty green. I wondered how many times they had been repainted in the last fifteen years and how many students had lived here. The two single beds and a bookcase were built-ins. There was a small desk, a tiny refrigerator, and a sink wedged into the twelve-by-fifteen-foot space. No bathroom. The room was littered with books and clothes and takeout cartons.

In the photographs I'd seen, it had looked much the same when Chambers, a fine arts major, lived here. *Fine arts.* Who majors in fine arts? A dreamer, I thought, and grief slammed into my chest like a two-by-four.

It was a ground-level room with two windows on the outside wall, flooded with light. I remembered studying the Ted Bundy murders when I had first been transferred to the Behavioral Analysis Unit at NCAVC. When Bundy was here in Florida stalking and killing more young women, terrified students at WFSU had piled leaves and crumpled paper outside their windows hoping to have advance warning of a prowler. Some planted cactus and nailed their windows shut. None of it helped. Bundy wasn't the type to climb

216

in windows. Good looks and charm and the sympathy con were his weapons. His victims came right to him. When Anne Chambers had been butchered here, had young women once again been terrified to cross campus alone or leave their rooms at night?

The walls were thin. Even through closed doors, music and sound seeped out.

The killing had taken place midday. The dorms would have been half empty, I guessed. Even then the killer was doing plenty of homework, knowing when to show up, when Anne's roommates were absent, class schedules. There had been a serious blow to the victim's head. It wasn't cause of death. It was merely the controlling blow. For at least a few minutes, Anne Chambers would have been incapable of defending herself, making noise, and this would have provided plenty of time for restraints and gags.

How did the killer get out without being seen? I looked up and down the hall. No way to get to one of the exits in the middle of the day without a resident noticing a person with blood all over his clothing. It was a violent scene. There was blood everywhere. A window maybe? No. The nearest parking lot was too far. The next building was too far. Someone on campus would have seen someone headed there. Perhaps the killer carries a bag or a briefcase with tools, a change of clothes. A bag would also solve the problem of what to do with the bloody clothes. No. Too much baggage. And then it hit me. The clothes come off. Of course. Being naked with the victim is part of the ritual.

I didn't want to be here anymore. I wanted to do what I had done in the past after imagining the unimaginable. I wanted to drink.

Instead, I spent a day pawing through a dead woman's life. I made lists of Anne Chambers's classmates, roommates, professors, and started the process of tracking them down, calling them. It had been so long ago, it was difficult to find anyone who remembered very much about Anne apart from her murder. No one seemed to know anything at all about her relationships, her dreams. She'd had three different roommates at different times. All remembered her as shy, distant, maybe even a little secretive. Mary Dailey lent me a stack of yearbooks from different schools within the university system covering the couple of years Anne lived here, and I packed them into my car for later viewing.

I had called Anne's mother and arranged a visit for the next morning. The trip to Jekyll Island would only take a couple of hours, even in a little piece-of-shit Plymouth Neon. I hoped I'd have time to take a walk on Jekyll's hard-packed sand. I loved it there, loved the smooth bleached-out driftwood that littered the beaches, the big gnarled live oaks bent like old men over the dunes from taking on the constant sea winds. At sunset the tangled black branches of those trees in silhouette is all at once so eerie and so beautiful it will raise the hair on your neck. Jekyll isn't one of those hosed-down-fluffy-white-sand islands. The Atlantic is choppy and white capped, and the afternoon thunderstorms will pound you into the sand. The locals were trying hard now to hold on to what they had left and fight back the developers, protect the wildlife and an island that had transformed itself into rolled-up shirtsleeves and artists and writers and shrimpers and fishing boats. Take any trail through the interior of the island and you are treated to deer and crabs and turtles, birds large and small, and alligators pretending to sleep in the shallow marsh. The feeling of belonging hits me there like no place else as if I sprang up barefoot from this earth and sand and weeds and made my way like a loggerhead to the sea. In my heart of hearts, I am a Low Country girl in a pickup truck and cutoffs, the sweet briny smell of the marsh filling my lungs. I did not look forward to meeting with Anne Chambers's parents, but how I longed to put my bare feet on Jekyll's dark sand.

I was driving over the causeway bridge toward the Jekyll Island entrance when my phone went off.

'This is Mirror Chang, Dr Street. Jacob Dobbs was my husband.'

I waited a second or two, but she didn't say anything else. 'I'm sorry for your loss,' I said awkwardly. It seemed an inadequate response and horribly unequal in empathy to what she must have felt in pain, but I didn't know what else to say to her.

'I know you worked with Jacob recently in Atlanta, and that you were a colleague of my husband's at BAU.' Her voice was even and betrayed no emotion.

'I was more of a student than a colleague.'

'My husband is gone, Dr Street. So I'd like to know the truth. I've heard so many things.' For the first time, I detected an edge of pain in her tone. 'What is it in us that needs to know if we've been betrayed even after we lose someone?'

'It's a way to postpone grief,' I answered softly.

A small, humorless laugh. 'That's something Jacob would have said. So tell me, Dr Street – what happened between you and my husband?'

'At the Behavioral Analysis Unit? I lodged a complaint. It wasn't taken seriously—'

'Because he had their loyalty and you were a drunk. Is that correct?'

I swallowed. 'That was my take on it, yes.'

'I remember his anger at you during that time. Too much anger. I sensed there must have been great feeling between the two of you.'

'I can assure you there was not, Ms Chang. Not like that.'

A few seconds ticked by. Then, 'His personal effects were returned to me. Isn't it interesting that one day your husband has clothes and things in his pockets and the next they're just personal effects?' It must have been agonizing for her to share with a stranger the things that had to have been so deeply painful in private. 'I found some of Jacob's notes. Your name was there. The usage was . . . well, sexual in nature. Did you sleep with my husband, Dr Street?'

'No. Not ever.'

'Some men aren't capable of fidelity,' she said. 'Jacob might have been one of them. My husband was not a perfect man, but something you may not realize is that he was a good father and a good companion to me for thirty years.'

I thought about all the times I'd seen Dobbs take off his wedding

ring and drop it in his pocket when he was flirting with someone –
the new girl in the unit, a woman in the cafeteria, a contact when we
were on assignment, someone in local law enforcement. He'd once
slept with both a female deputy *and* the sheriff when we were on a
serial case in Wyoming. I'd said something to him back then about a
tan line on his finger, and he'd laughed at me. '*Only a sociopath could
be unfaithful to a devoted wife while wearing a thing like that, Keye. I don't
remove it to disguise my marital status. I remove it out of respect.*'

'I'm so sorry,' I told Mirror Chang. 'What you're feeling must be
excruciating.'

'You must have been very angry at him for costing you another
job. In fact, you must have hated my husband.'

I waited, stung by the venom in her voice.

'Did you kill Jacob, Dr Street? Were you the whore who murdered
my husband?'

I pulled over before I reached the guard shack where I would have
to get a pass to enter the island. 'Ms Chang.' I hoped I could disguise
the shock and offense in my voice. She must have been crazy with
grief. 'I have worked for my entire adult life to stop the people who
inflict this kind of pain on others. It's no secret your husband and I
had a toxic history. Yes, I disliked Jacob. But he didn't deserve what
happened to him. And you and your children don't deserve the
misery you're feeling now. If it helps at all, we have capital punishment
in Georgia. And the Atlanta Police Department won't stop until this
bastard is on death row.'

A red-tailed hawk was circling above the wax myrtle and white
oleander on each side of the two-lane, surveying the marsh and mud
flats for prey. I didn't think I could have hated Dobbs any more than
I had while he was alive. But I was wrong.

'I had to know.' It was a broken whisper. I think she was crying.
The line went dead.

KNIFEPLAY.COM

Your Online Adult Edge Fetish & Knife Play Community blogs > beyond the EDGE, a fantasy by BladeDriver blog title > Crash Test Dummy

Hello friends and fans and thank you for your comments. I am so glad you are enjoying my dark fantasies. I love reading yours too. Perhaps we can play together one day, compare techniques.

Have you been reading the newspapers? They are listing the names of all my old partners. This has made me a bit nostalgic, I admit, remembering the early days when I was still sharpening my skills, the days before I could point my phone and take their sweet memory home with me. I want so to have these memories recorded and to share them with you.

Her name was Anne and we were both young, she younger and greener than I. She had a sour expression when she opened the door that day, said something about me being late. It was eleven-thirty in the morning. Everyone was at class. She was so needy and so desperate, always wanting time when she could be the focus of my world. She wanted sex too. Neither one of us was in love with sex with the other. It was just what she did, how she filled up that black hole of need she carried around. It never stopped. She always wanted it, wanted something, *want, want, want, me, me, me*. And when she wasn't painting her pictures or fucking, she was smoking pot or drinking or eating. Anne always wanted something going into her. Her requirements seemed endless, just vacuous, bottomless need. My mother behaved just like this with my father. I watched her suck the life out of him and everything else around her.

We won't have as much time now, Anne told me that day, maybe just an hour. That's plenty, I said, and she pressed her body against me. This was going to be easy. Let her feel my full attention. Let her be my sole focus. I was in the mood that day. I'd come prepared. She had said she wanted to explore with me. I deeply wanted to explore every inch of her with the point of my blade.

Oh no, she said. That wasn't exactly what she had in mind. It was too much. It hurt. *Poor baby.* Shut the fuck up, I told her. Just shut the fuck up.

221

She started to cry. Her face was red and she was bleeding lightly. I had barely run the sharp edge over her right breast just to see what kind of touch it would take to make a shallow wound. But she had to get all whiny and red faced. I was just getting started. I had planned this. I wasn't going to stop. It had been eight long years since that first time when I was only sixteen. It was so hurried back then, and I was so scared and so angry. I had not been able to savor it. That day in Anne's room, I needed it.

I kissed her and reassured her and when she turned her beautiful back to me, I slammed the base of her own table lamp into the back of her head and the bitch crumpled like a piece of aluminum foil. I checked the clock. Forty-five minutes to explore Anne. It wasn't as easy as I thought it would be. It was the first time I had worked any kind of restraint on a human, the first time I had used wire. But it was fantastic — ankles and wrists and neck wired to the chair. Her eyes got wide and the veins were popping out everywhere. The wire was twisted too tight. I had tied a scarf tight around her head to hold a washcloth in her mouth. She was gagging and crying. The wire cut into her each time she moved and each time she moaned. I closed my eyes and listened. Pleasure or pain — I couldn't tell from her sounds. It was fascinating. Really it was. I was so in love with her at that moment. For all her need, she was giving back at last.

She nearly tipped herself over in the chair when I took off her nipples. Big mess, urine on the floor, lots of drama. I should have waited. I have learned now what to do first and what to save for later, but that day I was so new. When I fucked her with the blade, she gave up. She just copped out, passed out, left me alone, so I whacked the fuck out of her again with that lamp and let my knife do whatever it wanted. It was like stabbing grapefruit. The point paused briefly, met some resistance, and then plunged inside. I did it until she had paid me back everything that she and women like her take from us. *Everything.* I did it until I got good at it. And then I sank my teeth into her warm flesh and I came so hard. So hard. I'll never forget her, my crash test dummy.

Chapter Twenty-Eight

Katherine Chambers had entered midlife plump and silver haired. They had not wanted children, she told me, but at thirty-seven she became pregnant and everything changed.

'It's not that I don't consider myself a feminist, I do,' she said with no accent whatsoever. I couldn't have guessed what part of the country she'd come from. She filled cups with flavored coffee from a glass coffee press. The scent of vanilla and hazelnut wafted through the room. We pulled out chairs at a round pine table. I could see the water beyond her kitchen window and the sand, golden brown and packed against the earth from last night's rain.

'It's just that I have this question about when life begins.' Katherine said it casually, as if we were discussing last evening's storm. 'No one seems to know. Not the scientists or the theologians. That put abortion way out of the realm of possibility for me.' She took a sip of coffee; a rueful smile played on her lips as she returned her mug to the table. 'We thought about adoption, but as time went by Martin and I became terribly excited about having a child . . . I'm sure you've heard this before, but you never expect to outlive your children. It's something that comes as a complete surprise. Although I don't suppose you could plan for something like that anyway.'

'No, ma'am. I don't suppose you could.'

She fell silent, looked out the window at the row of live oaks.

The ocean was full today, rolling dark green and acting up a little. Hurricane season wasn't over yet. So far this year the winds had all moved too far out to sea to make the Georgia coast. But there were reports of one not far off. Edward had formed near Jamaica, pummeled Cuba, ripped through the Keys, then moved back out to sea, where he was now patiently churning, regaining strength for another run at the coast. Watches were posted from West Palm to Jacksonville, Jekyll, St Simons, Savannah, Hilton Head, Charleston, and the Outer Banks. I wondered how this would affect my departure on the little two-lane strip that winds around the island. I could hear Rauser saying, 'It's not all about you, Keye.' But I knew the truth. Of course it was.

'Is it true that the person who killed my daughter is responsible for all these other murders?' Mrs Chambers asked.

'The evidence points to that, yes.'

'I read those awful letters to the police in the paper. They were very difficult to read.'

'I can't imagine what that would feel like,' I told her. 'I'm so sorry.'

Her eyes touched the ocean again, then came back to mine. 'How can I help you, Miss Street?'

She led me into her living room. There was an oil painting over the fireplace, Jekyll Island's lighthouse rising up above city skyscrapers, and below it, shadowy, gray-flanneled figures with briefcases, bent against the winter wind, heads down. Yellow cabs lined narrow streets.

'We moved here from Manhattan when Anne was sixteen,' Katherine Chambers explained. 'I think she missed the city very much. She painted this then.'

'Talented,' I said as if I had a clue.

Two boxes sat in front of a coffee table, Anne's possessions from her college dorm, Mrs Chambers told me. I looked through everything as delicately as possible. She sat watching me, her face a little pale.

'May I borrow the yearbooks and the journal? I have yearbooks from the university but I'd like to see Anne's.'

'Because they have messages inside from classmates and friends.' It wasn't a question. 'You think it was someone she knew.'

224

'Is that what you think?'

Katherine shook her head. 'Oh, I don't know. Anne was so secretive about her private life. Tallahassee might have been three thousand miles away for all we knew about our daughter's life there.'

Secretive was the word her roommates had used too.

'So you don't know if she was seeing anyone at school?'

'There were times when she didn't call for a while. I told Martin that I thought she was having some sort of romance. You know how it is when you're young and exploring. You don't think you need anyone else when you're involved. I had the feeling she was going from one relationship to another very quickly.'

I slid a picture of Charlie Ramsey across the table. 'Have you ever seen this man?'

'No.'

'How about friends here on the island? Anyone who would have kept in touch with her while she was at school?'

'She was only here for one year and she wasn't very happy. Anne couldn't seem to connect with the kids here. There was Old Emma, though. My daughter seemed fascinated with her, but then half the island finds Emma fascinating. Anne walked down there in the mornings sometimes with breakfast for her and a thermos full of coffee. Barefoot.' She hesitated. Her smile flickered. 'After dinner, she always gathered the leftovers and put them in the refrigerator until morning for Emma's cats. Now we do it.'

'So Emma still lives here?'

'Oh yes. I think she's been here her whole life, her and about a hundred and fifty cats. The road washed out some time ago, though. You'll have to walk if you want to see her.' She handed Charlie's photo back to me. 'You're not anything like they made you out to be on television. I'm sorry to bring that up, but I recognized you. We get all the Atlanta stations down here, you know.'

'Thank you for saying that. It's not who I am now, but I was a functioning addict for years.'

225

'I've been sober since we found out I was pregnant with Anne. Thirty-five years. That pregnancy was a blessing to us in so many ways.'

I nodded and smiled. 'Thank you, Mrs Chambers. I'll make sure Anne's things get back to you safely . . . I'm sorry about Anne. I'm sorry to come here and stir all this up again. If there's ever anything I can do, please don't hesitate to call.' I handed her my card. She took it, and then, to my surprise, her fingers closed painfully around mine.

'Find this monster,' she urged me. '*That's* what you can do for me, Miss Street.'

I followed the beach a quarter mile until it narrowed at a cluster of moss-draped oaks and a sandy path strewn with driftwood. As I walked, I imagined sixteen-year-old Anne Chambers coming here in the mornings, bare feet sinking into the sand, a foil-wrapped breakfast and a coffee thermos in her hands.

Emma knew I was there before I realized she was watching me. I was fascinated by her home – part folk art gallery, part salvage yard. Sinks and car seats, bumpers, bicycles, old windows, doors, high chairs – anything you can think of that might have once been abandoned – were piled, hung, or welded into elaborate sculptures in Emma's little patch of sandy front yard.

It was beautiful . . . and hideous, and must have taken thirty years to collect and construct. From every cool, flat surface, languid cats lounged and stretched and watched me steadily with cautious feral eyes. The air was warm and sticky and the mosquitoes clearly had not been given their breakfast. The house was decades past due for a paint job. Salt air and time had stripped it down to raw wood. When I reached out to knock on the screen door, something moved just on the other side.

'What you wont?' She slurred a little – a backwoods Ozzy Osbourne. She had startled me, but I tried hard not to show it.

'I only see about twenty cats,' I said, and smiled. 'I heard you had at least a hundred and fifty.'

A stained backwater grin glimmered faintly through the screen. 'You comin' for a readin' or you wanna stand out there countin' cats?'

'Oh, so you're a psychic?'

The screen door was pushed open. Emma, I noticed at once, looked something like the bad witch after she'd started to melt. She was perhaps five feet tall, but you got the feeling she hadn't started out that small. She gave me the once-over, pale eyes sharp and narrow and opportunistic, sized me up for what I was worth, from my shoes to my earrings and the watch on my wrist. She was curious about how much she could get out of me. I knew the look. I'd seen it in the city on people who live by their wits on the street. She sighed, disappointed, and stepped back inside. The screen slammed behind her.

I stood there on the other side for a few moments, unsure of what to do, then raised my voice a little. 'Excuse me?'

'Come on,' she said. It sounded like *Cah-moan*.

I found her sitting at a round table covered by a heavy red tablecloth with gold piping and tassels. She had a deck of tarot cards in front of her. The inside of the house was as crowded as the yard and not as clean. Emma was obviously a trash picker from way back.

'Mix these up for me.'

I took the cards and shuffled them a little. 'Actually, I just came to ask you some questions about Anne Chambers.'

'You don't want no readin', I won't give you one. Fifteen dollars either way.'

'Her mother said Anne used to come here.'

Emma was silent.

'The girl who used to live down the beach,' I pressed on.

'I know who,' she grouched.

I set the cards across the table in front of her and withdrew my arm before she took a bite of it. I wasn't sure Emma had had her breakfast either.

'Did Anne keep in touch with you after she left for college?'

No answer.

'Do you know if she was seeing anyone?'

She put the cards out and studied them for a long while. Somewhere in the back of my head the music to *Jeopardy!* began to play.

'I saw it. I saw it coming,' Old Emma said finally. 'I warned her when she came for a visit that she was in danger. She didn't believe me, said she was happy. Said they was in love.' She said it with a pinched smile, clasped her gnarled hands in front of her heart, and twisted her upper body back and forth as if she were hugging something mockingly. She drew it out too, the word *love*, so it sounded like *la-ooove*.

'So you're saying it was serious?'

'I suppose you could call getting kilt pretty serious, don't you?' She laughed. It was a wet, crackly laugh, and I was pretty sure she was now openly making fun of me. Her face split into a mass of deep sun wrinkles.

'Her mother didn't mention it,' I said.

'Nuh-uh. She wouldn't.'

I waited, but it didn't appear more was forthcoming, so I stood and dug around in the pocket of my jeans until I found a twenty. 'Do you know the name of the person Anne was seeing? She show you a picture of him or anything?'

'Nuh-uh,' Emma said. 'But you been real close lately too.' Her voice was gravel.

'Close to what?'

Her eyes narrowed again. 'Same one got Anne.'

A gypsy's cackle tumbled out of her and turned into a cough so deep and damp it startled me. I dropped the twenty on the table and headed for the door. It was half off its hinges like everything else I'd seen of Emma's world. I looked back at the filthy ashtray, the tarot cards on the table in front of her, the long curtain she used as a backdrop, the cheap claret rug. She was looking right at me when my eyes reached her sun-worn face.

'You eat pussy too?' she asked, and the dry lips split into a stained smile.

Eeewww! Okay, Emma's crazy. I slipped through the screen door, went back outside where there was air and yard art and junk and cats. I was trembling, I realized, and annoyed that I'd let the half-packed old duffel bag get to me.

Emma pushed the door open behind me, flicked a cigarette into the sand, where it lay smoldering. Smoke, heavy in the wet air, burned my sinuses. She held up a card. It was the Hanged Man reversed.

'Your Mr Fancy Pants, he don't love you. He can't love nobody but himself. But the po-lice man do. He love you,' she said, and having given me my twenty dollars' worth, disappeared behind the screen.

Chapter Twenty-Nine

Coming home with little more than you left with is never a good feeling for an investigator. Two days and what did I know? Anne Chambers was shy and reserved, according to her former roommates. Didn't make friends easily, according to her mother. In a relationship, according to a crazy old card reader. Studied hard, according to her records. Had some talent as an artist. Nothing there to help develop a clearer picture of her habits and routines, hangouts, lovers. No one seemed to have known the girl. No visible links to the other victims and no evidence yet that she'd ever crossed paths with Charlie Ramsey. But it was there somewhere. I knew it was. The first murder was always a road map to the others. This had all started with Anne. We'd find out why.

I thought about the hack job that had been done on Dobbs in a rental car in Midtown Atlanta. Sexually mutilated. What did it mean? To our knowledge, Wishbone had not performed his terrible sexual surgery on a victim since Anne Chambers. And why would he use a vehicle on a residential street? Extremely high risk. He'd left fiber evidence for the first time. No bite marks. Part of Wishbone's delight in killing was taking time with them. *How does it feel?* So why dispatch Dobbs so efficiently? The shock value, perhaps. High-profile murder. Add sexual mutilation and the media goes nuts. Was it that simple? Had I so deeply misunderstood the needs of this violent predator? At times it felt as if there were two Wishbones.

I wanted to beat my head against something. A bottle of vodka would have been nice.

I pulled the Neon into a service station in Brunswick. My directions told me to take US 82 or Seventh Street East or Georgia 520 West or Corridor Z, which was also South Georgia Parkway. *Huh?*

I needed a way to Atlanta without I-75, which would put me in Macon for the afternoon rush. No thanks. Macon's highways hadn't caught up with Macon's population.

'Afternoon, ma'am.' The patch over his shirt pocket told me his name was Grady. The grease on his hands told me he was the mechanic, a meat-and-potatoes man with his sleeves rolled up and wavy brick-colored hair. He looked like a lot of the guys I'd known in high school.

He smiled, rested his forearms on my door, leaned in through my open window. I liked his eyes, soft and dark coffee brown with little gold flecks. 'Like me to fill it up for you?'

Would I ever.

'Check under the hood? Never seen you around here. Just passing through?'

'You taking a survey?' I asked.

'Yes, ma'am. In fact I am.' His tone was swampy and rich, the accent Coastal Georgia. 'However, in order to complete said survey, I'll need your address and phone number and a few hours of your time this evening.'

I leaned closer to him and smiled. 'Grady, honey, I'm at least ten years older than you are.'

His teeth were straight and very white, but the smile veered off to the left a little, imperfect and utterly adorable. 'Well, that may or may not be true, ma'am, but I assure you I'm plenty grown up.' He pulled away from the car. 'I'll give you a minute to think it over.'

He made sure I got a good look at his butt in tight, grease-stained jeans on his way to lift the hood. I didn't really need the oil checked, but it was an opportunity to further objectify Grady and, well, how often does that happen?

I stepped out of the car and showed Grady the driving directions

I'd used. He got a kick out of this and told me he could keep me out of Macon and save me forty miles.

'Hey, I haven't eaten any lunch. How 'bout you join me?' We were leaning against my car. 'I mean, since you did end up here and all. Who knows? Maybe the universe is sending you a message.' His leg touched mine a couple of times and I felt it all the way south back to Florida. 'I can't leave until closing time, but I got MoonPies and RC Cola right here.'

RC and MoonPies? It had been years. Two disks made of graham cracker crumbs pressed together like cake with marshmallow wedged in between like a sandwich, and a thin shell of icing. God! I'm only human. And I needed a distraction. 'Vanilla or chocolate?'

Grady grinned. He knew he had me. 'Both.'

There was a picnic table on the side of the station in a little patch of grass. Some shrubs had been planted next to a trellis so loaded with flowering jasmine you could barely see it. We unwrapped cellophane-covered MoonPies and bit into them, chased it with ice-cold bottles of RC Cola that Grady had pulled out of an old red Coca-Cola cooler, the kind that stands about waist high and is packed with ice. He popped open the tops with the opener on the front, and in the heat of that day, I don't think anything has ever tasted as cold or as sweet. It was hands down the most fun I'd had in a while. Grady told me he'd lived here all his life and only traveled as far as the Lowcountry in South Carolina, and I was beginning to see how this might happen. He loved his mama's fried chicken, had two sisters who beat the hell out of him growing up, talked about walking home from church knowing there would be homemade banana cream pie, a staple to this day, he said, at his parents' table on Sunday. He liked to dance, and if I'd stay, he promised to show me how much. He liked to kiss too, he told me, and wanted to know how I liked it. His gold-flecked brown eyes were steady on me. I liked his mouth too. And then he did it. He leaned over the table and pressed his lips to mine just as my cell phone played Rauser's ringtone.

Rats!

232

'Goddamn Buckhead waiter that served Brooks that night never showed,' Rauser said.

I looked at Grady and he looked back, a long, knowing look. He might be a small-town boy, but he was clearly aware of his own charm. And in the most unpretentious way. His hair in the midday sun was like fire. He folded his arms over his chest and I saw his shirtsleeves tighten against his biceps. Good *Lord*!

'Guy's illegal. Took off,' Rauser said. 'I think his employer knows where he is. I let him know we're not interested in the guy's green card or what the restaurant reports. I'm looking for a goddamn murderer here, for Christ's sake. Thinking about a public plea in case someone else saw Brooks out that night. What if he was out with some woman and the killer got to him later, after she left the hotel? Then she's still out there, the last person to see him alive, and she might know something. But there's family involved here, you know? I mean, his wife and kids, they're suffering already. I don't want to humiliate them. It's just gotta be a last resort. Hello? Street? Are you there?'

I glanced at Grady. His grin widened. 'I'm listening.'

'News channels are trying to help by running pictures of the rental car Dobbs was killed in, plate number, pictures of Dobbs. We're just hoping someone will step up and say they saw him somewhere. Doesn't anybody look up from their fucking BlackBerrys anymore? Where are you? I got stuff to tell you.'

'I'm on the way back. I wish I had more for you.' I looked at Grady. 'Rauser, let me call you back.'

'Somehow I'm getting the feeling I won't be able to complete that survey tonight,' Grady said. 'Shame too. You could have had all this.' He gestured like Vanna White to the service station and the parking lot, that big smile never fading.

'Rain check?' I asked. 'Reality just called.'

Grady walked me back to the car, opened the door for me, and gave me a formal bow. 'Real nice meetin' you, ma'am,' he said, and waved as I drove away.

I punched in Rauser's number. 'You okay?'

'Uh-huh, sure,' Rauser answered. 'Four homicides linked to Wishbone in this city. I'm doing just fine. And it's not like the other shit stops just 'cause we got a serial, you know? Had a guy walk into an equipment company this morning and shoot three people. We been showing Charlie's picture around and guess what? He looks familiar to everyone. Bastard rides around the city all day every day. He's so visible we can't make an ID stick, but I can connect Charlie to three of the victims now – Dobbs, Brooks, and Richardson – so we're slowly building our case.'

'Wow, that's huge, Rauser.'

'When will you be back? Can we just sit down and talk through some of this stuff?' I opened my mouth to answer, but Rauser said, 'Oh shit. Hang on, okay?'

I turned on Martin Luther King Jr. Boulevard and followed Grady's directions toward the four-lane. I thought about Grady's lips.

'Keye, I got something to tell you.' Rauser sounded calm now. Bad sign. He could get real still when things turned nasty. 'There was a bomb scare two hours ago at the Georgian. Plain package came in. No return address. No postage, nothing. Looked suspicious. Bomb squad took the call, got the package out of the hotel, secured it, and it didn't detonate. It wasn't a bomb. But it was addressed to you, Keye. And, well, there was a severed penis inside.'

I had to pull over.

Chapter Thirty

I arrived at my office the next morning and spent several hours putting together a file for Guzman, Smith, Aldridge & Haze, something Margaret Haze had asked me to prepare for her. Neil had helped gather the intelligence. He was a natural snoop.

Diane was sitting at her enormous kidney-shaped desk in the reception area outside Haze's office. Her short blond hair was perfectly highlighted and a little spiky, as always, and her makeup was impeccable. Diane was one of those people who could be experiencing a private storm in her life without anyone ever knowing it.

I, on the other hand, am not as good at disguising my problems.

'Okay, you're tired and something's wrong,' she said the moment she saw me.

I told her about the package that arrived at the Georgian and its terrible contents. I told her about Mirror Chang's heartbreaking telephone call to me. I told her about Charlie attacking me in my office, and then it all spilled out of me. How I'd trusted and even cared for him, how violent he'd been, the strange and deceptive life he led, his past, the clippings I'd found. The police interrogation. How Rauser had apparently linked him to three victims now. How I felt I'd failed by not sensing, not seeing something sick and devious about Charlie. Diane disagreed. She knew Charlie too and she could hardly believe it.

'So.' I forced a smile. I was ready to talk about something else. 'Tell me something about the new guy. Is it still serious?'

Diane laughed. 'Still serious, but did I mention I'm seeing a woman?'

'Um, no. You left that part out.' I had known Diane since we were kids. I never had an inkling she was attracted to women. It wasn't exactly like hearing that Michael Jackson had died, but it did prove that you absolutely never know who is going to pop out of the closet and shock the shit out of you. 'Why didn't you ever mention this?'

'It never came up,' Diane said, and I gave her an *oh sure* look. 'Seriously. I don't know what it is about her, but it's about *her*.'

'I don't know what to say. Do you say congratulations at a time like this?'

'That would be nice,' Diane said, smiling. She picked up the phone on her desk. 'Ms Haze, Keye Street is here for her appointment.'

'Well, then, congratulations.' I hugged her. 'Movie or pizza night soon, okay? So you can tell me all about her?'

'Sure,' Diane said with a nod, and turned her attention to the work on her desk.

I followed the hand-woven wool runners through the lush reception area to Margaret Haze's office, feeling guilty. Diane had wanted something from me. I just wasn't sure what. Or if I even had it to give at the moment.

Haze stood and shook my hand. Behind her, the view from her windowed wall meandered south and east over suburbs and stretched across the city. CNN Center and Philips Arena to the right, Stone Mountain dead ahead twenty-five miles, Midtown's towers on the left and I-75 heading north.

She was wearing Chanel pumps. Power shoes. I wanted them. With the light streaming in behind her, she was almost a silhouette. I'd rarely seen her in anything other than black. Everyone in Atlanta always seemed to be dressed for burgling.

I opened my briefcase and, once Margaret was seated, handed her everything I'd managed to dig up on the dead owner of Southern Towing, whose driver – Margaret's client – had shot twenty-three times and, according to Margaret, in self-defense.

'You were right,' I told her. 'He was a scary guy. Long record of assaults, jail time, three arrests, lots of bar fights. Friends and coworkers say he beat his wife, he beat his kids, and sometimes he knocked his drivers around. Most everyone I talked to was afraid of him. His wife admitted that he had a temper but denies the beatings. I gave you copies of the hospital records. Four visits to the emergency room in two years. Cops have been out there six times on domestic disturbance calls. The guy was a bully. If he was coming at me, I would have used my weapon too.'

'I wouldn't have taken the case if I believed my client was a murderer.'

'Uh-huh.'

Margaret smiled. 'Careful, Keye, your bias is showing. Did all that time at the FBI turn you against criminal defense attorneys?'

It was my turn to smile, but also a very good time to remain silent. Something my mother always said about knowing who butters your bread.

Margaret looked at me for a moment, a slight flicker in her eyes, playful, nothing aggressive, just reading me. She then went back to the information I'd given her – neatly printed with times and dates, names, addresses, and statements, copies of the victim's extensive criminal record, hospital records.

I waited while she read. I looked out the window, drank water, looked at the picture on her desk of her with her parents, and studied the artwork on her walls.

'Well, with his background, it shouldn't be difficult to prove that he was dangerous, that my client feared for his life,' she told me. 'Whether or not the judge will allow it is a different matter.' She was quiet for a moment, still reading. 'I'll need witness subpoenas on these people. Will you have any trouble serving them?'

'I don't think so. Most of them will jump at the chance to testify to his character. Or lack of character. Not a lot of people in the community mourning this man your client murdered. Um, shot.'

'Excellent. I'll have Diane call you once we've filed the paperwork.'

* * *

I was sitting outside the Starbucks at 100 Peachtree, the old Equitable building, watching pigeons compete for popcorn in Woodruff Park. Couriers and people with briefcases and telephones and serious expressions rushed by me. From the loading docks just around the corner, I heard shouted instructions and the distinctive sound a big truck makes when it's braking.

Rauser plopped down in one of the metal chairs in front of me. He was twenty minutes late, wearing a suit and a light blue tie, which he tugged at as he sat down.

'You look nice,' I said. 'Got a date?'

'With the press,' he answered. 'I'll be the one standing behind the chief keeping my mouth shut. We're expecting a major leak in a few minutes.'

I smiled. 'Amazing how these leaks happen.'

Rauser nodded. 'Worked a deal with Monica Roberts after she ambushed us in the garage. Called her from the Dobbs scene and offered her first dibs, promised I'd confirm the suspect's name and leak Charlie's mug shot to her if she'd dump the footage of me and you together.'

'Smart,' I said.

'It's not as self-serving as it sounds. Maybe someone else will recognize him and we can connect him to more of the victims. This is what we know. The courier firm he works for had both David Brooks and the other dead attorney, Elicia Richardson, on their client list. Their records show Charlie making several deliveries to each office. Courier companies all over serve these big law firms. We also found a self-storage warehouse near his town house where he leases a big unit, big enough for a car. Unit's empty but the fluid on the concrete tells us there was a vehicle in there recently. He's lost my guys a couple times now. We think he's ducking into this maze of little warehouses, leaving his bike and driving out. We have it under surveillance. And the DA finally found a judge that would issue a search warrant.'

'You searched Charlie's place?'

'Early this morning. Didn't find a damn thing we can use. Circumstantial is piling up, but we got no knife, no blood, no pictures. This guy's a murderer. We'll get him. The special delivery to the Georgian is at the lab. Already matched the blood type, so we know it was Dobbs's dick. *Jesus.*' I saw the pain in his face. 'What's left of the package is there too. Still hoping we can pull some DNA off it. I don't know how he's doing it, but we *will* get him.'

I touched his hand. 'I know.'

He looked at my drink, ignoring my hand. 'What's that?'

'Chai tea latte, iced.'

'Thought that was some kind of martial art.'

'That's tai chi,' I said, and smiled.

He took a long drink from my plastic cup without asking, then took a couple more gulps big enough to leave me with nothing but some milky ice. Then he burped and leaned back in the green metal chair, tipping the front legs off the ground.

'*What?*' he said.

'I don't even know why I like you sometimes,' I said. 'You're such a guy.'

He grinned at me and made some adjustments to his crotch area with enough flair so I had to notice.

'And mature too,' I added.

'So, what's up with Dan?' Rauser asked suddenly. 'You back together or what?'

'No, we are not back together nor will we ever be back together. He just wanted to get out of his apartment for a few days and figured he could use my place.'

'That why he's walking around naked while we're on the phone?'

'Oh my God, you're jealous? That's so cute.'

'Get real. I'm just trying to look after you a little. Traditionally, Dan hasn't been a good investment.' We were silent for a few moments. 'You know, I was in the station when we brought in the guy who killed his boss at the tow company,' he said. 'That's the case you've been working for Haze, right? His pupils were bugging out, smelled like booze. He emptied into him twenty-three times. It's gotta blow, working for the defense on a case like that.'

'Pays the bills,' I said. I didn't like thinking about it.

'That's why I wouldn't want to go private, you know? End up working for the bad guys most of the time. When I retire from this, that's it.'

'If I waited for an honest client, I wouldn't be able to buy the groceries.'

'That's my point,' Rauser said. 'And why I couldn't do it. So now that you know how little I got on Wishbone, tell me what you got.'

'I've been looking at the first victim.'

'Yep, I know. Anne Chambers.'

'I've been going through her journal, tracking down friends, people who signed her yearbooks, study partners, stuff like that.'

'And?'

'I've located most of them. Made a lot of notes. Her diary talks about seeing someone, but she didn't name names. I showed Charlie's picture to Anne's mother, but she didn't recognize him.' I handed him the file I'd put together. 'Maybe something will jump out at you. I think I've looked at it too much.'

'Maybe. Or maybe there's nothing there.'

I shook my head. 'There are answers there. In her life. I'm certain of it. I just can't see them. You want to get an arrest and conviction, find Charlie's connection to Florida.'

'May not be an issue if we connect him to any more victims up here.'

'Promise you'll look anyway?'

Rauser smiled at me and his gray eyes were clear as rainwater. 'I promise. I'll take it home with me and have a look before I crash, okay? Look, nobody wants cold cases open. The families never really get peace until we close.'

We were quiet for another minute, watching the pigeons, thinking about the dead. Rauser drank milky liquid from the melting ice in my cup.

'I met an old lady who lived near Anne and her parents down on Jekyll Island. Her mom said they used to hang out. A card reader.'

'She tell your fortune?' Rauser snickered.

'Not exactly. Well, sort of.' I flushed, suddenly embarrassed, remembering what she'd said. *The po-lice man . . . love you.*

Rauser was smiling at me, waiting. 'And?'

'She said the last time Anne came to see her, she warned her that she was in danger.'

'Be easy to say now.'

'Be easy to say anything now.'

'You believe it?'

'No. I mean, I don't know. Really weird old lady, but I swear she knows things. She actually brought up Dan. She called him Mr Fancy Pants, but—'

'That's him.' Rauser laughed.

'She also said she felt the same vibe around me, which was pretty eerie given the whole car-wreck-hospital-stalking-bomb thing. But then she had said something about eating pussy, so I decided maybe she was just nuts.'

Rauser was nodding his head at me seriously and with absolutely no sincerity at all. He was fighting back a laugh and I knew it.

'It's a long story,' I said lamely.

He picked up the plastic cup he'd already drained and started eating the ice. 'She say you're a closet case too?'

I rolled my eyes. 'What is this obsession you have with my sexuality?'

'You're flattered. Might as well admit it.'

I thought about something Grady had told me while we ate MoonPies at the service station. 'Did you know that on New Year's Eve in Brunswick, Georgia, they drop a big ole papier-mâché shrimp into a huge vat of cocktail sauce?'

Rauser just looked at me.

'It's their version of the ball in Times Square.'

'Yeah, so?'

'Don't you find that odd?'

'I find it odd that you give a shit,' Rauser said.

'It's just very weird. Don't you think it's weird?'

'What are they supposed to drop it into?'

'I think you're missing the point.'

'Tartar sauce?'

I gestured to my empty cup. 'Why don't you go get us a couple of those since you drank all mine?'

Rauser blew out air like cigarette smoke and said, 'Ha! They oughta call this place Fivebucks instead of Starbucks. Besides, I am not standing up there ordering some pansy shit like that. Especially if I gotta say *latte* after it.'

I stood and slugged his shoulder hard on the way to the counter inside. 'I'll get it myself. You're such a dick sometimes, Rauser.'

He flashed his grin up at me. 'Bring me one too, okay? Lots of ice.'

Chapter Thirty-One

White Trash met me at the door, brushed up against my legs, looked up at me squinty eyed, and began herding me toward the kitchen. In her fantasies, I fully believed, White Trash was a border collie, obsessively tending her herd, keeping everything in a tight little circle. Her meager belongings – catnip mice and a catnip pillow, a ball – she leaves neatly under the table when she's done playing, and when she had occasion to encounter a helium balloon in the house on my birthday, she spent days pulling it by the string each time it drifted away and carefully stashing it back under the table. I indulge her. It's easier this way. She's very focused. There would be no rest until she had what she wanted.

I dutifully removed a slice of deli turkey from a bag in the fridge, tore it into little pieces for her, then leaned against the counter with a can of Reddi-wip and tilted it into my mouth. That couldn't have been more than a serving, I thought, reading the can for serving size. Two tablespoons. Hmmm. I did it a few more times. White Trash showed some interest in what I was eating, so I squirted a little on her plate. She tried it, liked it, stretched, and left me there in the kitchen, used and alone.

It was Thursday morning, five days since Jacob Dobbs died, and I was back in my office by eight after sleeping hard and entirely without dreams. I checked my voice-mail messages. Tyrone from Tyrone's Quikbail: '*Hey, baby. An absconder done absconded on me. Need you to haul his butt in. No big thing. A kid about twenty. Failed to appear on a DUI.*'

243

Diane left a message. *'Hey, you, witness subpoenas are ready on my desk. Seven of them. Cha-ching. You're buying dinner next time.'*

My mother called and extracted a promise out of me for dinner Saturday night. Saturday nights was homemade potpie, sliced tomatoes, mustard greens, and banana cheesecake. The only variations in this menu were seasonal, when we might have spinach or kale instead of mustard greens.

Before we hung up, she said, 'I know this is none of my business.'

Uh-oh. When Mother began a sentence that way, no telling what was coming next.

'Dan made some mistakes, Keye, but that's just the way men are. I spent some time with him after you left for your trip and we had a lovely talk. He loves you.'

'I'm bringing Rauser with me,' I said, astonishing myself. *Ha, take that.* She wouldn't push the Dan thing with Rauser there at Saturday dinner. She was unsure of our relationship. Hell, everyone was unsure of our relationship. Rauser had acted as protection against my mother's matchmaking many times.

I returned Tyrone's call and arranged to swing by to pick up the paperwork. It was a small job, not a lot of money, but it was important to be available to Tyrone now and then or he'd write me off, and I never knew when I might need the work. The law firms paid well, especially Guzman, Smith, Aldridge & Haze, but it was a competitive business and I could hear my daddy saying something about all the eggs in one basket. I still had a king-size mortgage to think about every month. I try not to burn bridges, no matter how small.

My mind drifted back to my trip to Jekyll. I thought about the water and the pure salt air and my heart lurched a little. I wanted that, wanted to walk the beach, adopt a dog, buy an old truck, maybe even introduce White Trash to sand crabs. How could I make a living down there? How could I leave Diane and Neil and Rauser? I let that movie play in my head for a few moments. Then I thought about Mrs Chambers living there in that beautiful spot, about her pain all these years. I thought about mine. It changes and dulls a little, but you never live without it once someone you love has been murdered.

Tyrone's Quikbail is in the 300 block of Mitchell Street, only a couple of blocks from the capitol, city hall, and the courthouses, on the fifth floor of a steadily declining yellow stucco building. There were at least a dozen more bail bond companies within the surrounding blocks. My personal favorite is Mama's Gonna Get You Free Bail Bonds & More, off Memorial Drive.

I took the stairs. I'd been in the elevator here before – fingerprints all over the buttons and filthy carpeting and the feeling of not wanting to touch anything. The stairway smelled like pee, but at least I knew I'd make it upstairs, something that was always in question with the elevator, which groaned at the slightest provocation. What if I was the last little bit of weight it could bear? I'd already had three Krispy Kremes today. What I like in an elevator is no element of surprise.

The outer lobby in Tyrone's office was quiet, the secretary's desk unmanned but neatly arranged. I'd seen lots of different faces at that desk. Tyrone used a temp service a couple of days a week.

'Yo, Keye. What up?' He was wearing a lemon yellow blazer over a red silk shirt. When he leaned back from whatever he'd been reading and crossed an ankle over his knee, I saw that his pants matched the jacket and his socks matched his shirt. In contrast to the drab offices, he was like a flare in a desk chair, a bright and shining light. Tyrone was six-four, with a strong jaw, square weightlifter's shoulders, and dimples when he smiled. I thought he was pretty. So did he.

'You gonna get the kid for me?'

I shrugged. 'What's it pay?'

'Come on now.' He laughed and dimples broke out everywhere. 'Don't do me like that.' He lifted a manila envelope up off his desk and held it out. 'Kid's name is Harrison. You take this and I'll make sure you get a good one next time.'

Lyndon Harrison had been pulled over on I-75 inside the Fulton

County line, the file said. He had agreed to a breath test, which put him just over the legal limit for alcohol. He'd behaved badly when the officer told him he'd have to go to the station, and the cop had promptly added resisting arrest to the DUI charge. His mother had put up her house to guarantee the bail. The house would have been quite a return for Tyrone on a six-thousand-dollar guarantee, but he wasn't that kind of guy, he told me, and grinned.

I took Mitchell Street to Capital Avenue, got over on Dekalb Avenue near Grady Hospital and drove east toward the Oakhurst section of Decatur. Oakhurst had once been a run-down area of shut-ins and crackheads, dealer infested and dangerous. In the last few years it had been undergoing a sort of face-lift. The combination of urban sprawl and soaring property values in Atlanta and Decatur, which now meet at several points, had changed the life of many longtime Oakhurst residents. Tiny frame houses on quarter-acre lots were suddenly worth hundreds of thousands, and residents began putting up For Sale signs in their yards. Gradually these neighborhoods were being renovated or razed. Still, some of the old residents stayed, so it was not uncommon to see renovated homes with towering additions and privacy fences next door to a weather-beaten shack in stunning disrepair.

The Harrison home was on Winter Avenue near the East Lake MARTA station, a little white brick with black shutters and a pampered square of green lawn. Lavender plants bloomed under the front windows and gerber daisies had been planted around the mailbox. A golden retriever spotted me through the front window when I rang the bell, and barked ferociously, but his entire body was wagging.

The boy who answered the door looked eighteen at the most. He didn't fit the picture I had of Lyndon Harrison, the bail jumper. I could smell pot smoke through the screen.

'Hi,' I said. 'Is Lyndon around?'

He smiled. 'Hang on, okay?'

'Okay,' I said, and as soon as he disappeared, I let myself into a small slate foyer with a coatrack and a mirror and a golden retriever who nuzzled my hand until I consented to giving him some attention. I knelt down next to him and rubbed his ears.

'Can I help you?' a male voice asked.

'Hi, Lyndon,' I said in the most non-threatening tone I could come up with. As I stood, my left hand moved to my back pocket, where I had a pair of cuffs. 'My name's Keye Street.' I held out my right hand to Harrison, but he didn't take it.

'Yeah, so?'

Lyndon Harrison was tall with the wire-thin body of a boy who hadn't quite begun to fill out the frame he'd sprouted. I smiled. I was still hoping he was going to play nice, but the sour expression on his face said otherwise.

'I was just wondering if maybe you forgot your court date.'

'Who the fuck are you?' he demanded, and the kid who had opened the door stepped into the room.

'What's wrong, baby?' he asked, and leaned his head on Lyndon's shoulder.

'She's trying to take me to court,' Lyndon whined, and wrapped an arm around the boy's waist. His eyes were very blue and bloodshot. His hair was white blond on the tips and he was wearing baggy blue jeans with the crotch nearly to his knees and a rope for a belt – Old Navy on pot.

'You're taking him to jail?' the boyfriend wanted to know. His eyes were bright – someone who appreciated a good drama, I could see.

I shook my head. 'He just needs to come down to the office with me so we can make up a new agreement and reschedule some stuff.'

Not.

'I don't feel like doing that today,' Harrison announced.

Oh boy.

'Your mom put up her house for you,' I reminded him. 'You know that she could lose it?'

He looked down at me as if I was the most pathetically boring human on earth. 'I'll do it tomorrow,' he said with a lazy blink, and turned away.

I grabbed his right wrist and clamped the cuffs on, and when he spun around, I got them on the other wrist. 'Sorry, but tomorrow just doesn't work for my schedule.'

'Who *are* you?'

'Bond enforcement,' I answered. 'Let's go.'

'*Cool*,' gushed the boyfriend as I pushed Lyndon out the door.

'Can Clifford go with us?' Lyndon wanted to know. We were heading down the sidewalk with his boyfriend and the dog trailing behind us toward my car parked curbside.

'Can't your boyfriend take care of him?'

Lyndon sneered. 'Clifford *is* my boyfriend. *Duh!*'

I opened the passenger door and helped him into the front seat, ran the seat belt through the cuff chain, and buckled him in just in case he had any bright ideas about a quick exit. 'What's the dog's name? John?' I asked.

'You're a total buzzkill.' Lyndon pouted.

In the rearview, I saw Clifford and the dog standing in the center of the oak-lined street. Clifford gave a little wave with his fingers as we pulled away.

Honey, I'm home.

The voice was loud enough to travel over the polished hardwood and through the quiet Morningside house. Setting the briefcase on the table next to the door in the foyer, the killer opened it and slipped into a skintight pair of surgical gloves. A four-inch fishing knife slid easily out of an unsnapped compartment.

How was your day?

The question was delivered loudly but pleasantly, standing at the refrigerator with the door open, a fresh bottle of water in one hand, searching for a snack. Really long day. No time to eat, to do anything. The intruder stomped on the kitchen floor a few times, hard enough and loud enough to be heard downstairs.

Why so quiet? Still mad about last night?

Something stirred. A fat cat was standing at the kitchen door watching the stranger he knew only from the street outside. He opened his mouth and a tiny squeak came out, nothing more.

Where have you been hiding?

The stranger knelt, peeled off a glove, and held out the back of one hand. The cat didn't hesitate, just walked right over and bumped into it.

Do you have food and water? Let's get you fixed up. And then I'll take care of your mother, your needy mother, your silly, stupid, needy fucking mother.

The killer sat at the kitchen table, drank the bottled water, sliced off a few pieces of sharp white cheddar, tried to shake off the day, relax a little while watching the gray tabby crunching dry food.

I'm so sorry to have to leave you alone, buddy, but I have so much to do. So many people are waiting. Time to deliver.

Melissa Dumas was bound to an old straight-back chair in the partially finished basement, where the washer and drier and all the yard tools were stored. She had been dragged down the hard steps by her hair a day ago, barely conscious, head bumping against each step, moaning quietly. She couldn't have known how many times she'd been stabbed, because she had faded in and out after the second wound. She had begged for water and received only a few drops, just enough to keep her alive.

Her eyes half opened at a sound. What she must have seen surely would have startled her – the intruder was standing in front of her wearing only a paper bonnet and booties and surgical gloves.

Do you know how long you've been here? Can you understand me? What does it feel like? Can you hear me? HOW DOES IT FEEL?

Melissa's head drooped downward and the killer tilted her chin upward, looked into her eyes and smiled gently. The smile was genuine, not meant to be taunting or malicious. A certain love for them sometimes developed during their time together, love for what they'd given of themselves, for the hours and the patience.

So tired, you poor baby. Don't worry. I fed your kitty.

A sigh, a twinge of regret. Not for what had happened there. Not for what was about to happen, but because it was nearly over.

Ah well, time to move on. Time to make my marks. Time to clean the scene.

Chapter Thirty-Two

'It's full pay plus expenses,' Larry Quinn told me. There was a hollow sound followed by dead space between words that let me know I was on a speakerphone. I glanced at Neil, who was leaning back in his chair with his feet propped up. I switched to speaker so Neil could eavesdrop. 'But you'll have to head up to Ellijay,' Quinn said.

Ellijay. Rural North Georgia. Yikes! Dueling banjos and Ned Beatty on all fours sprinted through my brain. But I needed the money and, truthfully, I was happy to have a reason to get back out of town. For one, I'd miss dinner with the parents Saturday night. And I thought about finding the picture at Charlie's place and what he'd written over my face. *Lying bitch.* I thought about the gruesome package that had been sent to me at the Georgian. So far the press hadn't connected me to the Dobbs murder, but it wouldn't be long.

'It's pretty up there,' Quinn continued. 'Be cooler. We'll get you a nice little cabin. You available?'

'What's the job?'

'Well, it's sort of a missing persons,' he said, and I heard someone in the background start to snicker.

'Uh-*huh.*'

'Actually, it's a missing cow,' Quinn said. Giggles erupted from somewhere in his office.

Oh boy.

'It's a cow case,' he added, and unsuppressed laughter broke out.

This got Neil's attention. He grinned at me and wandered into my office.

'Just one cow?' I asked, and winked at Neil. 'Or a whole herd of cows?'

This plunged them into hysterics. 'I'm sorry, Keye,' Larry said. 'It's our first cow case. Give me a minute.' Unrestrained laughter now complete with snorting sounds.

I looked at Neil and rolled my eyes.

Quinn said, 'Okay, sorry about that. A client in Ellijay owns some property and the family cow disappeared. The client asked us to find someone to find the cow, and you're our go-to girl.'

'I'm flattered,' I said. 'The cow's a pet?'

'Yep,' Quinn managed between sniffles and moans. I thought he might have actually been crying. 'Sadie the pet cow,' he said, and in the background his office became completely unhinged.

My cell phone played Rauser's ringtone. 'Larry, can I think about this for a minute and call you back?'

'Déjà moo,' Quinn said, and Neil finally lost it.

'Looks like we got another one,' Rauser told me. His voice was worn thin and weary. 'Housekeeper found her in the basement when she went down to do the laundry.'

'Oh, Rauser,' I said.

'Signature's there, scene staging, stabbing, wire, bite marks. As soon as we ran her name through the system, it came up that she had a lawsuit at Fulton. Discrimination, sexual harassment. Hefty settlement from an employer. Her name's Melissa Dumas. She had been restrained in a chair, stabbed repeatedly on the front of the body, moved to the floor and stabbed postmortem another dozen times on the back of the body. No weapons at the scene. ME thinks the injuries to the front of the body were sustained twelve to fifteen hours before she died.'

I let that fresh horror sink in. 'He really took some time with her,' I said, more to myself than to Rauser. 'Jesus.'

'Her wounds were sustained at different times. I think he came and went a couple times. Sadistic bastard let her suffer. I just keep thinking how scared she must have been down there in that basement waiting for him to come back. People next door couldn't remember anything about this girl except that they'd seen her jogging. They didn't even know her name. Keye, she'd lived there four years and they didn't fucking know her name.'

'Any evidence of sexual activity? Was there penetration? Or sexual mutilation?' I thought about Anne Chambers, about the crime scene photos I'd pored over of her bloodied dorm room. I thought about Jacob Dobbs, castrated in an automobile. 'Do we know where Charlie was when she died?'

'Charlie gave my guys the slip twice. I'm betting timeframes are consistent with what the ME's laid out. Did I tell you there was a cat in the house? Extra food and water bowls put out for it.'

'He wanted to make sure the cat was okay until somebody got there.' I sucked in air. I remembered Charlie bringing into my office a tiny orange kitten he'd found wandering. He'd held it close to his chest and waited for my mother to pick it up and take it to a foster home.

'Chief's talking about inviting the FBI in to help.'

Local cops hate federal interference. Rauser's department had a certain rhythm. They knew and loved the community. It was their investigation. This wasn't just another murder, for Rauser. I knew him. It was another murder *he* hadn't been able to prevent, another failure, another family torn apart. And now more shrieking headlines, more calls for the police to solve these murders. I wondered how many calls had bombarded APD after Charlie's mug shot was released, adding to the load this task force was carrying and Rauser's stress.

'I can be there in ten minutes,' I told him.

'I don't want you at the crime scene, Street. He's targeted you already. He could do it again.'

'I'm sorry, Rauser,' I said uselessly. I didn't know how to help him. My involvement seemed to only up the pressure on him. He was in trouble with his superiors and with the community and public opinion. And he was worried about my safety with Charlie still on the loose.

That cabin in Ellijay was sounding really good.

Chapter Thirty-Three

Georgia is a study in climate and backdrops, from the damp Low Country at the southeastern tip to the northern mountains reaching high enough to catch the winter snows before they turn to rain on the way south to Atlanta. Central Georgia is lush with kudzu and tall pine forests. I-75 runs for 355 miles from the swampy south and fresh seafood, past produce stands and cotton fields, country-cooking restaurants with homemade peach cobbler, truck stops and Waffle Houses, through Perry and Macon, until it merges briefly with I-85 and evolves into the Downtown Connector, Atlanta's main artery, then splits off again and weaves through the textile-mill mountain towns of North Georgia toward Dalton, the carpet capital of the world.

I exited I-75 just north of Marietta and headed toward Ellijay and Blairsville in the Neon, knowing I'd have to cut off the air conditioner if I wanted enough power to climb the hills that were coming. My Impala had been moved from the crime lab to a repair shop but still wasn't ready. Dad had taken charge of the body-shop details and I had a feeling he was armor-plating it.

It was Friday and warm, and it suddenly occurred to me I'd forgotten to cancel dinner tomorrow night with my parents. I picked up my phone and took a deep breath.

'What do you mean you can't come?' my mother wanted to know. 'You're not off on another wild-goose chase, are you?'

I hesitated and Mother, righteous as ever, leapt in. 'Oh, for heaven's sake, is this *dangerous*?'

I sighed. 'I'm looking for a cow, Mom. Unless she's packing, I think I'll be okay.'

'A *cow*! My Lord, Keye, that's not what we sent you to school for.'

'Tell me about it.'

'I made banana cheesecake with a special pecan crust.' Mother was a ruthless negotiator.

'Will you go by and check on White Trash this weekend?' I thought of Melissa Dumas's cat and the killer who'd left food out for it.

'Snowflake should just come and live with me and your father. Poor little thing—'

I crinkled the wrapper from the powdered doughnut gems I'd had for lunch into the phone. 'Mom? Mom? We're breaking up. I'll talk to you later.'

My first afternoon on the cow trail was uneventful, something that may or may not be a good thing when searching for farm animals. I did have an opportunity to meet Jim Penland, the man with the missing cow, and he seemed perfectly normal, a big friendly guy with a good crop of hair, brown eyes, and Wranglers. He owned about a bazillion acres of land and the largest apple orchards in the region. Gilmer County was some kind of apple-growing capital, something the folks up here take seriously, and first thing, Big Jim took me over to one of his retail locations, a tourist trap set up on the four-lane, which is what they call the highway up here, and treated me to homemade fried pies with two scoops of cinnamon ice cream.

'My *God*,' I said after my first bite. My toes might have curled up a little.

'Good, ain't they?' Big Jim was smiling at me. 'Almost nothing like a pie made right in front of you with good fresh apples and homemade ice cream.'

'It's unreal.' One of these every day and I'd never need sex again ... ever.

Big Jim had already finished his first fried pie and was working on the second. Steam was still coming off it and the ice cream was turning into sugary goo. We were sitting at a picnic table on the porch of Big Jim's log-cabin-style store. Tourists came in and left with hot pies in oil-stained brown paper bags and jars of homemade jam.

'So, what's your plan?'

Plan? I looked at him blankly for a moment. 'Oh, to find the cow, you mean.'

'Sadie,' he said.

'Right. Sadie. Well, I thought I'd just start by asking around, you know? Neighbors, employees, anyone known to be in the area when Sadie disappeared. Anything you can tell me that might help?'

'Sadie's a real sweet girl. We've had her four years. One day she just come out of the pasture and started hanging around outside the house. Couldn't keep her in a gate. She can open about anything. Came home one day and found her in the kitchen eatin' spaghetti napkins out of the trash. Nuzzled my little girl's face and that was it. We built her a small place nearer the house and she'd just trail around behind us all the time like a dog. Best dog we ever had, really.'

'So you just came home one day and she was gone or what?' I started on my second pie.

Big Jim nodded. 'Pretty much. I'd been up at the orchards most of the day. My daughter was off with a friend, and my wife, she was up here helping out at the counter when somebody didn't show up for work. Drove up and Sadie didn't come out to meet the truck. Knew right then something wasn't right.'

'And how long ago was that?'

'Last Tuesday. We done all the things you do when you lose a pet. Put up flyers, ran an ad in the paper, offered a reward. Truth is, we're all just broken up about it.'

'Does Sadie have a history of roaming at all?'

'Once we stopped trying to lock her in the pasture, she stuck like glue. She never liked being fenced in. After that, she never left the yard unless she was following one of us.'

'Any enemies?' I asked, and took the last bite of my second pie.

'Nope. Everyone liked Sadie,' Big Jim said, and grinned at me.

'Course *I* got enemies. I'm the richest sonofabitch in the county.'

'You make a list of them for me?'

'Ones I know about, I will,' Big Jim agreed cheerfully.

I spent the rest of the afternoon talking to Big Jim's wife, Selma, Big Jim's daughter, Kathie, and a few of Big Jim's employees. They all seemed to love Sadie the cow, but few had vivid recollections of when and where they had last seen her. One of them told me they had all searched the property and the woods while Kathie was gone in case Sadie had gotten sick and wandered off to die, but found nothing.

I drove a couple of miles up Blackberry Mountain Road and found the cabin Larry Quinn's office had arranged for me. I was sleepy and full of bad pie carbs and I didn't know what else to do until Big Jim finished his enemy list. A nap sounded good, I decided. Can't do that at home. Not ever. There's always something pulling at me, something that needs my attention.

There were three cabins on the property. The owners came out of the largest cabin and met me in a gravel patch next to the barn where an SUV and a Harley-Davidson were parked. 'Howdy. I'm Pat Smelly and this is Chris. You must be Keye.'

The Smellys? Really? I didn't say anything, but I wanted to. Chris was in pastel short shorts; the kind really large women should not wear and always seem to. Pat was in jeans with her hands dug deep in her pockets, skinny and butch with shoulders like a coat hanger and a handshake that nearly brought me to my knees.

'Should be everything you need in the cabin,' Pat told me. Her accent was anything but southern. The twang was distinctive, with that odd, almost Canadian rhythm. I guessed her for Minnesota. 'You're in that little one-bedroom loft over there. It's small but it's got a nice deck over the pond. Coffee beans are in the freezer and there's a grinder on the counter. You need anything else just let us know. Chris made some apple bread this afternoon and put it over there for you, and we just got Dish, so you can watch movies if you want.'

'Wow, thanks.' *Mmm, apple bread.*

THE STRANGER YOU SEEK

'Need help with your bags?'

I shook my head. 'I'm good, thanks. All I need is the key and a phone.'

'Door's unlocked. Key's on the table. Don't have phones up here. Sorry,' Pat said, and took Chris's hand.

No phones?

I watched them disappear back into their cabin. *Lesbians in rural Georgia? Who knew?*

An hour later I was balancing carefully on the deck railing, leaning as far forward as possible, the flat of one hand using the tin overhang on the tiny deck of my cabin as a brace, the other hand holding my cell phone toward the sky. I was trying not to look down. It was a thirty-foot drop to a slimy pond.

'Keye?'

I wobbled and nearly lost my footing. Pat and Chris Smelly were standing behind me with concerned looks on their faces.

'*Jesus,* wear a bell or something. You scared me.'

Pat gave an aw shucks shrug. 'I don't think it's a good idea for you to be up there like that. I don't think that's safe.' Chris nodded her agreement.

'I can't get a signal anywhere else. Do you always just walk in?'

'We knocked, but you couldn't hear us.' They looked at each other. Chris giggled, then covered her mouth. Pat held out a hand. 'We saw you from our place and thought maybe you were in some trouble up here. You can get a signal from our roof. And we got some lawn furniture up there.'

'Really?' I took her hand and climbed off the railing.

'We made it flat so we could enjoy the view of the mountains.'

'It's like having an extra room.' It was the first time Chris had formed a complete sentence in my presence, and it was deeply southern. 'It's our little terrace in the pines.'

'I don't want to be a lot of trouble,' I said as we walked through the cabin and toward the front door. 'Apple bread is really good,' I told Chris. I was embarrassed that I'd eaten half of it already. It was

259

on the kitchen table, and since the cabin consisted only of two rooms downstairs, we had to walk right past it. I wondered if they had noticed.

'Bread's my specialty,' Chris said, which came as no great surprise to me given the size of her ass.

The cabin I'd been assigned was furnished with gnarled-up raw wood chairs, an ancient futon, and lots of folksy chicken art. But the Smelly cabin had slate floors and a vaulted ceiling, stark modern furniture in a bright wide-open space, linen and leather, a towering A-frame glass wall that looked out at the Blue Ridge Mountains – *Architectural Digest* in the sticks. A basset hound and a tuxedo cat lay in front of the glass on a zebra rug. They paid me no attention at all.

'We did all the work ourselves. Bought the land about ten years ago, when you could still get it for a song,' Pat told me. 'Pretty much pays for itself now and we just hang out.'

She opened a door and we climbed a narrow pine staircase, then went through another door that opened onto a rooftop crammed with plants and a gas grill, Japanese lanterns and two chaise longues, an outdoor daybed, all in a deep espresso. Somebody has a West Elm catalog, I thought.

'We'll give you some privacy,' Chris said, and they left me standing on their roof with my cell phone.

Rauser answered on the second ring. 'Hey, you. Get my message?'

'No. I can't get a signal up here.'

'Where's up here?'

'Ellijay. Um. A missing-cow case,' I said, and laughed. 'My first, by the way. My mother is so proud. I'm on the Smellys' roof right now, which might take some explaining.'

'You know, I really want to ask,' Rauser said with a grin in his voice.

'I'll fill you in when I get home. How's it going?' I almost didn't want to know. Atlanta, the murders, at least for this one afternoon, seemed far away.

'The mayor's screaming. The press is screaming, and Charlie Ramsey's one slippery bastard. I told you he lost my teams a couple times. And my detectives are no dumbasses. The timeframes fit with when he started fucking with Melissa Dumas twelve to fifteen hours before he actually killed her. And if the ME's right on time of death for Dobbs, it's consistent too. We thought Charlie was inside sleeping before we picked him up the first time, but he must have slipped out.'

I thought about that day we'd left the station after Charlie's first interview with Rauser and the possible dead body call that came over Rauser's radio. Charlie must have known while he was sitting there being his goofy innocent self in the interrogation room that the call was going to come in any minute, that Dobbs's dead, mutilated body was baking in a hot, bloody car on Eighth Avenue. I closed my eyes. The killing no longer seemed so distant.

'You figure out how Charlie's losing you?'

'Uh-huh,' Rauser said. 'It was that self-storage warehouse. We set a honey trap for him, got the unit next to his and wired Bevins, put her in a wife beater and short shorts and an old car filled up with thrift-store crap.' Detective Linda Bevins was blond and curvy, a little wide eyed, the kind of woman guys really go for, the kind of woman guys usually underestimate. 'Charlie pedaled by a couple times on his bike, then went for it. Offered her help unloading. Bevins put some of the bait out, mentioned she was in a legal thing with a boss that had fired her. She played it, didn't push, waited for Charlie to ask the questions. I told her to say she had another load, so he'd know she was coming back and he could make his move. He was getting pretty comfortable, then he spotted a goddamn Salvation Army price tag on a lamp, and he put it together pretty fast. Threw the lamp down and rode off.' I heard Rauser hit his cigarette. 'Here's the good news: we finally got someone that recognized Charlie's mug on TV. Says he raped her. She had a rape kit done after the event, but no one was able to pull in a viable suspect. And Balaki's following up on another call. Same deal. Six weeks ago. This woman claims her attacker had a knife. If it pans out, I'll have him in custody by morning, and he'll have to submit to DNA testing for the rapes. Then I can get his ass off the streets while we build the Wishbone case.'

'That's huge!' I said, and thought about the day Charlie had grabbed me, the language he had used, sexual and angry. I'd worked serial rapist cases at the Bureau. Some of them started as peepers, then escalated as they began to fully realize their violent fantasies. 'Can you put him in Florida?'

'No. Not yet.'

'You're a good cop, Rauser. I wouldn't want to be the bad guy.'

Rauser's strategy with compliments was to deflect rather than accept. 'Tell me about the Smellys,' he said.

'They own the cabins where Quinn booked me. Nice. Well, *their* cabin is nice, anyway. Mine has a lot of embroidered framed roosters. Why do people do this to cabins? I mean, what is it about a chicken that makes you think cabin-in-the-woods? I just don't get it.'

'Yeah,' Rauser said. 'I think antlers and shit like that more than chickens.'

I laughed. 'Well, they're very nice people. They're letting me use their roof to talk to you because this wall of mountains is blocking my reception.'

'Straight couple?'

'Gay women. Why?'

'Have you noticed the lesbian thing is a continuing theme in your life?'

'In *your* life,' I told him. 'It's all you think about. What is it exactly with the two-women fantasy thing and guys? I don't get that either. It's not like that with women. Just so you know. We don't fantasize about men doing it.' I sank down into one of the Smellys' espresso-colored lounge chairs. It was just after sundown, and the stars seemed so close here in the mountains, away from the city lights. 'Okay, I take that back. We do think about it, but only if they're underage and you can bounce a quarter off their rear ends.'

'So are these real lesbians or just women you think are hitting on you?'

'They live together and hold hands and everything. And I'm sure they *would* hit on me. They're just obviously in love.'

'And we're monogamous,' Pat said from behind me. She had a cup of something hot in her hand. Steam was rising off it.

'And they're monogamous,' I repeated, and smiled at her, trying not to look as embarrassed as I felt.

'And what about the cow?'

I took the steaming mug from Pat. It smelled like herbal tea, minty and sweet. 'Long story.'

Rauser chuckled. 'I'll call you tomorrow, Street. Try to stay out of trouble until then.'

I closed my phone and looked up at Pat. 'I know how that must have sounded, but it's just this friend of mine who teases me because he thinks that I think women always want me, when, in fact, I don't think that at all, really. Just this waitress at Hooters and the forensic scientist he's sleeping with. Most women don't even *like* me, actually. And I don't really know any lesbians, although my best friend is sleeping with one, and Atlanta has about a million. And *Decatur*. Oh my God. Have you ever been to Decatur? It's, like, dyke central, perfect little short haircuts and athletic shoes.'

Pat was staring at me.

'I'm making it worse, aren't I?'

'Enjoy your tea. Chris made it with mint from the garden.' She paused and seemed to choose her next words carefully. 'Ever consider that if your friend's sleeping with a lesbian, she may be a lesbian?'

I shook my head and smiled. 'Absolutely not.'

Chapter Thirty-Four

I met Big Jim at Penland's Fried Pies and Gifts. He plopped down coffee for us both in monogrammed mugs and fried apple pies with ice cream. There were a few small tables and chairs near a stone fireplace inside, and Big Jim straddled a chair and smiled at me.

'They're best for breakfast,' he said. I had no problem with that. I'd been obsessing about the pie since I'd had my first two. 'Here's the list you wanted. Competitors mostly. And a few people I may have crossed lately.'

I took a bite of pie and ice cream, washed it down with some coffee, and picked up the paper he'd put between us. It was a long list. 'I didn't realize Ellijay was this big.'

'Well, I guess I have a particular way of offending folks round here.'

'You seem like a nice guy to me,' I said.

'Yeah, but you're kind of a pushover. It's all about the pie for you.'

I smiled. I liked Big Jim. 'You bring a picture of Sadie too?'

He nodded and pulled a wallet-size photo out of his denim shirt pocket.

'Nice-looking cow,' I said as if I had a clue. Big Jim's eyes got wet and he had to look away.

I started at the Cupboard Restaurant in downtown Ellijay. It was large and open, with vinyl booths and the look of a cafeteria. I was taken to a small booth to wait for Ida May Culpepper, the first person on Big Jim's list.

Two waitresses worked the room, both middle aged and friendly, both knew their customers by their first names. I glanced at the menu and saw chicken and dumplings, collard greens with pepper vinegar, fried chicken livers, and lots of apple products – apple pancakes, apple bread, apple pie, apple cake, fried apples, apple salads.

'Here ya go, hon,' one of the waitresses said to me. The thick white plate she set in front of me had a huge slice of apple pie. 'Want some coffee with that?'

'Oh no, I couldn't. I'm just waiting for Ida May.'

'Can't nobody sit at the Cupboard and not eat. How would that look? Pie's on the house. Ida May will be with you shortly.'

Ida May Culpepper was a tiny woman in her late fifties with smokers' creases above her mouth and dyed black hair. She slid into the booth and beamed at me. 'What can I do for you today, hon?'

'Ever seen this cow?' I asked it as seriously as one can ask a question like that.

'Oh my Lord.' Ida May laughed. 'You have got to be kidding me. Is this about Jim Penland's cow? Don't tell me he hired a detective to find that ole thing.'

'Afraid so.'

She shook her head in disbelief. 'I got four in my pasture and two of 'em look just like this if you want to come see. Maybe you can get a hoofprint or something.'

'Mr Penland mentioned the two of you had a run-in recently.'

Ida May sat back and looked at me. 'He tell you why? I got four home-cooking restaurants and one bakery in two counties up here and we use a lot of apples. We don't use his no more, though. We go to another grower. It's not personal. I got to make money and Jim won't come down on his price come hell or high water. It don't make a damn to him that I helped him out when he was just getting started.'

'Sounds personal to me,' I observed.

'Well, maybe it is a little, but I still wouldn't give two cents for that damn ole cow.'

Just outside Ida May's restaurant, I saw the stack of Atlanta papers in a wire rack near the front door with a handwritten sign putting the price for dailies at seventy-five cents and the Sunday paper at two and a quarter. The headlines screamed: **Gruesome Murder in Morningside Home. Wishbone's 8th**.

I went back inside and paid the cashier, stepped out on the street and walked with the newspaper. I needed to walk. It was barely ten-thirty in the morning and already I'd unbuttoned the top of my pants under my shirt. If I didn't get out of the apple capital soon, I'd have to hire a truck to get me home.

I spent the next three hours checking off the names on Big Jim's enemy list, which included the Snell family, who owned the second-largest peach and apple orchards in Georgia, claimed to have a town named after them outside Atlanta, claimed to have no ill feelings for their largest competitor, and claimed to be 'good God-fearing folks'. They happily gave me a tour of their orchards, their processing center, their home, and their horse ranch. They fed me pimento cheese sandwiches cut into little squares, what we call pamina cheese down South. They invited me to church with them, but I would have just as soon been beaten with a stick.

In the hills above East Ellijay, I discovered that Clyde Clower, the sixth name on Big Jim's enemy list, was not going to be as forthcoming. He slammed the door so hard that the double-wide shook, leaving behind him only the faint smell of Budweiser and marijuana. Big Jim had fired him a couple of days before Sadie disappeared. I snooped around outside a little, didn't find anything, but Clyde was the kind of guy who looked like he was perfectly capable of getting ripped and stealing a cow. I decided to come back later and keep an eye on him.

I was beginning to feel worried for Sadie. She trailed around behind Big Jim's family because she preferred them to the other cows. She opened doors and walked into the house. That cow was the best dog they'd ever had, Big Jim had said. And she was totally socialized now to humans. I hated to think of her in a strange place scared and with separation anxiety.

I decided to drive over to Ida May Culpepper's and have a look in her pasture. My Neon huffed and puffed up the hill to her ranch house and a split-rail fence, three posts high, a barn, and a few cows. I walked to the fence, took out the picture of Sadie. Looked at the cows, looked at the picture. Back at the cows, again to the picture. I had no idea. I called Sadie's name a few times. They all ignored me. It was more of a snub, really. They raised their heads briefly, appraised me, then went back to grazing.

There was a basket of apples Big Jim had given me in my car. Thinking that apples might be attractive to a cow, I got a few of them, put them on the ground while I climbed over the fence, and made my way out into the pasture for a closer look.

'Sadie, come on, baby. Want an apple?'

The cows started off slow, meandering toward me, then I heard hoofs galloping in the distance. I turned. It was a bull running fast, red clay dust boiling up behind him. His head was low and he looked mad. A flock of crows that had been pecking around in the fields lifted up at once. This startled the cows. They picked up speed, became deliberate and fast until they were all coming at me full gallop.

I started to run, turning to lob a few apples at them. They kept coming. Believe it or not, cows are fast once they get going. I wasn't getting paid nearly enough to get trampled in Ida May's pasture. Hurling my last apple at them, I picked up speed and made a leap for the fence, squeezed through just as the bull got there. He was milling around, snorting at me and pawing the dirt. The cows were all fired up too. *Good Lord*. I reached for my phone.

'Tell me about Clyde Clower,' I said to Big Jim. I was out of breath, but I had cell reception on Ida May's mountain and I didn't want to waste it. I gave the cows the finger and walked back to my car, still short on wind after the run. 'Does he have family up here?'

'His mama is a widow, I believe. Has a little place around here somewhere. You think Clyde took Sadie?'

'He's a candidate, that's for sure. Has a motive. But I know he can't keep her at the trailer park. He'd have to hide her somewhere. You have any ideas where that would be?'

'I don't. Clyde worked for me but only indirectly. I got lots of people working in the orchards. I don't know much about their personal lives unless there's a problem.'

'What was the problem with Clyde? Why did you fire him?'

'Came in drunk.'

'Can you get me directions to his mother's house?'

'Yeah, hang on. She's probably in the book. You talk to Ida May Culpepper?'

'Uh-huh. At the restaurant. Then I came to her house to check it out. Why didn't you warn me the cows would come after me?'

Big Jim chuckled. '*Warn* you? Cows ain't aggressive animals, Keye. I wouldn't worry about them.'

'Right, well, I was in the field with those apples you gave me and they just about ran me down.'

Big Jim's booming laugh came through so loud I had to hold the phone away from my ear. 'Well, they are goddamn *good* apples,' he said, and laughed again.

Forest Mountain Road, where Clyde Clower's mother lived, was tough for the Neon, a steady, winding incline into the North Georgia mountains. I couldn't get any speed up at all. In the rearview, I realized, a Chevy pickup was very close, too close to my bumper. I heard the roar of the engine and the gravel under the tires and tried to work my way to the right a little, but the road was narrow and I had no place to go. The truck swerved around me, zoomed by like I was tied to a stump. A horse trailer was hitched to the back. It fishtailed and nearly knocked my car into the ditch. Gravel flew all over the place.

'*Asshole!*' I yelled, and saw a hand came out of the driver's side window in front of me with the middle finger raised. The truck left me picking my way through a cloud of thick red dust to Mrs Clower's house.

I pulled over and walked toward the white frame house. It sat on an unfenced piece of land with a flower garden near the front windows and a vegetable garden next to the house. Backed up to a barn, I saw the truck with the trailer that had nearly wrecked my car.

'I know you're in there, Clyde. Might as well come on out with Big Jim's cow. I'm calling Big Jim right now.'

'Go fuck yourself!' he yelled from inside the barn.

I opened my phone and realized that I had no reception. *Crap*. A Gilmer County sheriff's car spun into the dirt drive. The sheriff and a deputy got out. Big Jim must have taken my suspicions seriously and called them. I waved my arms and pointed at the barn.

'I think he's got Jim Penland's cow in there,' I told the two men as they approached. 'I tailed him up here.'

Okay, so I only technically tailed him up here since he blew by and left me in the dust, but it was a detail they didn't need.

I reached for my PI license, which was clipped to my back pocket, and they drew on me.

'Whoa, take it easy, guys. I'm a private detective working for Jim Penland to find his cow.' I was annoyed to hear a wobbly little laugh come out of me.

Clyde Clower came out of the barn at that moment with a lead on Sadie the cow. He saw the cops with their weapons drawn. He dropped the lead and raised his hands above his head. 'It was just a joke,' he said, then spread out flat on the ground. This was clearly not his first arrest. His words were muffled from the dirt in his face. 'I just wanted to shake him up a little. I was just coming to get her and take her back home. I didn't mean nothing by it. Tell 'em, Kate. This here's my girlfriend, Kate Johnson.' He was looking at me.

'Would you mind taking your guns off me? My name is Keye Street and I am *not* his girlfriend. I told you, I work for Jim Penland.'

The deputy patted me down and cuffed me. 'Like Big Jim would hire a detective to find a damn cow.'

'I love you, Kate,' Clower shouted, and grinned at me.

269

'Check my ID,' I insisted, but the deputy pressed his palm against the top of my head until I folded into the backseat of the sheriff's car.

'Now sit back there and keep your mouth shut.'

The other door opened and the sheriff unceremoniously pushed Clyde into the backseat with me. Clyde smelled bad. He looked at me and smiled. His teeth looked like a picket fence. 'Whatcha in for?' he asked, and snickered. '*Kate.*'

'You smell like poop,' I said.

The sheriff shot me a look in the rearview mirror. 'Not a peep,' he warned us, and we sank back into the seat, me and Clyde Clower, shoulder to shoulder, in the back of a Gilmer County sheriff's car.

They did eventually look at my identification and Big Jim did convince them over waves of laughter that he really had hired a private detective from Atlanta to find Sadie the pet cow. I missed the reunion entirely, but Big Jim hugged me so hard he nearly crushed me before I started the drive back to Atlanta.

I'd made it as far as Canton, about an hour outside of town, when Rauser's ringtone went off.

'The women I told you about, it all checked out, Street. Rape kits handled right. We'll have DNA comparisons soon, and the composites after the attack look like our boy. And get this – one of the women said he used wire.' I knew how big this was. Ligature marks on the Wishbone victims always indicated he'd used wire, never fabric or rope. 'So we were able to get a warrant for the wire. Never found it, but we found the knife under the mattress. Human blood on it is consistent with Melissa Dumas and Dobbs. Knife fits the wound patterns on the other Atlanta victims too. And if that's not enough, we finally got the vehicle Charlie's been driving. A Jeep Wrangler. Carpet fiber's consistent with the fiber on Dobbs. He had it stashed in the garage at a rental house we found out he owns. Case is locked up pretty tight.'

I remembered the times Charlie had visited our office, about his little gifts, about watching him plant pansies in the planter outside our door. I couldn't think of anyone who wouldn't have opened the door for this man.

'But you'd already searched his place, Rauser. And you brought him in twice. He knew he was being watched. I don't get why you wouldn't have found this stuff the first time. Why would he keep the knife there? And where are his trophies – photographs, video, the stuff he's pilfering from the scenes? And these are rape cases, not murder. Why would he leave living victims?'

'Both these women used the same tactic. They were completely submissive, offered to comply, pretended they enjoyed it. Then they prayed for an opportunity to get away.'

'I don't get it,' I insisted. 'It doesn't fit.'

'Oh, come on, Keye. We got the knife and now we're going to have his DNA and we're going to pull that DNA evidence we collected at the Brooks hotel scene and connect him to that one too. Look, you knew something was up with him or you wouldn't have been out there on his street that night. Your gut told you it wasn't just Charlie forgetting his meds, and your gut was right. When are you coming home so we can go out for some grape juice? I'll be a big man after the next press conference. Very in demand. I'm afraid you'll have to call ahead.'

Chapter Thirty-Five

My days were once again consumed by nanny background checks and subpoenas and Tyrone's Quikbail, long surveillance hours on Larry Quinn's personal injury cases – all the things I'd once complained about. Getting so close to the violence again, to a violent serial offender, to something as sinister as the Wishbone murders, had put life in perspective for me. I knew now that I didn't want to go back into the darkness.

But I still had the feeling of waiting for the other shoe to drop. A sponsor of mine at AA once told me that that was a normal state for an addict. We learn to carry that foreboding when we live in the shadows, always hiding our interior life, our addictions and cravings and demons.

Charlie Ramsey was in jail and awaiting trial. I felt sure he would never again see Atlanta's streets. Two more women had come forward to identify him as their rapist. Charlie's list of crimes spanned almost two decades, and the blood and knife evidence found in his home had finally shut him down and sealed his fate. The DA was confident of a conviction in the rapes and at least two of the Wishbone killings – Dobbs and Melissa Dumas – where physical evidence had been found on the knife. The carpet fiber that matched to Charlie's hidden Wrangler wasn't much by itself, but it would add to the growing evidence, another nail hammered in. Most important, and I suppose most telling, the killing had stopped. The letters, the emails, the roses had stopped too, of course. I wondered what Charlie had had planned for me in his fraudulent and damaged brain. Had I been

272

destined to become another photograph on the War Room bulletin board? He went for Dobbs not because he fit into his selection process but because Dobbs was high profile. Charlie was expanding. He'd begun killing for the headlines and for the pure satisfaction of outmaneuvering law enforcement. It was not an unusual pattern for a serial murderer, but it was a terrifying one.

I had been so wrong about Charlie. My profile, in retrospect, had been shockingly uninformed. There was nothing in Charlie's background that pointed to abuse. I was so sure that Anne Chambers and David Brooks had been symbolic of parental figures. So sure. There were other characteristics that did fit, however. His achievements as a star in football and in the complicated field of biomedical engineering. My advice had been to look for an overachiever, a star in his field. I never imagined someone who had excelled to that degree would then settle for the kind of goofy social veneer that Charlie had settled on. But what choice did he have, really? The accident had left him incapable of a normal life. We had learned that after the accident, Charlie, who had early in life exhibited volatility and sexual aggression, had even more anger. Because of his brain injury and the way it had manifested in a cognitive deficit, Charlie experienced more impulsiveness and had trouble socially processing. He had chronic pain, head and neck aches, depression, trouble concentrating. After surgery and some rehab, he had tried to return to work but had become verbally abusive, even resorted to violent threats in heated moments with coworkers. The poisonous pattern that had trailed him through life deepened. I myself had experienced it. It explained a lot about Charlie and who he had become. Still, my analysis had been so terribly wrong in so many areas. Was it a sign? The universe has a way of telling you when to let go of something. Maybe I wasn't as great at my job as I thought I was. The universe has a way of telling us that too, doesn't it?

The days had grown shorter and cooler at last. Autumn was here and the trees had turned fluorescent. Brown paper bags bulging with yard clippings lined the curbs in Winnona Park, where my parents lived. The crisp air was perfumed with fireplace wood.

My brother, Jimmy, who had for years resolutely resisted my mother's urgings to come home, had flown in from Seattle for Thanksgiving. He did not bring his partner Paul with him, which was to me a disappointment. I loved Paul almost as much as Jimmy loved him. I scheduled a webcam date with Paul for later in the day.

Jimmy and Rauser had hit it off the very first time they met a few years back, just after I came out of rehab. Today the two of them had ended up in my parents' oak-paneled den watching football with my dad – Cowboys fans all of them. Mother, who had been hovering and fussing over Rauser and Jimmy since we arrived, turned them loose with a platter of sausage balls and cold beer while she finished dinner preparations.

My cousin Miki had come for dinner too. Miki was a photojournalist, sandy haired and blue eyed, and like our faces, our lives were worlds apart. She was the daughter of my mother's sister, Florence, and years ago when Miki began showing up for our holidays without her mother, we were told Aunt Florence had left for Europe. When we got older, we discovered that *Europe* was just code for the loony bin. Aunt Florence has been institutionalized since Miki was twelve. Once, before Aunt Florence left for 'Europe', I remember visiting their home. There was a houseboat in the backyard. No one offered any explanation for this or acted as if it was unusual, but I remember seeing Aunt Florence walking down the ramp of the grounded houseboat to greet us as if she lived there. Jimmy sneaked on the boat when no one was watching and later swore it was lined with full clothing racks and cosmetics and coffee cans brimming with coins. My beautiful and talented cousin had scars on her arms from wrists to elbows. She had begun the war against her own flesh at fourteen. Cutting, overdoses, institutions, drugs, eating disorders, and years of misdiagnoses followed. She was now thirty-five and I knew nothing at all about her life, but I'm very glad that the poison in her veins is not the same blood that pumps through mine. I have enough crazy of

274

my own. Thankfully, I seem to lack either the depth or the attention span for long-term depression.

Late Thanksgiving afternoon, we gathered in the dining room that hadn't changed since my childhood – high ceiling and arched doorways and plaster walls that had been dented and patched a million times over the years. The room was a very pale yellow, with an oak table and chintz-cushioned chairs and an antique china cabinet in the corner. My mother's taste ran to the traditional. She had packed the table with food; a leaf had been extended on each end. We joined hands for the blessing, as was the tradition in my Southern Baptist family. My father began, 'We're grateful to you, Lord, for all this good food and, well, for Miki and Keye being here, since they both damn near killed themselves with drugs and alcohol.'

My eyes popped open. My dad's head was bowed and his eyes squeezed tightly shut. Jimmy cleared his throat to cover a laugh. Miki's eyes met mine. She was grinning.

'Oh, for heaven's sake, Howard,' my mother said, hotly.

'And thank you, Lord,' Dad went on, 'for my wife still being pretty and for my queer son.'

We all raised our heads on that one.

'Well, amen,' Rauser boomed firmly, and sat down at the table.

'Amen,' we all followed enthusiastically, and took our seats too.

'That was interesting,' my mother said, and shot Dad a look. 'Potatoes, anyone?'

An enormous bowl of garlic mashed potatoes sat on the table along with a green bean casserole, chipotle sweet potato cakes covered with mango and cilantro and fresh chopped jalapeños, breaded baked goat cheese rounds on salad greens with fennel and bing cherries, and a stuffed Cornish game hen for each of us. For dessert, Mother had made Jimmy's favorite, deep-dish blackberry cobbler with berries she'd picked and frozen in summer, and the pumpkin cheesecake with maple glaze and toasted pecans I wait for all year long.

'I made something spicy just for you,' Mother told Rauser with a smile. She had watched him sprinkle red pepper over nearly everything she fed him.

Rauser nodded and reached for the chipotle sweet potatoes. 'You're the best cook I know, Mrs Street. You can't get food like this anywhere else.'

'Well, I love doing it,' Mom told him, and flushed. 'Especially for a man with a good appetite. It's a sensual thing, cooking. You can't peel the skin off a mango without realizing that.'

I stared at my mother, suddenly aware that she was *flirting* with Rauser.

'Awkward,' Jimmy muttered.

My dad seemed not to notice. I glanced at the water-size glasses filled with rum and eggnog and wondered how many of those they'd both knocked back today.

'Wasn't always true,' my father said. I had heard him say this for as long as I could remember about my mother's cooking. It was generally his sole contribution to our holiday conversation. 'When we first got married, it was so bad we prayed *after* we ate.'

'*Howard*,' my mother complained. 'That joke was not funny the first thirty years you told it. I frankly do not know why you think it would be now.'

'I think it's funny,' Miki said without looking up. She was examining the ceramic turkey-shaped napkin holder next to her plate.

Mother looked at her, then moved her violet gaze to my dad. 'Howard, you have turned my only sister's daughter against me. I hope you are happy,' she declared in her rich coastal accent – a betrayed Scarlett O'Hara. My mother seemed to become more southern as she became more of a martyr.

'Hey, Keye, where's Diane?' Jimmy asked, probably hoping to change the subject. My brother was a natural peacemaker and an expert at diverting my mother. 'I was hoping to see her while I'm here.'

I smiled. 'She has a new thing.'

'Ahh,' Jimmy said, nodding. We had all watched Diane cycle

through relationships for years. She was not the kind of person who could be happy alone.

Mother threw up her hands. 'The one woman on God's green earth you're attracted to and she's dumb as a box of hair.'

'Diane's not dumb, Mother,' Jimmy said. 'She's sweet. And you will always be the only woman in my life.'

Mother softened instantly. 'You're just about the most handsome thing I ever laid eyes on. Do you know that?'

I had to agree. My brother was a pretty man, fine boned, hazel eyed, with deep chocolate skin. His heritage was a mystery. Nothing at all was known about his birth parents, but he had been a calming force in our high-strung family since he'd become part of it.

'You should come home more often,' Mother told him. 'It's not like it used to be. We have several African American families in the neighborhood now, and China must have opened some gate somewhere, because there are little Chinese girls running around everywhere.' She patted my father's hand. 'Howard, we were ahead of our time.'

I made a big show of eye-rolling and Jimmy had to look away. We had been in trouble at the table for most of our lives, my brother and I. Generally during the blessing I'd make him laugh, and Emily Street didn't put up with laughing during the blessing.

It didn't take long for Rauser to practically annihilate his game hen and start piling on seconds. He reached for another heap of green bean casserole. Mother made it southern-style with rich mushroom cream, bread crumbs, and fried shallots piled on top. Her casseroles were always a heart attack on a plate. A bowl of Crisco had less fat.

'Keye, don't you ever cook for this man?' Mother asked. Then to Rauser, she said, 'I did teach her a thing or two, you know.'

Rauser touched the napkin to his mouth. 'We're big on takeout,' he said, and turned and looked into my eyes, smiling. 'And I'm just fine with that.' To my astonishment, he leaned over and very gently kissed the corner of my mouth. I felt his hand on mine under the table.

'Well, a man like you shouldn't have to eat takeout,' I heard Mother say, but my eyes hadn't left Rauser's.

My father suddenly announced into the silence that followed, 'I got something to show y'all after dinner.'

'He won't let me set foot in that garage,' my mother complained, and wagged a finger at my dad. Rauser squeezed my hand, then let it go and turned his attention back to his plate.

So after dinner and coffee we all ambled out into the front yard and waited for the garage door to open. Rauser was next to me with his arm draped over my shoulders. I looked up at him and he kissed my forehead. I was dumbfounded. He'd been gooey like this all day.

Mother had her arm around Jimmy's waist and he was holding Miki's hand. The neighbors from the houses on each side came out and joined us while we waited for my father to reveal his latest project.

The garage door began to lift and there was a collective gasp as Dad's new hobby came into view. All six hideous metal feet of it. We looked at it, squinted, looked at one another, and then looked at it some more. No one said a word.

My father seemed bewildered. 'It's a sculpture,' he told us. 'An eagle with a rat in its mouth.'

Someone said, '*Eeeww!*'And finally Jimmy had the good sense to clap. Then we all clapped and cheered and my father took a formal bow.

'Damn fool,' Mother whispered, and covered her face with her hands. 'It's not enough that he spells out *Leon* on the roof every year in Christmas lights. Now this!'

My father was dyslexic but would not admit it.

'Feel like taking a walk?' Rauser asked me after the unveiling.

We strolled silently to the end of Derrydown and crossed Shadowmoor Drive. 'By the way,' Rauser said as we walked over the wooden footbridge to the playground behind Winnona Park Elementary, 'I broke it off for good with Jo.'

'Who's Jo?' I said, and grinned at him.

'Keye, that night on the interstate when you went off the road, I thought my heart was gonna stop.'

We were standing near the swing set on the soccer field behind the school. Lights glared in the houses on Inman Drive and Poplar Circle, the two streets that bordered the school. It was an old neighborhood and full now of young families and renovated homes and new money. I saw a car pull alongside the park and cut its lights. Teenagers come here to make out. People park in the school lot at dusk and let their dogs run on the soccer field.

He turned and faced me, held both my hands. 'I just always thought there'd be time. But that night I started to think more about how short time is. I'm a true jackass, Keye. I've waited too long to tell you that I love you.'

I looked at the lines at the corners of his eyes, the ones that always made him look as if he was about to laugh, so familiar to me, so comfortable. I looked at all that thick silver and black hair and those wide shoulders and realized I wasn't numb anymore. Not even a little. I was on fire for him, this man who knew me so well and loved me in spite of it.

'When I called that night and Jo answered your phone . . .' I started.

'I knew you were jealous as hell,' he said with a smirk.

'No way was I jealous.'

'Uh-huh,' he said. 'And maybe Jodie Foster will just walk right up to us right now, right here in the friggin' park.'

'And? Where's the part where she gives us a lap dance or shakes her rear end or something? I love that part.'

Rauser looked at me as if I'd just pulled down my panties in church. 'It's Jodie Foster, for Christ's sake, Keye. Have a little respect.'

I leaned into him and we laughed. He wrapped his arms around me and I buried my face in his chest. He smelled like cold air and aftershave, and it crossed my mind that I hadn't seen him light even one cigarette all day.

I heard the tiniest sound come from him, just a small oh, so faint, like a puff of air. I looked up at him and saw the oddest expression: shock, bewilderment.

'Rauser? What's wrong?'

His brow furrowed and he took his hand away from his chest, held it out, palm up. Our eyes met just for a split second of recognition and horror. Blood. *Jesus Christ! Blood! What the hell?*

The second shot was just as silent and swift and pitiless, and ripped into Rauser's temple. His legs folded and he fell. I dropped on top of him.

Oh God, oh God, oh God.

I yanked off my scarf and coat with my right hand and found my cell phone with my left, used my thumb to punch in 911, then pressed my coat over the wound on Rauser's chest and used my body to apply pressure.

'Rauser, talk to me. *Rauser, can you hear me?* Stay with me. *Dammit, stay with me.*'

There was too much blood. It was coming so hard it was pooling before soaking into the dry ground. *Please God don't let him die I'll never drink again I'll never complain I'll never fight with my mother*

I scanned the street while I lifted his head just enough to wrap my scarf around it. My heart was slamming against his weak pulse, his blood seeping into my coat, my skin.

'Nine-one-one, what is the nature and location of your emergency?'

'*Officer down.*' I think I shouted but I can't swear to it. Time and sound and light, it all seemed to go haywire. I could hear my own breathing, like being underwater in a bathtub. 'Winnona Park Elementary. The playground behind the school,' I told the operator.

My God, we're in the playground. His arms were around me just a moment ago. Oh God—

'Unidentified shooter,' I said. My chest felt like a pallet of bricks had dropped on me. I was having trouble breathing normally. 'The officer is Lieutenant Aaron Rauser, APD Homicide. Oh God, he's barely breathing. *Rauser, stay with me.*'

I put more pressure on his chest. My scarf was soaked and crimson. The blood kept coming. The operator was trying to keep me on the phone. She wanted to know what I'd seen. She wanted to know my name. She needed me to be clear with the details. Was she sending officers into a dangerous situation?

'I don't know where the shooter is. On Poplar, I think. My name is Keye Street. Oh God, just hurry.'

And then I saw it. Headlights blinked on and the car sped in reverse away from us, past the school, and spun out onto Avery.

I was still screaming at Rauser, crying. *Stay with me. Rauser, I love you too. Stay with me.*

'There's a vehicle leaving the scene fast on Avery heading toward Kirk Road,' I told the operator.

'Can you make out the vehicle?'

'No, Jesus, it's too dark. *Where the fuck is the ambulance? Rauser, don't you die on me.*'

My phone beeped to let me know a text had arrived, and I held it away from my ear to look at the screen. Just habit pure and simple. I wasn't thinking anymore, just reacting. I felt utterly removed, as if I were watching someone else's shattered life, registering just this escalating, surreal sense of unreality.

My fingers were so slippery with Rauser's blood I nearly dropped my phone.

It's just the 2 of us now, the screen said. *Warmest personal regards. W.*

Chapter Thirty-Six

Chief Connor was livid. He had scored an enormous public victory and he was not going to let anyone take that away. He glared at newly appointed Homicide Lieutenant Brit Williams as if there were an ear sticking out of his forehead. 'That is absolutely not going to happen,' the chief growled. Williams had been put in charge the night Rauser was shot.

'Chief Connor,' I tried. I was standing next to Williams, in front of the huge mahogany desk in the chief's office. 'This text message I received, the rhythm and phrasing, it's very, very Wishbone. Charlie Ramsey is a criminal, yes. He should stay in jail, yes, but—'

'And you seriously expect APD to reopen the investigation after what this city's been through, Dr Street? I know you have a personal interest in this. I appreciate that. We want this person just as much as you do, and I have absolutely made it understood that we will use any and all resources APD can muster in order to bring this monster to justice, but I will not reopen this painful wound on a theory that has not the slightest shred of supporting evidence. We found a weapon at Ramsey's residence that tested positive for the blood of two victims, a weapon that had been present at every scene. The science is solid on this. We know it is *the* weapon. Not at *one* scene, not *two*, but present at *every* scene.' I looked down at my shoes. 'Our killer's in custody awaiting trial,' the chief stormed on. 'And four women have come forward to say he assaulted and raped them. One of them will even testify to the ligature being a thin wire.'

'Yes, that's exactly the point. She's alive to testify,' I interjected, and Williams shot me a look. I went on stubbornly. 'Chief, none of Wishbone's victims were raped. No other evidence linking him to the killings was found in Charlie's home or vehicle except an automotive carpet fiber that's consistent with carpeting in fifteen models. You didn't find photographs, no trophies, no bloodstains on any of his clothes, his sink, in his vehicle. You have fiber evidence *and* DNA linking him to the rapes. You'd have to believe that this very intelligent and organized offender is nearly flawless at one scene and stupidly careless at another. Frankly, he does not fit the profile, Chief. He never did.'

'First of all,' the chief boomed. He was on his feet now and red faced. Connor was a big, powerful man, and when his anger was directed at you, you felt it like a physical blow. 'You don't know that any other trophies existed or that photographs were ever taken. Criminals are liars, as you well know, Dr Street, and the only indication we have at all of pictures or video or whatever is in the letters, the boastful, lying letters of a deranged predator. Secondly, that text message you received at the park could have come from anywhere. The phone was prepaid, could have been picked up at any store for fifteen bucks. The MO of Rauser's shooting is all wrong for Wishbone. There has never been a gun. Not once at any scene. If this guy doesn't fit your profile, that's your problem, not ours. We did our job. The Wishbone case is closed.' He glared at Williams. 'There's a shooter out there responsible for putting a very good friend of mine and a fellow officer down. I expect you to pull him in. *Yesterday*. Did I make a mistake putting you in charge, Williams? Because the *Lieutenant* part of your new title can disappear real quick.'

'You did not make a mistake, Chief,' Williams answered quietly. I don't think he'd slept since Rauser had been shot. He looked like hell.

The chief turned back to me. 'Thank you for your services, Dr Street. If we're holding an invoice, speak to Eric Fordice in Accounts Payable. Lieutenant, I'll expect a report on my desk every morning *and* every afternoon until this is wrapped up.'

Williams's hands were tied. Chief Connor refused to commit any resources to reopen the Wishbone investigation. He would use everything the department offered to find the person who shot Rauser, I knew, but I was convinced they were going about it from the wrong angle. It would take too much time. It would put more lives at risk.

I wanted Wishbone so bad. I'd fantasized about blowing his head off, point-blank. He'd taken too much from me. When Rauser fell that night, when his blood soaked through my clothes and into my skin, Wishbone's serrated knife sawed deeper than ever into my life, and broke my heart.

The night of the shooting still has that old sixteen-millimeter quality in my memory, shadowy and jerky. Blurred one second, too crisp the next. I rode with one of the cops to the hospital. The medical techs wouldn't let me in the ambulance. Too much work to do on Rauser, they said, too small a space. All I kept thinking was, *What if you die and I'm not there?*

Jimmy and Miki came to the hospital and never left. My parents, Neil, and Diane put in their time too. Rauser was in surgery a long time that night. The doctor said something about the proximity to the front section of the brain, a traumatic injury, the dangerous chest wound, the loss of blood, the risk of infection, a minefield of warnings. I swear, as she stood there talking to us, it was like her mouth was moving but the words were bouncing right off me. She might have been speaking in tongues. A couple of hours later she came back into the waiting room, her expression grimmer than before.

Rauser had had a heart attack during surgery, she told us, and Jimmy reached out, held on to my arm to keep me steady. They had revived him, but he was fighting for his life. He'd slipped into some kind of vegetative state. He was breathing on his own, but that was it. And this is where the doctors shrug and look sympathetic and tell you to expect the best but prepare for the worst. How the hell do you do that? I felt like I had a hole in my chest like Rauser. Just keep moving, I told myself, just nail the bastard that did this. I was so heartsick I was stumbling, punch-drunk, but if I stopped I'd come apart. I knew it. I wanted a drink. I wasn't built for grief and loss. *Keep moving. Get this bastard!*

One of Rauser's children was in town, his son. The daughter was making arrangements to come in the next day. Aaron, named after his dad, was twenty-six and handsome, had a two year old at home. He was very kind to me, but he needed time with his father, especially now. No one knew what would happen. Rauser had a living will that specified parenteral nutrition was acceptable for a limited time, but he absolutely wanted to be let go if he could not breathe on his own. Every time I walked into his room, I prayed to see his chest rising and falling. How drastically life had changed since that stroll on Thanksgiving evening, leaning into him, us laughing at his stupid jokes. I'd replayed it in my brain a thousand times.

I finally left the hospital and faced the world without my best friend. I found my old Impala, which had been repaired with all the additions my father had arranged – new safety belts, an alarm system, and GPS tracking. I headed for home, a shower, food. I needed to make myself eat. I was so drained I couldn't think straight. How do you eat, how do you even swallow when you've been torn in half?

I closed my eyes and breathed in the cold air. The holidays. God. How could I do the holidays without Rauser?

Get this bastard, just get this bastard.

I fed White Trash and slumped on the couch. I was exhausted, but I didn't want to stay away from the hospital too long. I was terrified he'd die, just stop breathing while I was away. *It's just the 2 of us now.* No, it's not, you asshole. Your aim wasn't good enough. Rauser's still here and I'm not going to let him go. *I'm going to find you*, I vowed. But exhaustion got the best of me and I drifted off with White Trash curled up tight against me.

When Rauser's brick house was built, back when Eisenhower was president, a couple of bedrooms seemed like enough. He'd added a screened porch and French doors off the master bedroom and built himself a lower deck, fenced the yard for the dog he'd have when his life slowed down. There was an attic he hadn't gotten around to doing anything with. It was small, but he'd knocked out a couple of walls and it was light and open.

I walked into the bathroom and saw his razor on the edge of the sink, smelled his aftershave. He'd been so *absent* at the hospital, a shell I could touch but couldn't reach. In this house we'd shouted at Braves games and put away iced pitchers of sweet tea and every kind of to-go food Atlanta had to offer. I thought about him letting my mother know at Thanksgiving that he was just fine with our takeout habit. Thought about him looking at me when he said it, reaching for my hand.

I stumbled into the kitchen and turned on a gas burner. Rauser made cowboy coffee in the mornings. It was rugged and imprecise in the same way he was, and it hit your stomach like battery acid. No measurements, just drop some into a pot with water, bring it to a boil, and strain it directly into a cup. It was the best coffee I'd ever had.

One Saturday morning I had shown up early at his house. He opened the door in boxers and squinted at me. I had been crying, something stupid that had happened with Dan, another leap of faith, another crash of disappointment. Rauser must have been channeling Don King, because his hair was standing straight up. He yawned and put his arm around me, found a T-shirt and stood at his gas stove making cowboy coffee. He had been such a good friend to me. It was unbearable being here without him.

I made myself a cup of Rauser's coffee and looked for the file and journals and yearbooks I'd given him that day at Starbucks . . . Fivebucks . . . I found them in the back bedroom he used for an office. It was time to start again at the beginning, with the first killing. Was it a hundred years ago since I'd been to Jekyll Island, met Katherine Chambers, and left her home with this box of her murdered daughter's things? I had this wild impulse to take it to the hospital with me, comb over these again while I sat with Rauser, talked out my ideas with him. I didn't know if he could comprehend at all or even hear me, but if there was the tiniest chance that keeping him tied to the investigator he'd been in his life would bring him back, I would try. He'd already slipped too far away from me.

I gathered up the papers and Post-its, the journals and albums, made a neat stack of them. The yearbook from the College of Criminology and Criminal Justice was on top. I sat down in Rauser's desk chair. We'd suspected from the very beginning that the killer had comprehensive knowledge of evidence collection. The profile revealed he was schooled enough to leave a crime scene clean. He understood Locard's Exchange Principle, I remembered telling Rauser in the War Room a hundred years ago.

Was the university the source of that knowledge? Had Wishbone learned about forensics on the campus of WFSU? Was it possible Anne Chambers had met her killer there at the Criminology and Criminal Justice building?

I bent over the list of Anne Chambers's course studies. The curriculum included nothing at all that would give her reason to be in the criminology building. I got out the campus map. Anne had lived in Roberts Hall, one of the older buildings. I had already marked it in red on the map. I traced my finger down Tennessee Street from her residence, over to Smith Street and down to the College of Criminology. On the map it looked like a haul, but I thought about the campus. It was accessible, not as spread out as some rambling campuses could be. Still, it was a reach. How would a college sophomore and a serial killer have crossed paths? Where? If not in class, some other group or club, a rec center?

I opened a desk drawer for a pen and found instead a pack of unopened cigarettes and Rauser's tarnished Zippo. I remembered the smell of lighter fluid in the air each time he lit it. I'd noticed on Thanksgiving that he had never gone outside for a smoke break. He was trying to quit. I'd been pushing him to do this for years. And he'd broken it off with Jo. All during the Wishbone killings, I realized, Rauser was methodically preparing his life for me, and I had to push back tears.

I opened the album from the year that Anne Chambers was killed and just started going over it again a page at a time. I wanted to look again at every goofy candid shot, the teams and clubs and social groups, the individual class pictures, the group pictures, the faculty, all of it.

I went back to the map and it suddenly hit me. A few doors down Smith Street from the College of Criminology and Criminal Justice was the Fine Arts Annex, the Fine Arts building. Anne was a visual artist. The two buildings were practically next-door neighbors. If their schedules jibed, the killer could have easily seen her in passing, insinuated himself into her life.

I felt my heartbeat quicken hopefully. Was I looking for a student? A faculty member? I thought about Old Emma saying she'd warned Anne. I thought about Mrs Chambers saying Anne had bounced from romance to romance. I was getting close now. I could almost smell it. *I'm going to get you, you bastard.*

Chapter Thirty-Seven

I was in Rauser's office with his Zippo in my hand, the tarnished silver tight in my palm. My phone warbled. 'So,' Neil began. 'I was thinking about this blog thing again. What was front and center about the Wishbone killings?'

'Stabbing?'

'Exactly,' Neil said. 'And that's about what?'

'Power, penetration, control—'

'Dumb it down, Keye. Think nuts and bolts.'

'Um . . .'

'Sex and cutting, right?'

'Okay.'

'Look, I found these fetish websites where you can brag about all your freaky porn shit without getting kicked off some website or getting hauled off to jail. You can write about doing anything to anybody as long as you call it a fantasy.'

APD's detectives and Neil had looked long and hard for the blog I always knew existed but had never been able to locate. Maybe we hadn't asked the right questions.

'We weren't looking at hard-core porn and fetish groups. A search engine can only do what you ask it to do.' Neil had read my mind. 'Keye, I found all these online communities that call themselves edge fetish and knife play fans. Post after post from people turned on by blood and knives and shit.'

'You found the Wishbone blog?' I felt my pulse and my hopes climbing.

'I'm sending you the link. A website called Knifeplay. Look for a blogger called BladeDriver. Brace yourself. It's pretty hard to stomach.'

At Rauser's computer, I began to read the blog by BladeDriver at Knifeplay.com. It advertised itself as *the* place for the adult online edge fetish and knife play community, where sexual fact and fiction was posted without restraint. As Neil had warned, the specifics shocked and sickened me. The blog had about sixty entries over a period of three years. Twisted ramblings, some of it. Complaints about weak, needy people, about traffic, about greed. Some of the entries were chilling in their detail. I recognized descriptions of Lei Koto, David Brooks, Melissa Dumas, Anne Chambers, all of them written about as if they had sexually desired the kind of mutilation they'd had to endure as their lives ended. I read about him stalking Melissa as she took her evening run, and imagined Roy Orbison playing on the car stereo, him watching her, masturbating, thinking about driving his knife into her skin, and then boasting online and calling it sexual fantasy. It was revolting. Why hadn't this raised a red flag anywhere? I was reading details that had never been made public until the letters began hitting the newspapers. The Lei Koto blog was posted well before the first letter was published, and all of the entries offered details that would only later have been discovered at the crime scenes, details no one outside the investigation could have known about. The killer talked about William LaBrecque having no moral boundaries at all, about him being a bully and a wife beater and deserving a beating himself. No moral boundaries? This killer was judging based on morals!

A short entry talked about the first time he had killed, at sixteen years old, about remaining so unaffected by this that his grades had not even wavered. Wishbone had been killing since he was a teenager! He had bragged once to Rauser in a letter about being active longer than anyone was aware. Who fell victim to the young killer first? Was it Anne Chambers, as we thought? Had it been a crime of convenience that wet his whistle for killing or was

Wishbone already plotting out the murder in high school? So many people had been hurt. So many lives destroyed. My heart ached for all of them. But the last entry felt like that mean knife was splitting my flesh, like he was driving it into me, and I relived leaving that park with pieces of Rauser's skin and blood stuck to my face and hands while this killer must have rushed home to boast to his online fans.

KNIFEPLAY.COM

Your Online Adult Edge Fetish & Knife Play Community blogs > beyond the EDGE, a fantasy by BladeDriver blog title > Memories

It really is not much fun. In fact, it's a bit of a letdown once you get past the challenge of taking aim. It happens too fast, a quick pop, and it's over. Not like a blade. Not like seeing everything, every cut, every fluid that leaks out of the dying, the way pain pulls the skin tight and every expression line is exaggerated, painted on. Pop, pop. It's so ... impersonal. I saw his knees buckle. I saw her misery. Her pain was something anyway. However brief, her suffering is a memory to savor.

Soon that will be what I have, just memories. Videos will be deleted and all my beautiful photos, all those triumphant moments will soon be gone too. I hate to see them go, really. But it is time. And I know each picture by heart, cherish each moment with them, each sound, each smell. Tonight I will toss my pictures into the fire and watch them yellow, watch the corners turn up, watch the centers blacken and ignite. It's nice, actually. Never let it slip away – the first fire of the year, the turning leaves, the first snowflake – small pleasures. Life slips by so quickly.

Quicker than you think, you sonofabitch, I thought, and searched for a way to comment on this blog, read some details from the website. I had to sign up in order to comment. I left this message at the bottom of BladeDriver's last entry: *I won't rest until I find you. KS.*

I was worried for anyone close to me – Neil, my parents, my

brother, even Diane. I hoped issuing that kind of challenge would keep his focus on me. There had been too much collateral damage. I sent Lieutenant Brit Williams's BlackBerry the link with an email, explaining. *Neil found this blog, Brit. It's Wishbone, I'm sure of it. Check out the dates. At least one entry was after Charlie's arrest.*

I walked out of Rauser's house and locked the door, remembered the million times I'd left this house with him, us laughing or arguing. We'd been good friends so long it seemed we were always doing one or the other. I climbed in the Impala and pointed it down Peachtree toward Piedmont Hospital. I wanted a drink so bad I could feel the stampede of cravings all the way to my back molars.

I kept thinking about the knife at Charlie's place, the one the police had found under his mattress. The first search had turned up nothing, but the second netted them a bloody knife? Something was wrong. God, why didn't I listen to my instincts? Wishbone knew Charlie was our prime suspect. APD had gone out of their way to make that public. They'd even organized a leak of his mug shot. Had Wishbone seized advantage of this, framed Charlie, to keep the heat off? Charlie was a thug anyway. Send him off to jail and get some breathing room, rest and plan, kill again. I wondered if Wishbone had gone to the trouble of planting the serrated fishing knife that had ravaged so many lives. Or had he simply left it where Charlie was bound to pick it up?

The game was everything for this kind of killer, even more tantalizing now than the basic compulsions of a violent serial offender. Toying, evading, taunting those who were trying to stop him. That was the hook. That was the whole reason for killing Dobbs, for shooting Rauser. Entertainment. And it didn't matter who was in the way. The killer no longer needed a specific type of victim, someone who symbolized something. He could have stayed hidden. Charlie Ramsey had been set up beautifully. Wishbone didn't have to resurface and try to kill Rauser. And yet here he was, so driven by rapacious ego that he couldn't stay down.

My phone rang at the light at Fourteenth and Peachtree. 'Are you all right, Keye?' It was Diane. 'Are you taking care of yourself? What can I do?'

'I'm okay. Really. I'm heading back to the hospital. Rauser's getting better, I think.'

'The doctors are taking care of Rauser. You have to take care of yourself too,' she insisted, quietly but firmly.

I was silent.

'We all miss seeing you around here. Maybe getting away from the hospital would be good, you know? Take your mind off things. Margaret says we have a lot of work we could give you. And I miss you.'

I heard the chimes on my phone letting me know I had unread email. 'Hey, I gotta go. Don't worry, Diane. I'm fine. Really. I'll call you if I need you, okay? Love ya.'

I went through the light and pulled over in the passenger drop-off area in front of Colony Square. Brit Williams had sent an email saying the police department had contacted the fetish site publishing the BladeDriver blog. They'd requested all the details it stored on this user, including user name and passwords, addresses, phone numbers, but it would take a subpoena to get the records released and that would take time. Williams agreed that the blog was about the Wishbone killings but disagreed there was evidence Wishbone had written it. Anyone who was closely following the investigation could write fiction around the details and publish it. That the style and cadence were practically identical to the Wishbone correspondence Rauser and I had received was not something Brit was ready to accept as evidence. After all, the letters had been published for anyone to copycat. He had made the chief aware of a blog that had an entry the night Rauser was shot that was suspicious enough to warrant investigating. But there was nothing at all, Williams told me, in the vague ramblings of this blogger to link the attempted murder of Aaron Rauser to Wishbone. In his opinion, Wishbone was in custody and neutralized. The shooting in the park was about a thug who had a personal vendetta against Rauser or perhaps against anyone prominent in law enforcement.

I drew in a breath. I realized I was shaking. The air was crisp but still too warm to have stripped us winter bare; the leaves were hanging on and probably would through Christmas. A line of Japanese maples had turned cherry red up on Fifteenth. Colony Square and the High Museum were decked out head to toe for the holidays. NPR was playing the president's address on health care reform. There was a group of people waiting to get into a restaurant next door, laughing. Life ticked by, unstoppable despite heartache or tragedy. I felt removed from it all. Pain does that. It's utterly self-absorbed.

I was pissed at Williams. He'd let me down. I answered his email. *Bullshit, Brit. What would Rauser do if it was you in that hospital bed? Anything it took regardless of what the chief said, that's what he'd do.*

My phone went off a couple of seconds after I'd hit Send – a text alert, an unknown address. *Good to hear from you, Keye. Please do rest, my dear girl. What fun would life be without someone to challenge me? W.*

The message I had posted on the BladeDriver blog had obviously been delivered.

I sat there for a minute trying to collect myself before I went back to the hospital. I missed Rauser. I wanted to talk to him again about this. I wanted to hear his voice teasing me about getting so obsessed. *I won't rest until I find you.*

I put my nose to the aftershave I'd found in his bathroom, musky and quiet, not too sweet. The scent took me back to moments when he'd climbed in my car or I'd climbed in his, when he'd come for dinner and television smelling like that. I'd brought his razor and shaving cream too.

I stopped at the nurses' station to say hello. Another hello to the uniformed cop outside Rauser's door. APD guarded his room 24/7. I had gotten into the habit of coming late, trying not to intrude when his kids were there. His ex-wife came for a day and we had no idea what to say to each other.

294

Rauser was in the bed just as he had been the night before and the night before and all the nights before that, two weeks now. Eyes closed. Fresh bandages around his head, blue hospital blanket pulled up to his chin. His breathing sounded strong to me tonight, and that had not always been true. Those first couple of days it had been so thin, like winter air.

I found a kidney-shaped bowl and filled it with hot water, used the water to soften his beard, then rubbed shaving cream over his thick stubble. Very carefully, I ran the razor over his imperfect face. I was tired of seeing him look so ratty, like a vagrant, I told him, and whispered that I was frightened as I wiped shaving cream off his face with a warm towel, frightened and so, so angry. *Come back to me.*

Chapter Thirty-Eight

I woke around four to find a nurse in the room. She smiled gently and apologized for waking me, but she needed Rauser's vitals and to check the amino acids and glucose and electrolytes that flowed through a catheter and directly into one of the fat subclavian veins that twisted through a complicated maze of muscle and vein and helped deliver enough nutrition to keep him alive. I had been sleeping next to him when she woke me, squeezed into the bed on one side, my head against his chest, an arm thrown over his stomach. I listened for his breathing before I got up.

I nodded and said good morning to the officer on duty outside the door, then wandered to the elevator and downstairs, where I could find fresh air, even if it was on a bench under the harsh fluorescent light outside the emergency entrance.

Christmas music was playing as I walked through the main lobby. Happy holidays, I thought. *Happy fucking holidays.*

What had I been doing when Neil rang earlier? I'd been getting close to something before the blog had derailed me. What was it? WFSU, the criminology building and its proximity to the Fine Arts Annex. The first victim. Was Anne really the first victim? I was beginning to think not. If the killer was sixteen the first time he'd killed, as his blog had boasted, where had they met? I checked the pocket of my jeans to make sure I had my car keys. That whole pile of stuff on the Chambers murder was still in the car. Might as well get some decent coffee and go over it again. There was a Starbucks counter in the hospital. Fivebucks, I thought again, and smiled, though it hurt to remember his jokes and his laugh and to remember him teasing me, grumpy and scowling over the Wishbone paperwork.

The hospital café was nearly empty. It was not even five A.M. I took my double-shot, skim milk latte to a table, where I spread out Anne Chambers's photo albums, letters to home, yearbooks, everything her mother and Mary Dailey at WFSU had given me. I bent over the campus map and wondered again if the campus was where Anne Chambers had first met her killer. I'd been through the yearbook so many times and nothing had jumped out at me. Maybe it was time to begin running every name on that campus during Anne's last year. I imagined Anne coming out of the Fine Arts building and being spotted by her killer. What was it about her that had set him off? Had he stalked her? Did they meet, become friends? I thought again about Old Emma telling me Anne was seeing someone. Maybe it wasn't him. Maybe instead she had spurned his advances. A student? A professor? Maybe he was neither. I felt a spike of frustration.

An intern shuffled into the café in pale green scrubs and booties, looking as if he hadn't slept in a month. He paid the cashier for a muffin and coffee, then bolted when his pager went off, leaving his uneaten breakfast on the table.

I sent Neil an email and asked if he could get access to the university's enrollment information, then went back to the College of Criminology and Criminal Justice yearbook. This time I wrote down the names on each page, one by one. It forced me to focus on each individual instead of the group pictures and goofy gag shots and clubs, and it prevented me from missing anyone.

At almost six-thirty, when first light was beginning to seep through the windows and my second latte was gnawing at my empty stomach, my thoughts began to drift to Rauser upstairs in his bed. I could conjure him up, I realized, just by closing my eyes: every line in that rugged face, every way that his mouth moved, and his hands, his smells and sounds, food he loved and despised. I'd memorized him over the years. But all my will couldn't make him recover. I went back to making my list of names.

Then one of them leapt off the page and slapped me in the face. I studied the photograph. It was a group picture of twelve doctoral students who, according to the caption, had partnered with faculty members and won recognition for research in the field of criminal justice and behavior. The study was entitled 'The Biosocial Origins of Antisocial Behaviors'.

Sweet Jesus, could it be? A flood of thoughts, corrosive and incohesive, rushed through my tired brain. I stared at the photograph and thought about the campus, the dogwoods and palms and live oaks. Somewhere here Anne Chambers had met the person who would later beat her with a brass desk lamp until her face was unrecognizable, then slice away her clitoris and nipples. All along I had suspected it began there, the nurturing and feeding of a monster. The rage Anne Chambers was shown during their final interaction felt personal. Removing her nipples was a way to say 'I hate you, Mommy.' Anne symbolized a mother who for some reason was reviled. My mind was flying now, remembering things; fragments were adding up and beginning to solidify. Something with density and shape was being born at last, something more than theory.

I typed the name into my search engine and began to read, quickly following every link until I found background. The strange obsession with civil law, with turning plaintiffs into victims; it was all there. My throat had gone dry. Wishbone had been hiding in plain sight all along.

Florida Man Convicted in Brutal Killing of Wife. I searched for details of the crime scene. There were none apart from a brief description in the newspaper article, which stated in bold words that the victim had been stabbed several times with a fishing knife. Wishbone's father had killed his wife? Was Wishbone following an example set by a murdering daddy, copycatting? Or had Daddy simply taken the fall to protect a child who had discovered a passion for killing? Was I right? Had all this begun with a mother? Was that the kill described in the blog, the one that at sixteen never even caused a wobble in the killer's grade-point average? I'd been wrong about one thing. Anne Chambers was not Wishbone's first victim. We might never know how many had come before her. Wishbone's father had died in Florida's smoking-hot and overused electric chair after years on death row.

There was an article about the woman he'd killed. She had been a kind of celebrity in the southern art scene. *Local Artist Gives Back to Community*, the headline read, and I followed it until I found her picture. The resemblance to Anne Chambers, the student and artist, took my breath away. Now I could see it. Anne Chambers emerging one day from the Fine Arts building, young and vital and so naïve, an artist just like the murdered mother. Bearing a likeness to her so uncanny it must have set off a firestorm in the brain of the fledgling killer.

My eyes took in every detail of the group photograph in the yearbook. *Wishbone*. A terrible burning grew inside me, like drinking lava. It rushed through my bloodstream and made my face hot. It was counterinsurgent and infused with an utterly complete and vile hatred, this feeling. I thought about Rauser, about that night in the park, about his arms around me, and I was angrier and more helpless than I'd ever been in my life, even those days when I'd been too drunk to get out of my pajamas. This monster had taken too much from me. Too much from Rauser.

I reached for my phone and called.

'Keye, listen.' Brit Williams's voice was gentle. 'We all want to find out who did this to the lieutenant, but trying to reopen Wishbone – well, we really need to move forward now. If you want to help, help us do that.'

'You've got the wrong guy in jail, Brit.'

'See, here's the thing, since Charlie Ramsey's incarceration, we haven't had another murder with that MO and signature. So it's going to take more than a text message to move this forward. You're always all about physical evidence, Keye. Give me some physical evidence and I'll see what I can do. But I got to have more than my dick in my hand when I see the chief.'

Frustrated, I stuffed the urge to unload on him.

'I know you love him,' Brit added, and to my great irritation, I felt my eyes filling.

'And you love him too,' I said. 'He *trusts* me, Brit. He always trusted my instincts – you know that. I need you to trust me too. Look, even if you think I've gone completely crazy, just please humor me because Rauser would have. Get me the crime scene reports from this scene in Florida. I need the details. That's all I'm asking. I can get Neil to do this, but it's going to be faster and more complete if you'll contact the police down there. This would have been in Tallahassee PD's jurisdiction.'

Another silence, and then, 'What the hell. I don't have anything else to do, right?'

I went upstairs and checked on Rauser again, then waited on a bench in the hospital garden with my coat up close to my ears, blowing clouds of steam off my coffee in the cold morning. Fallen leaves from a Flame Maple clung to the dewy ground.

Nine-thirty A.M. I checked my phone for the third time. Power on. Volume up. No missed calls. Finally, when I thought I'd throw it on the ground and stomp on it, it rang.

'You have any idea how hard it is to get an archived case file from Florida?' Williams demanded. 'Can you meet me at twelve-thirty?'

We met at La Fonda Latina on Ponce de Leon, about five minutes from Brit's cube at the station. The place was packed. We sat on the patio upstairs. It was chilly up there but a place where we could talk. Only a few people had braved it. He ordered paella with squid and a waiter delivered chips and salsa to our table. I ordered coffee and, shivering, folded my arms over my chest.

Williams loaded a chip with salsa, crammed it into his mouth. 'You need to eat,' he said. 'You look like shit and it ain't that cold up here.' He pushed a letter-size manila envelope across the table.

'It's all there,' he said. 'Everything you asked for. Maybe some shit

300

you didn't ask for.' He ate more chips and washed them down with Modelo while I opened the envelope. He watched me as I went through the crime scene photos. 'Look familiar?' he asked. 'By the way, I emailed photos of the husband and his clothing to the spatter guys. Husband's the one who called nine-one-one. Bloodstains on his clothes were not consistent with the kind of spatter a murder like that would have created. In fact, a lot of the physical evidence didn't support the DA's case.'

I looked up at him. 'This man went to the chair for *murder*. How'd they get a conviction?'

'Confession, for one. And get this – teenager testified to finding the father leaning over the mother with the bloody fishing knife. That testimony and his confession – well, it would be pretty hard to argue against. And twenty-three years ago, they weren't reconstructing like we do now.'

'So many similarities to what we've been seeing at Wishbone scenes.' I was studying the photos. 'But less organized. Lots of emotion. Fury.'

'I didn't think a kid could do something like that.'

'It happens,' I told him, 'in some kids when they fail to develop affectional bonds.' I looked back at the crime scene photos. I'd studied child psychopathy in my career. It can be lethal for the parent of a fledgling psychopath. They can become the first victims of a deadly emotional cocktail – the child's lack of abstract reasoning combined with a driving desire for immediate gratification. The scenes are often terrifyingly violent and the children weirdly unaffected by their crime.

My grades never dipped a point.

Williams waited while the paella was delivered in a cast-iron pan. Picking up his fork, he shook his head. 'Chief's not going to reopen the Wishbone investigation based on this. We gotta build the case.' Then he grinned. 'Showed a picture of your suspect around the restaurant where David Brooks ate before he was killed and bingo. Immediate recognition by the manager. Still not enough, but it's a start.' He shoved some yellow rice into his mouth. 'You realize how fucking big a tiger you're poking at? Your suspect jogs with the mayor. You know that? APD can't rattle that cage.'

'But I can.'

'Yes, you can,' Williams agreed, surprising me. 'After seeing this stuff, me and Balaki and a couple detectives, we're willing to do what we can to help. On our own time.' He pushed his plate away and looked up at me. His brown eyes were serious and soft. 'Until this is under control, is there somewhere you can go? Rauser was right, whether you want to hear it or not. You need protection.'

I already knew the Wishbone blades were sharp. I'd felt them slicing deep into me as my car skidded off the road, as Rauser fell next to me.

'I have protection, Brit. And I won't think twice about using it.'

Chapter Thirty-Nine

Margaret Haze stood when I entered her office, nodded pleasantly, and offered me one of the chairs at her desk. She was wearing Helmut Lang, black, tailored, militant as hell, and so far out of my range that I couldn't even guess the price tag. She took her seat. I didn't. My nerves were sizzling. 'How can I help you, Keye?' She didn't seem at all surprised to see me.

'It would help if you'd stop killing people.' I wanted to slap cuffs on her right there, make sure she never got to see Atlanta's sapphire skies again. I wanted to make her suffer. Maybe then the bitch could experience empathy. *Do you feel anything?*

'You've lost me.' She was calm and, from my perspective, entirely unreadable.

'Can we cut the bullshit and have an honest conversation? No more games. I came here so you'd feel comfortable. I know you've had your office swept for bugs. And I'm not wired, Margaret.'

'My clients expect and deserve privacy in their attorney's office. By the way, I hope you don't mind that I've decided to no longer use your company for that service. We just don't seem to be a good fit anymore.' Her expression hadn't changed and neither had her tone. She was utterly confident. I heard the telephone ringing in the outer office and saw a light blink green on Margaret's phone. She ignored it. 'Diane didn't come in today. She hasn't missed a day in three years.'

'I called her. I told her not to come. I told her everything. She was devastated, Margaret. You've been a hero to her.'

'You never really know anyone below the surface, Keye. I would have thought you of all people had learned that lesson.'

'We need to talk, Margaret.' I held my arms out. 'Pat me down, if you'd like. See for yourself. No wire.'

Margaret laughed lightly. 'That's absurd.'

I ignored her. Instead, I stepped out of my shoes, removed my jacket, and began to unbutton my blouse. I removed one piece of clothing at a time and turned it inside out, shook it out for her to see, then dropped it on the desk. She was silent while I stripped, and I was intensely aware of her eyes on me, on my body, amused, arrogant eyes, openly appraising me. I knew what her victims must have seen, someone emotionless and far removed from anything with a beating heart.

Completely nude, I made a circle. She gestured to my earrings without speaking. I removed them, dropped them onto her desk. Margaret scooped them up in her palm, looked them over, then handed them back.

'Get dressed, Keye. What will people say?' She watched while I got back into my clothes. 'Are you here alone?'

I sat down. 'Lieutenant Williams and Detective Balaki are waiting outside.'

She leaned back, arms relaxed on the armrests of her high-backed desk chair. 'Do you really think I'm a danger to you? Is that why you brought them?'

I wanted to tell her all the ways she'd hurt me already, all the deep wounds, but I refused to give her that power. 'Honestly, I don't think I'm your type. But you do seem to be branching out . . .'

A smile played over her glossy lips. 'Exactly what type is that?'

I picked up the framed photograph on her desk, little Margaret with her parents, standing on the deck of a sailboat. 'The type that reminds you of him or his clients or your mother. That's it, isn't it? He gave them more than he gave you? Was he sleeping with them too?'

Margaret swiveled toward the window away from me. 'You know, if there was evidence – which there is not – they wouldn't be waiting outside. They would be in here with a warrant.' She said it without scorn or fear or anger. It was as if my response genuinely intrigued her.

'How did you see them?' I asked. 'As parasites? All their petty needs, petty problems, petty, greedy lawsuits.'

She was completely still. Through the windowed wall behind her, I could see miles of twisting highway, but not even a faint hum of the city reached her high glass office. The room was utterly silent.

'Who keeps a photograph on their desk of the man who murdered their mother? You did it, didn't you? You killed her. And then you let him die for it. Was that therapeutic, her paying for stealing his affections, and then him paying for what he did to you? He betrayed you, didn't he, Margaret? First he loved you. Then he left you for your mother.'

Her eyes seemed to be very bright green in the afternoon light when she turned back to me. 'Is this the part where I'm supposed to come undone?'

'That would be nice.'

She laughed quietly, stood and crossed to the bar, poured herself cognac and handed me a small bottle of club soda, unopened, and a dry glass. 'If I am the person you think I am, then I'd be a complete sociopath. You're the expert. You know that. I would be incapable of remorse. I would be able to tell you that I have never missed either of them. Their . . . passing, as violent and ugly as it was, would have been just another event. Nothing extraordinary. Don't you find that to be true about life, Keye? That it's just a thing that happens to us. Life doesn't really touch us. I think you get that. I think it's why you drank, it's why you've made the spectacularly stupid choices you've made. I think deep down, you're just as numb as I am.'

'I was,' I said. I could barely contain the hatred I felt for her. I thought about Rauser, about his arms wrapping around me, about feeling for the first time in so long that flesh-and-blood desire didn't have to exclude love and trust.

She sipped her cognac; her eyes never lifted from mine, never a quiver. 'It's amazing, really. With your education, you could have done so well. And yet you chose the *FBI*? Trying to make it right, are we? It must have been hard seeing your grandparents killed like that right in front of you. Still chasing down the bad guys?'

I opened the club soda and poured it into my glass, set the bottle down on the table next to my chair, took a sip. I wanted her to see that my hands were steady, that her observations hadn't rattled me. I was bluffing; my insides hurt like I'd swallowed a razor blade. But bluffing is something an addict learns early on. I'd gotten good at it over the years.

'How's Lieutenant Rauser?' she asked, and it felt like acid exploding in my veins. I didn't want his name on her lips. 'Someone really should get guns off the street.' She shook her head in mock regret.

'I'm going to get *you* off the street, Margaret. Whatever it takes to do that.'

This seemed to amuse her. 'Really? What are you going to do, Keye? Shoot me? Stab me? I don't think so. You have the handicap of moral borders. It leaves you ill equipped for real crime fighting, doesn't it?'

She was so arrogant I longed to reach across the desk and wipe that fucking smirk off her face. She'd exploited brilliantly a bias in law enforcement regarding women and violence, and she knew it. An unidentified perpetrator is always referred to as *he*, never *she*, and women are looked at last in violent and sexual murders. Like everyone else, I had looked right past her because she was a woman.

'You know, this feeling of being infallible, it's part of your illness, Margaret. It isn't real. You're going to pay for what you've done. The blog was a mistake. They *will* trace it back to you. Cat's out of the bag, Margaret. APD's watching.'

'Do you have any idea how much money our firm puts into local politics? No, of course you wouldn't. The mayor and the DA, the police chief, they'd all love to keep their jobs. APD isn't going to watch me, Keye. And if you're trying to scare me with those two cops you have waiting, well, it's not going to keep me up tonight.'

I laughed at her. 'I was just thinking what it's going to be like for you to trade in Helmut Lang for a nice little prison jumpsuit. I think they're blue in Georgia. Be nice with your coloring. I love the idea of watching your life pull apart at the seams.'

'Then we really aren't so different. You have an inner sadist just like I do.' Her eyes were steady on me.

'Let me ask you something, Margaret. Just to satisfy my own curiosity: did you know you wanted to keep killing after you butchered your mother? Or did it happen when you met Anne Chambers? I saw this picture on your desk and it ate at me. They looked so much alike, your mother and Anne. And they were both artists. Is that why you needed to kill her?'

Margaret thought for a moment. I might have been speaking to her about afternoon tea. 'To be frank,' she answered, 'I knew I had something that hadn't been quenched. I didn't know until I met Anne what it was or that it was permanent. It was like having an itch without fully understanding what an itch *is*. You'll have to forgive me. I've really never had an opportunity to verbalize it. I'm not sure there are words for it.' She held her drink up in a mocking toast, then took a sip. 'It is liberating, in a way, to try though,' she mused.

'Then maybe you'd like to make a statement on the record. Think how . . . liberating that would be.'

A light laugh. 'I like you, Keye. I always have. You're very smart and you're funny. I'm devastated that you think I might hurt you. It's no accident that you're alive, Keye. I *protected* you, if you must know.'

'Protected me? You made sure the media went after me so I'd get kicked off my APD consulting gig. You rigged my car and I was nearly killed. And you shot my best friend.'

'Don't be so dramatic, Keye – it doesn't suit you. You were not nearly killed. You had a lump on your head. And maybe, just maybe, you can open your mind enough to see that you'd have been safer

AMANDA KYLE WILLIAMS

out of the way. But you wouldn't back off. And you take the most ridiculous risks. LaBrecque, for example – we both knew he was a thug. He hurt you and threatened you and you went back for more. Don't you think he would have killed you that day at the lake house? Be grateful, Keye. I didn't want you hurt.'

That's why LaBrecque never fit in on the victims' list. I remembered coming to Margaret that day with my bruised wrist. I remembered her concern. 'What was the point of killing Dobbs like that?' I demanded. 'And sending that package to me, was that about knowing my history with Dobbs?'

'I thought you'd appreciate the package, Keye. You would have preferred cutting it off yourself? And the lieutenant,' Margaret told me. 'Rauser wasn't about you. Everything isn't always about *you*. I had a completely separate relationship with him before you started showing up at crime scenes.'

'Relationship? With Rauser? Margaret, get real. A bunch of crazy-ass letters to a cop doesn't put you in a *relationship*. That's your illness talking again. It tricks you, doesn't it? It's getting worse. Just so you know, Rauser didn't take you that seriously. He considered you another irritating thug.'

A smile. 'Sticks and stones, Keye.'

'If you ever get close to him again, I swear to God I will not wait for the police to take you down. If you can't control that itch, Margaret, I'll do it for you.'

'He's no challenge anyway. Unless you're into drool.' She checked her platinum watch, stood, and walked to the door, held it open for me. 'Thanks for stopping in. If you'll excuse me, I need to prepare for a client.'

La la, la la.

A child's song, without words. It went first high and then low. High-low, high-low. *La la, la la.* Over and over. Haunting and melodic. The tune never varied and little Margaret never tired of it.

She sat in front of her dollhouse humming softly. It was one of

308

those big dollhouses and she had begged Santa to bring it for Christmas. A three-story dollhouse with a front that opened out like a suitcase so Maggie could look inside, rearrange the tiny furniture, the little family.

La la, la la.

. . . Uh-oh. Little Maggie frowned, her brow furrowed. Something wasn't right inside her house.

She reached inside and carefully plucked the tiny daddy doll from the master bedroom. *That's it.* She wanted Daddy in her room. Away from Mommy. She used her forefinger to thump Mommy off the little bed. The doll clattered to the floor. *All better.*

La la, la la.

She remembered the dollhouse so well, remembered that moment just as clearly as she remembered the way her father smelled when he came to her in the night. Sleep and Old Spice. She looked at the photograph on her desk, her in her father's arms. She was five years old when the picture was taken. He'd been so busy all the time. No time for the family, for Maggie, except in the night when he touched her softly and kissed her. He told her it was about love and her body had responded to him, opened up to him. She couldn't help it.

Maggie had learned about love this way, in a small damp bedroom with a palm tree outside her open window and the wide Florida sky watching what they did together.

Even now she craved her father's touch. But she couldn't have that anymore. Sometimes she touched herself and fantasized that his hands were on her. She loved and hated him for this. But she hated them more, the ones who had taken him away from her.

La la, la la . . .

Chapter Forty

The sign on my dashboard identified me as a delivery person. No hassles that way from garage security and I could park in a courier slot directly across from SunTrust Plaza. I was in the Neon and practically invisible – *shields up*.

We'd been watching her for three days, switching shifts, dealing with day jobs and balancing personal lives, and all of us spending whatever time we could at the hospital. Thinking about Christmas being around the corner felt like jerking my guts out in my hand. Finding time with Rauser at the hospital and giving White Trash some sense of normalcy had been challenging. Rauser's children had called almost daily, but there was nothing for them to do here, so they had not returned, nor had his ex-wife. Neil had decided to end his office work boycott and really pitch in. He was doing his best to put the fires out until I could come back full-time. Diane was helping him and, he had reported, doing a great job organizing us.

Three days earlier, sickened and angry, I'd called Diane after leaving Margaret's towering office. I'd described the confrontation to her. Diane was stunned. I'd heard the bewilderment and fear in Diane's voice. She knew she could never return to Guzman, Smith, Aldridge & Haze after that, at least not while Haze was free. Apart from the obvious shock of knowing your boss and someone you'd admired had a dangerous secret career in murder, Diane now had the added burden of unemployment. I made her an offer that was nowhere near what Haze had paid her, but the benefits were in knowing there was almost no chance she'd be knifed to death by her new employer. Diane was worried about me. She and I talked every night. On days she hadn't been able to get to the hospital, she asked about Rauser's condition. She wanted to know what intelligence our surveillance operations had gathered about Margaret. She wanted to know about my emotional state and if I'd eaten anything besides doughnuts while I sat in front of 303 Peachtree these last couple of days. And on more than one occasion she'd gone to my place to hang out with White Trash and spoil her with half-and-half.

Margaret Haze stepped out of the revolving doors that empty onto Peachtree Center Avenue, and my pulse shot up like mercury. She crossed the street, headed for the parking garage where I waited in the dinged-up Neon and where she kept her silver Mercedes. I sank down low in my seat, ducking my head so that my face was in the shadow of my hat brim. I was wearing a blue Braves cap. I saw Margaret stride past in the rearview mirror, slim and erect, briefcase at her side. A pair of seven-hundred-dollar Jimmy Choos clicked against the concrete and reverberated throughout the enclosed garage.

The silver Mercedes took Peachtree from downtown past the Georgian Terrace all the way through Midtown into Buckhead. I kept my distance; let her get a good lead. She turned onto Piedmont and we drove past the executive hotel where David Brooks had been murdered. I thought about that hot summer night – the fireplace, the wine, the single wineglass – and what we now knew about David's final hours. They'd had dinner a few blocks from here in a Buckhead restaurant. And while Brooks was naked and sexually aroused, Margaret Haze had shoved her knife deep into the cavity above his sternum. I imagined her lips brushing against his ear as she reached around from behind to murder him.

Haze pulled into a Mercedes dealer and I waited for twenty minutes. Finally, she emerged and climbed into a cab. I ran inside to the service department, where Margaret had left her car. There were several counters. Parts, service, rentals, leases. It took too many minutes to work out what had happened. I called Brit Williams when

I knew. 'Haze just dropped off her car at Buckhead Mercedes. It was leased.' Outside, I looked right, then left, and spotted a cab turning onto Peachtree from Piedmont Avenue. I thought it was the one Haze had taken. Buckhead isn't like downtown. It's not wall-to-wall taxis. Chances were pretty good I could catch up to it. 'Why would she give up her car? Brit – she's leaving town.'

'It's the holidays, Keye. Everybody's leaving town except us. And she doesn't have any travel restrictions on her.'

I jumped in my car and pulled out onto Piedmont. 'She's trying to hide something. If there's evidence in that Mercedes, you'll need it for the court case once this breaks. Can you seal the car before it's contaminated?'

'*Shit*. Chief finds out, I'm gonna get my ass handed to me.'

The taxi returned Haze to her office building and she disappeared inside. By seven that evening, there were five of us on duty to keep an eye on Margaret: Lieutenant Williams, me, Detectives Balaki, Velazquez, and Bevins. I parked in one of the courier slots on the Peachtree Center Avenue side of the building and put up my fake dashboard sign.

She came out at 7:32. Her auburn hair was pulled back tightly off her forehead and temples. She wore a high-collared black coat that clung to her and opened in an upside-down V, exposing soft black boots that rose up over her knees. If she had any concerns about being watched, it didn't show. Not in that outfit.

She stepped out onto the sidewalk, walked twenty feet, and turned left into the restaurant there, a two-hundred-dollar-a-meal steakhouse.

I left my car, crossing the street and dodging traffic, and went into the restaurant. Low lights, warm, the hushed murmurs of a well-dressed clientele. I asked to sit at the bar. I needed to keep my eye on her.

Chief Connor still didn't consider Margaret Haze a viable suspect. That Margaret had openly discussed her savage double life with me in an unrecorded conversation was not credible evidence, he reminded me, pissed that I wouldn't go away. Neither were the Buckhead restaurant employees who recognized Margaret's photograph. Balaki had made some excuse to Brooks's wife for showing her a picture of Haze. Yes, Haze had attended the backyard barbeque she and her husband had hosted around the swimming pool last year – another connection to David Brooks and now a connection to the BladeDriver blog. *I met his wife and fucked him twenty minutes later behind his own pool house.* I hoped the stack of circumstantial evidence would soon grow too tall to ignore. But as Williams had pointed out over paella at La Fonda and Margaret had so arrogantly confirmed in her office, Guzman, Smith, Aldridge & Haze was a giant shark in Atlanta's political ocean. And the chief was fully convinced the right person was in custody for the killings. We had no proof against Margaret. The murders had stopped. And Margaret, having a pipeline to the mayor and therefore knowing everything that was happening inside the police department, was cleverly biding her time. But I was certain she would not be able to resist the itch for long.

The bar was high-glossed cherry and reflected the glittering wall of liquor bottles and glasses behind the bartender. I parked myself in one of the cushion-backed stools and scanned the restaurant until I spotted her. *Wishbone.* Our eyes met and she smiled, gave a little finger wave.

The bartender came for my order. I could smell the Dewar's he'd just filled with soda from the tap in front of me. I ordered a drink and saw Larry Quinn walk in the door. He was alone. He always looked dressed for court. He glanced around and broke out his famous smile when he saw me.

'Keye! I been meaning to call you. Big Jim was so pleased everything turned out. I told him up front we didn't usually do missing cows.'

I glanced at Margaret. She was nursing a martini. 'Are you meeting someone, Larry?'

'Date. Wish me luck.' He shook my hand. 'It was nice to see you, Keye. Hey, there she is now.'

To my horror, he walked straight to Margaret's table. They

embraced. I couldn't let Larry have a date with Margaret Haze! I knew far too well how her dates turned out. And Larry was famous for his television advertising and personal injury suits – too close a connection to Margaret's headline-greedy attorney father. I thought she had been trying to finally extinguish her father's memory when she'd murdered Brooks. I didn't want her working out her issues on Quinn too.

I whipped out my phone and found Larry's number. I heard it ringing from my end but not in the restaurant. Was he carrying his phone or was it simply silenced? Then he pulled it from a pocket, glanced at the display, and put it down. *Damn.* I didn't want to make a scene in the restaurant, but I would if I had to. Quinn wasn't leaving with her. I quickly typed out a text message. *Do not leave with that woman. Murder investigation. Danger.*

A few seconds later, Quinn picked up his phone. If he'd read my message, it didn't show. He returned the phone to the table next to his plate. A waiter appeared and they ordered. Quinn had one drink before he got up. He didn't look at me on his way out but my phone vibrated almost as soon as he'd stepped onto the street.

'What the hell, Keye? You know how long it's been since I had a date?'

I watched Margaret gathering her things to leave. 'You'll thank me one day, Larry.'

He cursed. I snapped my phone shut.

Haze stopped by the bar and touched my arm, squeezed it affectionately as if we were old friends. 'Might as well go home, Keye,' she whispered. 'Looks like I'll be working late. Seems my date had an emergency.' She glanced at the glass in front of me. Her green eyes lit up. 'Don't go back there, Keye. Drunks are no challenge.'

I lifted the fluted whiskey glass to my lips. It was heavy and felt right in my palm. More right than anything had in a while. I left it on the bar. The ice was beginning to melt into the remains of my Diet Pepsi.

* * *

In the evening, the elevators at 303 Peachtree, SunTrust Plaza, require a key card. The elevators and elevator lobbies on all floors are equipped with security cameras. Getting to the elevators requires signing in or out at the guard station on the main lobby level. Margaret was accustomed to this routine, as were most of the occupants – investment bankers and attorneys whose jobs necessitate long hours. She knew most of the guards by name, was always careful to be pleasant, to take a moment to speak, to remember them on holidays.

Behind the desk at the guard station, a row of monitors displayed shots of the elevator lobbies from all fifty-three floors. Usually, one guard watched the monitors while another handled the sign-in sheets and traffic. Margaret had studied their routines carefully, had asked about the building's security systems and how they worked, where the cameras were located. All in the interest of safety, of course, since she was a woman who, on many occasions, worked long after others had gone home to their families. She had quietly picked the guards' brains over the last couple of years, and they had taken her concerns seriously, happily answering questions to make her feel more comfortable. Margaret Haze was, after all, one of the most famous criminal attorneys in the city and also one of the best tippers. Each and every security guard and cleaning person had received an envelope from her last Christmas.

Margaret had taken a break, enjoyed a drink, then greeted the guards downstairs with small talk upon her return. She wanted them to remember her tonight. She carefully signed back in at 8:52 before taking the elevators to her fifty-third-floor office.

It was a weekday evening and the fifty-third floor was empty. The lower floors, occupied by the hundreds of young lawyers and legal assistants, would still be humming, but tonight she had fifty-three all to herself.

In about an hour, she knew, the cleaning crew would begin to arrive, having entered through the loading docks and parked in the basement. One person would sign in for the entire crew, then they'd all come into the building via the freight elevators, which were located away from the main elevator lobbies in a hallway on each floor. Their routines, uniforms, and the tools they used had all been of great interest to her.

The freight elevators' location on the main floors had made it easy to slip out of her office wearing the blue scrubs of the crew, flat shoes, head down, no makeup, hair pulled into a bun and hidden under a bandanna. Many of the cleaning women wore them that way to keep their hair out of their faces while they worked. She could come and go using the loading docks while still signed in at the guard station in the main lobby. Later, when she was finished with her work on the outside, with the thing that drew her, called her out into the city, she could return. She could change back into her corporate clothes and leave through the main lobby. She'd done it many times.

Two nights ago she had walked right past Detective Velazquez and he hadn't even looked twice. Just another cleaning person. Nobody special. *Idiot*.

My phone rang and I saw Balaki's number on the screen. I thought about Rauser. I missed his calls. I'd never told him that I chose Aerosmith's 'Dude' for him or that it made me laugh every time he called.

'Keye, go home and get some rest. Me and Williams got this. And Bevins is at the hospital with the lieutenant, so everything's handled.'

I looked at the dashboard clock. Ten-thirty-six. 'Andy, I don't how to tell you guys how much I appreciate what you're doing—'

'Listen here, girl,' Andy Balaki interrupted in his South Georgia drawl. 'He's our family too.'

I didn't argue with him. I wanted to go home, needed to rest. I hadn't been there since early that morning, just a quick visit to feed the cat, scoop the box, change clothes, and shower. Diane had made a midday visit to White Trash to help relieve my guilt.

Traffic was at a trickle. Lamp-post wreaths lit up Midtown and reminded me again that Christmas was coming. I flipped on the gas in the brick fireplace in my bedroom, turned out the lights, and curled up with White Trash and *Dexter* on Showtime. It took me no time at all to fall asleep. This was normal. The problem usually came in *staying* asleep.

It was White Trash who first alerted me. With a strange low growl deep in her throat, she scurried over my head and leapt off the bed, nudging me awake.

Then a darting prism of reflection. The streetlights filtering through my cracked curtains had caught something, and when I realized what it was, when I understood that the light had reflected off a knife blade, when it hit me that Margaret Haze must be standing over me, she struck me hard, with something heavy. My whole world went abruptly cobalt blue. Pain tentacled out of every nerve. *Hurt. I hurt.* I fought to keep from losing consciousness.

She slid gracefully onto my bed, straddled me between her knees, leaning so near my face that I smelled her coffee breath. What was she doing? I struggled to get my vision, my senses back. What the hell had she hit me with? She was on top of me, bending over me. My body hurt. It was the lamp. She'd hit me with my bedside lamp.

Then raking pain – a cold, thin wire digging into my wrist. I needed to get my bearings, needed to get free. *Wire*, my fuzzy brain kept warning me. Wire, struggling, ligature abrasions, the victims, Rauser telling me they all had the abrasions. I was going to die. This silent killer was wrapping wire around my wrist and fastening me to the slats under my bed.

Too late, I started twisting and bucking, desperate to get her off my body, desperate to find some strength. I hit at her with my one free hand.

Margaret pressed down on me. She was watching me as the reality fought its way past the blow she'd delivered, watching as each thought, each realization, each new terror crossed my face. She knelt over me, studying me as if I were a laboratory experiment. Nothing I could say now would touch her, would alter her plan in any way. I wasn't human to her anymore. Not real. Just a thing to be toyed with.

Then she leaned over me and reached for the wrist she had already wired to my bed, and in one precise stroke, she sliced it with her knife. Jagged pain like a saw splitting my skin cut a headlong path to my nerve endings. Blood poured from my wrist and spattered off my fingertips.

'Can you feel her power now, Keye? And mine?'

I was beginning to shiver. My lips were tingling. I knew what it meant. I was losing calcium and blood too quickly. How quickly, I couldn't be sure. It's impossible to keep that kind of time.

She hit me hard again, and the room spun. I thought I was going to vomit in terror. 'You never took me seriously,' she said, and I saw her pick up a spool of wire and with great efficiency slice off a section with her knife.

'*You?*' I gasped.

I had changed my locks to protect myself, then given her a key. *Jesus.*

She leaned forward to pull my arm up and get her wire around that wrist too, and I struck her with every bit of force I had left inside me. She tumbled off me and hit the bedroom floor.

'Diane, why?' My voice was a mutilated whisper. 'Why would you do this?' Blood and saliva gushed out of my mouth.

She was on her feet, screaming at me. '*Because you fucking won't stop, will you? Not until you ruin everything!*'

She launched herself at me.

I squeezed the trigger.

In the darkened room, it looked like black oil exploding out of her neck. Blood and tissue sprayed my face and filled my mouth and nostrils. It was rusty and warm. She made a sound like a straw at the bottom of an empty cup, and dropped.

The last thing I remember is my gun, the one I'd pulled from beneath my pillow, hitting the floor.

Epilogue

It was the second time I had spent my days with the excellent nursing staff at Piedmont Hospital, courtesy of Margaret Haze. Yes, I blamed her for this and for what had happened to Diane. I knew Haze had manipulated and changed my sweet friend. I felt in my heart that Diane had been a victim too, though I would never have the facts. I'd killed my childhood friend. This wasn't fully sinking in. *It's no accident you're alive*, Margaret had told me that day in her office. Indeed. I'd fought to live. And why? There were moments now that the emptiness just seemed to sweep me downstream. Diane was dead. Charlie was gone. Rauser was in some terrible purgatory.

I don't remember that second emergency trip to the hospital, nor do I remember much about my first days here. I'd lost a lot of blood, they tell me. I slept. The great escape.

The scar on my right wrist would be with me forever. There would be no escaping the constant reminder that a killer had come to me in the night with a serrated knife blade and in one merciless, furious movement sliced me open.

Do you feel her power? Yes, I feel it still. But I didn't think Margaret had ever wanted me dead. She told me in her office that day that she had protected me. She warned me too when I mentioned Diane, but I didn't get it. *You never really know anyone below the surface, Keye. I would have thought you of all people had learned that lesson.* I've learned it now, Margaret, and learned it well.

The doctors said I had another bad concussion, lots of bruising on my face, some teeth jarred loose that would need attention as soon as

I was released. I would be spending some time with chiropractors and osteopaths and oral surgeons. My doctors advised that I should stay for a few days. They wanted to make sure all the wounds were healing properly. But we all have wounds, don't we? We are all scarred. Wasn't that Margaret's real message?

Mother had been to the loft to feed White Trash and had taken her home, something she had been plotting anyway. She was probably calling her Snowflake by now, carefully reprogramming her. I fully intended to take my cat back when I was well, but being well seemed far away right now.

Neil was taking care of the business. Rauser was still in a coma, and I didn't care if I ever left the hospital. I didn't know how to go back home. I was so close to him here.

None of this had worked out the way we'd hoped. I suppose the good news was that Chief Connor had finally acknowledged the mounting evidence. He'd authorized a full investigation into Haze. They had located the gun that was used on Rauser, a nine-millimeter that had originally belonged to Cohen Haze, Margaret's father. She had done a thorough job of cleaning out her home, but the Mercedes she'd left at the dealership tested positive for trace amounts of human blood. The blood matched that of Elicia Richardson, Lei Koto, and William LaBrecque. Haze's prints were all over Diane's place. So was Jacob Dobbs's blood – saturation amounts on Diane's clothing. The carpet in Diane's vehicle was also consistent with the fiber found on Dobbs's body. Diane's Toyota had Dobbs's blood and lots of it. APD reasoned that Diane had murdered Dobbs in it. How many other murders she'd participated in or committed herself, no one knew. CSI believed they could figure this out with time.

Personal items belonging to Diane were found at Haze's Tudor in Buckhead. The affair had been going on long enough for sleepovers. So this was Diane's new person and the real reason her voice trembled when I warned her that day about Margaret.

Soon after I had regained consciousness, Williams stood next to my hospital bed with a grim expression. 'Haze disappeared,' he told me.

Margaret Haze was the FBI's problem now, and Interpol's. They would monitor the globe for her signature characteristics. Others would die, I knew.

'She'd been preparing for this for years, siphoning money out of the country every month. Amounts less than ten thousand don't raise an eyebrow, Keye, and the shit's been moved so many times now, well, it's just gone, essentially untraceable,' Williams told me glumly. 'She must have had escape passports and identification ready.'

I sat with Rauser every day, reading to him the way Mother and I read to each other when I was a kid. Each day, he got the morning paper with a massive dose of my own personal op-ed. I insisted on keeping him connected to life, to me, to my voice, to news about the city he'd sworn to protect. I'd gotten into the habit of creeping back into Rauser's room late at night when it felt like everything was crashing in on me – the terrible memories of Rauser's shooting, of Diane's voice as she tried to kill me. *Because you fucking won't stop . . .* I'd snuggle up to him and my mind would race back to a million small moments with him. I should have been nicer, I thought. I'd teased him so ruthlessly sometimes. Did I ever even tell him how smart I thought he was or how handsome or how funny or how extraordinarily hot he looked in those stupid wife beaters? Why hadn't I admitted I was jealous of Jo Phillips? And that Jodie Foster thing, him just going on and on, drove me a little nuts. God, what I would give to have just one of his irritating little quirks back.

I thought about that night at the playground, about Rauser touching his chest, looking so utterly surprised when he realized he'd been shot. Anger and grief knotted my stomach. I should have known. I was the expert, wasn't I? I could have stopped her.

I slipped out of bed and reached for my sweatpants. I absolutely refused to walk hospital corridors in my pajamas. It was pathetic enough that I had to look like this, bandaged and bruised.

My phone went off. I sighed. My mother had only today unraveled text messaging and unfortunately she was getting quite good at it.

I looked at my phone. Caller ID was showing an unavailable

321

number. It felt like a fist slammed into my heart. Part of me had been expecting this since I learned that Margaret Haze had gotten away.

Shame about Diane. So unstable. How did it feel to watch the life drain from her? Sorry I had to leave so abruptly. New life beginning. But don't worry about me. They always open the door. M.

I forwarded the message to Williams. The wheels on tracing the text would start turning at once, but I knew she wouldn't have done it if she wasn't very sure it was safe.

How does it feel? Like being torn apart, Margaret, that's how it feels.

I pushed open the door to Rauser's room and squeezed in next to him. I lay there for a moment, mourning him, and then I whispered, 'Nothing makes sense without you.' My heart ached, but I had no tears left.

I missed him so much, laughing with him, talking to him. We had told each other the stories of our lives, our real lives, the things that marked and changed and elevated us, the stories you save for that one person fate hands you like truth serum. And when that person's gone, grief wells up without a channel, like a river jumping its banks.

'Rauser, you son of a bitch,' I told him, 'if you don't wake up, I'm going to dedicate my life to making disparaging remarks about Jodie Foster.' I kissed his cheek and brought his arm up around me. Then I closed my eyes.

It was still dark when I woke. Fingers were clutching my shoulder. Strong fingers. This wasn't the limp arm I'd put around me every night before sleep in the hospital.

I was frozen for a moment, my heart trip-hammering, and then I realized that Rauser was holding me. His chest was rising and falling.

I lifted my head slowly.

'I was beginning to wonder if you were ever going to wake up,' he said.

About the Author

Amanda Kyle Williams has worked as a freelance writer for the *Atlanta Journal-Constitution* and owned a small business. She is active in the humane community and one of the founding directors at LifeLine Animal Project, a nonprofit, no-kill animal welfare organization based in Avondale Estates, Georgia.

The Stranger You Seek is Williams's first mainstream crime novel and the first in the Keye Street series. Williams currently lives in Decatur, Georgia, which produces unending fodder for her fiction.